She began to struggle mightily against Tol Shaddock's grip. "Dammit, let go! Can't you see Pa's still alive?"

Ducane's eyes were still open, staring glassily. But there was no other movement, none at . . . no, wait! The man's chest rose just slightly, then fell. "By God," Tol whispered, "he is breathing at that!"

"Breathing, yes," said No Moon. "Alive, yes. But living? No. He is hollow. His spirit is gone. Only the shell remains."

One of the demons slowly turned its attention away from their circle of sanctuary and back to Russell Ducane. It watched him as if expecting movement, then it leaned over, unfolded an ethereal forelimb, and extended it deep into the man's chest cavity. In response, Ducane's body began to quiver, to twitch . . .

"What the hell is it doing?" Tol whispered.

"It knows," the old Indian reported warily. "It can take on flesh by possessing the man's body. Then it will be able to cross into the circle. Prepare yourself, Shaddock. The time of greatest danger grows near. . . ."

Demon Dance

T. CHRIS MARTINDALE

POCKET BOOKS

New York   London   Toronto   Sydney   Tokyo   Singapore

An *Original* Publication of POCKET BOOKS

POCKET BOOKS, a division of Simon & Schuster Inc.
1230 Avenue of the Americas, New York, NY 10020

ISBN: 0-671-70452-4

First Pocket Books printing September 1991

10 9 8 7 6 5 4 3 2 1

POCKET and colophon are registered trademarks of
Simon & Schuster Inc.

Printed in the U.S.A.

To my niece
Brandie Martindale,
for a real good name

Demon Dance

Prologue

The night wind was to the old Indian's back. It blew soft and cool . . . whispering to him. Telling him things.

He stopped walking in the middle of the dirt road and turned to look behind him across the rolling Nebraska plain. The grassland was well lit by the autumn moon waxing high above the horizon, and his view was unfettered; it reached far into the distance, at least a mile, maybe more. But a flat shelf of sparse clouds was sliding in from the west, just overhead. They were so low they all but seemed within reach as their splotchy shadows rippled across the landscape.

He watched those shadows for several breathless moments, waiting for a sign that they were something more, all but praying for it. For after three nights of being stalked, he had yet to see his pursuers. Not even when they ambushed him the night before, or when he fled into the darkness on foot. But he wanted to see them now. It was an irrational need, given the risks: to his recollection, no one had ever seen the spirits known as They-Who-Follow-Behind and kept mind enough to describe them. But the blood of a warrior people burned in his veins, and it demanded that he at least know his enemies. Whatever came of it, good or bad, would be better than not knowing or thinking that the night itself had turned against him. So he watched, and he waited. And ultimately he learned nothing. The only movement on the plains was simply shadow after all.

But the wind still whispered. It told him to be cautious, that they were out there. Somewhere. And they were coming.

The old Indian turned up his coat's collar and pulled the

1

worn old derby with an eagle feather in its band down around his ears. And when he started walking again, his pace was more urgent than before.

He wished he still had the horse with him, and not just to save his sore feet from the long walk ahead of him. That mare had been a good mount and had served him well ever since he snuck away from the Pine Ridge agency and "borrowed" her from a ranch along the Niobrara. She had carried him all the way to the mountains in the southwest and back again . . . or at least as far as the Platte River, where he had decided to camp beneath the shadow of towering Chimney Rock. He hadn't sensed their presence until they were already upon him—he barely had time to leap onto the mare and try to flee. But then those ghostly pale hands came groping out of the darkness. He ducked beneath those meant for him.

But the horse . . . she went another few steps from momentum alone before she went down, her heart still beating but her eyes empty of life. And behind him, he heard the terrified neighing of her stolen soul. The old man did not waste time looking back; he simply ran, casting a hurried spell to confuse them and cover his flight. He'd been running ever since.

The Indian frowned. He did not want to remember an ally that way. He thought instead of the mare's strength and spirit. Yes, she'd been a good horse. If he had dared to camp and make a fire, he would have sprinkled bits of food into the flame as offering to her noble spirit . . . if it still existed, he thought ruefully, remembering the plaintive wails he had left behind. He thrust the thoughts from his mind. It mattered little in the end. There would be no fire. He had learned that lesson the hard way—that was what had attracted them the last time. That was why he now walked and mourned instead of rode.

He shivered and pulled his coat around him tighter, tried to blame it on the chill in the air. But deep down he knew better. He was frightened, and that kind of chill went right to the bone. It had taken him a long time to admit he was afraid, even to himself. After all, he was not some quaking adolescent on his first hunt in the night. He was No Moon,

2

revered mystic and medicine man of the Oglala, with more than sixty years of pride built up in his breast. But despite all his experience and wisdom, he was ill prepared for the events of the past few days, or for the dangers that now stalked him with unerring tenacity. He trembled at the recollections and the mere realization of his plight; it gave new strength to his stride where there had been little remaining.

The road stretched out before him relentlessly, like a dark and infinite serpent, and it conveyed a seeping hopelessness that No Moon fought hard to resist. There was an end to this road, he assured himself, trying to bolster his already flagging spirits. For he had passed barbed wire fencing not too far back—that meant there were ranches nearby—and on one of those fenceposts had been a sign. BARLOW it said. FIVE MILES. Not much farther, he told himself. And there you should find—

A scream pierced the night behind him, long and ululating as it swept across the plains on the eddies of a cool breeze. Only the bare edge of an echo reached him—it was obviously miles away—but it still prickled his flesh and called the hairs on his neck to attention. It was not a cry of fear or pain—there was no mistaking that. This was unnaturally shrill, almost abrasive to the ear, and it cut through the distance with startling clarity. So startling, in fact, that No Moon began to run. His lead over his pursuers was no solace to him. He knew who they were—*what* they were—and a few miles was no margin of safety. He ran despite the knotting muscles in his thighs and the fire that burned through his lungs and side, because he had seen what such *nagi* could do. His horse was just an example. He had to get away, far away, before they caught sight of him. For once that happened, there would be no escape. Fatigued as he was, he would have to stand and fight.

And die.

He felt naked and vulnerable in the road. He had no cover at all, no way to elude them. But off to the left, over a gentle rise, he spotted a line of trees standing black and isolated against an infinite field of yellow-green, their limbs waving, beckoning to him. For an instant his suspicions flared. Was

3

this another of *her* traps, another dark ambush like that which claimed his mount? Perhaps the witch had sent other assassins besides They-Who-Follow-Behind after him—perhaps the trees themselves were her agents now, their spirits blackened and corrupted by her evil, just waiting to scoop him up in their knotted, powerful limbs and crush out his opposition. He hesitated, unsure and afraid. But then the wind caught up to him, buffeted his clothes, and rustled the bristling gray mane that stuck from beneath his derby. And it told him that the spirits were that much closer. There was no choice. He left the road and waded into the dark, lapping ocean of grass.

Even before he reached the top of the knobby rise, No Moon had an idea of what he would find. The light trickle of water had already reached his ears. Beyond the gentle slope was a creek that meandered through the meadowland in long, crooked coils, and the trees he had spied from the roadway grew all along its banks. But the stream was faltering, drying up. It was barely a shadow of its former self, for now only a rivulet of dark water dribbled through a creek bed that stood almost four feet deep in places. That left the roots of the trees exposed through the eroding bank.

No Moon's senses bristled. He needed no scream this time to tell him that they were getting close. But where could he go? Where could he hide?

He dropped into the creek bed and crouched against the bank, just below the base of a great gnarled oak whose roots broke the surface behind him. The old man tried to calm his nervous wheezing but couldn't; the panic was flooding his throat and choking him, filling his mouth with the bitter taste of terror. His long fingers fumbled with the straps on the leather pouch over his shoulder as he tried to conceal himself even further, sinking into the bank, wedging himself back into the exposed roots of the oak.

He quickly turned and looked at what he had stumbled onto. The tree's central root was partly visible above the soil, and its tendrils stretched out into the stream bed for water that no longer ran within reach. But beneath that sprouting base was a dark pocket of shadow. It could have been a hollow carved by the stream when its waters were

4

high and the current strong, or perhaps it was an animal's den burrowed deep beneath the tree itself. The animal could still have been there, for all No Moon could tell, but he had no time for caution. He stuck an arm into the darkness there and felt around, half expecting the fur of a sleeping badger beneath his palm or the sting of a serpent's tooth as he invaded its nest. When he was sure there were no obstructions, he quickly took off his hat, ducked his head beneath those gnarled fingers of deadwood, and slithered into the hollow. The dank odor of dirt assailed his nostrils, that and the stink of fresh offal. He could feel it beneath him now, still warm. So it was a den of some sort after all. But the occupant must have been away, for the old man would have brushed against it by now. There was barely enough room for him to squeeze into, and even then his head was pinned to his shoulder and his legs folded against his chest like a newborn. At least he was hidden and out of sight.

But would that be enough?

He could take no chances. Carefully, he slipped his hand into the leather pouch and sorted through the powerful implements he kept there. His fingers went right to the items he sought, or perhaps they came to his hand on their own? He drew them out and held them before him. One was a long, flat piece of obsidian that tapered to a spear point and had chiseled serrations on either edge. It was the spirit knife, handed down from his father and possessed of much power. A last resort, in case his plan did not work. At least with it he could die fighting.

The other piece was more innocuous, at least to the untrained eye. He held up the rabbit's foot and stroked the soft fur. It was from the first long-ear he had ever stalked, now more than fifty winters past, and it was very special to him. He knew of white men who kept such things, but they were ignorant of the ways of nature and carried them all wrong. There was no "luck" in such a piece. But there was something else . . . something mysterious, sacred. Powerful. Something *wakan.* "Wise old hare," he whispered in a coarse, dry voice that cracked with fear. "Friend of the Oglala, may I conceal myself in your image, may I share in your wily ways when the hunter comes stalking . . ."

5

EEEEEEIIIIIAAAAAAAOOOOOOOOO!!

No Moon's words caught in his throat, choking him. His breath would not come at first, and he pressed a hand to his breast to make sure the scream had not stolen his heart. It was as shrill and piercing as before, just as inhuman, but much louder. Much closer. Sweat beaded on the old man's brow and slid down his face. His hands were shaking and for an instant he couldn't remember what to do. *Think, you fool, think!*

He closed his eyes and ears to the outside world and focused his concentration, tried to see the spirit he sought, the grandfather of rabbits. He stroked the small foot reverently and mouthed his words in silence. Grandfather, many times have you offered yourself up to me when the hunting was scarce, and many times did I leave offerings of your favorite clover and wild carrot. This I will do again should you watch over me now and secret me from harm.

He could feel his pursuers now. They were very close. He opened his eyes and dared to peek out through the tangle of roots. There was nothing there . . . at least nothing he could see. But he could still feel them. It was as if they were watching him even now, staring straight through the earth at him with huge owl eyes that burned with unnatural fires, and never once did they blink. No Moon recoiled inwardly at the image and choked back the urge to cry out. He fought to convince himself that he was safe, that he was no longer a man at all but a long-eared hare deep in his burrow, safe and unseen. And slowly the hollow seemed to grow larger around him. He felt there was finally room to stretch and relieve the pain in his legs and back but he dared not move. He stayed completely still, and he waited. And the silence of the night stretched on.

The sky was beginning to lighten in the east before he heard another scream, or at least the fading echo of one. They-Who-Follow-Behind were moving away. Leaving. No Moon breathed a sigh of relief. But he still did not move. He stayed perfectly still for hours yet, until the sun was well above the edge of the world. When he did try to stretch he found he couldn't; he was a man again and too large for the burrow. Only then did he wriggle into the open and collapse in the stream bed, his cramped muscles crying out from the strain of movement. He lay there on his back, breathing the clean air and letting the sun warm his flesh. But part of the chill just wouldn't go away. It was deep inside him, in his bones, and at times it rose like bubbles to the surface and made him tremble. Those eyes he had imagined, the unnatural fires that burned there . . . he knew that they would never give up. They would find him as surely as the setting of the sun. And he would not be able to hide again. He would have to face them.

He sat against the stream bank and reached into his pouch, took out the handbill he'd found the day before, tacked on the same fencepost as the Barlow road sign. No Moon unfolded the paper and studied the drawing of a man's face there, read the strength and courage in those features. Then he read the white man's words again for the twentieth time, and for a while he was reassured.

Perhaps when he finally made his stand, he would not have to do so alone.

Chapter 1

Willie Ducane was up early Saturday morning. The freight wagons had just come in from Omaha the day before, bringing a whole raft of new supplies to her father's general store, and she had to get everything stocked and presentable before the crowds came in. Saturdays were always the most hectic, what with the ranchers and homesteaders coming into town for supplies or to socialize over a drink or two at McKinney's Saloon. But with the weather holding to a brisk but tolerable nip in the air and a Wild West Show come to town, she knew there would be more people today than ever.

The show, she thought anxiously. It starts tonight. But just as quickly she chastened herself. Think about that later. You've got work to do.

She propped open the front door to the day's business, though it was just a bit early. The small town of Barlow, with its one muddy thoroughfare and high-plank sidewalks, was just rousing to the dawn. The people from the outlying areas wouldn't make it in till noon or thereabouts. This early there were only a few people in sight: Sheriff Tuttle, strolling along the storefronts, his colorful vest bulging from an extra-hearty breakfast; Mr. McKinney sweeping out the tavern across the way; and a few other passingly familiar citizens.

But there was one man Willie didn't recognize at all. An old Indian was coming down the street. She couldn't tell what tribe he was—they were all just red to her—but he was sturdy-looking for his age. He wore heavy jeans and thick moccasins and a hand-me-down coat, more patches than original material. There was an Army-issue wool blanket draped around his shoulders for added warmth. And on his head, of all things, was one of those fancy derby hats like they wore in the big cities. Only this one was old and fraying and sported a single eagle feather in a snakeskin band. It was an odd sort of headpiece for an Indian: where were the feathers, the fringes and beads? The strange old man held her attention a moment or two longer, just until that pragmatic voice in her head told her to get back to work before Pa came out to check.

As Willie turned, her eyes fell on the colorful handbill pinned to the door frame, the same one she'd read over and over for days now. But she forced herself to pass it by this time, to go back into the store. The Wild West Show can wait, she had to remind herself once again. Get busy.

She set about her chores methodically. She was not afraid of hard work. Stocking and organizing the store was an old habit by now, since she'd been helping her father for the last five of her seventeen years. Ever since Ma died. And often she looked over its operation even more closely than he. First she stacked the nail kegs, four high and in a pyramid, then she arranged a bouquet of rakes and hoes and shovels in an empty barrel nearby. She put the heavy bags of flour and salt and coffee and seed along the far wall, then laid out the bolts of new material on the dressmaking table, in front of the full-length mirror so the local women could hold the fabrics up against them and see how they might look in finished form. There were chambray shirts and several sizes of good stout jeans to display, some work boots and cowboy boots and children's shoes, as well as rubbing liniments and castor oil and other medicinals for the shelves behind the counter. She diligently put them all away, but such work was strictly a rote exercise for her—she could do it with her eyes closed. Of course that left her thoughts free to wander, and her eyes were not long in following.

Back to the door. To the handbill still precisely where the fat man in the John B. Stetson hat had hung it three days before. She studied the drawing there, of a man with long blond hair and handlebar mustache, sitting proudly on horseback. And then her eyes took in the words printed in big garish letters:

**The Wild West at Its Best!
Presenting
Col. Bill Brady's Old West Event**

**Re-live the riproaring days with those that
blazed this great Western frontier! Bring
the women and children! Fun for all!
Fancy shooting!
Trick riding and roping!
Knife throwing!
Authentic Apache fire dance!**

**IN PERSON: TOLMAN SHADDOCK,
Western Legend.**
Soldier/Buffalo Hunter/Lawman/Army Scout!
Killed the infamous Orlen Brothers!
Sole Survivor of the Creekmore Indian Massacre!
Watch him shoot and ride! Hear the stories!

**September 29th of this year, 1890
Barlow, Nebraska**

The thought of it thrilled her. The first show was tonight —they're already here! Willie had stood in the street at sunset and watched them roll in, the fancy fringed carriage and several wagons, about a dozen men in all. They put up a big show tent at the end of town and readied their gear, and before it got too dark she even caught a glimpse of one of them practicing trick mounts on a fiery Texas pony. It only fed her hunger for more. Imagine, a Western show here, in Barlow! That would finally give her something worthwhile to put in her journal. It wouldn't be anything big, she could tell that from the limited number of the ragtag troupe. Pa even sneered at them, said the whole thing was nothing but a snake-oil show. But Willie was more optimistic. After all, big trees grow from little acorns. And it wasn't that long ago, just fifteen years or so, that Mr. William Cody started his own Wild West extravaganza, and not that far away either. Just over in North Platte. And now

10

where was he? Playing for the crowned heads of Europe, no less.

Who knows, she told herself. This Colonel Brady could end up the next Buffalo Bill. Even if he doesn't, at least you'll get to see Tolman Shaddock. Maybe even shake his hand!

She wondered if the legendary frontiersman had been among those she watched ride in the previous night. It had been too dark and they were too far away to tell. And it was hard to say whether the poster drawing would match him very much; Lord knows it didn't look anything like the painting of Shaddock on his adventure books, the two best editions of Beadle's Half-Dime Libraries. Of the twenty or so periodicals she owned, those two had chronicled the exploits of Tolman Shaddock. And they both pictured him on the cover as a strapping bear of a man with flowing locks—dark hair, not blond—and with no mustache at all. Now that she thought of it, the handbill drawings looked suspiciously similar to pictures she'd seen of William Cody himself.

Compared to that august adventurer, Shaddock was a minor legend, barely a footnote in the recent annals of the American West. The dime novels had more extensively covered the lives of John Wesley Hardin and Wild Bill Hickok, Cole Younger and the James boys and that rascal Harry Tracy. But that did not diminish the man's exploits. At least not in Willie's eyes. After all, the Orlen brothers had been some of the killingest bastards the West had ever seen. It took a special kind of man to bring them three to justice, yessir. And then there was the Creekmore massacre in the Dakota Badlands. Everyone knew about that—how one Indian scout stood alone against the horde of Red Cloud's murderous savages that had slaughtered the rest of his patrol.

She marveled. That's grit, all right.

In her mind Willie tried to picture that scene just as it had been on the cover of one of her thin novels. The grasses painted dark with blood. The butchered cavalrymen lying sprawled all around, pin-cushioned with arrows and great stout lances. And in the middle of it all, that hulking figure of a man. Shoulders back and chest out. Chin held high. Bloodied but never bowed. He faced at least a score of heathens with his infamous LeMat grapeshot pistols in hand, still smoking. And he just dared them to come ahead, to come taste a little more .44-caliber justice. . . .

Willie smiled. For as the scene unfolded before her mind's eye, the look of Shaddock's face shifted. The line drawings from the cover of the Beadle's Half-Dime extravaganzas took on depth and color, grew smaller and younger as she watched. Even changed gender. Until the face was finally her own. Yes, it was Willie Ducane out there, facing the whooping throng of red devils. They charged down the bluff to engulf her as she drew her Colt in a blur of motion and set it to blazing. . . .

She stopped stacking the new cook pots and looked around to see if there was anyone watching. Once sure of her privacy, she stepped over to the big mirror by the fabric display and untied the work apron that covered her from chest to knees. Underneath she wore a cotton shirt with the sleeves rolled up and a worn pair of jeans. And one other article. Around her waist was a wide leather belt, complete with fancy scrolling and loops for extra cartridges. It hung just off her hip on the right side, so the holster there rode low and the polished grips of her Colt .45 Peacemaker were right about palm level when her arms were at her sides. The holster was tied down with a leather thong, just like all the fancy pistoleros wore in the books she'd read. She stepped back and judged her reflection, how the revolver looked there. Not bad, she thought. She even made a few mock fast draws, though never actually pulling the pistol from its cradle. She'd read once that a gun should never clear leather unless it was to be cleaned or fired. And she was not one to break with the tenets of the American West.

Willie turned sideways, posed with her hands loose and ready to draw. Yessir, not too bad at all. She was a big, strapping girl, not fat, but big-boned and healthy. In that she was like her father and grandfather and the rest of their Germanic bloodline. She also had their thin lips and broad features. With the baggy shirt hiding her modest bustline and her long auburn hair tied back with a ribbon, she looked deceptively like a boy of nineteen or twenty, every bit as rugged as those cocky young ranch hands who were always riding in on the weekends with their fancy chaps and polished spurs. Without doubt, she could cut just as mean a figure, if she was of such a mind. Still a little young, but then, so were the men she'd read so much about, when they were first making names for themselves. John Wesley Hardin was an accomplished pistol fighter in his late teens, when he almost faced down Wild Bill Hickok himself in rowdy Abilene. And there was always the notorious Billy the Kid. The West had beckoned to those men, the same way it now did to . . .

"Wilhelmina!"

She flinched. The voice was loud and reproachful, and it made Willie immediately grab for her apron and try tying it back in place. But it was too late. She knew her father had already seen the gun and holster. So she just turned slowly and faced the man's stern gaze.

Russell Ducane was big and stocky, even more so than his daughter. In fact, he looked more suited to smithing than to tending a general store. His rolled-up shirt-sleeves revealed more hair on his forearms than on his scalp, and his hands were broad and blunt-fingered. But he also wore small wire-framed spectacles, and that lessened the overall impression of his size, giving him a more educated demeanor. He could also peer over them disapprovingly, which was the way he looked as he reproached his daughter. His thick arms folded across his chest, he tapped his foot impatiently as he glared at the girl. Or at her Colt, to be precise. "What have I told you about that?" he said in a hard whisper.

Willie just shrugged. She was never good at arguing with her father.

"Take that gun off right now, young lady. This isn't some cowtown from one of your dime novels, you know."

"But I thought . . . well, the Atwood gang's been sighted again," she stammered, trying to construct a feasible excuse. "They raided a ranch over by Alliance, stole the horses and everything. I thought if they headed this way, you never know, they might stop here. . . ."

"That was a month ago, girl. And if that trash does head in this direction, they won't be coming into town for supplies. They'd just raid the supply wagons between here and Omaha, like they did that once." He looked at her with a patronizing smirk. "Do you really think you could outgun real outlaws such as they?"

"I think I'd do fine. I've been practicing, you know."

"Oh, so I've heard." Her father sighed. "A girl your age shooting cans out on the prairie . . . you should be giving thought to more important things. Folks are starting to talk, you know."

"I don't much care what they have to say. Ain't none of their business anyway."

Russell Ducane walked over to his daughter and took her by the shoulders. "Willie, this isn't the Wild West anymore," he told her adamantly. "It's 1890, for pity's sake. Times have changed. The gunfighters and cowboys are a thing of the past. This land is settling, the population growing larger all the time. It's a place for business and industry now, not crazy outlaws and Indians on the warpath."

"But what about the Atwoods—"

"There's always a few who won't face up. But you know better, Willie. You'd do well to get your nose out of the past and start looking to the future."

He turned her toward the mirror and then took the ribbon from her hair and fluffed it out around her shoulders. "See that face?" he said, pointing at a reflection that softened considerably when framed in auburn curls. "That's a beauty, isn't it? Just like your mother, God rest her soul. You know, I'll bet there's a lot of young men in this town who've never even seen this face before. Eligible young men. Why, I was just talking to Jacob Walker over at the bank the other day and he said his son's had an eye on you for some time now—"

"Pa, please!" Willie pulled away from him. "How many times do I gotta tell you? I ain't interested in Lute Walker! I ain't interested in nobody right now. I expect I'll be married someday. But not right now."

Her father scowled. "How long do you expect to put it off,

huh? A year? Five years? And in the meantime, you'll strengthen up your gun hand, blasting away at prairie dogs in the middle of nowhere? I swear, girl, sometimes you are the most contrary . . ." He tsk-tsked her silently for a moment. Then he finally put out his open hand. "Give it to me," he said, snapping his fingers for emphasis. "Now, Willie."

Begrudgingly, the girl unbuckled her holster and surrendered it. He wrapped the belt tightly around it and tucked it under one arm. "I'll just keep this until you start acting like you've got some sense. Do you hear?"

"Yes. Sir."

"That's better. Now, sweep up around here. There's a lot of dust on the floor." He went back behind the counter and headed for the stairway that led to the apartment upstairs where the two of them lived. But he paused when he passed the cash drawer. Tacked to the back shelves, in plain view, were two postcards and a sheet of paper. The former showed images of death; one card had the lifeless remains of train robber Harvey Clay, propped up for photographic posterity, a bullet in his chest, while the other showed an accused backshooter named Eustace Weems. The Kansas lawmen that had brought him down were posed around him, smiling. Russell Ducane did not recognize either outlaw by face or name. But the wanted poster hanging beside them was more familiar. It offered a five hundred–dollar reward for the capture of the half-breed Clancy Atwood, otherwise known as Kolo, along with his white half brother, "Stutterin' George" Atwood.

"What the hell are these doing here?" Willie's father said angrily. He pulled them loose, tearing the paper, popping tacks across the floor. "A store is no place for such things. Do you want to upset the women who come in here?"

"No, sir."

Pa shot her one last wearisome glance. Then he stalked out of the shop, past the narrow stairway, and into the storerooms in the back.

Willie stood there, fuming as well. But her anger was more at herself than at her father. Why did she never stand up to him? Why did she stay here at all? Sometimes she wished she could just leave this place and head west, as she'd always dreamed, see the country and the people that she'd read so much about. She was sure she could make it out there, if she could just find a cattle ranch with smarts enough to hire her. She didn't have any experience to speak of, but she knew how to ride a horse and use a six-gun. She'd read so much about roping and droving that she was sure she could pick up the particulars in short order. And if any of the other cowhands gave her trouble or if rustlers ever crossed her path . . .

She went back to the mirror and posed with her hands at hip level, prepared to slap leather that was no longer there. But that's when her eye drifted up, past the shoulder of her reflection, to find a man standing in the open doorway behind her.

It was not a local man. Willie did not recognize him at all. She turned quickly, flushed with embarrassment. "Good morning, sir," she said in greeting. "What can I do for you?"

The man took off a hat with a drooping brim that held little life these days, wiped his boots before stepping inside. He was a good head taller than the girl and half of that again. But there was not much meat to his frame. His worn old mackinaw hung loose around him and his trousers were baggy and fraying over bony knees. He was of grandfatherly age, if not sixty, then damn close to it. His face was wrinkled by the sun and the years, and his stringy hair and droopy mustache were both shot through with gray. He wore an odd expression, confused and numb. And that's when Willie caught the pungent smell of alcohol in the air, noticed the stubby neck of a whiskey bottle peeking from the man's coat pocket. A drunkard, then, she surmised. Better watch him close. Sots like this were always trying to palm something or other, saving back their money for another round of spirits. "Sir?" she asked once more. "I said, what can I do for you?"

The man closed his eyes and scratched his stubbly chin, wavered unsteadily on his feet. For a moment Willie was afraid he would pass out right then and there. But finally he looked at the girl again, right at her this time. He rolled his tongue over his teeth and grimaced from the sour taste. Then, in a low croaking voice that held the barest echo of a

South Carolina accent, he said, "I am in need of tobaccy. You do carry such a thing?"

"Indeed we do. Right here in the case. Will it be pouch or plug?"

"I believe I'll have the plug," he said, stepping slowly over to the counter. "I once smoked a pipe. But the noted bastard Eli Miller shot it from my mouth one fine day over a gambling transgression. I don't believe I ever had another."

Willie rolled her eyes. "Yeah, right," she said, just to placate the old man. She opened the case and took out several blocks of chaw. "How many are you needing?"

The man opened his fist and laid a handful of pennies on the counter. The change from buying his bottle, Willie guessed. For she'd known a few drunkards in this town, and with them the liquor always came first. Willie counted up the coins and laid out six pieces of tobacco. "Sorry, but that's all you've got money for."

"It'll do." The man shrugged. He picked up one right then and bit off almost a third of it, till his cheek bulged noticeably. Then he held out the plug. "Will you join me, missy?" he said with a crooked half smile.

"No, thanks. I tried it once, when I was younger. 'Bout made me sick."

"There's a trick to it, all right." The tall man nodded. "You gotta know what you are doing, and that's a fact. But at least it keeps your mouth busy. More people oughta chew these days 'stead of talking. Too much talking going on."

The man leaned over and spat into the brass urn at the foot of the counter. Then he considered his actions. "You know," he said whimsically, "back when we was droving over the ol' Chisholm, sometimes you'd have to rub a bit of tobaccy juice in your eyes just to make them sting and stay open. Couldn't go to sleep. You'd lose too many head."

"In your eyes?" Willie winced, feeling her own tear up at the mere suggestion. "You really did that?"

"A time ago," the old man said. "I did a lot of things."

She looked at the old tramp again. Maybe she'd judged him too quickly. "So what are you doing now? Are you still droving? Or did you come into town to see the show?"

"Say what?"

"The Wild West Show." She went over and pulled the handbill loose from the door, brought it back to the counter, and laid it before the man. "It's gonna be late this afternoon, just 'fore dark. And it's gonna be a lulu, I'll bet. We don't get many things like this through Barlow, us being so tiny and all. So I expect there'll be quite the crowd. 'Specially with Tol Shaddock being there. You've heard of him, ain't you?"

"I believe so, yes."

"He's a famous tracker and Indian fighter. He fought off the Sioux in the Creekmore massacre all by himself, him and his ten-shot pistols. Have you ever heard of a LeMat grapeshot revolver? I believe a few confederate officers carried 'em during the war, like General Beauregard and J.E.B. Stuart. He's the one who gave Shaddock his brace, right 'fore he was killed at Yellow Tavern. Boy, I'm telling you, I'd sure like to take a look at those beauties. . . ."

The man sighed wearily, as if tired of the girl's prattling. He casually swept back the tail of his mackinaw to reveal a high holster on his right hip. He drew a big horse pistol from there and pointed it square at Willie Ducane's chest. The girl's eyes grew as large as saucers as words clogged her throat and wouldn't let her gasp in surprise. *I'm being robbed,* she thought with horror and excitement at the same time. *It may not be Kolo and Stutterin' George, but it's a robbery just the same.* Her hand dropped instinctively to her thigh and found no holster there. *I told you, Pa,* she wanted to call out. *I told you. . . .*

But then the man reversed his grip on the pistol. He was suddenly offering it to her, butt-first. "I thought you might want to look at it," he said. "Go on, have a peek."

Willie sighed, half from relief and half from disappointment. "You had me going there for a minute." She laughed as she took hold of the revolver, almost dropped it when the stranger let go. It was very heavy, which was understandable given its size. The cylinder alone was a handful, much thicker around than that of Willie's own Colt. But then, it had to be to accommodate nine separate .44 rounds.

Nine rounds . . .

No, she thought, it can't be.

She looked over the weapon more closely. Sure enough, it

18

was an old cap-and-ball arm, and there was a second barrel just beneath the first. A smooth bore tube for a .65-caliber ball and patch or a small shot load. That, combined with what was already in the cylinder, made for ten shots in all.

"God amighty," she whispered. "It's a LeMat, isn't it? A grapeshot pistol, just like Tol Shaddock . . ." She suddenly looked up at the man with his tobacco-stuffed cheek and his glazed eyes. And in Willie's mind the Beadle drawings tried to superimpose themselves over the rangy old features before her. But the hair was too thin and stringy, the mustache too limp. The images were too discordant to mesh properly. "You can't be him," she stammered. "You just can't be . . . Tolman Shaddock?"

The tall man wiped a hand on his shabby coat before offering it in greeting. "That would be me, all right."

Chapter 2

Willie just stood there, slack-jawed. It couldn't be him, she thought. Not this skinny old man with the stink of whiskey about him. But the girl held the proof in her very hands. A LeMat ten-shooter. There couldn't have been that many of the old pistol made. What were the chances of anyone else around Barlow having one? Anyone but Shaddock, that is.

Still, it could have been coincidence. "Tol Shaddock carries two of these pistols," she baited.

The old man gave a cluck of laughter and pulled back the other tail of his coat. There was the second of the brace, this one in a cross-draw holster on his left side. "You sure know a lot about me, young'n," he said with a big uneven grin. "I take it you've heard a story or two?"

Willie knelt down behind the counter and took out the small stack of dime novels she kept on hand. There were six of them there, heralding the adventures of Wild Bill Hickok and Lariat Lil and Fancy Frank of Colorado, among others. And the two Tol Shaddock copies as well. She held up *Orlen Brothers Shootout* for the tall man's appraisal. "I've read that thing at least a hundred times."

"Is that right?" He took the thin book in his long, leathery hands and looked it over, studied the garish cover, where the three-against-one gunfight was played out in dramatic line drawings. Then he gave a big horse laugh. "I don't know that I ever looked like that. Missy, you gotta take these things with a grain of salt. What the bastards don't know, they'll make up."

She held up the LeMat pistol. "It told all about these. Did Jeb Stuart actually give these to you himself, like they said?"

Shaddock puffed out his chest. "He did at that. The general gave 'em to me as reward for courage on the field of battle. Hell, he knew I'd always fancied his brace, so—" He furrowed his brow. "That's the God's honest truth, now, so don't you let nobody go and tell you different. If'n they do, they're a goddamn liar. There has been some speculatin' that I just took 'em off the general's body, but I say no sir—swear to God and spit on the ground. I was wounded at Yellow Tavern myself and dragged to safety by some of my pards. So I wasn't nowheres near the general when he fell."

"I believe you." Willie nodded. She returned to admiring the pistol, held it out with both hands to sight down the barrel. But it was just too unwieldly for someone her size. She handed it back. "It's a fine piece," she said appreciatively. "You know, I've got me a pistol."

Shaddock grinned. "Do you now? What would you be needing a gun for? 'Less you're fixin' to press some young buck into matrimony."

"Hardly." She rolled her eyes. "I just like to shoot. Honest. Mostly just cans and bottles." She went over and unlocked the gun case at the end of the counter, and from the few pistols on display, she produced another Colt. "Mine's out back," she explained, "but this one's just like it."

The tall man examined the smaller gun with a wan

expression, then nodded. "Very nice. A little stubby for my hand, but not bad."

"It's a cartridge gun, you know," she told him, opening the loading gate for his inspection. "You'll get a lot quicker reloads with one of these than those old cap-and-ball horse pistols. Loading the powder and the shot and all separately's kinda old-fashioned."

"Well, missy, there's some sense to your words. But I'd be a fool if'n I wasn't prepared at the get-go." The tall man laid the Colt aside and hefted one of his own pistols. With practiced speed, he unpinned the cylinder and let it fall free into his hand. "You see this?" he said. Then he pointed to the two leather pouches of relative size hanging on his belt. "I keep me a couple extras already loaded. All you gotta do is drop the empty one and put in another. That way I got nine more shots 'fore you can yell Sadie Lou." He laughed and replaced the cylinder in the gun without looking, holstered the big pistol in one fluid motion. Despite his drunken demeanor and obvious unsteadiness, his movements with the gun had been quick and dexterous. A lifetime of experience had seen to that. "Doesn't matter all that much in the long run, though," he continued. "It's usually the first one out of the gun that gets the job done, if you'll pardon my poetry. You know, I don't think I can remember but a handful of times I ever had to reload in a hurry—"

"Not even during the Creekmore massacre?"

"Well, that's a whole 'nother story. I'll tell you, missy, I . . ." Then the tall man's eyes locked onto the rifle rack on the wall behind Willie. "Good gawd," he gasped, trying to blink his vision into focus. "Is that what I think it is? A big-bore Sharps?"

Willie looked around. "Oh, that." She went to the rack and lifted off the bottom rifle, struggling with its obvious weight. It was a big single-shot with an overlarge hammer and two triggers. She handed it over to Shaddock. "We had a sore-footed jake come through here about two years ago. The sorry fool had come out here to hunt buffalo, only to find out the hunts were long over, that those animals are done gone. Well, he was in bad need of supplies but a little short of folding money. So my pa agreed to trade for his rifle and two boxes of shells. Trouble is, nobody these days has much of a need for a gun like that. It's been gathering dust ever since."

"Now, don't you believe it, little missy," Shaddock told her. "There's always a need for big guns. Why, my old Sharps 44-70 was good for the game whether it was shaggies I was hunting or two-footed lizards with a warrant for their arrest. A big-bore'll bring down both horse and rider when you need to, and from a considerable distance at that. I put it to just such a use on many an occasion. Damn, that was a real pisscutter of a rifle!"

"Do you still have it?"

Shaddock shrugged, pulling the bottle from his pocket. After a big swig he sighed, "Nope. 'Fraid not."

"What happened to it?"

Another shrug. Another swig. "Don't rightly remember. Probably a poker game or the like. Shame too. I miss that rifle." He took a moment to study the big Sharps Willie had handed him. He hefted it, raised it to a shoulder. "Damn, and I thought my old longarm was heavy. But this one's got it beat." He looked closer at the manufacturer's engraving on the top of the receiver. "You know what you've got here, young'n? This is a Sharps Big Fifty, .50-90 caliber. You almost need three men and a boy just to pull back the hammer on these things. By God, you shoot some poor bastard with this and his daddy's gonna feel it. Should pack a helluva punch, even more than my old piece." He raised the tall Vernier sight to the rear of the breech, peered through it and imagined squeezing off a shot. "By gawd," he said again. "I'd almost give up the bottle to put a few through this."

Willie could see how taken the old man was with that rifle. "It's for sale, you know," she told him. "Pa'd be glad just to be rid of it. I'll make you a deal. The gun and both boxes of shells for fifty dollars. Are you interested?"

The old man got a sheepish look on his face and laid the rifle back on the counter. And it was then that Willie remembered him laying a bare handful of coins on the table, just enough for his tobacco. She felt bad for him then, and was ashamed that she'd brought it up. "Maybe after the show," she said, "once you've been paid."

"This is my pay these days, as often as not," the man said softly, holding out his whiskey bottle. He looked at it with contempt, and for a moment Willie thought he might dash it against the foot of the counter. She even urged him silently to do just that. Instead, Shaddock pulled the cork once again and took another swig, drowned his anger in the very thing that sparked it. "Aahhh," he sighed with a forced smile. "That's goooood!" But it didn't sound convincing.

"Wandering off again, eh, Shaddock?"

The brusk voice came from the front of the store. The girth of the man standing there filled the doorway from jamb to jamb. He was so large, in fact, that there must have been three or four yards of fine fabric just in his fancy waistcoat, let alone the tight vest beneath. The cuffs of his pleated trousers were tucked in unblemished snakeskin boots—even the metal toe caps shined. He must have polished them religiously, Willie noted. And in a town like Barlow, where the street turned to a quagmire every time it rained, it would have taken some real high-stepping to keep them from getting grimed.

The man's size, the way he was dressed, was all somehow familiar. She then pictured him with a stack of handbills under one arm, and the pieces fell into place. She remembered him riding into Barlow three days before in his fringe-topped buggy, posting the signs all around town. He'd been dressed much the same then, like some big-city dandy, though at the moment he appeared to be a very belligerent one. He stood anxiously rubbing the silver knobhead of his walking stick as it supported his ponderous weight. His secondary chin was bloated and red with indignation like a great big bullfrog. And he glared straight at Tolman Shaddock. "I expected to find you in the saloon," the fat man huffed, "but you'd already beaten me there. The bartender said you staggered in this direction." He eyed the bottle in Shaddock's hand. "You have a show to give tonight, or had you forgotten?"

"I didn't forget, Colonel," Tol stammered, scuffing the

plank floor with his boot sole like a mischievous child caught red-handed. "I just can't abide the waiting around. So I thought I'd just have a little look around the town, and, well . . ."

Bill Brady stormed across the store, not bothering to use the cane for support—it was more a fancy affectation, an accessory to his wardrobe. A little too highfalutin for Willie's tastes. He went right up to Tol Shaddock, had to rock his head back on a plump neck to look up into the taller man's face. "Give me the bottle, Shaddock," the fat man demanded. "Now."

"But Colonel—"

"Now!" He slammed his walking stick down on the counter, startling both man and girl. Willie was sure that she saw a flash of anger in Shaddock's eyes, and he almost took a menacing step in the fat man's direction. But then he bowed his head and silently offered up the bottle. Brady's face remained red and angry, but the slightest bit of a grin played on a corner of his mouth. Triumph. "Get back to the wagons," he ordered the taller man. "Let's see if a bucket or two of black coffee'll sober you up."

Shaddock nodded slowly. Then he turned back to the girl and managed a slight smile. "I'm obliged for the tobaccy, little missy," he said, doffing his floppy hat in respect. Then he obediently followed after his employer.

"Wait a minute," Willie called. She picked up the heavy Sharps and went out after them, caught up to them on the sidewalk just outside the store. She went right to Shaddock, held up the big-bore. "If you're interested in this, I'm sure Pa would just about let you have it for next to nothing. If you really want it."

Tol's eyes shone as he looked over the piece admiringly. But then Colonel Bill Brady gave a humorless laugh. "It would have to be nothing itself, child. This man's been advanced his salary for the next two months. And it all goes to the same place." He uncorked Tol's bottle and poured the remainder into the dirt, right before the cowboy's eyes. Then Brady looked up and down the nearly empty street to see if anyone else had been watching. "Here, girl," he said in a conspiratorial whisper as he took a ticket from his vest pocket. "Free passes to tonight's show. Bring a beau if you want. As long as we keep all of this under our hat, all right?" He looked around once more, only this time he was startled to find someone right behind them, leaning against the front wall of the store. It even surprised Willie. There stood the old Indian she had seen earlier, wearing the coat and blanket and single-feathered derby. He was just watching them. The colonel gave him an intolerant glance but handed him a free ticket nonetheless. "Here you go, chief. Remember, you didn't see any of this." Neither Willie nor the Indian replied, but the man took their silence as an agreement. He smiled and patted the girl on the head as if she were a small child. Then he turned and ordered Tol Shaddock along as they walked toward the camp at the end of town.

Willie watched after them and wondered if Colonel Brady had been lying about Shaddock. Was he a common drunk these days? Even she'd thought so upon first seeing him, though learning his true identity had softened that harsh first impression. Once they'd started talking, she'd all but forgotten about it. Until now.

No, it can't be, she assured herself. Not Tolman Shaddock. He just likes a nip now and then, just like Pa and that bottle he keeps under the counter. Social drinking, that's all. You wait until tonight, you'll see. He'll show you what he's made of. He'll show everybody.

She looked down at the tickets in her hand. And despite her adamant confessions of faith, somehow she wasn't as eager to see the show as before.

Willie hefted the big rifle and turned back to the store, only to realize the old Indian was still standing there. He looked at her and held up his ticket, smiling.

She forced a smile in return and stepped quickly past him, shutting the door behind her.

No Moon turned the ticket over and over in his hand, watching the big tent and wagons at the edge of town. His smile was gone; there was no pretense of humor about him now. He took out the handbill he'd been carrying, the one for Bill Brady's event. The words matched; they were for one and the same. Satisfied, he wondered whether he should have spoken up when the men were right next to him. But his inner voice told him no. Wait for tonight. Make sure he is the one you seek.

Yes. Wait for tonight. And hope there's time.

He looked at the position of the morning sun and wished for it to pass quickly.

Chapter 3

The sun went down on Barlow, and the air grew even cooler. But there was no wind this night, and for that late in September the weather was considered most tolerable. If anything, it helped to attract the crowds at the end of town.

Torches were lit all around the big tent. The show was about to begin.

There were quite a few people present, about sixty or so in all, though it could have been more had these festivities been held in the daytime hours. Several families had left town well before dark, hoping to make it home at least by midnight. Besides, people did not travel easy after dark these days, not with the Atwood gang still on the loose.

Even with free tickets, Willie Ducane almost didn't show up for the Brady event. Her father had insisted that she wear something ladylike and "fetching," and, as always, she gave in without argument. The calico print felt baggy and uncomfortable compared to a tight pair of jeans, and she would have preferred wearing her hair tied back instead of loose. But Pa knew best. He had even decided to go with her, despite his contempt for anachronistic shows such as this. She suspected it was more to keep an eye on her, to make sure she didn't slip out and change clothes after leaving home.

There were more than enough benches in the big tent for

the entire crowd. Willie and her father sat in the front row for an unrestricted view of the showground. It was all well lit by the pole lanterns standing all around. Once everyone was settled, Colonel Bill Brady rode out on a short stallion that seemed ill at ease beneath so much weight. The showman was dressed in some gaudy military uniform replete with medals, though it was unclear from the appearance just what army he had served in. In a booming voice he announced the first act.

Twin brothers named Birdwell or something similar came riding into the tent. They specialized in fancy mounts and trick riding, and Willie thought they were quite good. They did headstands in the saddle and dismounted and re-mounted at a dead run, which seemed to please the audience. There was not enough room in the tent for the horses to really cut loose and gallop, but maybe that was the idea. When they were finished, next came Tuscaloosa Sam, the knife thrower. He could hurl knives and tomahawks and even full-sized axes, and most of them stuck in the target. He was even better received than the trick riders until he asked for a volunteer from the audience and up stepped Lucy Walker, the banker's daughter. She stood against a wooden target and held up balloons for Sam to pop, which he did with eight-inch blades. But on the last throw Lucy flinched, and the knife nicked her hand. It was not a bad cut to Willie's eye, but Lucy was a pampered young lady and fainted dead away at the first sight of blood. Tuscaloosa Sam apologized but was still booed from the tent. Immediately the crowd was abuzz with dissatisfaction. There was liquor on his breath, one woman announced. She'd smelled it all the way across the tent.

Willie sighed. If they think that's bad, she thought to herself, wait till they get a glimpse of Tolman Shaddock.

The old cowboy stood at the rear of the show tent, listening to the unease of the crowd inside. He was dressed in the fringed white uniform that Colonel Brady insisted he wear for these exhibitions, with the white Stetson and leather gauntlets and boots to match, even a long blond wig to make him look more like the famous Buffalo Bill. He felt stupid and sick to his stomach, and he waited for his time to go on with an icy dread. Just a drink, he wished. All he needed was one. That would be enough to calm the pounding in his skull, ease the tremors that ran down his arms and into his clenched fists. Just one . . .

He turned to Mose, his faithful paint. The horse snorted softly as he patted its powerful neck with affection and checked the saddle, made sure the straps were secure. Methodically he worked his way back to the saddlebags, which had been his destination all along. There was a secret pocket inside the left pouch, where he kept a small silver flask . . . but to his chagrin he found that it wasn't there. Then he remembered Colonel Brady had taken it at the last small town they'd visited. In fact, it dawned on him that all of his bottles were gone now, either drunk or confiscated. There was not a drop left. And his shakes were getting worse. How are you going to perform like this, he wondered. You won't be able to hit the broad side of a barn.

There was a smattering of applause inside the tent. A moment later the flaps suddenly parted and Chief Eaglefeather came out, rank with sweat. It was hot beneath those heavy hides, and with the full Indian headdress to boot. He'd just finished his Apache fire dance, where he twirled a long torch that was aflame on both ends, accompanied by the standard chanting and wailing. But Tol knew the dance itself was about as authentic as the man's identity. The chief's real name was Joe Corkle, a Texican with barely a smidgen of Apache blood. What he knew about that part of his heritage could have filled a thimble. And what Joe didn't know, Joe made up. He was a good dancer, though, Tol thought, and he faked it well enough to satisfy the equally uninformed ranch hands and storekeepers who came to these shows. Except for tonight, that is. The sparse clapping from inside suggested that this audience was a little more demanding.

"Rough crowd," Corkle said, sighing in disgust as he jerked off his feathery headdress to wipe the running warpaint from his face. "Damn yokels don't know quality entertainment when they see it. Best be on your toes, Tol. They'll go for the throat the minute they smell fear." He looked over at the older man, leaning on his horse for support. His fists were doubled at his sides and visibly trembling. "Hey, Tol. You look like shit. You able to go on tonight?"

"I'm not all too sure," Shaddock stammered, wincing at how loud his own voice seemed, how it thundered in his ears. "I could really use something to calm my nerves about now. Hey, Joe, you wouldn't have a little nip in your wagon, would you?"

"Sorry, Tol." The almost-Indian waved him off. "The colonel cleaned me out too. This show's dry as dust. I'd like to help, but . . ." He listened for a moment to the sounds from inside the tent. Accordion music—Bill Brady was addressing the crowd, making his nightly pitch, hawking questionable elixirs and carbolic salves and camphor balms before bringing out the main attraction. "That's you, old man," Joe said. "You're up next. Sorry, but you're on your own." The chief draped his feathers over one shoulder and headed back toward his wagon. He passed a real Indian along the way, a small, wiry man who looked to be at least Tol's age, maybe even older, clad in baggy trousers and a wool blanket and an out-of-place derby. This stranger stared at Joe Corkle's outfit and just shook his head in exasperation. Then he came walking over to Shaddock.

"That one is not Apache," the old Indian said. "And he dances like a woman."

"I suppose you're right." Tol nodded. He looked straight at the smaller man; there was something very familiar about him. "Ain't we met before?" he asked. Then it finally came to him through the miasma surrounding his brain. "Oh, yeah. Outside the general store today, right?"

"Yes." The Indian nodded. "You were drunk at the time."

"Well, I'm paying for it now, believe me. Say, friend—"

"I am called No Moon."

"All right, No Moon. You wouldn't have a little sip of firewater anywhere around, would you?"

"You mean whiskey?"

"That'd do."

The old Indian just shook his head. "I do not drink your liquor. It is bad for the spirit."

Shaddock groaned. "Figures."

No Moon stepped closer. He took out the handbill he'd been carrying, unfolded it, and pointed to the face drawn there. "You are this man Shaddock."

Tol leaned heavily on Mose, touched the brim of his hat as if too weak to doff it. "What's left of him, that is."

"And you were at this Creekmore massacre?"

"Yup."

"And you alone survived?"

"Yup."

"Then you are the man I seek. Provided you are telling the truth."

Colonel Brady came storming out of the tent just then, his face red in anger. He took off his Stetson and wiped the sweat from his forehead. "Damned ignorant clodhoppers," he grumbled. "Their wallets are tighter than birch bark. I didn't sell but one bottle." He waved a stubby finger at Shaddock. "You'd better be good, old man. Leave these folks in a better mood or we'll never sell nothing 'round this shithole." He noticed for the first time the Indian standing there, though he didn't appear to recognize him from earlier in the day. "Local color, huh? What's your name, chief?"

"No Moon."

"Well, you want to earn some money? I'll give you two dollars folding money if you let Shaddock here shoot a can off your head. What do you say to two whole dollars, huh?"

The Indian reached out to take Tol's wrist, held up his hand. The shaking was very evident. "I do not think so," No Moon said. "And I did not come here for money." He turned to the taller man. "There is not much time. We must talk. . . ."

"Not now you ain't, Crazy Horse," Brady snapped. "We got a goddamn show to do. Now, get in there, Shaddock, before the crowd wanders off completely."

Tol nodded and pulled himself up into Mose's saddle. The simple movement made his head pound all the harder and his vision began to swim. But he just gritted his teeth and gave the horse a gentle heel in the flank. The old paint was accustomed to the act; it knew right where to go without further instruction. Mose trotted around to the front of the tent, and by the time they reached the main opening, they were to a brisk canter. That became an all-out gallop as they burst into the tent, into the light that burned from a dozen poled lanterns. Then the horse stopped abruptly and reared back on two legs, neighing dramatically. It was all Tol could do to hang on.

The crowd clapped halfheartedly at his entrance, showing a bit more enthusiasm than before. After all, this was the man they had come to see.

He watched the audience from the corner of his eye. It was a sparse gathering. He'd played for larger crowds. But then again, some a lot smaller than this. At least it was a family crowd, mostly townsfolk with their children. They made the best audiences in Tol's opinion. Too many times the cowhands from the nearby ranches would come in, all liquored up and spoiling for a rowdy time. Then there was always one or two who wanted to put the Western legend to the test. He was too damn old to deal with pups like that.

You're too damn old to be out here at all, the voice of common sense said bitterly.

He saw a familiar face in the front row, a young lady in a calico dress with her hair hanging loose around her shoulders. She smiled and waved and he waved back, though he couldn't quite put a name to her. Wait a minute . . . the general store. Could that really be the smudge-faced girl behind the counter, the one who was so interested in his guns? It didn't even look like the same person. This little thing was downright fetching, in a big-boned sort of way. She waved enthusiastically again, but this time the stout, bald man sitting next to her gave a terse command and she begrudgingly settled down.

Another recognizable figure was sitting at the end of the bench behind them. The old Indian No Moon had perched himself there, watching intently.

Tolman dismounted and shooed the paint away, then turned back toward the large opening to the tent. Some of the local boys hired by Brady had moved two long sawhorses into the open, and atop their main beams they now propped white china plates. There were eighteen in all. One for each round in the cylinders of his pistols. Shaddock felt the eyes of the crowd burning into him as he faced the targets. He drew one of his big LeMat pistols in a smooth motion, at least as smooth as his shaking would allow, then thumbed back the hammer. He fired on the first plate, filled the tent with a crack of thunder.

And missed completely.

The audience was silent. But he could feel the accusation in their stares. They burned into him, hotter and harder than ever. He cocked the pistol again, aimed steadily this time. But the barrel would not stay on target; he couldn't even focus his eye on the front sight. He tried to gauge the tremors and compensate. But when he pulled the trigger again, not one of the plates shattered.

The audience let out a collective sigh. Someone gave a mocking laugh, and another man groaned "he's a fake" loud enough for all to hear. Shaddock stood there, gun in hand, staring at the plates that taunted him with their mere presence. How could I have missed? he asked himself. I've done this a hundred times, drunk or sober. Maybe I'm just trying too hard. That's gotta be it. Just relax, nice and easy . . .

He slid the gun back into its holster and let his arm hang limp, let himself tremble freely. He took a deep breath and let it out, tried to steel himself against the grumblings of the crowd and the roaring between his own ears. In his muddled mind there flashed pictures from the past, fading daguerreotypes of a wild and unrepentent life, and he saw himself in just this same position as a man of twenty-five, and twenty-nine, and again and again in his thirties. Only there weren't just plates facing him in those days . . . there were wild-eyed criminals like the Orlen brothers, itching to draw their guns. Painted natives of many different tribes, from the Kiowa to the Comanche, bearing down on him with arrows already nocked and ready to release. And the cocky young pistol fighters, grinning with confidence, always eager to make a name for themselves at the cost of another life. Namely, Tol's. They were all standing before him at the entranceway of the tent, their mouths twisted into sneers, and the look in each one's eyes said he was ready to fire.

Shaddock drew the pistol again, not with lightning speed,

but with a sure and even hand, thumbing back the hammer as he did so. He didn't aim as before. He just pointed and fired, over and over as fast as he could manage. The harsh reports filled the tent like a string of firecrackers, and were immediately accompanied by the tinny sounds of china shattering. They went down one after another, all the way down the line.

He holstered one pistol, drew the other, and continued to fire. And when that one clicked on an empty chamber as well, there were only two plates remaining, the ones he'd missed with his first two shots.

Shaddock cocked the pistol once more. But then he paused, just long enough to adjust the striking nipple on the hammer, from its uppermost position to a lower one. When he leveled the pistol and fired again, this time it was the secondary barrel that belched smoke and flame, just beneath the first. The smooth bore was stoked with a shot load, so there was little need for accuracy this time. The fifteen yards were more than enough distance for the shot to spread. That gave the china little chance of escape. The storm of pellets struck true, shattering the stubborn plates with distinction.

The crowd was silent a moment, stunned by the display. It had taken only moments for Shaddock to mow down the entire line of plates. Finally, when they began to clap, they did so vigorously.

Young boys came out to clear away the sawhorses and debris as Tol removed that pistol's cylinder and replaced it with a fresh one from his belt. But his hands were still shaking badly, noticeable even as he skillfully restoked both guns. So to cover any fumbling, he began to talk directly to the audience. "I am indeed Tolman Shaddock," he introduced himself with a dramatic bow that almost left him dizzy. "And when you look into my eyes you will see images of a time almost gone. Wilder days filled with even wilder people, a time when you could go months in the wilderness without seeing another soul, or go into the cowtowns and play cards with the cheatinest lizards to ever wear a pair of boots. I have seen much and done more, killed many men and committed many a sin and never repented once. For I was young and so was the West, and God always forgives rebellious children."

Several people laughed, cheering the man's folksy audacity. One of the boys present yelled, "What about the Orlen brothers?"

The glazed look of Tol's eyes was excusable as he appeared to think back. "Funny you should mention the Orlens," he ruminated, "for without a doubt they were three of the meanest mother's sons to ever ride out of the Texas Panhandle." And just that quickly he was immersed in the telling of his most famous capture, some twenty-five years past when he worked as a lawman in the Texas town of Waco. He did not have to think about it much, for he had recounted the same tale perhaps a hundred times in the last two years, the same words strung all across the Near East. He did not gloss over any details; they were all there, right down to what each person said and how he moved, how he drew his guns and which of the three he shot first as they rushed his campfire that fateful night. He even demonstrated his draw in slow motion. No one seemed to notice the slur in his voice or how unsteady he was on his feet. The locals were caught up in the sheer drama of the story.

As he was finishing the Orlen brothers tale, Brady sent a boy out into the tent. The teen threw an empty quart can out into the open behind Shaddock and then headed for cover. As soon as the can struck the ground, Tol whirled about with his pistol already drawn, and it barked just like before, in steady cadence. The can jerked and jumped, bounced across the ground as each round struck home, one right after another, not allowing it to stop. The smoking LeMat kept the can dancing all the way across the tent and out the main entrance.

Tol turned immediately back to the crowd, nonplussed. "Now," he said with a faint smile, "where was I?"

The people laughed and cheered, visibly stunned by his performance. It never occurred to them that the act had been rehearsed, that he hadn't simply heard the can fall but had been waiting for it.

Tol swayed slightly, his balance going awry. It felt as if the reports of those gunshots had cracked his already tender skull like an eggshell. He could feel the nausea growing within him, and he knew he'd have to get to an intermission soon. So he launched straightaway into the legend of the Creekmore massacre. "Nigh about fifteen year ago I was working as a civilian scout for General Crook on a reconnaissance of the Black Hills territory up in the Dakota, which ain't too awful far from you people hereabouts. This was during the gold rush up there, in the days of the Indian unrest, and just a couple months before Custer's stand at the Little Bighorn. That day myself and a squad of twenty raw recruits under the young Lieutenant Nathaniel Creekmore were sent out to count the number of miners who were sneaking into the hills along Custer's trail, what Red Cloud's Sioux called Thieves Road. So we went. But little did I suspect that I alone would return . . ."

Tol wasn't completely cognizant of what he was saying; as before, he told the stories rote, regurgitating the details unconsciously. It was a practiced skill. He could just as well have been talking in his sleep. And in a way, he was.

The audience listened in rapt silence, conjuring mental pictures to match Shaddock's words. In their minds they saw how he and his men had been quickly surrounded by more than sixty screaming Sioux warriors, and though they fought bravely, they were cut down one after another. Butchered by the heathens. Scalped. Women gasped at the details and children listened slack-jawed as Tolman Shaddock stood before them, straddling the imaginary corpses of his dead comrades and facing the oncoming horde with guns blazing. The crowd hung on his every word, completely caught up in the story.

All save two.

Surprisingly, Willie Ducane was one of the latter. Unnoticed by the rambling Shaddock, her enthusiasm had seemed to wane the more she listened. She just seemed puzzled, wearing an uncertain expression. Not far from her sat No Moon, still stoic as ever, but the old Indian's mouth had turned down at the corners just the slightest bit. As close to an actual frown as he would allow.

"Mose was what saved me," Shaddock concluded. "My guns were long empty and I was just using 'em as clubs, just flailing at the scoundrels for all I was worth, screaming and spitting like a wild animal. I will be frank with you, ladies and gents; I was beginning to think my ass belonged to ol' Joe Hayes for sure. For the way it looked then, I didn't stand a hope in hell of getting out of there alive, not against that many braves. But then a strange thing happened. Them injuns, they just pulled back aways. They musta thought I was crazy, and that's heap big medicine among them primitive people. So while they were trying to decide what to do with me, I jumped on ol' Mose and give him the heel, and we shot out of there like our asses were ablaze." He gave a whistle, and the old paint came obediently to its master's side. "Mose was a young colt then," he said, stroking the horse's withers, "and nothing on four legs could catch him at a dead run. So we just rode hard and kept riding, for a day and a night in no particular direction. Not until another cavalry patrol finally found us about thirty miles away. And that is how I escaped the massacre in the Black Hills of Dakota." The audience began to applaud and he took a deep bow, almost toppling over onto his face. But no one seemed to notice.

"Do some more shooting," a boy called.

"Tell some more stories," came another.

But Shaddock did neither. He swung himself up into Mose's saddle and held up a hand to calm the audience. "I must take leave for a few moments," he explained to them. "But I will return after a short intermission." As if on command, Mose rose up onto his back legs once more and gave a powerful neigh. Then horse and rider bolted across the tent and out into the night.

Colonel Brady met him just outside, ranting angrily. "What's wrong with you!" he barked. "The show isn't over yet!"

"I need some air." Tol brushed him off in passing. "Besides, they're in a mood to buy something now."

Those words more than anything else seemed to pierce the colonel's bluster. His eyes lit up. A greedy smile slithered across his face. "Don't go far," he ordered, but was already turning away, eagerly looking around for his accordion player.

Mose wandered leisurely away from the tent and town, out into the bright moonlight where the open prairie stretched as far as the eye could see. The paint went about sixty yards and then slowed to a halt, waiting for a command from the man in the saddle. But Tolman didn't give one. He was slumped there, lying half across the horse's powerful neck, holding his head and wishing he would retch and get it over with. The report of each gunshot he'd fired still reverberated inside his skull like the pealing of a great bell, till his eyes bulged and even his hair seemed to ache. I'm dying, he thought with certainty. I've gotta be, 'cause I don't remember ever feeling this bad before. . . .

"You lied."

It took a moment for the voice to make its way through the tender matter between his ears. But finally he acknowledged it and glanced up from under his wig and fancy hat. The old Indian was standing right in front of the horse. "Where the hell did you come from?" Tol groaned.

"You lied about this Creekmore massacre. There were no sixty warriors. Only six. Against twenty of your pony soldiers."

"Is that right? What, was you there or something?"

"No. But I am an Oglala, one of the tribes of the Lakota Sioux. We know the truth, unlike those in the tent."

Shaddock cradled his aching head in his hands. "They've heard the stories before," he explained. "I was just telling 'em what they expected to hear." He looked up at the Indian. "You don't believe I was there, do you?"

No Moon's expression did not change. "On the contrary," he said. "I am sure you were. But you still have not told what happened to your men. How did they die? What really killed them?"

Tol grumbled. He didn't like this questioning. It was like the old red man was calling him a liar. Even worse, the look in this No Moon's eyes said that he knew something.

Maybe he knows about the nightmares.

Hogshit, Tol thought adamantly. He couldn't. That's all in my head, mine alone. He doesn't know nothing. Don't let him bluff you. "I have spoken the truth," he replied, "all I can remember. And I don't like you inferrin' otherwise.

37

Besides, what is it to you, injun? It was a long time ago. None of it matters now."

"Oh, but it does." No Moon stepped closer. There was a dread seriousness about him. "It is the reason I sought you out. Most men would not believe what I am going to tell you. Even many of my own people would scoff. But you have seen the *wakan* ways. You will know what I say is true."

Shaddock just blinked at him. None of this was making any sense. "*Wakan?* What the hell is that? Just what are you talking about?"

The Indian looked away, out across the rolling grasslands. Tol thought he saw a shiver rack the smaller man's wiry frame. "There is evil on the wind this night," No Moon said in a hushed tone. "And I fear it is growing. It threatens your people—perhaps all people. Even my own. Together we may be able to stop it."

The man on the horse gave a bitter chuckle. "I don't know what you're talking about, pard. But if you're looking for help with something, you've come to the wrong place." He held up a trembling hand. "Do I look like I'm in any shape to do anything?"

"You shot well enough inside."

"Practice. You do something long enough and sooner or later you can do it with your eyes closed. Or with a hangover."

The Indian shook his head adamantly. "That is not what I saw inside. You are still a great warrior. These liquor spirits that haunt you will subside with time. Then you will see."

"Shaddock!" It was Colonel Brady, standing outside the show tent. "Get back here!" he yelled. "You don't want to keep these good people waiting, do you?" From clodhoppers to good people. The elixir sales must have improved the second time around.

Tol looked back to the Indian. "I don't know what you want, friend. But if you're determined to talk about it, I'll be in my wagon over there after the show." He reined Mose back toward the tent. But then he called over his shoulder, "Bring a bottle, old man. I guarantee the shakes'll fade after—"

A sound erupted from the distant prairie, stopping him in midsentence. It was the barest periphery of an echo, faint but definitive enough to reach his ear. A high-pitched wail, long and ululating, unlike anything he'd heard before. The fine hair along his neck stood taut against his collar. "What the hell . . ." he stammered. Then he looked back to No Moon. "What was that?" he asked, for somehow he suspected the Indian would know.

The old Sioux said nothing. He just stood there, staring out into the moonlit distance. Tol wasn't close enough to see him tremble.

Chapter 4

One of the canvas-covered wagons in Bill Brady's entourage belonged to Tolman Shaddock. But he very seldom slept there.

It was small as far as wagons go, and didn't allow very much room inside. There was a cot that was none too comfortable, and a place for his saddle when it wasn't on old Mose. And the old steamer trunk he'd won in a card game in St. Louis sometime back, which now held the few belongings he could call his own. Between those three items, there was not much space for moving around, especially not for a man as large as he who'd spent most of his years beneath the stars, traveling both plains and mountains where the openness could steal one's breath with its grandeur. After that it was stifling to stay inside. So most nights found Tol Shaddock's bedroll pitched out where he could breathe, or beneath the wagon if he thought there might be rain.

That is where he was this night, lying between those big wooden wheels. The air didn't carry the scent of rain as it most often did. But he could feel something there nonetheless . . . an odd sensation. Maybe a storm was coming.

It was almost midnight, and the Brady show had been over for some time. The big tent was empty and silent and the crowds gone, having returned to their homes and the monotony of small town life. But the brief respite that the show offered had been well received. The audience had been satisfied with the entertainment, what there was of it. Colonel Brady was satisfied with the receipts from the elixir sales. And Shaddock had survived another performance without shooting his foot off. So far, so good, he thought. Now, if only he could make it through this latest brush with sobriety. The battle was still raging, even at this late hour. He lay on the blanket beneath the wagon, twisted into a ball by the burning in his stomach and gullet, covering his ears in vain against the still-echoing clamor of the audience. Each breath made his head pound all the harder. He had to fight down the urge to retch, though there wasn't anything left in his stomach anyway.

If only I had a bottle . . .

But he knew there was no way of getting one. The colonel had warned everyone else in the show against him—not one of them would risk sneaking him a nip, not with the fat man watching. And he would be alert, what with a second show to do tomorrow night. Tol thought about walking into town for a drink, but the saloon was closed by now and he had no money, not even something worth bartering. Except for his pistols, that is, and he wasn't about to part with them. Not unless he just had to . . .

Nope, he thought, no bottle tonight. And that gives you just three alternatives. You can lie and moan like a fractured coyote. You can put a pistol barrel to your ear and blow that throbbing head clean off your shoulders. Or you can just go to sleep.

The last was the only reasonable option. But it was the one he fought the hardest.

He knew what would await him there, in the arms of slumber. The dank memory of those nightmares had been stirred this day, just when he thought he'd outrun them. They were flitting around his subconscious like black and bothersome gnats. He could feel them, waiting, eager to take him in their dark folds as they had so many times in the past. But he couldn't allow that.

Ultimately, he found his will lacking, not nearly as strong as it had been in his younger days. Or maybe his fatigue was just that much stronger. Within the hour Tol's eyelids became increasingly heavy, impossible to hold open. No matter how much he struggled, he couldn't stop the inexorable descent that followed.

Or the dark images that awaited him.

The sun was setting steadily over the mountainous Dakota wilds, birthing shadows that joined together and spread across the rugged landscape like a tide of running oil. Tol Shaddock, already forty-five and trail scout for the United States Army out of Fort Randall, noted the harbingers of night from the corner of his eye and nudged his strong young paint to a quicker pace. He had wanted to catch up to his quarry before the daylight was too far gone. But he began to realize that it just wasn't going to happen. Before long the settling gloom of evening would obscure what few signs he could still ferret out, and the hunt would be over for the night.

And a savage killer would still be out there in the darkness. Watching.

The thought did not sit well with him. Not at all. In fact, it sent a tremor of unease fluttering up his backbone. He took the reins in one hand and rested the other on the butt of one of his holstered revolvers, ready to draw at the slightest provocation.

Hooves clacked loudly on the exposed bedrock as Mose ambled out of a stand of box elder and onto a broad limestone shelf, where they had an unhindered view of the surrounding lands. This was the first time he'd been in this part of the Black Hills in his two years of Army employment, and he found the landscape to have a rather dramatic face. Massive shards of granite seemed to jut from the earth as if pushed up by some ancient cataclysm. They loomed above the treetops, where there were trees, at least, and would have dominated the geography completely were it not for the even more imposing formations beyond. Framed against the burning sky and wrapped in cloaks of ebon pine were the Black Hills themselves. They towered above the world, mute and eternal, and bore scowling witness to the white man's trespass.

Shaddock did not deny their disapproval. In fact, he agreed only too well. It was precisely why they were there— to support the Treaty of '68 and tell the miners in the hills to get out. At least that had been the Army's mission. Before this hunt began. "Tolerate us a might longer," he whispered to those stoic palisades. "We'll be out of your hair just as quick as we can." He looked around, fought down a shiver. "Even quicker if I can help it."

Sitting alone and surveying the area without the clop of the horse's hooves or the creak of shifting saddle leather to occupy his ears, he was quickly reacquainted with the unnatural silence that seemed to permeate this entire region. And with it his unease intensified, for in all his years on the frontier, he'd learned never to trust the silence. When the crickets didn't chirp and the birds held their songs in check, it meant that something was wrong, that danger was close at hand. And with this quiet lingering for two days straight, ever since they rode into these mountains, his wariness was beginning to show signs of strain. . . .

Especially after finding those butchered miners early on the second day. The bodies of the men whose killer he now stalked.

The blood-spattered image of that murder scene still played before his mind's eye, just as it had repeatedly throughout the day. It brought a frown of disgust, dredged the bile in this throat. Tol Shaddock was not a man of weak constitution, not after having his baptisms by fire on the battlefields of the South. There he saw the horrors of war, men skewered on bayonets or gutshot and screaming for their mamas. Pieces of humanity scattered about by the fury of an artillery shell. But even that had not prepared him for the savagery that these killings evidenced. Shattered limbs. Disembowelment. Decapitation. The bodies were barely recognizable as human anymore.

But not so the heads. They were unmarked, having been separated and placed all in a line facing the camp as if to witness their own slaughter. Their faces still wore masks of frozen anguish. Those staring eyes, the gaping mouths . . . they still haunted him as none had before, their silent screams echoing in his mind. . . .

There was movement in the trees behind him. Subtle sounds—the snap of a twig underfoot, the tread of something heavy in the leaves and dirt. But the silence magnified such noises, enough to pierce the veil of memory that clouded Shaddock's mind. He snapped alert and in one fluid motion a LeMat was clear of its holster, the hammer already back and his first knuckle whitening on the trigger. He held it there, trained on the approaching horseman's chest, for one second. Two.

"Well?" the black man asked. "You gonna shoot me or what?"

"I's thinking about it," he grumbled. "Maybe staring down a gun barrel'll break you of a bad habit, sneaking up on people like that."

"Sneaking's what we do for a living, Tol." Jubal Turner laughed lightly. "Ain't you figured that out yet? 'Sides, I made enough noise coming up that trail to wake the dead. If you couldn't hear that, well boy, you'd best give up this here field of endeavor." Then he gave that big horse grin that Shaddock had come to know so well. The Negro was almost fifteen years his senior in age and five in scouting for the Army, and time was beginning to tell on him. What hair he still had was frosted gray as winter, and wire-frame spectacles were perched atop his nose. Indeed, his failing eyesight had forced some changes in his life, like trading in his sharpshooting rifle for a close-up scattergun. But he refused to give up the trail. He had been a tracker for too long now, and still had the nose for it. That's why he and Shaddock made such a good team. As he often put it, Tol was the eyes and he was the brains. Tol never refuted that claim.

Shaddock finally lowered his pistol and holstered it. But he never returned the other's smile. "Sorry, Jube," he said softly. "I guess this whole thing's got me a little on edge." He took a plug of chaw from his coat pocket, bit off a wad, and tossed the rest to his friend. "Find anything?"

"Naw," the older man muttered around his own jawful of tobacco. "I came in from the south. But I couldn't find a damned track 'ner nothing. How about you?"

"Two spots of blood back aways, 'bout quarter of a mile. Hoped the damned thing might be wounded somehow, maybe from fighting the miners. But I didn't find any other signs. Means it was probably just trailing blood from the dead men." He looked around, sighed with frustration. "Dammit, there's gotta be a trail here somewhere. No animal can just disappear like that."

Jubal was looking to the west, watching the day's descent. "It'll be dark 'fore long. Maybe we'd best call it quits, go find the lieutenant and his men, and make camp for the night."

Tol was still searching the landscape, scouring each rock and tree with an eaglelike stare. "You go ahead. I want to find this bastard."

The old black man was bewildered. "Are you crazy, boy? This thing, it's killed six men that we know of, left 'em in tatters like in a slaughtering pen. Six men, you hear? And you want to tackle that thing all by yourself? And in the dark at that?"

Tol was confident, or at least he tried to sound that way. "I expect it's a rogue bear," he said with a nod, "wandered down from the hills. And I've taken plenty of bears before." He patted the butt of his Sharps 44-70 in its saddle scabbard. "This'll bring it down, sure enough."

"If it is a bear, that is," Jubal muttered. "I ain't so sure."

"Oh, yeah? Well, what do you think it is, old man? You agreeing with Lieutenant Creekmore now, are you? Think it's Red Cloud and his Sioux on the warpath? The little half-wit wouldn't know an Indian if one snuck up and bit him on the ass. Dammit, Jube, you know the Sioux better'n me. You've seen 'em fight. And kill. Couldn't you tell this weren't no Indian massacre? Where were the signs of a struggle, huh? Where were the broken arrows or lances? There weren't even any knife or hatchet cuts—them miners were torn apart, plain and simple. Weren't no men that did that, red or any other."

"I know that, Tol." The older scout shrugged. "Don't go getting your back up. I'm agreeing with you. No man did that. But it wasn't no bear either." He saw the other man roll his eyes. "Okay, Mr. Expert Tracker. Was any of them bodies eaten or carried off for later? Did a bear line them heads up like birds on a fence rail? Come on, Tol, I learned you better than that."

"Then what do you think did it?"

Jubal just shrugged again. He reined his horse alongside Shaddock's, closer to the edge of the rocks, and looked out over the jagged countryside. And for a moment the younger scout would have sworn he'd seen a look of apprehension, of dread, play across those dark, leathery features. "Do you know where we are, boy?" Jubal asked. "The Sioux call this place Paha-Sapa. The Black Hills. This is their most sacred place. Their warriors come here to prepare their eyes for the brilliance of the Happy Hunting Ground. This is native land, Tol. Holy earth. And now, thanks to that strutting peacock Custer, sounding the reveille for gold, these hills are starting to crawl with miners. Us too. It's trespassing, pure and simple. And someday somebody'll pay the price." He looked around at Tol. "Maybe it's started already."

"But Jubal, you just said that it wasn't the Sioux. It—" He looked at his friend, realization setting in. "Oh, I get it. Native land. If it's not the red man, then maybe his spirits, eh? We got us some Indian devils running around killing miners, right?" He spat a stream of tobacco juice and shook his head. "Are you gonna sit there bald-faced and say you believe that horseshit? I swear, Jube, you sound like some scared kid."

"I am scared," Turner muttered under his breath. "And maybe you should be too."

"Well, I ain't, old man," Shaddock announced. "'Cause there ain't no ghosts 'ner spookies in these hills. Just some damn big bear. And I'm gonna prove it to you by running that bastard to ground." He tugged the rein, pulled Mose into a turn, and left the outcropping at a quick canter. Jubal cussed and spat; he had to hurry just to keep up. Shaddock was already skirting the large rock shelf, looking for a path where the incline was not so severe. Mose, though, was a sure-footed mount and found his own way down with little effort. They waited at the bottom for the older scout, still cursing under his breath, to catch up, then they rode back along the base of the limestone ridge.

It was darker down where the lingering sunlight did not reach. A shadowy realm that already held the damp chill of nighttime. "I don't like this," Jubal was grumbling. "Don't like it nary a bit." But he stayed right behind Shaddock just the same.

The steady gurgle of running water reached their ears, growing louder, until they abruptly came upon a natural spring spurting from a cleft in the rock itself, feeding a weed-choked stream. The vegetation was very dense along the water's edge, and it combined with the settling dusk to obscure their vision even further. Plenty of places to hide in there, Tol thought. His hand settled on the butt of one pistol for reassurance. But he just as quickly thought better of it. For as big as the LeMat was, it just didn't seem like enough. Without further thought he drew the Sharps 44-70 from its saddle scabbard. The big-bore was just a single-shot, but it felt more reassuring in his hand. And if it could bring down an eleven-hundred-pound buffalo at a dead run, it could surely handle a rogue bear.

If it was a bear . . .

He cut the doubt off at its root, reined his horse out into the middle of the stream and began to follow it through the weeds. Jubal was close behind him, muttering again, cursing the gathering darkness.

The creek wound around the base of two of the rocky spires they had seen earlier from that higher vantage point, and then it meandered into a small meadow ringed with trees. But Tol's eye could reach no farther. What little sunlight remained lit only the sky above; it could not breach the barrier of the Black Hills that surrounded them, leaving all of the land within, even open space such as the meadow, cloaked in a palpable gloom. Even the trees that awaited them were no more than a stunted line of shadow.

"Let's get out of here," Jubal said from behind him, his voice quavering as he spoke. That was something Shaddock had never detected in his mentor's voice before. Fear. "It's too dark, boy. Ain't gonna find nothing now. We gotta call it off, you hear?"

Tol frowned, started to bark at him for a decided lack of backbone. But the image of those dead miners came back, those heads all in a line, their dead eyes watching him. That chill ran along his spine yet again, but this time it latched on with spider arms and refused to go away. That thing—bear or whatever—could be anywhere in the dark. Hiding in the trees. Hunkered in the grass. Just waiting for you to ride past . . . "Maybe you're right, Jube," Tol finally, begrudgingly, agreed. "We'll go back to that high shelf and camp there for the night. The moon'll keep it well lit; won't nothing sneak up on us there. Then come morning, we'll—" He saw Jubal stiffen suddenly, his senses alert. "What?" Tol whispered. "What is it?"

Turner put a finger to his lips. "Listen."

Tol complied, and the silence that resulted—no buzzing insects, no sighing breezes, nothing—seemed to magnify the soft popping sounds in the distance. At least enough to reach their ears.

Gunfire. Tol knew immediately. "Creekmore and the soldiers. Think they've found our critter?"

"Maybe." Jubal swallowed hard. "Or it found them."

In unison they gave their mounts the heel and set across the meadow at a full gallop, following the faint echoes of the gunshots. Neither hesitated at the dark treeline ahead; rather, they plunged straight into the shadows, where the underbrush snagged at their clothing and tore their skin. Tol laid the big rifle barrel right along Mose's thick neck to keep it from being caught by a low branch and jerked from his grasp. The woods were dense but not deep; within minutes they emerged into the open again, this time a much wider area that skirted the base of a sheer butte. The grassland they rode into was no longer distinct in the gloom, just a field of grayness. Except for the pale spot at the far end. At the speed of their gallop, it did not take the two long to reach that spot and recognize it as a white shirt. The body wearing it was facedown in the grass. Not moving.

"Ain't wearing soldier blue," Jubal said, dropping to his feet. "Who you figure it is?" He knelt down, grabbed a shoulder, and rolled the body over. It was a young Indian boy, a Sioux probably, no more than twelve and clad in fringed trousers and a white cotton shirt. The boy was obviously dead, no two ways about it. There were two bloody wounds through his chest and a ragged hole just over his left eye, showing brain and bone where the bullet that killed him had exited. He was lying on gathered sticks, the same bundle he had doubtless been carrying somewhere when he was shot from behind.

Shaddock fumed. "That son of a bitch Creekmore! I told him it weren't no Indians that did it! They killed this boy for nothing!"

"He was gathering wood for a fire," Jubal observed. "That means there's an injun camp near here somewheres." And no sooner had the words left his mouth than shots rang out again. More of them this time, and not as far away. In fact, the echoes sounded as if they'd traveled only from the far side of the butte.

"Yah!" Tol spurred his mount onward with explosive suddenness, even before Jubal could get a boot up into the stirrup. The big paint thundered across the open ground toward the butte, then shifted course and followed along the rock's base. He rounded the bend and came upon another meadow, this one longer and stretched in the shadow of one of the Black Hills' craggy peaks. The mantle of night had already settled in that flat lea, so he could not see much at first. Just the conical shapes of tipis backlit by a smoldering campfire, two of them in flames themselves. Indistinct shadows skittering about in the flickering light. A flash of dark skin, then the blue of swarming uniforms. There were screams and more shots, and this time he could see their muzzle flashes like fireflies winking in the darkness. In that instant Tol Shaddock knew he'd found the Sioux encampment . . . and that Lieutenant Creekmore and his men had gotten there first.

The shooting and screaming had ended by the time he reached the tipis. He could see the soldiers of Creekmore's reconnaissance force milling around the campfire, laughing raucously over their obvious victory. But there was not much victory to it when Tol realized there were only six Indians in the camp to stand against them. Their bodies were now piled by the fire. Nathaniel Creekmore sat nearby on horseback, watching over the tableau with a grim satisfaction. He was a small, lean man, like a banty rooster to Tol's way of thinking, with his back ramrod straight and his uniform conspicuously free of grime and gore. His hawkish features and haughty air had earned him the nickname Little Custer among the enlisted men at Fort Randall, something the young officer did not attempt to dissuade too strenuously. Rather, he seemed to encourage the comparison, right down to his wavy blond hair and carefully cultivated mustache.

He looked up as Tol came riding into camp, and his expression was a smug one. "Well, if it isn't our trusty Indian scout," he sneered contemptuously, and the men chortled in agreement. "It would seem that we didn't need you after all, Mr. Shaddock. I'd say we have the situation well in hand."

Tol looked slowly from the cocky young officer to his men. They stared back at him, all twenty of them, and their evident zeal was disturbing to him. Especially McGuinn, the beefy sergeant. He stood amid the bodies of the murdered Indians, holding the lieutenant's saber in his hand, its blade stained black in the firelight. His smirking expression betrayed the horror of his task. Three of the bodies had not only been shot multiple times but decapitated as well. Their heads were now lined up along the campfire, the dance of the flames reflecting in open glassy eyes.

"Jesus Christ on his throne," muttered Jubal Turner, who had ridden up alongside the younger scout without his noticing. The old black man cast a disbelieving eye on the men and then their leader. "What the hell have you done here? Are you mad, is that it?"

"Just doing our duty, that's all," Creekmore replied. "I promised those miners on their graves that I'd bring their

killers to justice and, by God, that's just what we've done."
He motioned to the line of detached heads. "Let this be a
warning to the rest of their heathen breed."

"But these people were innocent," Shaddock objected as
he swung out of the saddle, the butt of the Sharps still
propped against his hip. "We done told you, it was an
animal that killed those miners. You killed them for nothing."

"Just injuns," grinned Sergeant McGuinn. "They had it
coming, one way or another."

Tol knelt down beside the fire. To his dismay, one of the
three heads propped there on the dirt lip of the firepit was an
older female. Another was a boy even younger than the
wood gatherer they'd found only minutes earlier. "You're
wrong," he muttered, fighting the urge to bring his rifle butt
across the sergeant's grinning mouth. "No one deserves this.
No one."

"Uh, Lieutenant," called one of the younger soldiers
standing nearby. He was staring off to the side, in the
direction of a larger circular lodge at the rear of the camp.
Pliable saplings had been bent and tied to form a dome, and
old buffalo hides stretched across the frame. The heavy flap
was hanging open just a few inches, enough to glimpse the
darkness within. "I think I saw someone move in there," the
boy reported. "I'm almost positive."

All eyes turned to the lodge. "Who checked in there?"
Creekmore questioned his men. When no one answered, his
brow furrowed. "McGuinn! Didn't you have anyone check
out this lodge?" The brawny sergeant was blank-faced for a
moment, then turned angrily on his men in search of his
own scapegoat. "Oh, never mind," the young officer snapped
as he drew his pistol for the first time and dismounted. "I'll
handle this personally." He moved through the crowd of
men with a stiff, authoritative stride. The two scouts fell in
close behind him.

"What are you gonna do, Creekmore?"

"Leave it to the Army, Shaddock," the lieutenant warned
him off. He approached the lodge with his Colt ready.
"Awright in there," he called through the partially open flap

in the most menacing voice he could muster. "You get out here right now with your hands empty. You hear me? Do it now, or we'll burn you out right quick."

There was immediate movement in the lodge. Shuffling sounds. A distinct dragging gait. And then the flap pulled back farther and a small, thin figure came out into the flickering firelight. The Indian was probably in his sixties but looked much older, due mostly to the gray hair and deeply lined face. His frame was withered nearly to the bone, and he had a painful, hampered walk. But the latter had nothing to do with the infirmities of age. Rather, it was the result of a physical disability; the old man's spine began to bend to the side just above the hips, giving him a distinctly crooked posture. It was that deformity that seemed to bring the soldiers up short. Even Lieutenant Creekmore was somewhat taken aback by his appearance.

"So that's one of your killers, huh, Creekmore?" Shaddock laughed. "Is this cripple the one who tore those miners' heads clean off their shoulders?" The young officer didn't respond. He just glared at the scout with unconcealed enmity.

Jubal Turner stepped forward to face the Indian. Their eyes met, and for the first time Shaddock saw the glimmer of the red man's eyes. A spark of hatred, glowing deep and bright. Which was understandable, he supposed, given that his small band had just been slaughtered right in front of him. The old black scout muttered something under his breath, meant for the Indian, but Tol caught enough not to recognize the tongue. He just watched the Indian for a response. Unfortunately there wasn't any. Even after Jubal was finished, the old man still did not reply.

"What did you ask him?"

"His name," Turner said. "If I'm not mistaken, this is Sky Falling Man. At least he fits the description, all twisted up like that. They say he's a great medicine man among the Lakota tribes." He asked his question once more. But the Indian gave only his baleful glare. And silence.

"Never mind that gibberish." Creekmore waved them off. "The chief here savvies our talk good enough, else he wouldn'ta come out of there when I told him to. Isn't that right, chief?" He stepped closer to the Indian. "Heap big medicine man, are you?"

No answer.

"Go ahead, tell 'em. It was you that killed those miners, wasn't it? You told your braves to butcher 'em, didn't you? Didn't you!"

"That's enough, Creekmore," Shaddock warned.

The officer glared at the Indian, furious at being disobeyed so. He raised his pistol and laid the barrel against the crooked man's temple. "You're gonna talk, you goddamn savage. Or I'll drop you right where you stand."

He'll do it too, Shaddock assured himself. He's gonna kill him, just like he said, just like he had the rest of them killed. Butchered. Are you just gonna stand here and watch him do it?

No.

Then do something, dammit.

The words were out of his mouth almost before he could give it another thought. "Put the gun down, Creekmore," he warned in a steely voice. And when the officer paid him no heed, Tol raised the Sharps with one hand and pointed that gaping bore at the center of the smaller man's chest. "I said put it down. Now."

The lieutenant turned to look at him, and at the big buffalo gun staring in his direction. And then a confident grin came across his features. "That's treason, Shaddock," he said. "And this man's Army doesn't look too favorably on traitors." The grin grew larger as Tol heard the familiar sounds of multiple hammers being cocked behind him. There were twenty guns on his back now, he could feel them. But he wasn't about to lower his own. They'd just kill you anyway, he told himself. You're committed now, pard. You'll have to ride this horse till it drops.

"Where do you stand, Jubal?" he said to the other scout beside him. The old Negro's double barrel would not equalize this standoff much, but it was better than nothing. Still, his friend did not immediately respond. "Jubal? You with me or not?" He dared to take his eyes off the lieutenant just long enough to cast a sideways glance in his mentor's direction.

Turner stood gripping his shotgun so tightly that his arms and shoulders quaked. His expression was wide-eyed, slack-jawed, and Shaddock could have sworn he'd turned a shade whiter from shock. "Shadow . . ." the old scout finally stammered, pointing. "Shadow . . ." Tol followed his gesture to Creekmore and the Indian, the former still holding a pistol to the latter's head. It took a moment for him to realize what had startled Turner so.

Shadow?

That's when he saw it. The flickering campfire cast the young officer's shadow all across the side of the lodge behind them. But his was the only one emblazoned there. The crooked man had none.

Tol didn't react right away; he was numbed to silence by the sight, same as Jubal, as his mind struggled to provide a suitable explanation, all in vain. By this time even Creekmore had turned to notice his own shadow and the absence of the other. "What the hell . . ."

Shaddock caught a subtle change in the Indian's expression. His lips twitched, then curled back into a gleeful smile.

The flap of the lodge suddenly blew wide open and a dark shape loomed over them, blotting out the side of the sapling and hide structure as it came. In a split second something slammed into Shaddock like a cannonball, jarring the gun from his grip, sprawling him on his back. The impact left him stunned, with starbursts of pain dancing before his eyes, even through closed lids. He could barely make out indistinct sounds through the miasma of his dulled senses. Faint pops of gunfire. The cries of horses and men alike. But after a while they died away, and then there was nothing.

Sensations returned to him slowly; the pain from a gash in his forehead, a lung-straining weight on his chest that kept him pinned to the ground. A warm wetness was spreading across his legs.

He opened his eyes, blinked the fuzziness away, and found himself staring into another face bare inches above his own. It was Lieutenant Creekmore lying atop the scout, his own forehead gashed open from where their heads had collided. He did not move. Or blink. Or breathe. Tol was repulsed by the dead man's closeness and shoved him away. That's when he realized there was only a torso pinning him down. Creekmore had been torn in two just above the pelvis; only the upper half had landed atop Shaddock. He kicked the horror away from him with disgust, disentangling his legs from the officer's ropy entrails. Then slowly he got to his feet.

The campsite was silent. The only sound was the crackle of the fire and his own labored breathing. When he looked around, he found himself surrounded on all sides by death. There were uniformed bodies and pieces of bodies and mounds of horseflesh littering the grass, steaming in the chilled night air.

But I couldn't have been out that long, he thought. What could have killed this many so fast? He tried to count the bodies, but he couldn't tell how many men there were, not shredded that way. But there can't be twenty out there. Not all twenty. Surely some of them got away—

A man's scream suddenly echoed in the darkness somewhere. It was long and shrill, a cry of absolute terror. Then it strangled off abruptly, and the silence returned.

It's after them, Tol realized as a cold dread touched his heart. The few that got away. Whatever slaughtered Creekmore and these men is after them now, and it's catching them. But what the hell is it?

There ain't no Indian devils here. . . .

Shaddock turned back to the Sioux lodge where this nightmare began. And there he found three more figures. Or two and a half, to be precise. First was the old Indian, Sky Falling Man. He was not only still alive but standing precisely where he had before, a wan expression playing on his craggy face. Directly beside him in the grass was Lieutenant Creekmore's missing lower half, a pile of crumpled trousers and boots and glistening intestine. And not far from that he located Jubal Turner. The old Negro scout was kneeling on the ground with his back to Shaddock, his head bowed, still holding his shotgun in both hands.

"Jubal?" Tol whispered, rushing to his side. "Jube, did

you see what . . ." But then he saw that his friend was beyond words. Whatever monstrous blow had driven him to his knees had also pushed his head down into his chest till his mouth and nose were hidden from view and his spectacles now rested on his collarbone. A drop of blood hung from each spattered lens.

More sounds from out there somewhere . . . the mingled screams of horse and rider alike. Both died suddenly, with nothing in their wake. That left Tol's ears empty except for the words Jubal had spoken to him earlier. They kept echoing, over and over.

Trespassing, pure and simple . . . somebody'll pay the price. . . .

He turned to find the crippled Indian still watching him, still glaring with eyes that reflected the firelight. Eyes that wouldn't blink. "It *was* you, wasn't it?" Tol said, drawing one of his big pistols. "You did have the miners killed, just like Creekmore said. Didn't you!"

Sky Falling Man still did not reply. But he did smile again. And that wicked expression, devoid of humor or of any human emotion at all beyond simmering hatred, said more than words ever could. Then the medicine man's steely gaze flickered a moment, shifted just enough to see past Shaddock's shoulder. In response to the view, his smile grew even larger.

Tol swallowed hard. He knew what the Indian had seen. He could feel it himself now, as if its mere presence caused ripples in the very air around him. The unknown killer had returned.

A cold sweat broke on Tol's neck and slid down his spine as he turned to face this new enemy. The thing standing at the periphery of the campfire's glow was unlike any animal Tol had seen. This creature was several heads larger than he and three times as broad, especially across its barrel chest and shoulders. It stood upright like a man on powerful goatlike legs, its feet a curious blend of hoof and talon, and its powerful arms trailed so low, they almost dragged the grass. It appeared to be covered in black hairlike quills like a porcupine, and the flesh beneath must have been dark as well, for there was no other color to the beast at all. Only black, as if covered in a thick coat of oil. It even had a glistening sheen to it. Tol could not locate a face or even a head for that matter—there was nothing at all sitting atop those massive shoulders. But he could feel it watching him nonetheless. An icy, merciless glare that sliced straight to the bone.

The thing moved abruptly, took a quick and silent step farther into the light. Tol could see the head now, if indeed that's what it was—a small black knob that protruded straight out from the shoulders at a right angle to the chest. But there were still no features evident there.

Shaddock didn't wait for it to move again. He raised his pistol and fired straight at the center of its chest. He even saw the round strike home, caught the ripple of the impact across the thing's torso. It clutched at its chest just where he'd fired. But only a moment later it took that massive hand away, and he could see no wound there at all.

The thing took three quick and silent steps, moved right through the middle of the campfire. It stopped between Tol and the flames and stood silhouetted by their light. And there it watched him.

A spark of panic began to burn in Tol's stomach as he drew his second pistol with his left hand, began firing both guns one after another, as fast as he could cock them and pull the trigger. But the effects were no different, and the spark in his gut became a roaring flame of fear. He knew each and every shot was on target. But they did nothing. Not even a flinch this time.

"What in the hell . . ." he whispered. And then he realized how close that phrase probably was. Hell indeed . . . and who do you think called this thing up, an inner voice asked.

Behind him, as if in answer, the crooked man started to laugh, a grating sound full of hatred and venom.

Tol didn't have to look back at the Indian's face; he could picture it in his mind, split by a capering grin of triumph. As the mad cackling grew in pitch and intensity, echoing across the meadow and throughout Paha-Sapa, the hulking shadow-beast came forward again. Coming for him.

The scout's pistols were empty now, even the shot loads

under the main barrel, and there wasn't time to reload. He cast them away and began a frantic search for some other weapon, any at all.

Find Creekmore's pistol or pry the shotgun from Jubal's dead hands or . . . there!

His eyes fell across the trusty Sharps lying on the ground halfway between himself and that oncoming nightmare. He did not hesitate an instant—he simply rushed forward and grabbed up the rifle, even as the devil bore down on him. It loomed not more than six feet away, blotting out the fire entirely. As he watched its inexorable approach, two eyes seemed to open on that small, knoblike head. Not normal eyes, but two ragged slits that gave witness to an inner blackness even darker than the rest of its being. A mouth opened as well, extending downward and doubling and tripling in size until it was larger than the head that produced it. And Tol would have sworn that Sky Falling Man's maniacal laughter now issued from that gaping maw as well.

"C'mon then, you bastard!" Shaddock dared. "Come on, take me straight to hell. But I'll promise you one thing. I won't be going alone." He wheeled around, lined up the rifle's iron sights with the medicine man's forehead. The Indian's laughter seemed to catch in his throat; his eyes widened with shock, and Tol took some satisfaction in that.

The massive hand caught his shoulder just as he jerked the trigger and *fired*—

Tol awoke with a start, wincing from the pain in his forehead. He touched it and was surprised to find no gash where Creekmore had been thrown into him. But then he remembered that there was none, never had been one to his recollection. *You've been dreaming again, that's all. Probably banged your head on the axle when you woke up. Yeah, that must be it.*

He lay back under the wagon and took a deep breath of midnight air, tried to calm the rapid pounding of his heart. *Just a dream,* he told himself. *It's always just a dream. It never happened like that. It was the Indians who slaughtered those men, no two ways about it. Just like I told those folks* at the show. But despite his denials, the coldness in the pit of his stomach refused to subside.

He was shaking badly now, and he tried to blame it once again on his enforced sobriety. *Lord, I need a drink now more'n ever. And by God, I'm gonna get me one.*

He crawled out of his bedding and into the bright moonlight, where he stretched and scratched. Then he retrieved his hat and his gunbelt, strapped the latter at his hip. He went over to Mose, who was grazing fitfully a few yards from the wagon. "Gonna get me a bottle, pard," he told the horse adamantly, "even if I gotta do something drastic."

He was trying to decide where to look first, to his fellow performers or straight to the closed saloon in town, when he turned and saw a figure sitting against the rear wheel of the wagon.

Chapter 5

Shaddock first glimpsed the figure from the corner of his eye. It made him flinch, for in that instant he was sure a phantom from his nightmares had followed him here, crawled forth to plague him in the flesh. It was Sky Falling Man sitting there, wasn't it, watching him with eyes that nearly glowed in the dark. Tol's hand was shaking as it reflexively grabbed for one of the pistols at his hip. But then his eyes began to see more clearly. The man seated against the wheel of the wagon was indeed an Indian, but it was not Sky Falling Man. The face was all wrong—the nose was not as large, the features much less pinched. Those differences became even more apparent when the man abruptly stood. He was slightly taller, more fit, and his spine was straight and strong. He brushed off his woolen blanket and the seat of his pants and put his hat back on, a derby that he pulled low around the ears. Then he slung his pack over one shoulder and approached Shaddock. "Your sleep was very restless," No Moon observed. "You cried out many times."

The old cowboy cast a suspicious eye on the equally aged native. Something wasn't right here, he thought. First the nightmares had come back after all this time, and now this Indian shows up. It was all too coincidental. "You red bastard," he growled. "You put that dream in my head, didn't you?"

"No," the Sioux replied. "What is in your head has always been, whether you choose to see its face or not. I have many skills, Shaddock. But sometimes truth is the most powerful magic."

Tol shrugged him off with disdain. "Well, I don't want no part of your magic, you hear? I got no use for you people or your witchy ways."

The Indian gave that some thought. After a while, he nodded his head. "This is understandable," he said, "your having been to Paha-Sapa and all. Seeing what you have seen . . ."

Shaddock stiffened. "There you go again about that massacre. Look here, I told my story at the show earlier. You were there, you heard it. There was twenty of our soldiers against upwards of sixty screaming Sioux. And I was the only one to come out of that alive. Now, that sure sounds like a massacre in my book."

"Yes, it does," No Moon nodded, "and you tell the story very convincingly. So much that perhaps over time you've convinced even yourself. But that is not the way it happened."

"Oh, yeah? Then why would I say it?"

"To keep from facing the truth. To avoid seeing memories so terrible that you've sought refuge in a bottle for these many years."

Shaddock's teeth grated with anger. "I don't have to take them kinda words, not from the likes of you. I was there and you weren't. I guess I oughta know."

The Indian leaned back against the wagon, cast a knowing eye on the cowboy. "Tell me about your dream."

"What?"

"The dream you had while I watched you sleep. It was about the massacre, wasn't it?"

"I don't see where it's any of your—"

"And it made you cry out. Why? Were you frightened?"

"I ain't never been scared a nothing—"

"Was there an animal in your dream? A beast, large and black, that moves and kills like a whisper? Like a shadow?"

Tol felt his stomach twist at the mention as images flashed before his mind's eye, of a knoblike head split into a grinning maw, and eyes blacker than the night itself. "Dammit, it's just a dream," he growled, as much to himself as the Indian. "Just a dream!"

"No!" No Moon snapped, and there was an urgency in his voice. "You know deep down that it is the truth. And you must face it before they arrive." He abruptly looked out across the open plains, his body tensed as if he'd heard something. But after a few moments his attention returned to Shaddock. "It is precisely this reason that led me to you. In the hills of Paha-Sapa you faced powerful magic, and yet you survived. Even the spirits were impressed by such courage. And if that courage were combined with my *wakan* ways, we would be powerful medicine indeed. Together we may yet survive this night." He started again, stared out across the prairie.

"I don't pretend to know what the hell you're talking about, old man," Shaddock said. "But what are you looking for out there anyway? You hear something?"

No Moon remained stoic and silent, ignoring the other's words. When he did speak, it was in a whisper. "Has your head cleared of the liquor yet?"

"Well, more or less, but—"

"It will have to do. They will be here soon."

"Who is this 'they' you keep talking about?" Tol fumed. "Dammit, you better stop with the riddle and put your business flat on the ground 'fore I get any more riled."

No Moon kept his wary vigil on the moonlit expanses beyond. But he slowly divulged his story just the same. "There are things going wrong in the mountains to the west," he whispered. "Bad things. I was suspicious and tried to stop them, so they—she—sent assassins to kill me. They will be here soon."

"Oh, so that's it," Tol sighed in relief. This territory was more familiar to him. "So somebody's after you, old man? Well, hell, why didn't you say so. I've been known to hire my gun out at times. Sure, I'll keep an eye on you, if'n you've got a little folding money, that is. Services like this don't come cheap, you know—"

"You still do not understand," No Moon snapped at him. "Do you think I could not handle a few renegade braves or pistol fighters by myself? I am an Oglala warrior as well as a shaman. I would not need your help unless it were otherwise." He paced back and forth alongside the wagon, as if searching for the proper words to explain. "These are not men pursuing me. They are *nagi,* spirits who have never been men. These particular *nagi* are known as They-Who-Follow-Behind. They have been summoned to find me, and they will not stop until I am dead."

Shaddock took his hat off and tiredly ran a hand through his stringy gray hair. "You expect me to believe . . ." Then he gave up, sighed, and shook his still-throbbing head. "Lordy, I need a drink."

"No, you mustn't!" No Moon was almost agitated. "You must be clear-headed for what is to come. This is not just for me, Shaddock. I am not the only one in danger. You are as well, and all of your people. Perhaps all people everywhere."

"Look, friend," the cowboy said slowly, trying hard to retain his patience. "I don't want to hear no more about your Indian craziness. If you got real problems—real people after you other'n ghosts and spookies—then I might be able to help. But if you're gonna keep up this magic nonsense, well . . . so, what's it gonna be?" He waited for the Indian to reply. But there was nothing forthcoming. No Moon simply returned to watching the emptiness, staring into the vast Nebraska flatland. Tol sighed again, put his hat back on. "Suit yourself. I'm gonna go into town and see if I can scare up a drink. I don't want to find you here when I get back. You understand? And don't you bother my horse neither."

Still no answer. The Indian appeared to be in a trance as he stared into the distance. Shaddock just shook his head and ignored him. He gave Mose another pat on the neck, then set off for Barlow on foot. Spirit beings, he grumbled. What a bunch of horseshit.

But he knew the dream. How could he know the dream . . .

To hell with the dream! I guess I oughta know what happened all them years ago! Jubal wasn't pounded into the ground like some penny nail. He took three arrows in the back on the Sioux's second charge, and he was still shooting as he went down. And that pantywaist Creekmore, he was still screaming as they peeled the scalp off his noggin. It was an Indian massacre, no two ways about it. And no dream's gonna change that!

Still . . . just the fact that No Moon had known about the dream, and the goblin that haunted it, kept niggling at him, pricking the soft tissue at the back of his mind. That just served to quicken his pace a little more. The faster he could get him a bottle and immerse himself in blessed numbness, the faster the doubts would leave him in peace.

Barlow was asleep beneath the cold eye of the moon. The single wide street was empty of man and beast. The few pole lanterns in view had been extinguished long before, and the window lamps in individual houses and apartments had followed suit shortly thereafter. Not a single candle burned —not in the general store or the bank or the church at the end of the street. Not even at McKinney's Saloon. Tol's spirits sank at the sight. He'd hoped there would be a light burning somewhere in there, in a backroom poker game or a bedroom to show the proprietor was still awake. But no such luck. If he wanted a bottle bad enough, he'd have to wake someone to get it.

He climbed up onto the high wooden sidewalk and bypassed Tooly's Emporium, went to the big picture window of the tavern which was right next door. But he found only his own moonlit reflection in the glass there; the darkness inside was so absolute, his eyes could not penetrate it, and he had to dredge his foggy memory to imagine where the bar was located. He mustered a faint impression of solid oak with brass hand and footrails, of mugs and glasses hanging on hooks over the bar, of a fancy mirror on the rear wall behind the bar and the rows of bottles lined up before it. Before he knew it he was banging on the door frame, harder and harder until the glass panes jiggled in their slots.

There was the sound of a window sash being thrown up on the second floor. "What the hell is going on down there?" shouted a stern voice still thick with sleep. Tol had to back out from under the narrow secondary roof before he could see Mr. McKinney's long face poking out the upper story window and into the chilled evening air. "Who is that down there?" the saloon owner said, wrestling with a wiry set of spectacles. "What do you want?"

"I apologize for waking you," Tol called up to the man, while trying not to be too loud and disturb anyone else. "But I was wondering if I could make a small purchase . . ."

The man in the window just gaped at him, unsure of what he'd heard. "Who the hell would try to . . . Wait a minute. Ain't you the cowboy from that medicine show?"

"Yessir, as a matter of fact—"

"Well, what the hell do you want?"

"I already told you, I'd like to—"

"Lord a-mighty, don't you know it's the middle of the night? Go away, come back in the morning!" He pulled his head back in, made ready to close the window.

Tol began to panic. "No, wait! I just need something to help me sleep. I promise, I'll make it worth your while. Look . . ." He drew one of his pistols, started to hold it out for the man to see. But Mr. McKinney had already seen God's plenty. At the sight of the gun he quickly slammed the window, then hid himself back behind the jamb. "You get out of here," he called, the glass muffling his voice. "Get now, 'fore I call the sheriff!" Then he jerked his drapes closed.

Shaddock quaked in frustration. "I was just fixing to swap you," he tried to call. But the man was no longer listening. "Grubby little coward," Tol muttered as he holstered his gun, "I wasn't gonna hurt him." He stood there in the street, looked around the dark little town. He could see faces in some of the other windows, peeking out to see what the disturbance was. But when his eyes met theirs, they just as quickly pulled their own shades and disappeared from sight. Well, Shaddock, he thought to himself. What are you gonna do now? You could surely take what you want—a good solid kick would almost knock that saloon door right off its hinges. But it ain't hardly worth spending time in jail for a couple bottles of cheap whiskey. 'Sides, after a time the booze would wear off and you'd be right back where you are now, needing some and having none. But where else you gonna go? Ain't a person you know in this town . . .

Wait a minute, he thought. There was somebody here after all, but his memory was so fuzzy these days. A girl, wasn't it? No, not *that* kinda girl. A young thing . . . yeah, the one from the general store—oh damn, what was her name now . . . Billie, I think. She was at the show too. And the way she went on about the guns and those stories and all . . . she thinks you're a real Western hero, Tol old boy. Yeah, she might be just the one to help.

He located Ducane's General Store and headed across the street. The windows were dark there as well, but that was not enough to detain him. As before, he rapped on the door frame over and over, progressively louder each time. Then he backed out into the street to watch the windows along the upper floor.

A dim glow filled one window, growing steadily until someone balanced a candleholder on the sill there. Tol's hazy mind cleared long enough for a lucid thought: What if it isn't Billie? What if it's her ma or pa and what would I say then, what? But then the sash rose and a face appeared there, framed in a cascade of dark hair. Tol breathed a sigh of relief as the girl wiped her eyes and tried to focus them on him. Then recognition sank in and she smiled. "Mr. Shaddock?" she asked. "What are you doing here?"

"Good evening, Billie." He doffed his hat and bowed dramatically.

"That's Willie."

"Oh. Sorry. Of course. I was wondering if we could parlay for a minute or two. You know, talk."

The teen looked perplexed. "Now? It's kinda late, isn't it?"

"It's important."

She finally shrugged. "All right. I'll be down in a minute. But be quiet, okay? If my father wakes up, he'll have both our heads." She turned away with the candle in hand, and the window darkened once again. But in a few moments he could see the flame through the store windows on the main floor as it danced down an unseen staircase and grew steadily brighter. Willie slid the bolt and opened the door, stepped across the threshold and hugged herself against the night chill. She was wearing a long cotton nightshirt with a coat around her shoulders. "What do you want, Mr. Shaddock?"

"Call me Tol, please. I was just wondering . . . how did you like tonight's show?"

Her smile returned. "It was great. You can really make those old pistols talk, I swear. You're not as fast as I woulda figured, but I guess everybody slows down sometime."

Tol wasn't sure if he'd been complimented or insulted. "Missy, I was never very fast. But the first man to get his gun out isn't always the winner. You gotta be willing to shoot once you've drawed. Not everybody's prepared to do that."

Willie nodded. "I'll take your word for it. You know, everybody liked those stories you told, especially about the Orlen brothers. That was great."

"Thanks. Willie, I was wondering—"

"Yeah, you tell them stories darn good. Except . . ."

"I was just over at the saloon, and—" He stopped himself. "Except? Except what?"

The girl looked at the ground, hemmed and hawed before going on. "Well, you told about the Orlen shootout real good. It was almost like being there. And you included a lot of details I'd never heard, like about Elmo Orlen's tattoos. But when you got to the Creekmore massacre . . . I don't know. It almost sounded like you was reading it. It was still entertaining, don't get me wrong. But I checked the Beadle's book as soon as I got home and it was almost exactly the same. Like you'd memorized it or something."

"I didn't."

"I know you didn't. But I was wondering if you could give me a few more details, you know, like you did with the Orlens. Tell me a little more about what happened."

"I done told you—"

"Who was it that got hit first, huh? With the first arrow?

Was it Jubal Turner, or the sergeant, or who? Didn't Jubal cry out when he was first shot? I can't imagine being stuck with an arrow and not yelling my head off . . ."

Shaddock was trying to oblige her, searching his memory for bits and pieces of the past, shreds that would satisfy her somewhat lurid curiosity. But he couldn't remember who got hit first. He couldn't remember anyone getting hit period. All he saw were dead bodies, pieces of bodies littering a dark campground. There were no arrows piercing Jubal as he kneeled in the grass, his face sunken into his chest all the way to the eyes. . . .

"You don't have to worry about me being squeamish or anything, Tol. I may be a girl, but I can take it. Was Lieutenant Creekmore actually scalped alive? Imagine that, while he was *alive* . . ."

. . . not scalped but torn in two and half of him lying on me and his innards hot and wet on my legs—and goddammit I need a drink!

He reached out and grabbed Willie by the arm to silence her, a little harder than he intended. But it had the desired effect. Her cascade of questions ended abruptly, and for a moment she looked a little frightened. So Tol just as quickly let go of her and forced a weak smile to put her at ease. "Sorry there, missy. I didn't mean to startle you. But I need to ask a favor."

"What's that, mister, er, Tol?"

"I was having a little trouble sleeping, you know, and, uh . . . I could use a little nip, to relax me. But you saw Colonel Bill pour out my last drop. And I need it, you see. You know the saloon owner, don't you? I was wondering if you could get him to open up for me just long enough to get me a little bottle. Just a little one."

The gleam of hero worship in Willie's eye dulled a bit, became tempered with suspicion and disappointment. A point that wasn't lost on Shaddock. "I don't know," she said slowly. "It's pretty late. I didn't think you had any money to be buying booze, anyway. Colonel Brady said he'd advanced your salary clear for the next two months."

Tol's need outweighed his embarrassment. "You've got a

good memory there, hon. I am a bit short of money. But I thought I could barter a little with the barkeep."

"Barter? What have you got that Mr. McKinney might be interested in?"

Begrudgingly Tol drew his off-side LeMat, half cocked the hammer so he could spin the cylinder. "It's a good gun. Maybe a collector's item for all I know. They never made a whole lot to begin with. And I figure if Colonel Bill wants to keep the show a-moving, he'll probably come in to the saloon tomorrow and buy it back, so . . ."

"You'd pawn your pistol?" Willie was incredulous. "One of your LeMats? For a bottle?"

"Well . . ." Tol tried to think of an excuse, to make it sound less desperate. But no words would come.

Willie looked at him knowingly. "That's what happened to your Sharps rifle, isn't it? There wasn't no card game, never was. You pawned it for a bottle, didn't you?" She waited for a response, a denial, anything. But the cowboy just lowered his gaze and said nothing.

Willie abruptly turned and went back into the store, her candle showing the way to the counter. There she knelt down and retrieved something from a lower shelf. When she returned to the door, she was carrying a half-full bottle of whiskey. "It's my pa's," she told him. "Sometimes he takes a nip before bed. He doesn't think I know about it, but . . ." She held it out to him. "Go on, take it."

Tol reluctantly accepted the bottle, then offered her the big LeMat. But the girl wouldn't take it. "Keep your gun, Mr. Shaddock," she said. "Go back to your wagons. It's late."

"I appreciate this, missy," he whispered as he reholstered the pistol. "And I'll make it up to you, I promise. I can get you more tickets to our final show tomorrow, and I can bring you out in front of all your friends and let you ride old Mose and, uh . . ." But he could see the lack of enthusiasm in her eyes. There was no longer a gleam of hero worship there. Just disappointment and a profound sympathy for the drunk that now stood before her.

"Good night, Mr. Shaddock," she said. Then she went

back inside and closed the door, slid the bolt back into place. Soon the candle flame was dancing back up the stairs, where it disappeared from sight.

The old man stood on the wooden walk, holding his coveted bottle in both hands. But he could not forget the look in the girl's eyes. "I ain't no drunk, you know," he muttered sullenly. He looked at the bottle. "I don't need this. I don't. I could just throw it away right now if I wanted. I could."

Tell me more about the Creekmore massacre . . .

No arrows. No whooping Indian hordes. Just the silence and darkness, and the smell of death. And then that damned laughter, growing louder and madder, issuing from the grinning maw of the night itself . . .

His memorized dime-novel past was quickly crumbling, leaving real memories with a stink and a taint too unpleasant to recognize. But Tol Shaddock's instincts for self-preservation had been well honed over time. Reflexively and without conscious thought he uncorked the bottle and took as big a gulp as his gullet could manage.

"Shaddock!"

The whispered voice broke not only the silence but the cowboy's train of thought as well, waking him from the past so that he gagged on his precious liquor and spat a stream of it all across the walkway. He whirled around with his hand near his holster and searched the shopwindows and doorways, looking for whoever had called him. That's when he saw the man standing in the street. He recognized the blanket and derby right off.

"I thought I told you to leave me alone," he said rather heatedly as he stepped off the high wooden walk and into the dirt of the roadway. But the Indian didn't seem to be paying much attention to him. He was bent over at the waist, sprinkling some sort of white powder from a small leather pouch and muttering to himself as he did so. "See here," Tol said. "What the hell are you up to anyway?"

No Moon ignored him still, at least until the two ends of his powder line met each other and formed a large white circle in the dirt. When he looked up finally, it was not at Shaddock. Instead, he glanced nervously to the edge of town where Colonel Brady's Western show was camped. "Come, get into the circle," he told Shaddock without looking his way. "Quickly! There is not much time!"

The man's anxiousness made the fine hairs on Tol's neck stand up. "All right now," he glowered, "I've had just about enough of your—"

AAAIIIIIIOOOOOOOOO . . .

The sound came from the open fields just beyond Barlow's edge, high and ululating, like no animal Tol had ever heard. The shrillness of it made every hair on his body stand alert. The whiskey bottle slipped from his numbed grasp and thudded to the ground, began bleeding into the dirt.

"They are coming!" No Moon called, and there was terror in his voice. "Get into the circle now!"

Chapter 6

Despite the Indian's urgent warning, Tol remained stock still in the middle of the street. Half of him wanted to run, not to some powder circle drawn in the dirt, but to the other end of town and beyond, just run and keep on running. For there was a danger inherent in the scream he'd heard that he couldn't describe but could most definitely feel. Yet the other half of him, the pragmatic side imbued with the stubborn will of a frontiersman, made him stand and watch, downright curious to see what kind of throat could birth such a noise. "What the hell is that?" he wondered, taking a step in the direction of the wail. "Sounds like it's almost to Brady's camp—"

"Shaddock, stay here!" No Moon called behind him. "There is nothing you can do for them now!"

He turned to look at the Indian. "What's that supposed to

mean?" he wanted to know, suddenly alarmed at the hopelessness in the other's words. But he found no reassurance in the old man's face. He could tell this No Moon was frightened. And whatever was making him that way was close to his camp. "What is it?" he demanded to know. "What made that scream?"

The Indian didn't answer. He had taken a gourdlike rattle the size of his fist from the leather pouch on his side and sat down cross-legged. Now he was holding it in both hands and muttering to himself. . . .

Praying?

Tol felt a spark of panic burn his insides, hotter and sharper than the liquor ever had. For he could already hear the horses growing restless down amid the ring of wagons, snorting softly, pawing at the ground in their unease. Probably Mose among them. Why didn't you bring him with you, he cursed himself as he started walking in that direction, his pace much more determined than before, picking up speed with each step. One of the horses let out a deep-throated neigh that cut through Tol's heart like a knife; it was a terrified sound, and it was joined by two other horses and then more until the entire camp's animals seemed to be crying out all at once. That should be waking the men, Tol thought as he broke into a run. Why isn't it waking them up, why aren't they doing something . . .

The sounds stopped abruptly, cut off in mid-cry. Then only silence.

Shaddock slid to a halt halfway to the edge of town, his eyes locked on the campsite, on the wagons and tent where he'd yet to see a single movement. An icy dread had hitched a ride on his back and was now clambering up his spine like a ladder, scrabbling for the base of his neck. For he'd heard those sounds before, the sudden cessation of terror. Of life. Suddenly he wasn't standing in the main street of Barlow anymore but the lea of Paha-Sapa's peaks, watching the charnel stillness of the Indian camp, listening to the death cries of the few soldiers who had managed to flee. They strangled off midway, just like the horses in the camp.

"Shaddock!" No Moon called to him. But Tol was too far away and his attention fixed on the wagons, frozen there in terrified expectation. He knew for certain that any minute now a figure would step out of the night, a powerful shadow with no source, come back to haunt him after fifteen long years.

As if in answer to his fears, something did appear from behind the big show tent. But Tol was shocked to see it was not his inky goblin. The two figures he saw were not black, but instead just the opposite. They almost glowed in the moonlight like will-o'-the-wisps, their edges blurry and diffuse. But from where he stood, Tol could see enough that it made his throat constrict and his scrotum cinch up in fear. The specters there appeared almost birdlike in some aspects, yet reptilian in others. Their legs were long, thin stalks with too many joints, and the feet were three-toed and splayed out wide. The arms were much shorter, folded close to the body like a praying mantis, and tapered to small hands sporting bladelike talons instead of fingers. The torsos of the creatures were stunted and fowlish, almost chickenlike. But that impression was just as quickly negated by the serpentine necks that writhed above their shoulders. Their heads were so repugnant, so constructed of mismatched parts as to look incapable of life. Tol was mesmerized by the round owl eyes that never blinked, flanking a crocodilian muzzle so full of teeth that they jutted out in all directions even when closed.

One of those snaky necks swiveled around, and the big saucer eyes locked onto Shaddock. The other creature saw him right after that. They-Who-Follow-Behind bared their teeth and let out a banshee wail that echoed everywhere, rolled up the street like a wave and engulfed the cowboy.

AAAAIIIIIOOOOOOOOOOOOO!

And before Tol could react, the apparitions came rushing after him, those sticklike legs churning madly.

Tol's natural reaction was to grab for his guns, to stand his ground and fight as he had all his life against Union soldiers and Missouri border gangs and a half-dozen of the southern tribes alike. But this went beyond mere reflexes. That scream sliced right to his very core, stirred the deepest instincts for survival. They told him *run*, run as hard and fast as your weathered old muscles can carry you. He started back up the street even though he felt impossibly slow, as if his arms and legs were mired in molasses, and he was sure the demons would be upon him at any minute, those hooked talons and fanged jaws digging into his back. Then another scream came, just as hair-raising as the first, but at least it told him they were still several strides behind him. Coming fast, but he still had time. The thought galvanized his actions, stoked his heart and lungs with blind panic, and forced his already-aching legs to pump even harder. No Moon was just ahead, still sitting in his circle, clutching the leather pouch and rattle and singing a chant that Tol couldn't hear over the pounding of his own heart.

This is crazy, he thought, looking at the circle that surrounded the old native. How will white powder keep these things away—

Just shut up and trust somebody for once! He knew they were coming, didn't he? He tried to warn you. So he must know what he's doing. Besides, where else you gonna go?

The wail came again, sharp and punishing to the ears. Tol ducked his head and made ready to dive into the circle—

And that's when the door to Ducane's General Store opened. Willie stepped out in her nightshirt again, this time forgetting her coat and boots, and she looked around in confusion. "What the hell is going on out here?" Her eyes fell on the running cowboy and, a split second later, the ghostly images speeding after him.

Without a conscious thought, Shaddock veered toward the wooden walkway where the girl stood transfixed. He grabbed her in passing, jerked her off the sidewalk and into his arms, and was just as quickly headed back into the street. But he could sense the presence of the demons behind him, felt the chill of their talons as they sliced the air behind his neck. He knew they would not miss again.

Three steps more, long ones that bespoke the lanky cowboy's stride. And then he made a desperate dive for the boundary of white powder, even as the wails pierced the air around them and he was sure he had failed. . . .

The impact with the ground told him otherwise. He tried to absorb the brunt of landing, but he and the girl still sprawled in a tangle of arms and legs. His momentum alone almost carried them out of the circle on the other side, but a restraining hand caught his shoulder. No Moon held him down, kept them anchored within the lines. A look of relief was evident on the Indian's face. But it was there for only an instant. He quickly returned to sitting cross-legged, held up his rattle, and continued to chant in a low, throaty voice.

From the corner of his eye Tol saw a flash of movement, of ghostly whiteness, and he knew those creatures were still around.

The *nagi* lingered, seemingly stymied by the circle. They would back away a few steps and then rush forward, but always stopped just short of the powdered line and wailed in frustration. Up close, Tol had a much better look at the apparitions, and it all but made his blood run cold. They were not completely tangible; at times he could see completely through them to the opposite side of the street. And though their legs moved as if walking, he noticed that their feet never actually touched the ground.

They rushed the circle once more, as fast as an eye blink. Again, they stopped just short. But it startled Tol enough to draw one of his big pistols. "That will not stop them," No Moon said. "Not as they are now."

"I'll keep it out just the same," the cowboy replied. "It makes me feel better."

There was a soft moan from right next to him. Willie was hunkered against Tol's side, watching their pursuers with a numbed sense of shock. "Wha-what are those things?" she stammered.

"Spirit beings," the Indian said without casting her a glance. "Demons."

"And this circle will keep them out?" Shaddock knelt down, almost touched the powder but thought better of it. "What is that stuff?"

"Dried herbs," No Moon told him. "Sweetgrass. Buffalo bone and excrement. Some secrets too. They-Who-Follow-Behind are minor *nagi*. This should hold them."

"Should? You mean it might not?"

"It will if they remain as they are now, in spirit form. But should they choose to become living, to take on flesh . . . I am not so sure."

"Can they do that?" Willie asked.

The Indian shrugged. "I don't know. But if they do, at least we can fight them then." He looked past the ambient demons and was suddenly alarmed to see an open door down the street. A man and woman were peeking out, looking for the source of the commotion. "Go back!" he called to them. "Back inside! Quickly!" But the people only stepped farther out onto the sidewalk to see who was yelling.

Shaddock thumbed back the hammer on his LeMat and fired once in their direction, blowing a large chunk of the doorjamb to pieces. The curious heads abruptly ducked out of sight, and the door slammed immediately shut. "It gets the point across," he told the Indian as he fired a few more shots at other doors and windows along the street where more faces had appeared.

Willie suddenly gasped. "Daddy, no!" she called. "Stay back!"

Russell Ducane stood in the open doorway of his store, his pants pulled on hastily over his long flannel underwear, carrying an ax handle he had picked out of a display barrel along the way. He stalked out onto the sidewalk in a huff, eager to find the ones responsible for ruining his sleep. But instead he walked straight into a nightmare that had yet to play itself out. "What in God's name . . ." was all he could muster.

Still, it was enough to attract attention. The two demons turned in his direction as one.

"Run, Papa!" Willie screamed, and would have dashed from the circle herself were it not for Shaddock's powerful hands holding her in place. "Run, before they—"

But it was too late. The demons were already scuttling after him, across the road and up onto the porch before he could retreat a step.

"What the hell? What the hell?" Russell kept saying in a shocked whisper as the transparent creatures closed in around him. And just as he turned to run back through the door of the general store, one of them snapped outward with those long saurian jaws and *into the storekeeper's back*. There was no crunch of teeth on bone or the tear of flannel and flesh. The great fanged maw slipped through the man's torso like a hand through water, with no ripple or physical contact at all. Just as one would expect an ethereal spirit to do. It was inside him for just an instant, and then it jerked back like a buzzard tearing its share of carrion from the bone.

The moment it did so, Russell Ducane's muscles went slack and his body sagged, struck the plank porching with a heavy thud and did not move again. But the thing hanging from the demon's toothy muzzle certainly did. It looked like a long, fibrous bit of gossamer, as white and transparent as the creature that held it. It approximated the shape of a man, and they saw a flat face imprinted there. It thrashed about wildly in the grip of the Indian demon, and when it gave a mournful wail, it was a hollow, displaced version of the storekeeper's own voice.

"Pa!" Willie cried, fighting Tol in vain. "Papa, no!" She turned to No Moon, screamed, "Do something, please!" But the Indian said nothing.

The demon reached up with those taloned front limbs and grasped the flailing spirit, held it firmly between them as it bit through the filmy substance and tore a long strip of it away and gulped it down even as Russell Ducane screamed anew. The other demon abruptly joined in, snapping and tearing and fighting over the prize, until the ghostly wailing finally stopped. The feast itself didn't last much longer than that. Once they were finished, they immediately returned to the circle and its occupants.

"Bastards!" Tol muttered, his fist white and bloodless around the butt of his pistol. "Is that gonna happen to the whole town? Isn't there something we can do?" But again No Moon didn't answer. Shaddock felt a flush of anger at him as well but tempered it; remember, he counseled, you're in his circle. Don't push your luck.

He went back to watching the demons again, and this time he was surprised to find they no longer rushed the circle as before. They had not even moved off the high wooden walk. They still stood over Russell Ducane's motionless form, watching the circle with unflinching interest. Those eyes, Tol thought with unease, those damnable eyes . . .

Willie suddenly gasped, began to struggle mightily against

Tol's grip. "He's alive!" she cried, squirming to get loose till he had to lock her in a bearlike hug. "Dammit, let go! Can't you see he's still alive?"

Shaddock saw that Ducane's eyes were still open, staring glassily. But there was no other movement, none at . . . no, wait! The man's chest rose just slightly, then fell. Rose again. "By God," Tol whispered, "he is breathing at that!"

"Breathing, yes," reported the old Indian flatly. "Alive, yes. But living? No. He is hollow. His spirit is gone. Only the shell remains."

Tol looked back at the storekeeper's blank, mindless stare. *Only the shell remains.* The thought sent a chill through him, worse than when he'd simply thought the man dead. For somehow this seemed infinitely worse.

One of the demons broke the unison link with its twin. For it slowly turned its attention away from their circle of sanctuary and back to Russell Ducane. It watched him as if expecting movement, though it must have known there would be none. It glanced back to the circle only once. Then it leaned over and unfolded an ethereal forelimb, extended it deep into the man's chest cavity. In response, Ducane's body began to quaver.

"What the hell is it doing?" Shaddock whispered.

"It knows," reported No Moon warily. "It can take on flesh by possessing the man's body. Then it will be able to cross into the circle. Prepare yourself, Shaddock. The time of greatest danger grows near."

The second demon abruptly turned on the first, saw what it was doing, and wailed its contention just as it had when they fought over the man's squirming spirit. That struggle started anew, but over the body this time, as it, too, thrust its transparent talons into Ducane's chest, as if to claim its rightful share. Between the two of them, the storekeeper's shudders turned progressively more violent. His stare did not falter, nor did he mutter a single groan. But his body jerked about like a man stricken with seizures. Before their eyes he began to change.

First the right leg banged on the planks once, twice, three times before suddenly bending back on itself, just above the ankle, where there was no joint to bend. The brittle snap of bone had barely filled the air before it folded back again and then again, past the knee this time, looking like a fat length of human rope. His other leg was rigored and flailing and the arms as well, twisting and malforming, and the chest had begun to bulge and undulate with inner movement. His face, still wearing that tranquil expression, bent too far to one side until the flesh around the neck ruptured and the carotid artery spat a stream of crimson into the air. But it did not travel far. The blood seemed to hang there as if suspended in water, spreading slowly, forming a red haze that all but glowed in the moonlight. It obstructed the demons and their victim from view. But it did not hinder the sounds, the ghastly commotion that unsettled them just the same. The snap and crackle of bones being reworked. The tear of fabric and flesh alike.

Willie forced her fists into her ears to block it all out. "Make it stop!" she cried. "Please, somebody . . ."

No Moon tensed. "It has stopped," he reported. "Listen." He was right; the horrible clamor was over. But the pregnant silence that followed seemed to hold even more potential for horror. Not knowing made them more wary than ever. Especially the Indian. He stood as rigid as a board, his concentration so focused that he didn't appear to be breathing. In a slow, steady movement his hand slipped beneath his blanket covering and the tail of his rag coat, returned with a long, flat shard of obsidian that resembled a crude knife. "Stand with me now," he murmured in Lakota, and not to the man or girl beside him. "Aid me now as never before."

The blood haze was subsiding, roiling slowly and turning back on itself as if drawn up by a sponge. It became an arching jet of crimson again and reversed its trajectory, returned to the body that released it. A body now grotesquely different.

Of Willie's father, at least as he had been in life, there remained nothing beyond a tattered pile of denim and flannel. But where the *nagi* had stood, floating a hair's-breadth above the sidewalk, there was now a single figure sculpted in living tissue. At least one of the demons had taken on flesh, constructing a physical form to approximate its own. But it had not counted on the limitations of the medium; how skin and muscle and tendon would stretch only so far and in so many ways. What resulted was an abomination, a nightmarish hodgepodge even more disturbing than the specter that came before. Its long, stalklike legs were the same, but built from reworked bone and a taut wrapping of human flesh. Only one of its folded front limbs had formed; there was not even a stump to mark where the other should have been. Its serpent's neck was not as long, and the head atop it little more than a fist-sized knot of bone and tissue. An eye was up there, bulging from a makeshift socket, and a mouth below that. But no reptilian snout this time; just a lipless hole lined with what teeth Ducane still possessed and with jagged shards of bone to make up the difference. Yet that was not its most ghastly aspect. For on the creature's henlike torso, ingrained across its bulging belly, was the unmistakable image of Russell Ducane's face. It was stretched and distorted, and the orifices sealed over to give it strength. But it was there nonetheless.

Tol was numbed by the sight. Somehow his mind kept questioning, though, trying to affix some sort of logic and sense to this unnatural scene. The storekeeper was bigger than that, the cowboy remembered.

So why is the flesh stretched so tight, with one arm not even formed? Where's the rest of him?

At that moment there was movement behind the monstrosity. Something shifted in its shadow, pulled itself across the planks and into the glare of the moon. And in that instant Tol not only had the answers to his questions, but knew where the second demon had gone as well. Only this one had come out the loser in its struggle for flesh, and had barely claimed enough to take physical form. It amounted to a twisted torso half the size of the other, a creature with both of its taloned arms but not a leg to stand on. There was no head either, or even a snaky neck. Just a leering, toothless maw, a gullet between its shoulders, and above that Ducane's other eye, glaring with lidless malevolence.

The larger demon moved slowly, hesitantly, forward, testing its newfound corporeality. The planks creaked with its first solid footfall, then a second. That must have been enough to familiarize it. For the thing abruptly turned and leapt down into the dirt of the street. Starting toward them.

"Shoot!" No Moon urged. And when Tol failed to react immediately, he turned and grabbed his shoulder, shouted urgently, "Shoot!"

Shaddock raised his pistol without even realizing he still held it. His thumb reflexively drew back the hammer and his finger squeezed the trigger of its own volition. And his unconscious aim was dead on. The .44 round tore a ragged hole in the demon's newly formed chest, releasing a spray of pilfered blood. The impact shook it, made it sway off balance for a moment. But then it righted itself and kept on coming.

Just like the black goblin, said a dread voice in the back of Tol's mind. They're coming for you and your guns won't stop them, not now any more than fifteen years ago. But Tol refused to listen. He drew his other LeMat with his left hand and cocked both pistols, fired them in unison. The volley shredded the tissue on its trunk, destroying Russell Ducane's face once and for all. But the thing kept coming. He fired again and again, blowing holes in its coiled neck, blasting away that staring eyeball. Still, nothing could stop its relentless advance.

"Its legs!" Willie pointed. "Shoot for its legs!"

Shaddock obeyed, snapped off a round at one of those reed-thin limbs. Missed. Fired again with the other hand. This time the bone there shattered like cordwood beneath the ax. The demon toppled sideways and flailed in the dirt. But it still continued to crawl toward the circle.

"Die, damn you!" the cowboy cursed as he kept firing, destroying both its legs and then its single arm as well. When he finally clicked on empty chambers, the thing was little more than a riddled mass of tissue. Yet it still moved. Inched through the dirt like a grub. Up to the white powder. Into the circle . . .

Tol frantically adjusted the hammer on each pistol and fired the secondary barrels at point-blank range. The shotloads blew away what was left of the creature's skull, leaving its neck to thrash wildly and spray blood all around. But a shudder finally racked the creature's spindly frame. It went rigid, and then slowly the muscles relaxed, ceasing all movement.

Tol stood over it, triumphant and terrified, until he remembered there was still another demon on the loose. He whirled around with his empty pistols at the ready, expecting its attack. But he found the other nightmare still squatting on the sidewalk. Watching them.

"Keep an eye on it," he called as he fumbled for his backup cylinders.

"It does not attack," No Moon observed. "We are a threat now. It is having second thoughts."

Indeed, the last demon seemed unsure of what to do. It looked at the empty street around it, then at the three enemies in the circle, each of them now larger than it. It looked at itself, at the malformed limbs and stunted body it had pieced together. And right then and there it seemed to recognize the futility of continuing. The hole that was its mouth let out a deep bellowing cry that hung in the air, steadily rising in pitch and treble till it became the same ghostly shriek as before. Almost immediately, tendrils of ghostly matter began leaking through the very pores of its flesh, gathering in the air like swirls of midnight fog. The cast-off body sagged and ceased to move as the retreating specter hovered above it, slowly returning to its spirit form.

No Moon suddenly leapt out of the circle, his age belying the spring in his legs as he bounded across the roadway and up onto the walk. The *nagi* was too preoccupied with abandoning its earthly shell; it did not see the wily old man until he was already close at hand, and he did not give it time to react. He dove past the thing and into the doorway of the general store, slashing with his stone knife as he passed. No contact was made; the obsidian sliced as if through curls of simple smoke. But it had an effect just the same. The creature's ghostly wail became strident, filled with otherworldly pain as it clutched its side where the weapon had passed. No Moon darted in again, this time from behind, and thrust with his crude black weapon. It pierced the translucent figure, straight through the torso, and the demon's cry strangled away to nothing. It stiffened, limbs splayed and trembling, and then it simply faded from view.

Only the moonlight remained.

Tol and Willie were still tensed, cautiously looking around. But No Moon breathed a sigh of relief and leaned against one of the porch beams for support. "It's over," he told them. Then he added in a somber tone, "For now."

"What's that supposed to mean?" Tol wanted to know. But the Indian didn't answer, and Tol thought maybe that was for the best.

The silence that had resettled around them now invited the rest of the townsfolk to peek out into the night again. To open their windows and doors and emerge fearfully into the street, to find out what those noises were, what was all that shooting about, what in heaven's name was going on there. Tol saw the sheriff coming, now that the calamity was over and it appeared safe to be in charge once again. He sighed with frustration. How was he ever going to explain all of this? Hell, he didn't understand it himself.

He holstered his pistols, put an arm around Willie's shoulders. "Are you okay, missy?" he whispered in as soothing a voice as he could muster.

The girl didn't answer. She was staring at the mass of pulpy flesh that had barely breached the circle, staring at what had once been her father. There were no more tears, just a faroff look in her eyes. Confusion, he wagered. Shock. Maybe even a hint of madness. After what she'd seen, he couldn't blame her.

He just wondered if the look would ever go away.

Chapter 7

Sunlight fell through the jail's high barred windows, leaving stripes of brightness and shade across Tolman Shaddock's chest as he leaned against the rear wall of his cell. But despite its warmth on his skin, he just couldn't shake the chill inside him, couldn't calm the tremors in his stomach. He knew it wasn't the liquor anymore, sure enough. And it wasn't just fear, either. He'd been afraid in his life; no sane man who lived on the frontier would deny that. He'd dreaded everything from Indian attacks to buffalo stampedes to young gunfighters with a reputation to build. Fear was a necessary ingredient back then. It kept him on his toes, never let his guard slip too much. But what he felt now went well beyond that careful wariness. This was closer to panic maybe. Or sheer terror.

He had felt that only once before. . . .

Images and sensations came flooding out of that abyss of fifteen years ago, things he'd tried hard to forget and almost convinced himself that he'd succeeded. But now they were back, as fresh and vivid as the new nightmares he'd fought just last night. The stench of death on the cold night air. The crackling of the campfire. The crooked man's maniacal laughter. And, worst of all, this time he knew it wasn't a dream. It had never been a dream.

"Thinking about last night?"

The voice startled him, brought him back to the reality of his imprisonment. The old Indian was sitting on the cot of the cell next to his, his legs pulled up beneath him so he appeared to be meditating. Indeed, he hadn't said three words since the sheriff and his deputy had hustled them into jail just as the sun cleared the edge of the world. Tol had assumed he was sleeping. But now he was looking at Shaddock with genuine curiosity. "Last night?" he said again.

Tol shook his head. "Further back. I'm remembering everything now. About Creekmore, that is."

The Indian nodded. "Sometimes the truth is hard to face," he said solemnly. "But even the fastest horse cannot outrun a memory for long." He leaned closer to the bars that separated them. "At least you won't need the liquor anymore."

"Well, I don't know about that. 'Cause I could sure use a drink right now . . ." Then he saw the knowing expression on No Moon's face. He gave a mischievous grin of his own. "Yeah, I guess that's what I have been doing, ain't it? Crawling into a bottle. But old habits are hard to break. I'd still like a good stiff drink. Especially since I can't get those damned Black Hills out of my mind."

"You remember all now?"

"More than I care to." He nodded. The memories were still sharp, playing before his mind's eye even as he spoke. "The . . . thing that killed the soldiers was huge and black and spiny like a porcupine. And it killed 'em in a heartbeat. Slaughtered them. And it was that crooked little bastard that caused it."

"Sky Falling Man."

"Yeah, that's right." He looked at the Indian. "You knew him, did you?"

No Moon just nodded. "The most powerful of the Lakota *wicasa wakan.*"

"The what?"

"Wicasa wakan means holy man, magician. Medicine man. He had much power."

"Not enough, evidently," Tol said. "'Cause I'm here and he ain't. Now, I wasn't wanting to bother him at first. I don't cotton to killing cripples, you know, and I even tried to hold back that snip of a lieutenant from hurting him. But when that thing came back from killing the others and I emptied my pistols into it to no good, I thought to myself, well, old son, it's finally time to step up and shake St. Peter's hand. 'Cause this thing's gonna kill you for sure. But then that crooked little bastard set to laughing, just a crazy kinda laugh that makes your skin crawl. And because of that, I was less scared than I was pissed off. So right as that big thing latched on to me, I whirled about and put a buffalo round into Sky Falling Man's forehead. That shut him up, sure enough."

No Moon nodded in understanding. "So you are the one who killed him, then," he said in a monotone, though Tol couldn't tell whether it was a question or a statement.

"It was me, all right. And good thing too, 'cause the minute that his lights went out, so did his goblin. That thing just dropped to the ground like all the air had gone out of it. When I finally got up my courage and stuck it with my rifle, there was nothing left on the inside. Nothing but that empty, oily black hide. Damn thing wouldn't even burn, you know? 'Cause I tried. All I could do was bury it, deep as I could get." He looked at the Indian in the next cell, tried to read his blank features for a reaction. "The thing that killed those men . . . you know what it was, don't you?"

No Moon nodded. "It is called Siyoko, but it is also known as the Black Heart Devil. You are lucky to have survived, Shaddock."

"I figured that. Devil, huh? Is it like those *nagi* things we fought last night?"

"No. They-Who-Follow-Behind are spirits from the world beyond the Far Pine. But the Black Heart Devil is not a living thing. It is simply a hide, a demonskin. It is empty. It is the one who summons it that gives it life."

"And just how's that done?"

"The medicine man puts his own shadow within the skin to give it purpose. He sees what it sees, knows what it knows. For his own shadow has become the black heart within."

"His shadow?" Tol laughed. "Well, excuse me, friend, but that sounds like the biggest load of horseshit I've—" But before he could finish his thought, the image of Sky Falling Man flashed before his mind, standing alongside Lieutenant Creekmore in the glare of the firelight but with only one shadow between them. He remembered the maniacal laughter echoing not only from the crooked man but from the

Black Heart Devil's gaping mouth as well. He swallowed hard, realizing No Moon's tale wasn't quite so ludicrous after all. "So when I killed the medicine man . . ."

"You killed his shadow as well," the Indian finished. "It is too bad you buried the skin. There is much magic in such an item. We could have used such big medicine against her."

"Against who?"

"Dee-Bo-Ha. She is a witch, the one who sent the *nagi* after me. And she will send more, do not be mistaken about that. As long as we are here, imprisoned and unarmed, we are in danger. And this town with us."

Shaddock spat in disgust. "I don't like this, I don't like it one bit. Demons, spirits, ghosts. I wish I'd never heard any of it. I wish you'd've just stayed out there on the prairie and left me outta this."

"I could not fight Dee-Bo-Ha alone," No Moon told him. "Had I drawn my circle out there, they would simply have waited until hunger or fatigue drained my will. Then my magic would have been weak, and they would have overcome me."

"But you killed one of them, I saw it."

"With the spirit knife," he said, nodding. "It belonged to my father's father. It is from long ago, when the spirits first formed the world. It has much magic. But I could strike only when the *nagi* were distracted. If I had confronted them straight on, I would not have stood a chance. My soul would have been consumed, same as the girl's father."

Shaddock didn't like remembering those images. He tried to force them from his mind as he went to his own cot and sat down tiredly. But his lack of sleep was catching up to him, making it hard to fight the dread images. "How do you think the girl's doing?" he wondered. "I thought if she'd be able to tell 'em what really happened out there they'd believe her. But it's been hours. Maybe she's worse off than I expected."

"She watched her father die before her," observed the Indian. "Very bad indeed."

"Which reminds me," Tol said suddenly. "When they herded us in here, I was a-running off at the mouth about ghosts and spirits and such. But you didn't even say a word. What was in your head then? They thought I was a damned fool talking that way."

No Moon appeared very solemn. "You didn't tell them about just ghosts and spirits. It was Indian ghosts. Indian spirits."

"It's the truth, ain't it?"

"Perhaps. But I have lived a long life, Shaddock, and I have learned much. And I know that the white man's justice does not extend to my people. It has always been this way. If a few young braves went on the warpath and killed a settler or two, the Army would come and slaughter whole villages. They would not care whether the guilty ones were punished as long as Indians died. And it would be this way today. Go out there, Shaddock, and tell the sheriff again that it was Indian devils that entered their town last night, that killed one of their own. I promise you, they would not be content with just my death. They would gather together and march to Pine Ridge or Standing Rock or one of the other agencies. And the innocent would suffer yet again." Then the old man closed his eyes and bowed his head.

Shaddock gave thought to his words, and he knew the truth in them. He had heard many times of Indian slaughters like that at Sand Creek, and he couldn't blame the old man for his fears. "But how else are we gonna get outta here?" he wondered aloud. "They're not gonna let us walk away, that much I know." But No Moon had no reply. He just sat there, silent, which made Tol very nervous.

He stood and began pacing again, prowling the eight feet of his cell over and over. *More of them are coming, the Indian had said. How soon? How many more? We've gotta get out of here. I've gotta get to my guns. . . .*

There were voices from out in the sheriff's office, muffled by the heavy door that stood between there and the cell-block. But the deputy should have been the only one on duty. Maybe some of the townspeople came to gawk and ask questions, he guessed—there had been a lot of speculation and hysteria out there once the screams stopped and the people of Barlow felt it safe to look outside. Or it could be the sheriff returning. That thought brought Tol to his feet. Roscoe Tuttle had gone down to Colonel Brady's camp to check things out there, and the old cowboy was especially eager to hear what he'd found. He didn't give a damn about any of his fellow employees, or even Bill Brady himself— they weren't friends of his by any stretch of the imagination. But Mose was, and he had a bad feeling about that old paint. He kept hearing the screams of the horses as he ran back toward the wagons, just before those things . . .

The door to the cellblock swung open just then, and Deputy Leeds stepped through. He was a rangy youth, barely out of his teens, and would have looked more at home fielding cattle on a family ranch. He wore a tin star and carried a shotgun, an old greener just like the sheriff. But it seemed to grant him little solace. For the last few times he'd looked in on his prisoners, he was wide-eyed and anxious, visibly shaken. Downright scared. Tol knew then that the boy had snuck out sometime during the morning to see the remains of Russell Ducane. The larger grotesquerie was too shot up to look like anything, but the stunted legless one was still in one piece. Still alive but soulless, staring glassily with its one human eye. It had been wrapped in a canvas and carried to the livery stables, there to become the object of eager glimpses and horrified whispers.

"You sure you want to do this?" the deputy asked, looking warily at Shaddock. But despite his gaze, he wasn't talking to the prisoner. His voice was directed back to whoever stood behind him. That person finally followed him through the doorway, and Tol was surprised to recognize the visitor as Willie Ducane. The girl had been cleaned up and dressed in jeans and a flannel shirt, didn't look quite as frazzled as she had in those pre-dawn hours. Her eyes were puffy and red from crying and a lack of rest. But she did not look as fragile as he had expected. Rather, she had a determined look about her that told him she was one strong young woman, one who had come with a purpose.

"I don't know, Willie," Deputy Leeds was saying. "I don't think you oughta be in here without the sheriff present. He'll be right back if you'd like to wait and talk to him—"

"It's all right, Luther," she said in a calm, even voice. "I'll talk to Roscoe when he gets back. But before that, I have to talk with these men. Okay?"

Leeds hemmed and hawed for a moment, uncomfortable with decision making. But he finally gave her a grin and shrugged. "Okay, but just for a little bit."

"I appreciate it, Luther." She stared at him a little longer, expectantly. "Privately, Luther."

He finally caught on, gave another shrug. "I'll be right out here, Willie. Just give me a shout." Then the deputy slipped back into the office and pulled the door shut in his wake.

"Morning, missy," Tol said, reaching to doff a hat that had been taken away with his guns and knife. "How're you getting along today?"

Willie did not smile. Nor did she respond to his pleasantries. She just walked up to the bars and fixed the old cowboy in a harsh gaze that contained not even a hint of her earlier hero worship. "I want to know what went on out there last night," she said flatly. "We all saw it. Didn't we?" The old cowboy agreed with a nod. "Then I have to know what it was. And why my father died."

"And I'd love to tell you, missy," Tol commiserated. "But I know only half the story. That man over there's the one with all the details. But unfortunately he ain't talking."

"Not to the sheriff," No Moon suddenly said, taking Tol by surprise. "I always intended to explain everything to you, Shaddock. How else could I gain your aid for that which is to come?"

"And what about me?" Willie said, moving over to the Indian's cell. "I deserve to know. My father's dead, damn you. You owe me that."

"She's got a point," Shaddock agreed. "She's already seen enough to haunt her for the rest of her days. The truth can't be that much worse."

No Moon smiled without a hint of humor. "You haven't heard it yet, Shaddock. You had best not judge until then." He motioned to a stool sitting in the corner outside the cells. "Best seat yourself, girl. I'll have to start back aways." As she obeyed, he unfolded his legs for the first time, stretched them, finally stood from his cot. He stalked the cell with small, silent steps while he measured his words, and in that time Shaddock remembered his quickness last night when attacking the last spirit. No Moon was as old as he, but from the springiness in his step it appeared the years had taken less of a toll.

"The heads of my people have hung very low for months now," he told them, "not just among the Oglalas at Pine Ridge but at other agencies as well. Last year Three Star Crook, the white general that lured us out of the Powder River country, came back to see us again with yet another peace commission from the Great Father in Washington. We respected Crook, for he gave us a good war. But we soon learned that he had no such respect for us. They came not wanting peace but more land. They were not content with the Powder River and all the good hunting ground that once belonged to the Natural Human Beings. Now they wanted pieces of the Great Sioux reservation as well, the land that they had promised us. They sought to split us up into just the lands where our agencies were located. And with the help of that snaky-tongued agent at Standing Rock, they managed to trick many of our brothers into signing papers that we could not read. That left us with barely the ground we stood upon, and many feared that they would return for even that. It appeared the Human Beings would sink and disappear in the ocean of whites. Red Cloud, our chief, was very sick at heart for this, and so was the Hunkpapa chief, Sitting Bull. First our guns and then our ponies and now this. There was no food on the reservations, and the agencies cheated us of our government money. Our children wailed in the night from hunger. Bad times indeed.

"A few weeks ago, a Cheyenne brother to the Oglala came to visit us in Pine Ridge and he brought news of a new belief in the West. He said he had been beyond the shining mountains to a place called Walker Lake, and there he had seen an Indian Messiah. This Christ, whom he said was a Ute named Wovoka, said he had been in the world before, but the whites mistreated him. So he was back now as an Indian and would save us if we were faithful to him. Dance for the ghosts, he said, and the old ways will come back. The land will be new again and the buffalo will return in herds too big for the eye to hold. Our loved ones will come back as well, all who have gone before, and the white man will be swept away forever.

"This story gave the Lakota tribes the hope they had lost. Some from the other agencies, including Kicking Bear and Short Bull, were sent to consult with this Messiah directly. But I was slow to show my thoughts. This was not the Indian way to my mind. This sounded like the beliefs of the whites—I know this because Agent McGillicuddy and I once argued on this long and hard at the Pine Ridge agency. I was not so sure about this Ute holy man. But then I had a vision of my own.

"A bird came to me in this vision. It was a curious bird, without a feather at all and with the face of a lizard. It whispered to me in a soft, girlish voice and it said 'Come to the West, wise man. Seek not, for you will know when you are there. Come. The ghosts of the past are calling you. . . .'

"I honored this vision. I slipped away from the agency and traveled west, walking at first until I could find a horse in need of a rider. I rode it into the land you now call Wyoming, and to a range in the Rocky Mountains that is not so far from the white town of Laramie. There I found others already waiting, one for each of ten tribes. And they were all medicine men, very old and powerful like myself. I recognized many. There was Cold Eyes of the Southern Cheyenne, the man who blinks but once a year. His northern brother, Buffalo Hump, was there, whom I knew from the war with the pony soldiers in the Powder River many years ago. That is also true of the Arapaho called Two Horses. Men of power from my own Lakota tribes had received like visions, for they were there as well; Longer Tongue of the Minneconjou, Spotted Wolf of the Hunkpapa, Tall Bear of the Brule. I even saw my old enemy Smoke there, the Crow medicine man. We had warred with them in the past, but such feuds were behind us now since there were not enough warriors left to fight them. The Navaho and Cherokee there I had never seen, but the others told me they were Atawai and Running Thunder. It was a *wakan* gathering indeed, very powerful. But we still did not know why we were there.

And there was no one at the foot of the mountains to greet us. So together we climbed up the rocks and into the cold of the higher ground.

"The bare trail led us to a low canyon in the shade of a tall, flat-topped tower, and in that canyon we found two lodges. One was large enough to house a small tribe, the other a warrior and his children. None among us could decide which tribes these were from, for the paintings on the lodges were strange to our eyes. Perhaps it was the Messiah, we thought.

"The flaps turned back on the smaller lodge and a girl stepped out, wrapped in a long cloak made of eagle and crow feathers and some from birds I did not know. There was nothing else we could see, not even moccasins, despite the cold of the rocks where we stood. She was one of our people, though I could not decide which tribe, and she looked to be not many years older than you, Willie. But she was very beautiful with long hair like the night and green eyes that flashed when she looked our way. She carried herself with much authority. She smiled at our approach and held out a hand to us. "Great medicine men," she called in a soft, willow voice, which was the same I had heard from the lizard-faced bird in my dream. 'The Savior Wovoka could not be here to greet you. But I am Dee-Bo-Ha and he has sent me to bear his word to you.'

"Well, the others with me began to grumble. For their chests were full of pride, and they thought the Savior should have greeted them in person. Besides that, these old men were not very respectful of holy women. Though I have known a few in my years, women are not usually accepted in the medicine circles and certainly not among the highest of the shamans. And this woman, Dee-Bo-Ha, must have sensed our displeasure. For when she spoke next, it was not in her own talking, but an older voice. A man's. 'Brothers,' he said through her, 'I am your Savior, the Paiute called Wovoka. This is my servant and these are my words. Give her your ear and your hearts. There are important things to hear this day. Remember, the ghosts are calling. . . .'

"This took much of the pride from us. For though none of

us had heard this Wovoka before and could not be sure it was he, she still had much power, this was evident. So we agreed to be silent and hear her out.

"She led us into the larger of the lodges. It was circular and had seating around a firepit which had yet to be lit. But it was already very warm in there, almost hot. The cold of the outside was suddenly forgotten as sweat broke down my sides and along my brow. That was when I first felt my unease begin to build. Where was the heat coming from, I asked myself. I have always accepted mysteries as the work of Wakan Tanka, but this felt somehow different.

"We were seated around the firepit, and Dee-Bo-Ha took her place at the head of the circle. Then she clapped her hands twice. In answer, the lodge flaps opened and two figures came inside then, hunched and furtive, bundled from head to foot in long robes till we could not even see their faces. One bore a pipe, while the other carried a large earthen bowl. They sat these down next to the woman and then scurried from the lodge.

"The pipe was lit and passed about, so that the air became even heavier and hard to breathe. During this time the woman watched us closely, from one man to the next. And my discomfort continued to grow. For when she looked in my direction, I felt those eyes burn right through me, into my spirit itself. It is hard for you to believe, I imagine, but I felt this.

"Then the woman regarded us and spoke. She said, 'Brothers, a sad tale has been told. The original people who held this land and cared for it like kind fathers are almost gone from the world now. Where once our people covered the land like grass, now there are only patches of green in a world of dust. The whites have taken our land and our buffalo and our lives. Is there a man here who has not been touched by their greed, their treachery, their cruelty?'

"Of course, the medicine men could not say this. For though each of us have known whites who we would call friends, we could not forget the ways we have been cheated of land. I myself have given up fighting since they moved us to the northern reservations, for there are no more ponies or guns and no more warriors to stand beside. But at her words I could feel the old anger coming back, poking its head from just beneath my skin, where it has always hidden.

"The smoke from the pipe had begun to swirl above our heads as if stirred by a gentle breeze, yet there was no wind inside the lodge. It curled back on itself and went round and round, and as it did we could make out images in its midst. Pictures formed there, growing clearer to us. And especially to Cold Eyes. 'You of the southern Cheyenne were at Sand Creek with your leader Black Kettle,' she said to him. 'And Two Horses of the Arapaho was also there, were you not? When White Chief Chivington's soldiers came riding in.' She directed our eyes back to the images dancing above our heads. Images of slaughter. Indians were running in all directions as the soldiers rode into camp, shooting at anything that moved. I saw Black Kettle there; I knew him only because of the stories I had heard of him standing beneath an American flag he had been given once, and the others of his tribe huddled around him in hopes that the soldiers would not shoot someone under such a flag. But they were wrong.

"The Cheyenne warriors had gone to the south to hunt buffalo on that day, so there were mostly women and children and old men in the camp. But that did not matter to the soldiers. They killed all they could and they butchered the bodies, cut out the privates of the dead to make tobacco pouches and hat bands. I had heard of this many times in hushed tones over the campfire. But to see it before my eyes—my anger grew even stronger, till my shoulders quaked.

"The images changed as Dee-Bo-Ha spoke again, became different places, different tribes. But the pictures were just the same. Treachery, injustice. Murder. 'A sad tale indeed,' she said, 'retold too many times. And often what followed was even worse. For at least the white man's gun kills quickly.' At that the pictures changed yet again, and we saw two small children kneeling by a stagnant pool, lapping at the black water like dogs. She told us this was Navaho suffering from the Bosque Redondo reservation far to the south. But each of us had known similar suffering at our own agencies. Starvation. Disease. No clothing to fight the cold. But perhaps the shame was worst of all.

"The smoke swirled again and the images faded, went away to nothing. But the anger stayed behind. We all had tears in our eyes at the sights we had seen, tears of rage. Our hate was as thick as the smoke had been. And I saw that Dee-Bo-Ha seemed pleased for that. This troubled me, and I was reminded of what my Cheyenne brother had told me: that the Messiah had preached peace with the whites. 'Why do you stir our rage so?' I managed to ask. 'Does this Messiah not wish us to be peaceful, to dance and make no more war with the whites?'

"She looked at me as if I had said some strange words indeed. 'The Ghost Dance is not working,' she said to me. Her voice was not soft and whispery. There was a hard edge to it. 'The spirits do not hear the songs, they do not hear such small voices crying out in the night. But your voices are strong, and they will ring even louder with your anger and your cries for justice. When you dance for the ghosts and sing the secret songs, the spirits will hear this time. And the world will be made new again.'

"She clapped her hands once more and this time the stones in the firepit grew bright before our eyes, and the lodge grew even hotter. Then she lifted the bowl that had been brought to her. 'Come and walk the Peyote Road with me,' she said as she offered the bowl to the Navaho called Atawai. 'This plant will bring on visions to show you what must be done, to instruct you in the special Dance of the Ghosts and the songs we must sing.' She put the bowl in his hands and whispered, 'The ghosts are calling. . . .'

"The bowl was passed from man to man, and each of them in their anger took some of the peyote eagerly. But I was less sure of my actions. I tried a bit, but it was bitter on my tongue and I spit it out. Besides, I have never needed such a plant to bring on visions. This was making no sense to me. If we medicine men were indeed the last hope for the Ghost Dance to work, why did the Messiah not meet us in person? And this was not pride speaking in me, but caution. My anger eased as my suspicions grew stronger. And that is when I felt it. Another presence in the lodge. I could see no one besides the other old men, but I could feel something still, growing stronger, feeding on the thick anger. I felt very sick at that moment and my hair was standing. I knew I must get out of there. This was not right at all.

"By now the peyote was taking affect on the medicine men seated around me. They had begun to sway to some unknown rhythm, and they grunted and barked and called out in strange tongues that hurt my ears. I could not imagine what kinds of visions this plant had produced for them, and I did not want to know. I did not want to be a part of such a ceremony. I looked to Dee-Bo-Ha and saw that she was swaying and crying out as well. Her eyes were closed. I don't know if I would have had the courage to leave had they been open, for despite her youth there was something about her that unsettled me and made me fearful in my heart. But she could not see me now. So I quietly stood and slipped through the flaps of the lodge.

"It had been daytime only a few minutes before, when we went into the lodge, but now it was night, and the full moon was high in the sky. How long was I in there, I asked myself. How long had I been under this witch's spell? This night was very cold so that the sweat froze on my skin. But it awakened me, chased the anger from my soul, and rid me of whatever magic the witch had cast upon us. I half expected to see the covered servants she had summoned earlier, that they might try to stop me. So I put my hand on my knife to be safe. But there was no one in sight. So I started toward the slope that would take me out of that canyon. But I had taken no more than a step before I felt breath on my ear, and a whispered voice that said, 'Do not leave, No Moon.'

"I whirled about to find Dee-Bo-Ha standing just at my shoulder, her feathery robe billowing around her thin form. And I had never even heard her approach. My heart crawled into my throat, for despite my own *wakan* skills, I was very afraid. Those eyes . . . they held me as fiercely as the strongest hands. 'You cannot leave me, wise man,' she said boldly, as if I could never refuse.

" 'I do not want any of this,' I told her, even as I pulled my eyes away. 'Something is not right here. I do not know you. I do not know your Messiah. You ask for too much on faith alone.'

" 'But is it not worth it?' she said, moving closer still. 'To see the white man gone forever? To have justice finally? Vengeance for those killed by their bullets and their greed?'

"But I ignored her and tried to walk away again. She caught my arm. 'There is more,' she offered, as if those things had not been enough. 'You are the most powerful here. We need you. And in the world that is to come, you may have anything you desire. Your own pony herd will match the buffalo in number. You will be chief over all the tribes. You will be as a king among all men. And you will have anything.' A strange smile came across her face then, and she took a step back, let the feather robe fall from her shoulders despite the cold. She was naked there in the moonlight, so beautiful and desirable; the sight of her aroused me more than I had felt in many years. Anything you desire, she whispered again, and reached out for me. But I did not give in to her witchy ways. I made myself remember the unease I had felt inside the lodge, the heat and the gathering rage and that strange presence there, the way it made my skin crawl. I remembered the wrongness of it all, and how she was behind it. This allowed me to see through her spell and resist her, to step beyond her grasp.

"In that instant, Dee-Bo-Ha's face seemed to change. I saw something there that was dark and inhuman, a vision of coarse hair and long teeth, the face of a coyote and yet like no coyote I had ever seen. Then, just as quickly, the image was gone, as if it had never been. She was a woman once again, just as young and beautiful. But one thing had changed—her expression. Her features were twisted and hard, and her eyes burned with fire. For she knew I had looked within her, had glimpsed whatever dark secrets she holds. And this angered her.

'Those who are not with us,' she said in an icy tone, 'are against us. Hear me, No Moon of the Oglala. You will not stand in our way.' Then she scooped up her robe and stalked back into the lodge, leaving me alone in the night.

"I stood there, shaking, and not just from the chill in the air. I had no idea what was occurring there, what I had stumbled into or what I had seen behind the woman's face. All I wanted was to be away from that place, to get as far as possible. So I ran down the mountain, and I did not look back.

"I found my horse and rode hard to get away from there. But once I was out of sight of the mountains, I slowed in my flight. The images and bad feelings were fading now, and I asked myself had I really seen and felt those things. Or was it just the imaginings of a foolish old man, or jealousy toward a girl who held such power. But then, in the night, the wind came. And it told me of my pursuers. And this made me think hard. I remembered how she had looked, and how something seemed to feed on the hatred in that lodge. And I knew whatever it was could not be good for my people. I decided then that if I survived these spirit stalkers, I would go back and confront her. That is when I found the poster along the road for Colonel Brady's show, and noticed the name of Shaddock. This was the man who faced the Black Heart Devil and survived, I told myself. Such courage is big medicine indeed. So I came here looking for you."

Tol and Willie had listened quietly to the Indian's whole story. They were still silent for a moment after he finished. Finally Tol spoke. "So you came here to save the white man from the Ghost Dance, is that it?"

"No," the Oglala said flatly. "I owe the white man nothing but my rage and bitterness. If someone fights for them, it must be you. I care for my own people, and at this moment I fear for them. We all hunger for revenge, it is true. But from the badness I felt in that lodge, the evil—such vengeance may have a price too high to pay."

"The way she tempted you . . ." Willie considered aloud. "It sounds like the Bible, you know? Where Jesus was tempted by Lucifer. Is that it? You think this woman's in cahoots with the Devil?"

No Moon considered her words solemnly, then nodded. "Someone's devil," he said. "I am not sure whose."

Tol threw up his hands in exasperation. "This is all hogshit, you know that? It's crazy. I mean, what are we really talking about here? Ol' Scratch, come a-calling? Joe Hayes himself, in the flesh? C'mon!"

"You saw those things last night," Willie replied. "You explain 'em."

The old cowboy nodded as if taking up the gauntlet. But no reasons would come, and he finally just fell silent.

The heavy door to the cellblock suddenly swung open and Deputy Leeds came in. He was not alone. This time the figure behind him was larger and older and had a stomach that a waistcoat and vest could barely contain. Sheriff Roscoe Tuttle was a big man about ten years Shaddock's junior, but nowhere near as weathered or hard. Instead, he was well fed and soft, looked as if he'd never been in a saddle. He had a droopy mustache that had strained many a meal and his eyebrows were equally bushy. At that moment his brow was knitted in exasperation. His expression changed a bit when he regarded Willie, trying to take on a friendly mien. But he had seen too much this day to look anything but frustrated.

"Hello, Willie," he said, putting a hand on the girl's shoulder. "Are you feelin' all right, darlin'?"

"Well, what'd you find!" Tol said impatiently. "Did you see my horse? How's my Mose?"

The sheriff turned and gave him a troubled look. "No better than Colonel Brady himself or any of the other men or animals at the campsite. Oh, they're all still breathing. But it's not what I'd call living. It's the damnedest thing. The Devil's work, I'd say." He didn't see Willie and No Moon exchange looks at his words. He was looking straight at Shaddock. "What I want to know is, what the hell went on out there last night? And I want to know now."

Tol could hear only the Indian's words from earlier, his predictions of what would happen if these men knew the truth. And this time he kept his mouth shut. Neither of them said a word. And that left the sheriff to fume with his own impatience.

"What's wrong, Shaddock? You sure was chomping at the bit to talk when we brung you in. So how about going over that again?"

"I was outta my head then," the cowboy said with a nervous grin. "To tell you the truth, I was a little drunk at the time, so I couldn't tell you right off what went on last night."

Tuttle frowned, then turned to No Moon. But one look at the Indian's impassive face told him he wouldn't get a word in reply. Finally he went to the young Ducane. "Willie, honey? You want to tell me what's become of your daddy, an' what happened out there last night?"

Willie stood from her stool and steadied herself against the bars, holding her forehead with mock fragility. "I'm . . . feeling kinda faint, Roscoe. I think I'd best go lie down for a while. We can talk later, if that's all right. . . ." She didn't wait for his answer but instead brushed past him and Leeds and went out into the office area.

Tuttle just glared at the two men in their cells, biting his lip in barely controlled anger. "Lookee here," he stated plainly. "We've got a storekeeper who's missing and about fourteen or so men and almost that many horses a-sleeping like the dead out at the end of town and who knows what the hell that thing in the livery is. And by God I'm gonna have some answers 'fore long or somebody's gonna be swinging from the rafters! You can count on that!" Then he turned and shoved his way past young Leeds. The deputy followed obediently after him and pulled the door shut in their wake.

Tol sighed. "Well, at least the girl held her tongue. She's got grit, that one." Then he leaned against the bars. "Still, we're no closer to getting outta here."

"That is true," No Moon concurred. "And we must get away, that much is certain. Dee-Bo-Ha said the Ghost Dance would last a week. That leaves us only three days to reach the mountains and stop them." He perched himself back on his cot, pulled his feet up under him as if to meditate a while longer.

"What do you mean, us?" Tol muttered. "I never said I was going, you know. You can't make me go."

But No Moon was not paying any attention. He knew in his heart that Shaddock would help him in the end. That was never in doubt. No, the only problems confronting them at the moment were the bars of these cells. "Three days," he said again, and closed his eyes. "We will leave here tonight."

Chapter 8

The sun had gone down three hours earlier, leaving the town of Barlow in the grip of an oppressive silence. The memory of the previous night's strange goings-on was still fresh in every citizen's mind, the echoes of those screams still ringing in their ears. The communal worry that it might happen again was tangible indeed, so much so that the slightest sound seemed capable of cracking the night air around them like fine crystal.

There was tension in the jailhouse as well, for much the same reason. But the two men within knew something would be coming, sooner or later. And that made their fear all the more urgent.

Shaddock paced his cell constantly, his muscles taut as coiled springs, his ears primed for any sound that might seem out of the ordinary. He prowled all corners of his cell over and over, always ending up back at the window, where he'd stood countless times before. But nothing had changed. All he could look at was the twinkling expanse of night sky overhead. His vision was limited by the weathered clapboard of the next building—his cell was on the side of the jail facing into a narrow alleyway, so he had a clear view of neither the street nor the open prairie. He didn't like that at all because if someone were coming after him—some*thing* —he wouldn't know about it till it was too late.

Unless they scream again, he thought sullenly. Unless they howl like the dead, like the last two. And that notion alone sent a chill wriggling along his spine.

What does it matter whether you see them or not, an inner voice said, mocking his wariness. If more of those things like They-Who-Follow-Behind come, they'll go through walls if they want 'cause there's nothing to 'em. And there won't be any magic circle to hide in this time because the Indian's powder and knife and bag of tricks are out in the sheriff's office along with your pistols. Nope, there won't be no fighting 'em this time. Just dying, the same way that Russell Ducane died. Or at least the way his soul did.

Shaddock remembered that delicate thing pulled from the storekeeper's body, a wispy butterfly in human form, and how the demons tore at it ravenously. . . .

"We gotta get outta here," he muttered, pacing again. "I ain't going that way, no sir!" He flashed an impatient glance into the cell next to his. "I thought you said we'd be getting out of here tonight . . ."

The Indian sitting on the floor ceased his muttered chanting and cast the lanky cowboy with an irritated eye. "I am doing my best," he said in a controlled voice. "But you keep interrupting me. Please, let me concentrate."

"Yeah, well, hurry up." More pacing, more fidgeting. "You never did say exactly how you're gonna pull this off, you know."

"It would be easier if I had my pouch," No Moon confessed as he tried to regain his composure and return to the vision-state. "There is much magic in that. But without my things I can only ask mercy from Wakan Tanka."

"Wakan Tanka? That your God or something?"

A faint smile crossed No Moon's features. Just like Agent McGillicuddy—the whites were ever trying to understand others by imposing their own limited view on the subject. "This is the Great Mystery," he said. "Wakan Tanka is many spirits such as Maka the Earth and Inyan the Sky and Wi the Sun. But all of these together are one. This is why it is the Great Mystery, do you see?" But apparently he didn't. Shaddock was just staring at him numbly, uncomprehending. So he gave up trying to explain. "The Great Spirit," he finally said in surrender. It was a phrase he seldom used because it was so Americanized and it did not capture the scope and majesty of Wakan Tanka. But it seemed the only way for simple minds to understand it. "If I please Wakan Tanka, one of the spirit servants will be sent to free us."

"Spirit?" Tol felt his insides go cold at the notion. "You

mean you're actually calling one of those *nagi* things like last night?"

"Different ones," he said with a nod. "But still spirits."

"And you're wanting to bring one here? No sir!" Tol was adamant. "I don't want any more of them things running around me. Who knows what they'll do. You said it yourself, 'If I please Wakan Tanka . . .' Well, what if you don't? What if he's downright pissed and he sends those Follow-Behinders back again?"

The Indian listened to his worries and took them in stride. His expression was so stony that he appeared completely unflappable. But to Tol's surprise, he offered no reassurance. "What you say is true," he agreed. "You can never tell how one of the spirits will behave. Another part of the Great Mystery." He looked at Tol then, and an uncharacteristic grin split his features. "You could cross your fingers, you know."

"Very funny."

"Do you have a different plan?"

"Just let me think a minute, okay?" the cowboy snapped. More pacing. More staring helplessly out the window. Then he abruptly stopped, glanced in the Indian's direction. "You say you got other magic in that pouch, huh?"

No Moon nodded. "The powder I drew the circle with out there." He gestured toward the street. "It has many uses, depending on the spirit I call on for aid. I could sprinkle a bit in the lock of the cell. Then, if I call on Fire to help me, the metal will melt. If I call on Ice, it will freeze and turn brittle. I could also—"

"That's good enough," Tol cut him off. "All we've gotta do is get Tuttle to bring the damn thing to us. Lay down on your cot and act like you're sick. Do some moaning and groaning, and make it sound good. I'll tell the sheriff to get the bag, that you need your medicine from it. That way you can pocket whatever things you need."

"And why should he care whether I am well or not?"

This time Tol grinned. "Simple. They'd rather hang a live Indian than a dead one."

No Moon considered that, and could not argue with Tol's logic. He went to his cot and did as Shaddock had instructed. There came a long painful mewl, followed by a questioning glance. "Good enough?"

"A little more pitiful," he said. "And louder this time." When the next groan came, it was more to his liking. "That's it. Now, just keep that up and I'll yell for—"

Suddenly the door to the cellblock swung open, taking Shaddock and No Moon both by surprise. No Moon even forgot to moan, but in a moment resumed his role and became mortally ill once again. Tol's own reaction was a little slower. He was staring at the sheriff, who stood in the doorway, and wondered what had brought him so quickly. *It couldn't have been the Indian's cries, not that fast.*

Tuttle looked bleary-eyed and was dressed only in his longjohns, which meant he'd already turned in for the night on the cot that sat just to the side of the jailroom door. So what got him up, Tol wondered . . . until he saw the stranger standing behind him. He was shorter than the sheriff, a stocky man in a wool coat and Stetson, pulled down low over the eyes. Whoever it was wore a gunbelt low on his hip, and the holster tied off at the thigh was empty. And from the mortified look on Roscoe's face, the gun that rode there was presumably stuck in the sheriff's back.

"Don't do this," Tuttle warned his assailant. "Why don't we just sit down and talk about this—"

"Just move inside, Roscoe," came a low whisper in reply, nudging the fat officer forward.

There was something familiar about the voice to Tol's ear. The stranger forced the sheriff into the cellblock and followed close behind, but the lighting wasn't good enough for the old cowboy to make out his face. It wasn't until the man turned sideways and Tol saw the long hair sticking out beneath the big Stetson that recognition finally sank in.

Willie Ducane caught Tol's slack expression through the bars. "Don't look so surprised, Mr. Shaddock," she said, keeping the gun trained on Roscoe's ample tummy. "What'd you two think? That I'd run out on you?"

"Didn't think nothing at all," the cowboy replied. "You don't owe us nothing. I just figured you'd gone home." He looked over at No Moon, who was still on his cot and groaning fitfully. "You can stop now. It's just the girl."

The Indian looked up at her through the bars, strained his eyes. "Girl? Are you sure?"

"It's me, all right," she said, tipping back the brim of her hat so he'd see. Then she jabbed her pistol barrel into Roscoe's belly a little harder. "The keys, please."

Tuttle picked the key ring off his belt, held it out to her. "Now, just think about this, Willie. We can stop this right now and I'll forget it ever happened. I know you've been through a lot. . . ."

She didn't reach out for the keys—she was extra careful, wary that the officer might not take her seriously and try overpowering her. So instead she gestured with the barrel of her gun for him to throw the keys to Shaddock. "I'm sorry to have to do this, Roscoe," she said with sincerity. "I really am. But you don't know what the hell's going on here."

"You could tell me, Willie. . . ."

"You'd never believe it," Tol said as he opened his own cell and then tossed the keys to No Moon, who did the same. "Take my word on that." When he came out from behind the bars, Willie held out a coil of rope and a bandanna that she'd been carrying in her other hand. "Put him in the cell," she said, nodding toward Tuttle, "and tie him up. Make it tight, and gag him too. We gotta have time to get away."

"What about the deputy?"

"He's already gone home for the night. Won't be back till morning."

Shaddock cocked his head to the side and studied her quizzically. "You're a pretty steady hand at this, missy," he commented. "You ever lead a jailbreak before?"

"Nope," she said, "but I've read enough about 'em. Now, are you gonna stand there flapping your jaws or get moving?"

"Yes, ma'am."

She turned to the Indian, but his cell door was already standing open and No Moon was nowhere to be seen. Just then he stepped back through the cellblock door, startling her. Somehow he'd slipped past her before and now came back carrying his shoulder pouch and Tol's gunbelt as well. He handed the latter to the cowboy.

"Much obliged there, pard," Tol said, then motioned to

the Indian's leather pouch. "You still got that rattle in there you was shaking around in the street last night? Well, better leave it here. We're gonna hafta run hard and fast, and the sound's liable to give us away."

"That is the *wagmuha,*" No Moon told him. "It will not speak unless I ask it." Then he turned to Willie. "We will need horses to make good time."

"There's some out back. If Shaddock'll just hurry up . . ."

"I'm hurrying, girl!" the cowboy said, finishing with Roscoe Tuttle. The sheriff was lying on the cot in Tol's cell, on his stomach. He had been hog-tied, his wrists and ankles bound together behind him, and the bandanna was stuffed into his mouth. "That oughta do it. No offense, Sheriff." He came out of the cell while Willie went in, knelt down next to the cot to look the angry Tuttle in the eye. "Listen to me, Roscoe. These men saved me last night. I can't say how, but they did. And there's still something that has to be done. Something bad's gonna happen unless they can stop it. So don't come after them, all right?"

"Let's go already," Shaddock said, impatient to leave. The jail was closing in around him, cutting off his air, and he just wanted to get out in the open so he could breathe. Willie came out of the cell and relocked it, then followed the others out into the office and closed the jailroom door as well. Tol's eyes had already locked onto the gun rack on the wall, filled with small double-barrels and a couple of Winchesters. But a padlocked crossbar prevented their extraction. "Where'd you put those keys, girl? We'll be needing some supplies—"

"It's taken care of," she urged, physically pushing him toward the side door of the office. "I took what we'd need from the general store. The gear's all on the horses."

"But the guns—"

"Get moving already!" The much smaller girl took the task of shoving him through the door and into the open alleyway. They looked to the main street of Barlow and found no one there, not even the light of the street lamps, which had been extinguished only an hour after sundown. The way was deserted to the rear of the building as well, and that was where Willie led them. When they rounded the corner there, Tol saw that she was a young woman of her word—she had indeed taken care of things. Three horses were waiting for them, a bay mare and an Appaloosa and a spirited pony that perked up the minute she came into sight. All three were already saddled and stocked with bedrolls and canvas sacks and everything else that the girl had thought to pack.

"Where'd these come from?" Tol whispered.

"The livery," Willie replied as she swung up onto the prancing pony. And when she said it, there was a look in her eye, a flash of the little girl that was hiding behind this cock-sure exterior. Tol knew what had been carried to the livery, wrapped in canvas. It must have taken a lot for her to go in there. Real grit. He found himself liking this girl more and more all the time. "This'n is mine," she said, stroking her pony. "The others I had to borrow. And I mean borrow." She put special emphasis on that, in case they had any notion to the contrary.

"We will return them when we are finished," No Moon agreed. He had already picked out the Appaloosa and stepped into the stirrup; it reminded him of the fine animal that had carried him halfway to safety a few nights past. If it had half as much spirit, he would be satisfied.

That left only the mare for Tol. She was stout and solid as a draft horse but seemed ill chosen for the swift flight that lay before them. She certainly wasn't old Mose. "Beggars can't be choosers, I suppose," he muttered as he climbed aboard. To the horse's credit, she accepted his weight without a misstep or snort of any kind. The three of them reined their mounts around and pointed their noses into the Western prairie. But suddenly a thought occurred to Shaddock. "We can't leave just yet," Tol whispered suddenly, drawing one of his big pistols. "I'll need to be reloading after that fracas in the street. And my powder and shot's all in the wagon down yonder—"

"Not anymore," Willie said impatiently. "It's in your saddlebag. Now, can we get going? Please?" Without waiting for their answer, she started her pony off at a steady canter, keeping him under tight control for fear that galloping hooves would announce their escape. The other two followed after her, and they left Barlow behind gradually, at least until they were out of earshot. Then the girl gave her mount the heel and it bolted across the open grass like a bat out of hell. The older men both stayed right after her. The Appaloosa was a natural runner and took the lead, staying not far behind the fleet pony for most of the way. Even though Tol brought up the rear, he was still more than impressed with his own heavy horse. It had a lot of muscle and was not shy to use it, yet it rode well just the same. No, you ain't Mose, he thought as he patted its straining neck appreciatively, but I think we'll be getting along fine just the same. Yessir, just fine.

They did not slow until the little town was no longer in sight behind them. There was nothing but the waving oceans of grass, frozen in perpetual ebb and flow and cast silver by the moonlight. "Down, Buck," Willie ordered her pony three times in his ear to make sure he heard her. And immediately the faithful animal slowed his mad gallop, coming to a stop at the crest of a gentle rise. Shaddock and No Moon reined their mounts alongside hers.

"It's good to be outside again," Tol said gratefully, dragging in all the cool night air that his lungs could hold. "But what the hell are we stopping for? I wanna be as far away from that town as possible."

"I thought you might be wanting these," Willie told them. She unlashed a blanket bundle from the back of her saddle, unwrapped it to reveal several rifles and handguns from her father's store. "Here you go," she said, handing a short Winchester carbine to No Moon, followed by several boxes of shells.

He held the gun up before him, worked the level on it, lifted it to his shoulder with obvious joy. "I had such a rifle once," he said nostalgically, "before they made me give it up at the reservation. I was a good hunter with it. The children ate well then, you know."

"I have something else for you." She dug into her cache again, took out a double-action Thunderer that had sat in the store's display case for almost a year now. "It's a tad on the fragile side," she told him. "But it shoots fine. I tried it once." She offered it to the native butt-first, then pushed a box of .41 Long Colt ammunition into his hands as well.

"This one's mine," she said, taking out the extra Peacemaker, the same one she'd shown to Tol that first day. She stowed it in the pouch of her saddlebag. "Now for Tol." She went through her trove again. "I know how slow those big horse pistols are to reload. So I brought you a cartridge gun just in case." She handed him a chunky-looking pistol with a short barrel and a birds-head handle. "It's a Merwin and Hulberd Pocket Army in .44-40. It ain't the most accurate in the world, but it's small and it carries a big bullet."

"Thank you, missy," Shaddock said, taking the pistol and extra ammunition. He studied the fistful of steel, nodded appreciatively. "You never know when a little piece like this might come in handy. But I was kinda hoping you might've brought me some kind of longarm like his. . . ."

"I was getting to that," she said as she peeled away the blanket completely to show the final weapon in her lot, the Sharps Big Fifty that he'd admired so much.

Shaddock's eyes almost popped; he reached out and took the big-bore almost reverently. "That'll do the trick," he whispered. "That'll do for sure. I appreciate this, missy. I really do. It almost seems like the old days."

No Moon finished loading his pistol and thrust it into his waistband, then set to loading the Winchester in earnest. "We should be moving on," he said solemnly. "West. We have only three days."

"Whoa down there, friend," Shaddock said. "I never said I was going off to the Rockies with you."

"What?" Willie was incredulous.

"Look here, girl. I don't know about you, but after last night I have no desire whatsoever to mess with any more of them *nagi*. And that's what we'd be doing if I was to go, isn't that right?"

"Chances are," No Moon said with a nod.

"Well, thank you but no. That is not for me."

The Indian's expression did not change. If he was surprised by the cowboy's attitude, he did not show it. But Willie was another matter. She gaped at him outright, her jaw hanging slack. "I don't believe it," she said slowly, "I just do not believe my own ears. Tol Shaddock—*the* Tolman Shaddock—turning down a good fight?"

"Against witches and spookies? Honey, you bet your sweet little ass I am. I may not matter much no more, I'll grant you that. Just an old piece of leather a few years too long on the bottle. But at least I'm alive. And I intend to keep it that way as long as I can."

"And how long will that be, Shaddock?" No Moon asked point-blank. "If the witch is not stopped, you may have only three more days of life. You and the rest of the white men everywhere. Three days."

Tol didn't have an answer for that. After what he'd seen, he had no doubt that the Sioux shaman was telling him the truth, at least as he knew it. This Dee-Bo-Ha must have been a real threat to rattle the old man as she had. So when No Moon threatened the entire world of the white man, his words carried a great deal of weight. But Tol had seen the *nagi* with his own eyes, had felt the cold fear it birthed within him. And that personal terror had eclipsed even the genocidal warnings.

Willie's disbelief had turned to exasperation. "Never mind him," she said to the Indian. "You've still got me. I'll go with you."

"You?" Tol laughed. "You ain't going out there, little sister. What could you do besides get yourself killed deader'n hell? You're not a fighter—you're a storekeeper, for chrissake!"

"Not anymore, I ain't. Bustin' you two out pretty much sealed my fate in Barlow. I won't be going back there ever. I took what money there was in the store and anything else I'd need. Let Mr. Walker take care of the rest. Hell, the bank owned more of it than we did anyhow. Look, the point is that I got you out of jail, didn't I? I got guns for you, didn't I? I'm plenty useful. And I'm not too bad with a pistol, I can tell you that. Besides, I want this Dee-Bo-Ha woman. I owe that bitch for my pa's life. So you never mind me, Mr. Shaddock. You just ride on and find you another Western show so you can keep on telling people about the old days and your greatest adventures." She leaned closer from her saddle as if sharing a secret. "But I'll promise you one thing,

Mr. Big Western Hero. Deep down in your heart you'll know that you missed out on the last big adventure. Maybe the greatest of all."

She could see in the cold lunar light, from the look on his face, that her words had struck home. Perhaps it was a combination of No Moon's grave warnings and her own appeal to his ego. But she saw a gleam in his eye, the way his lean jaw set to the challenge at hand. "Aw, hell," he sighed dramatically. "I suppose somebody's gotta look out for the little lady here. Count me in." He gave an ironic laugh then. "Some team we make. A couple of dried-up old farts and a baby girl. I'll tell ya, this witch sees us coming and the sight alone's bound to scare her to death."

Willie chuckled as well, and even No Moon cracked a half smile as they reined their horses westward and set off at a gallop.

The wise men of the nine tribes still sat in the lodge where the Oglala had left them three days past. They had sought visions and chanted and sang every moment since then, sleeping only when their minds and bodies could no longer endure. At various times each man lost consciousness and slumped over, exhausted. But the robed assistants did not let them rest for long. They would pull them back up and give them food and water, along with more of the peyote. Soon the visions began anew.

The words that poured from their fevered lips were hoary and arcane and hadn't been heard on the earth in millennia, not since before their common ancestors first crossed the land bridge in the far north. But they did not hear themselves. Instead, their ears were filled with the voices of the past, the screams and lamentations of the thousands who had died beneath the white man's heel. Likewise, their eyes saw only the injustices, the rapes and massacres that fueled their anger, and nothing of the present. So they did not notice the changes that had occurred around them, especially the creatures that appeared on the second day.

Birthed in flame and smoke, the grublike creatures crawled from the firepit itself and lay among the unknowing humans. And as their glowing skins cooled, the things began to change. To grow. Long, sticklike arms sprouted from their sides, reached out with boneless fingers to touch the stuporous medicine men. To stroke them and to peel away their sweat-soaked clothing so that they may join, man and monster, in blasphemous union. But the nine old men were oblivious to their hot and inhuman touch. They felt only the hatred burning in their hearts, filling the air around them like an ever more palpable presence.

The woman behind all of this knew that the ceremony was going well. The power was building. The arrival of the slithering harbingers was a clear sign of that. They in turn would prepare their mortal charges for that which was to come. Two more settings of the sun and then the Dance would begin.

But for now her mind was not on the ceremony at all. Neither were her eyes.

Dee-Bo-Ha sat at the head of the circle, staring glassily into space, unmindful of the obscenities around her. Instead, she saw rolling moonlit meadows from on high, watched them ripple in the light breeze. That same breeze sought to carry her eastward; the leathery wings that bore her had to beat all the harder just to maintain their present position. She watched her enemy and his newfound allies far below, riding to the west. Coming here. That was very unsettling indeed.

We underestimated the Oglala, she thought in bitter silence. He was powerful, this one; she'd known that right away, when she first laid eyes upon him. He'd thwarted They-Who-Follow-Behind, compounding her grave failure in not securing his aid in the first place. It was her fault and hers alone, and her punishment would be severe if this one old man somehow managed to interfere with the ceremony. Severe indeed.

The thought was so disturbing that her concentration lapsed and she lost control of her distant eyes—the images distorted and darkened and she was suddenly back in the lodge again, watching the tendrils of smoke that curled snakelike from the glowing coals of the firepit. No matter. She could bring back such visions whenever she wished. Besides, she had seen enough. She knew that the Oglala was coming, and he now had aid. They may have been just an orphan girl and a creaking old white man, but she knew better than to dismiss them out of hand. She had learned that the hard way. These two, they had not been scared easily. Indeed, even after facing the *nagi*, they still came, which made them threats to be reckoned with. Deal with them decisively, she decided. Destroy them all in one swift stroke.

She stood abruptly, picked her way through the moaning, undulating ranks of old men and inhuman attendants before stalking through the flaps and into the night beyond. The thin air was crisp and startling, especially after the smothering heat she'd just stepped from; it swept beneath her cloak and caressed her nakedness with hands of ice. But aside from an initial wince of surprise, she did not fight the chill or pull her cloak any tighter about her. Instead, she reveled in it. She had not experienced such distinct sensations before. Any feeling at all short of outright pain was a marvel to her, something to be experienced. That notion lent a sense of urgency to the task at hand, gave a new meaning to her step. The Oglala would stop all this, she thought with sudden anger. He would take this away from us. But we will not let him. We will not!

The robed ones finally noticed her standing outside the lodge, and they must have sensed that something was amiss. They immediately huddled around her and groveled there, waiting for a command. But she ignored them, continued her trek for the small lodge nearby.

What should I use, she asked herself as she walked. What should I call on to do my bidding this time? So many to choose from—a thousand different demons from a thousand different beliefs. Some went by many names in many tongues, while others were known to no one, at least in this time and place. She'd thought it amusing when she called upon They-Who-Follow-Behind, to use the Oglala's own beliefs against him. But he had been too well prepared for that, and the spirits themselves too simple-minded. That was always the case with lower demons, she thought—either fickle or unruly or uncooperative, making such poor assassins. But the more powerful forces were too cunning and crafty to allow themselves to be used—they demanded more for their services than she was willing to pay. If only I could do this myself, she thought, with my very own hands. But she knew full well that she could not leave this place, not when the plan was so close to fruition. But if I could, I would deal with them once and for all. Their screams would linger on the night wind, and I would save the Oglala for last.

She stopped just short of the lodge, felt a rush of anticipation course through her like liquid heat. Perhaps there was a way after all. And the delicious thing about this sudden solution was that it sprang from the old man's own beliefs, just like the *nagi* had. A smile formed on her lips, a hard and cold expression to match her austere surroundings. No Moon will know, she told herself gleefully. He will know what is coming and that I am to be his killer, and he will be afraid as I tear the life from his chest. Very afraid.

She swept back the hide flap of the smaller lodge and went into the darkness there. And at her entrance a small candle sparked to life, cast the limited space there in a flickering orange glow. It was a sparse structure with few amenities, not even a sleeping mat. Just a small buffalo skin for sitting that was worn from age and a second even smaller hide rolled into a bundle beside it. That sat directly before a firepit much like the one in the other lodge, though far smaller. A long wisp of acrid smoke still hung above it, just as it had after she summoned the *nagi*. Indeed, the stench of conjuration was still heavy there, nauseatingly strong . . . to anyone except Dee-Bo-Ha, at least. She did not even give it notice. She went right to the hide and seated herself upon it, taking off her feathered robe and laying it aside to face the pit unadorned. Immediately the coals in the shallow hole began to glow as if triggered by her mere presence, and the cold retreated from around her like the waning of the tide.

She unfurled the hide bundle beside her, revealing several sewn pockets on the underside which held herbs and powders and other materials few medicine men would have recognized. She took a pinch of sulfurous powder and flung it into the pit, followed that with bitterroot and mullen and wildwood shoots. In response there was a hissing in the pit as white smoke curled up from it. The woman was satisfied;

she began to murmur deep in her throat, chants and incantations all slurred together like a steady monotonous drone. Another pinch of powder, another belt of smoke, though this one changed in hue. It became darker. Angrier. The air grew thick and clogged her lungs, made it hard to breathe. But she endured.

Dee-Bo-Ha closed her eyes, and her expression grew taut with concentration. Beads of sweat broke on her brow and lip, rolled across the flawless skin of her face and onto her heaving chest. She began to sway to a primal rhythm that no one could hear save her. It was hard to tell how long she continued that way, perhaps an hour, maybe three. She was no longer cognizant of time or space or anything except the firepit and her own voice.

Finally her hand moved away from her lap, slipped into the bundle beside her, and returned with a long thin-bladed knife.

She held it aloft, presented it to the coils and folds of multicolored smoke that now hovered before her eyes, taking shape one moment, then melding back on itself the next. She held it in both hands, the hilt in one, the blade laid across the other. Then without a second thought she closed that hand around the blade and swiftly drew the knife away, letting the steel slide deep into her palm. She did not flinch. She merely held her clenched fist over the pit, watched as the rivulets of crimson leaked from between her fingers. They popped and sizzled on the glowing coals below. And almost immediately the cloud of smoke before her turned bloodred.

"Hear me," she said in a longdead tongue. "The bargain has been struck. Give me that which I crave."

The cloud of lingering redness answered her. Soundlessly it spat something out onto the ground beside the fire, a wad of sputum that glistened wet in the candlelight. And as she watched, it began to move, to writhe. It seemed to swell. A knot formed on the side of it, stretched, grew until it looked as if it would split from the original entirely. But instead, another knot appeared and the process started all over again. The substance was spreading quickly across the ground like running oil, taking on a shape that seemed remotely human and yet grotesquely different. It finally stopped moving once the form was complete. But there was no life there. Only a thing.

Dee-Bo-Ha knew what to expect next. For a brief moment she was afraid, but that fear itself was new to her, and she did not fight it.

Tendrils of the red smoke extended from the central cloud and came toward her, ethereal in makeup but somehow threatening nonetheless. But she did not shrink away. They circled around her, touching her tentatively here and there before caressing her with abandon. And it was only an instant later that the tremendous ripping sound occurred, if nowhere else than within her own mind. Pain shot through her like a firestorm; it felt as if a part of her were being torn away. The sensation was hot and ragged and nothing she wanted to savor at all. She tried to force the anguish into submission by sheer will alone. Finally she succeeded, but leaving her senses still throbbing from the pain.

She fought her way back to a seated position. Her muscles burned and ached and her mind was numbed beyond her understanding. She held her head, closed her eyes, and tried to get her bearings. . . .

Suddenly she was no longer in the lodge at all. She was outside in the moonlight, moving across the canyon with amazing speed, heading up the slope toward the trail that led out of these mountains. . . .

She opened her eyes. She was still in the lodge after all, the firepit smoking lazily before her. The red cloud was gone. And so was the glistening black form in the dirt next to it.

She laughed then despite her pain and, closing her eyes again, watched the landscape fall away beneath dark, tireless legs. The Oglala will be afraid, she thought. Very afraid.

Chapter 9

"Wilhelmina . . . help me . . ."

Willie peered all around her, searching for the source of the haunted voice that kept calling to her. But it was no use. She was standing in a vast twilight wasteland, a void of gray and black that seemed to stretch to infinity. And there was no one else in sight. "Who is it?" she yelled, her uneasiness building. "What do you want with me?!"

"Here," came the whisper again. "Over here."

She whirled around to find a man standing some distance away. He was cloaked in shadow till only one side of his face was visible to her. But it was enough to recognize her father. "Pa?"

"Why . . ." Russell Ducane said softly. "Why didn't you help me, Willie?"

The girl's vision began to swim with tears. "I wanted to, Pa. But they were holding me. And there was nothing I could do anyway. I mean, those things, they would have killed me too and—"

"You could have tried," he interrupted, his tone just as decided and unreasonable as ever. "You could have saved me. But you didn't want to."

"No, Pa. That's not true. . . ."

"You wanted me gone, didn't you, Willie? You wanted me out of the way so you could go west, just like you've always wanted. Isn't that right?"

"But Pa . . ."

"Isn't that right!"

"No! I never wanted to hurt you, Pa! You gotta believe me!"

Russell Ducane took a single step toward her, just enough

116

to take him out of the shadows for her to see him. To see that he was changing. The side of his body that had been obscured in gloom was writhing and shifting, the arm folding back on itself like a hose, with new mantislike appendages sprouting from the rib cage beneath. There was also a toothy maw growing from the side of his squirming face. "You got what you wanted, Wilhelmina," the nightmare told her. "I'm out of your way. There ain't nothing holding you back now, girl. You're free. Free . . ." He turned away, shuffled back into the darkness.

"No, Pa! Don't go! Please!" She ran after him as hard as she could, determined to reach him this time. Dammit, she had to reach him! But to move through this realm of shadow was like slogging through quicksand; with each step she took she could feel herself falling farther and farther behind. "Pa, please! Don't leave me here! I don't want to be alone! You can't leave me alone!"

"It's just a dream, Willie. Wake up."

It was a new voice, not her father's, which brought the girl out of her slumber with a start. She sat bolt upright, jerked in reflex. But strong hands caught her shoulders and held her in place. She didn't fight; she just looked up at the face above her and waited for recognition to sink in. The Indian . . . it was No Moon who knelt beside her bedroll, stared down at her with concern. "Are you all right?" he asked. "You were crying out."

She steadied herself, wiped the dampness from her face. Whether it was perspiration or tears, she couldn't be sure. "A dream," she stammered, sitting up. "Or a nightmare more like it." She thought a moment. "That's funny. I can't even recollect what it was about. Ain't that something?"

The Indian started to repeat what she had called aloud before he woke her, about being alone and all. But he stopped himself. Her eyes still seemed wild and uncertain, and he couldn't be sure whether she actually didn't remember or chose not to. So he just nodded and motioned to the fire. "Come warm yourself."

Willie nodded and followed after him, even as she took in their surroundings. The sun was just peeking above the horizon, the birth of another day, so there was more light now than when they arrived and she could see their campsite clearly. It had been a cabin once, many years ago if the present condition was any sign. These days it was little more than a wooden frame on the ground with two log walls left standing to the north and west. It was hard to tell its history just from looking at it; perhaps the remains of an ill-fated farm, whose hopeful builders had failed to realize that the eroding soils of Nebraska's Sand Hills were just too unstable for crops. It had happened many times in the past, as settlers sought to carve a niche for themselves from this new frontier. The husks of their mistakes, like this one, dotted a sometimes harsh and uncompromising landscape. The cabin had been dismantled over time, log by log as others sought building materials in a tree-poor land, till the two adjoining walls were all that remained.

But it was a good place to camp. The walls provided a break against the cool prairie wind, and as Tol pointed out, it also gave them something at their backs in case of attack. The girl and the Indian couldn't tell just who he was worried about the most, spirits or posse, nor did they care at that moment. It was the dark of the early morning then, and they all needed rest. Just a few hours. That should be enough.

Willie sat by the fire, feeling its warmth chase the morning chill from her bones. She closed her tired eyes and almost couldn't will them open again. Okay, it hadn't been enough, she sighed. She was more tired than ever. She hadn't been able to sleep at all the night her father was killed, and afterward the jailbreak and all. Add to that all the time in the saddle, which was the most she'd ever ridden at one stretch and the hardest she'd pushed little Buck before. But the pony had proven himself equal to the task. She just wished she could say the same for her backside. It felt tender and swollen, much like her eyelids. She looked to the Indian then, watching for a sign of the same kind of aches and pains that nagged at her. But he exhibited none of them, even at his advanced age. He still seemed fresh, obviously accustomed to hard times and the abuses of the saddle. "Did you get any sleep at all?" she asked.

"A few hours," he nodded. "Enough for now."

"And how about Shaddock? How's he doing?" She looked around. "Better yet, where the hell is he anyway?"

Her answer came with the crack of a rifle, one so loud that it seemed to ring in her ears for several moments. She could see No Moon sitting nonplussed as if he had been expecting it. His lips were moving, but she couldn't hear what he said. She rubbed her ears until the echoes of the gunshot faded from them. "He's just on the other side of the wall," the Indian repeated. "He wanted to sight in the rifle you gave him."

"What the hell's he shooting way out here?"

No Moon pointed off to the east, beyond the wall to her rear. "There's a row of old fenceposts out there. I believe he's trying for the last one. He said it was about seven hundred yards." He leaned forward, whispered, "I have seen men make longer shots."

"I heard that, you heathen," called an unseen Tolman from behind the wall.

Willie yelled to him, "So how about it? How's it shoot?"

"Just fine." There was pain in his voice. "But I'll tell you, missy, I'd almost forgot what a joner these things are to shoot. They'll play hob with your shoulder till you're onto 'em."

"Did you hit anything?"

He hesitated before admitting, "It pulls to the left. I'll have to adjust for that." A moment later another thunderclap rang out. But this time it didn't seem quite so loud to Willie's ear. "Aha! Got'er that time, by gawd!"

"Great," she muttered under her breath as her stomach twisted on itself. *The great hunter bags a fencepost. How do you cook those things anyway?* But just as quickly she felt ashamed for mocking him, especially since the hunger gnawing at her belly was her own fault. Real smart, girl, she chastised herself. You remembered the guns and the ammo, and you remembered the blankets and bedding and matches, the cook pot and coffeepot and a fork for each of you. You even thought to raid Shaddock's wagon so he wouldn't have to take the time to do it himself. So why, for God's sake, didn't you remember to bring some food? It was so stupid. So unforgivably stupid.

"I have something to eat," the Indian said, mimicking her very thoughts. She turned to look at him suspiciously, unsure whether this old man was somehow able to read her mind. But his expression was open and friendly, and it convinced her to lower her guard. He opened the leather pouch that hung on his side, took a cloth bundle from within. Inside it was some sort of food, a dry cake that was thick and dull-colored and looked none too appetizing. He broke off a hunk, held it out to her. "It is *wasna*," he told her. "Some meat pounded with berries and kidney fat. It will get you by."

The girl did not seem overly eager to try the proferred morsel. But her stomach burned again, urging her on. She took it and bit off the smallest amount. It had a strange taste and texture. Not bad. Just strange. But at least it quelled the tremors within her. "You carry a little bit of everything in that bag, don't you, old man?" she said between bites.

He grinned. "All that I need."

"You know, you're a real mystery to me. I mean, here I am, following after you and Shaddock, believing every word you tell me. And I don't even know you, except for your name."

"What more would you like?"

"Well . . . for starters, how is it you speak such good English?"

No Moon thought back, letting moments from the distant past return to fill his mind and eyes. The memories must have been pleasant, for he smiled upon seeing them again. "When I was a young brave among the Oglala, there was a white man, an Englishman from across the great ocean. His name was Elias Childers and sometimes he wintered with the Natural Human Beings. He was a hunter and trapper, but he was not very good at either. So we took him in and showed him better ways. In return he taught me the white tongue and let me hunt with his rifle. And he gave me this hat." He took the derby from his head, admired the weather-beaten old thing. It was the first time Willie could actually remember seeing the old Indian bare-headed, even during the mad flight from Barlow the previous night. The hat had stayed in place at a full gallop, and she had begun to think it had grown onto his scalp. "It is a white man's hat," he said pragmatically, "so there is no magic in it. But Elias said it made me look quite dashing." He replaced the hat on his head as reverently as a crown, cocked it to one side with a rakish flair. "So? What do you think?"

Willie laughed. "Yeah, you're a regular city man."

Another bark from the Sharps interrupted them, and after a pause to reload came still another after that. He better take it easy, Willie thought. He's got only two boxes of shells for that piece. Once they're gone, he's not likely to find any more out here.

One more blast. This time it was followed by a victorious whoop. Tol suddenly came around the wall of the cabin, wearing his biggest grin. Like No Moon, the old cowboy didn't look the worse for their midnight ride. He wasn't even shaking from withdrawal anymore. If anything, he seemed invigorated. "I got one," he told them.

"Another fencepost?"

"Nope. A buzzard. There's been a bunch of the critters circling around out there, gotta be at least eight hundred yards out, maybe even nine. And I picked one out of the air. A clean shot." He turned to the Indian and bragged. *"In the air,* Pappy. So put that in your pipe and smoke it." He laughed and started around the back of the cabin where the horses had been tied up. "Yessir, there'll be meat for the stewpot tonight."

"Buzzard?" Willie almost retched. "You expect me to eat buzzard?"

"I have eaten worse," No Moon told her.

Shaddock reappeared a moment or two later, steering the bay mare around the cabin. He hadn't even taken the time to saddle her; he just clung to her main and slapped her rump, set her off across the dew-laden grass at a dead gallop.

"But buzzard?" Willie said again, and grimaced. The thought just wouldn't leave her alone. Hell, that even made No Moon's *wasna* sound good. She looked to the old man's leather pouch again. "What else do you keep in there?"

The Oglala held it up proudly. "I am a *pejuta wicasa*—a medicine man and healer. And I am also a *wicasa wakan,* a holy man. So I carry the implements of both. There are powders and herbs here, cedar and calamus root and yellow leaf medicine and many others, very powerful. But I also have my *wakan* tools—"

"*Wakan?*"

"Mysterious. Magical. Here." He began to sort through the pouch, showing her the things he found there. "This is the spirit knife, which you've seen before. It is truly *wakan*. And this is a *wagmuha*, the sacred rattle I used to strengthen the circle." He held it up for her to see. "It is made from the scrotum of a buffalo," he said with a smile. "As you can see, it was a small buffalo." Then he stowed it back into his poke, kept up his search. Finally his hand closed around that which he sought the most. "And here is my heart," he said, holding out a small bundle of fawn skin. Like the *wagmuha* rattle, Willie remembered him carrying it inside the protective circle. "It is my *sicun*, the thing of reverence. When one becomes a *wicasa wakan*, the holy men of the village construct this for him. It is very sacred. It allows me congress with the spirits. Brings me magic."

"What's in it?"

He shrugged. "That is part of the mystery. I have my suspicions, of course. But to mention such things aloud would be to rob them of their power." He held the *sicun* up before his eyes, appeared to whisper to it. Or maybe he was praying, Willie thought. Then he placed it back in the larger pouch carefully, as if it might have contained the most fragile crystal.

"I don't have nothing valuable like that," Willie said, a bit forlorn. "But I do have a few things. Keepsakes, you know." She took a bundled kerchief from an inside coat pocket, unfolded it to reveal another wrapping, this one treated oilskin to keep the contents safe from rain. She unwrapped that too, laid the items within on her lap. The first was an ample wad of money. "My part of the store." Next she picked up two small photographs. "This here's my pa. And this one, that's my ma." She held it out for him to see. "Wasn't she beautiful? Sometimes I wish I'd turned out more like her."

She went back to sifting through her trove. "I got other things, too—uh, this here's the casing from the first round I

122

ever fired. That was five years ago. I woulda kept the bullet too, but I missed the target by a mile and couldn't never find where it went." She held up a hair ribbon after that. "You see this? My pa got me that last year, for my sixteenth birthday. Ain't that pretty?" She rolled the length of blue satin around her fingers, rubbed it as she remembered. But it stirred other memories as well, like a haunting monotone from a wasteland of shadow. So she quickly discarded it.

In the ribbon's place she picked up a large piece of folded paper. "Well, you'll probably remember this," she said, straightening the handbill for Brady's Western Event with Tolman Shaddock's visage emblazoned there. "I took this out of the store window before I left," she said. "I don't know quite why. In fact, I don't know why I keep any of this. They just please me, I suppose." She finally put it aside and held up a small book of paper. "This here's my journal," she explained. "At least the latest one. The other two're in my pack. I been keeping one ever since I was little, when Ma died. It don't say much—Lord knows there was precious little to speak of in Barlow. But I've wrote in it good and faithful for so long that it just wouldn't feel right to stop now." She dug in the pocket of her jeans and produced a handful of pencil stubs, along with a little folding knife to sharpen them. "I ain't put down nothing for the past few days, what with everything happening and all. But I'm gonna catch up first chance I get."

She leaned closer. "You know what else? I kinda thought about writing down what happens as we go along. Sorta like the latest adventure of Tolman Shaddock? He's had books wrote about him, you know. And I figured they might pay me for another one. Worth a try, right?"

No Moon nodded, as if he really understood what she was talking about. But Willie saw that he didn't, and she realized that she'd just been running off at the mouth. Pictures and shell casings and a stupid journal, she thought. Do you think an important medicine man would give a hoot in hell about the things you pack around? He's got magic in his bag. While you got nothing but junk.

She was just refolding her oilskin bundle when the pounding of horse's hooves broke the silence, growing steadily louder. That'll be Tol coming back, she figured. And he'll have that damn bird with him. Maybe if I don't look at it . . . After all, meat's meat once it's in the pot.

The cowboy rode right to the edge of the cabin. He was carrying something big and limp in his hand, but he no longer whooped and crowed. In fact, his expression was just the opposite. Deeply lined. Deadly serious. "No Moon," he said evenly. "We got us some trouble."

The Indian rose in alarm. "What is it?"

"You tell me," Shaddock said. He abruptly lobbed his heavy trophy onto the dirt floor of their camp, for both of them to see. "What the hell is it?"

It was the size of a buzzard; that and the distance at least explained why Shaddock had been mistaken earlier. But up close there was no confusing this carcass with a bird or anything else they had ever seen before. It was lying on its back with its leathery batlike wings extended, so their view was unencumbered. It almost looked like a dog whose front legs had been replaced with wings, traded for the power of flight. Its sinuous body had a mottled gray-green coloring to it like bad meat, and closer inspection showed that the flesh was covered in small lizard scales that overlapped everywhere. Except where Tol's bullet had struck. There were two holes, one on either side, just under the wings. The wound was two fingers wide going in and four where it came out.

Shaddock knelt beside it, frowning with disgust. The thing's neck was long and heavily muscled, and it tapered to a triangular head that was fringed in coarse hair, hanging from the jawline and crest like tufts of black moss. The eyes were open; they were silver and reflected the astonished expression of the three looming over it. Tol took the skinning knife from the back of his gunbelt and slipped the blade into the creature's beakish snout, pried it open just enough for them to see the needlelike teeth lining its jaws.

"Hell if I know what it is," the cowboy told them, backing away from the thing in disgust. "But at least it ain't no spirit, 'cause a bullet killed it sure enough." He looked at No Moon. "You got any answers?"

The old Indian was silent for a moment. But then he gave a slight nod. "I am just as puzzled as you—there is nothing in my beliefs to explain this. But I have seen such an animal before. This is the same featherless bird that came to me in my visions, the one which spoke with Dee-Bo-Ha's voice. It must be one of the witch's spies."

"How many of these things did you see anyway?" Willie asked.

Shaddock couldn't take his eyes off the grotesque carcass. "I don't know . . . four, maybe five."

No Moon's brow furrowed. "Five of them," he repeated, his expression troubled. "The wind did not tell me of this. Either I am growing too old and weak, or this witch is even more powerful than I had thought."

The girl walked to the edge of the camp and stared out across the prairie. "That means she's still watching us. She'll know every move we make." Her eyes scoured the emptiness out there, both above and below. "If only we could find the rest of them. If only . . ." Her voice trailed away then. She tensed, squinted her eyes against the glare of the morning sun.

The girl's silence attracted Shaddock's attention faster than words could have. "Willie? What is it?" He hefted the big Sharps. "You find another one of them critters?"

"Nope. But there's something else out there. Look."

The old men both joined her and followed her gaze across the rolling meadowland. Then they too saw the horsemen coming. Shaddock couldn't tell right off how many of them there were; they were still too far off to count. But he could tell there was a passle of them . . . and that they were coming their way.

Chapter 10

The sight of the riders in the distance gave Tol a queasy feeling. "Is it a posse?"

"Hard to tell," No Moon said. "I count seven."

"Wouldn't be a posse," Willie affirmed. "Not this quick. I doubt they've even found Roscoe yet. Maybe it's some local ranchers or cowhands. Maybe they heard the shooting."

Shaddock was sure of that; they most certainly were attracted by his gunshots. But the strange gnawing at the pit of his stomach told him these were not simply landowners coming to check on a neighboring spread. It was the old lawman's nerves acting up, a paranoia he'd acquired while sheriffing down in Waco so many years before. That same hinky feeling had saved his skin many times since, and he'd learned better than to question its origin. "I don't know what they want," he said, "but we'd best be ready all the same."

"Ready for what?" Willie asked, feeling her excitement and anxiety grow in equal portions. But neither of the men took the time to answer.

Tol dropped his rifle next to the campfire, then unbuckled his gunbelt and laid it on the ground as well, at least two feet from where he finally sat down. He saw No Moon watching him. "Puts 'em more off guard if they think you ain't armed," he said as he drew the Merwin and Hulberd pistol from under his coat, double-checked it, and then put it back in its hiding place. The Indian nodded in understanding. He sat down and laid his own Colt Thunderer out in plain sight, then put his short Winchester rifle on the ground beside him and covered it with the wool blanket he wore around his shoulders.

Willie motioned to her own guns. "Should I take off mine too, or . . ."

"Keep them," Tol told her. "Nobody expects trouble from a kid. And make sure all your hair is pushed up inside your hat. A man's unpredictable when there's a female around . . . especially if they're shiftless to begin with."

Willie's eyes widened as she poked her auburn curls up inside the Stetson. "Outlaws?" she repeated, the idea crackling through her like lightning. "You think . . . could it be the Atwood gang?"

"Who the hell's Atwood?"

"Stutterin' George and his half-breed younger brother, Clancy," Willie explained, "only they call the half-breed Kolo too. Two of the most cold-blooded bushwhackers this side of the Platte." Her excitement was suddenly overruled by the unexpected fear that seemed to overtake her. It was like a cold slap in the face—this isn't a book, a voice reminded her. This is real and Pa's not here to help you and you might wind up on one of those grainy postcards yourself with a couple of silver dollars covering your eyes. She stared out into the open lands, her gaze locked onto the horsemen as they grew steadily larger.

"Whoa down there, girl," Tol said. He pointed to her hand, which was unconsciously gripping the butt of her Colt. "Relax yourself," he told her. "Nobody said this was trouble. 'Least not yet. We're just being ready. So don't you make a move or even flinch until I tell you to, understand? And if there comes some shooting, you forget about them silly books you been reading. You get down fast and you stay down. You hear? Young lady, I said, do you hear me?"

"Uh, yeah." She nodded, though still unsure of what he'd said over the thundering of her heart.

"What about this?" No Moon was pointing to the carcass of the lizard bird.

"Leave it." Tol shrugged. "If we're lucky, their attention will be on that instead of us. If there's trouble, that would give us an edge. And judging by the odds, we can use it."

They fell silent then, waited as the riders came upon them. There were indeed seven of them, just as No Moon had counted. They lined their horses along the southern and eastern perimeters of the cabin remains, effectively blocking any escape.

Tol looked them over thoroughly and took the measure of each man by the look in his eye and the manner in which he wore his gun, all the time smiling and trying to appear unalarmed by their arrival. It wasn't easy though. For Willie had been right—this was no posse, not by a long shot. The seven were trail-hardened desperadoes—not the meanest-looking bunch he'd ever come across, maybe, but dangerous just the same. Most were young, barely out of their twenties if that old, except for one grizzled veteran in faded buckskin britches who was almost Tol's age. He had a crooked eye that looked a bit off to the side, and that struck the cowboy as somehow familiar—he thought maybe he'd known some-one like that once but couldn't put his finger on it.

Anyway, there was no nonsense about this bunch; they wore sour expressions beneath low-brimmed hats, and they regarded the three with the cold demeanor of wolves closing in on wandering sheep. Tol felt an old urge to go for his pistol—go on, do it now while you've got the chance, you can kill at least three before they even clear leather—but he had to remind himself that this wasn't the old days, and that his speed wasn't what it used to be. Besides, there was No Moon and the girl to think about. . . .

He glanced over at Willie, hoping that she was under control like he'd warned her. He was relieved to see her hand nowhere near her gun. But that relief slipped away when he saw the wide-eyed look on her face. And in that cold moment he knew she recognized one of them, or at least she knew who they were. His eyes followed hers, crossed the lean, hard faces of the strangers before them, and came to the youngest of them all. The boy on the stout palomino had barely cleared twenty-one, if Tol was any judge, for whiskers grew along his jawline in fits and starts, just as coal black as his hair. His skin had a dark bronze cast, almost as ruddy as No Moon's, and yet his eyes burned bright blue like no Indian Shaddock had ever seen.

Half-breed, he realized.

They also call the half-breed Kolo . . . two of the most cold-blooded bushwhackers this side of the Platte. . . .

"Good morning," said the one in the middle of the pack. He was a skinny man, slightly older than the others. He already sported gray lines in his beard. He spoke slowly and pronounced each word carefully, as if unfamiliar with the language. Or trying to control a bothersome impediment. "We heard shots," the man continued. "Thought we'd r-ride over . . . see if you n-needed help."

"Thank you kindly." Tol gave them a big disarming grin. "But I was just trying to scare up a little breakfast. Afraid my luck ain't running too good, though. Only varmint I managed to take was that thing over there."

The horsemen's eyes were directed to the twisted gray-green figure sprawled out before the fire, its leathery wings spread to give them an ample view of the body. And their expressions showed that they had never seen anything like it. "W-what the hell is that?"

Tol shrugged. "Your guess is as good as mine."

The gang's spokesman turned to a beefy man at the end of the line, dressed in a heavy overcoat and flat-topped hat, wearing spectacles over his nose. "You know animals, Hinch," he said. "What do you make of it?"

The man stepped down from his saddle and walked over to the thing, nudged it with his toe before bending down to study it further. "Well, I'll be dipped in it," he said, scratching his head. "I ain't seen nothing like it before, I'll tell you that." He looked at the fire, then back to Shaddock. "You don't plan on eating it, do you?"

"I don't hardly think so. Seeing that thing's all but killed my appetite."

The big man grinned, showing a notable lack of teeth. "I can imagine." He looked the lizard bird over again. "I'll tell you what. I'll give you two dollars cash money for it."

"What the hell you gonna do with that?" asked one of the other men, a tall, rangy sort with a nose so broken that it bent to one side.

"Aw, I don't know. Maybe I'll have it stuffed. What do you say, mister? Two dollars?"

"If you want it that bad, fine." He looked at the other men still mounted. "You're all welcome to share the fire. I'd offer you some coffee, but somebody forgot to bring some . . ."

He looked to Willie, hoping his jab would somehow snap her out of that trancelike staring. But the girl hadn't even heard him.

The man with the stutter noticed her, though, and the way she was looking at him. It made him uncomfortable. "W-what's the matter with the b-boy?"

"Don't mind him," Shaddock explained. "He's a little touched, that's all."

"Well . . ." He managed to pull his attention away from Willie for the moment, turned back to the cowboy with his friendliest grin back in place. "Where w-was I? Oh, yeah. I was ab-bout to introduce m-myself. My name is George, and this"—he motioned to the silent half-breed—"is my brother C-Clancy. And these are our p-partners—Mr. Lansdale, Mr. Rexer, Mr. Garton, Mr. Hinchberg." He turned to the crooked-eyed old man. "And we just call him Grandpa Sipes." The old man frowned at the name, shot an irritated glance in George Atwood's direction.

Shaddock watched each man as his name was mentioned, searched their faces and eyes more thoroughly this time. He'd already figured the odds in his head and he knew for certain that he'd be killing them in a few minutes, as many as he could manage. The only question in his mind now was which one to shoot first. Stutterin' George was a good candidate. He was shifty-eyed and fidgety, and from the way he kept glaring back at Willie as he talked, Tol could tell he was volatile, easily angered. There was violence in his eyes, and no telling when it could ignite. His brother Kolo was a big threat too, though for completely different reasons. Where the older Atwood was noticeably antsy, the half-breed was stoic and motionless, almost detached. It didn't matter that the only weapon they could see on him was an enormous Bowie knife on his belt. He simply exuded a cold danger that put Shaddock on edge.

Of the five others, Tol dismissed two fairly quick. Garton was a dirty sort with wild hair that his hat couldn't contain, and he looked no less shifty than the rest. But his only weapon in sight was a Henry rifle, and it was still in its scabbard on the saddle. He would never clear it in time for a fight. And Hinchberg, the bearish figure who'd dismounted to study the lizard bird, was still too caught up in its mystery to play much of a role. But the last two, Lansdale and Rexer, they were going to be problems.

The former was the man with the broken nose who spoke to Hinchberg earlier. His eyes were specks of black coal in a hard, chiseled face, surrounded by muscles that had never been disturbed by the act of smiling. He had a crossdraw holster on, worn on the front of his left hip so when his hands rested on the saddle horn before him, the gun butt was already halfway in his palm. And from those cold, flinty eyes, it was plain that he would not be shy in bringing it to bear. That is, unless Tol stopped him first. Rexer, on the other hand, was a tall, lanky man who slouched in the saddle, and his perpetual squint made it hard to read his intentions. But the way he wore his pistols made Tol think twice. His coat was open in the front, so Shaddock could see that he had two Colts stuck down his pants, with the open loading gates simply hooked on his waistband. Most tenderfoots went for the fancy fast-draw rigs like Willie's. But not this one. Tol had a feeling that this Rexer was the real thing.

Kill him first. Put one right in his heart and then only a couple of inches to the left and you'll take Lansdale, maybe even the stutterer, since his horse stood between them. That would be three down, and he could then concentrate on Kolo and hope that No Moon could get to his Winchester to cover the rest. . . .

But what about Grandpa Sipes? He'd almost forgotten the old man with the nest of gray hair framing his scalp and jaws. Tol turned to regard him, found a man who had obviously been large and powerfully built once, almost as tall as Shaddock and probably twice as broad. But age had withered his arms and legs and sheathed a muscular torso in layers of drooping fat. But he still looked capable in a fight, and he carried a short brush-flusher of a shotgun, which could always mean trouble. He could spray the lot of us with that, Tol thought.

He saw the old man's left eye wander away from the right so that he looked in two directions at once, at Tol and Kolo at the same time. And that struck another note of familiarity in the cowboy. Where have I seen that look before, he wondered . . . and abruptly a name broke loose and popped to the surface of his subconscious.

"Hephaestus Sipes," he said aloud.

The bearded veteran looked at him suspiciously, his brow furrowed but glaring with just the one eye. "That would be me, mister," he said in a ragged growl of a voice. "Do I know you?"

"Depends. Tell me, Mr. Sipes, has your ear growed back over these twenty-odd years?"

The man glared at Tol suspiciously. Slowly he took off his hat, touched the hole on the left side of his head where an ear once hung. "How would you be knowing something like that? Unless . . ." His eye widened with recognition finally, and he looked at the Sharps rifle and twin LeMats lying on the ground as final proof. "Well, I'll be a suck-egg mule," he whispered as he stepped down out of the saddle, holding the double-barrel in the crook of his arm. He walked straight up to the cowboy, till they were no more than a foot apart. And he looked him straight in the eye. "That was some kinda shot," he said, nodding. "I musta been more'n a mile from that butte you was on."

"More like a mile and a half," Shaddock said. "But it wasn't all that good a shot. I was a few inches off."

At that Sipes let out a loud gust of laughter and cuffed the taller man on the shoulder, grabbed his hand, and shook it vigorously. "Son of a bitch!" he kept muttering over and over, still pumping away at Shaddock's arm. "It's been a loooong time, ain't it? Son of a bitch!"

"You kn-now him, Sipes?" George Atwood asked.

"Are you kidding?" Hephaestus called back. "This is the bastard what shot me. I pulled a bank robbery down Texas way 'bout a score back, and this beanpole with a tin star pinned on it chased me all the way across the Indian Territory." He looked back to Tol. "I lost you in them wilds sure enough, but not without this little souvenir." He touched the stub of his ear again, then laughed some more. "You never did catch me, old hoss."

Tol shrugged. "You was the only one. Ruined a perfect record."

"Tin star, huh?" said Lansdale, and the others were visibly restless at the mere words. "You still a lawman, mister?"

Before Tol could answer, Hephaestus turned to scold them. "Don't you'uns know nothing? This here is *the* Tolman Shaddock his ownself. Hell, he's a frontier legend these days. Sheriff, Army scout, Indian fighter . . ." He looked over at No Moon a moment, as if his quiet presence somehow brought the exploits into question.

"I heard'a him," Garton said, showing a gold front tooth when he talked. "I saw his name on a poster alongside the road a few days back." Then he grinned at the others, quite proud that he'd been the only one able to read it. "Colonel Brady's Western show, it was."

"Frontier legend, huh?" It was Rexer who said that, in a molasses-slow voice that rolled from his lips in monotone. He fixed his squint on Shaddock and let a grin curl the corner of his mouth. "Just looks like an old fart to me." He looked at Sipes. "Why the hell are you so friendly with somebody who done shot you?"

Hephaestus brushed off the younger man's words. "I'll tell you, boy. When you get to be as old as I am, even an old enemy is a sight for sore eyes." He looked back to Shaddock. "Them was wild times, right, Tol? I tell you, I miss 'em. I surely do. . . ."

"D-d-dammit, stop s-staring at m-me!" It was George Atwood again, still focusing his anger in Willie Ducane's direction. The girl had averted her eyes, now hid them beneath the brim of her hat. But that wasn't enough for the outlaw. "Y-y-you l-looking for t-trouble or something? Huh?"

"George," came a soft but steely-edged voice, Kolo speaking for the first time. "He's just a boy," he said. "Pay him no mind."

"B-b-but he k-k-keeps s-staring at m-me. . . ."

"Let it go. Business, remember?"

George begrudgingly nodded. "R-right. B-b-business." He took a deep breath, fought to control his deteriorating speech. But his composure was slipping, and his face was red with either indignation or embarrassment. He turned back to Shaddock, tried to pick up where he left off. "We r-r-represent the r-r-r . . . we r-r-repres-s-sent the r-r-r . . ."

After several long moments of struggle, the half-breed finally nodded to the others, and Garton took over for their frustrated leader. "What George's trying to say is, we represent the Ranchers Association for these parts." A smirk played on his lips, and a like expression spread among the rest of them. They obviously enjoyed the new title that Atwood had made up for them. It gave them self-respect, and it sounded a lot better than "border gang." "As such," he continued, "it is up to us to see that nobody trespasses on private property in this area. And to punish those who do."

"Is that right? And do the ranchers know you are providing this service?"

Garton's smile widened, flashing gold again. "We never took the time to ask. But I know they'd appreciate it."

"We want nothing," No Moon abruptly said. He still sat by the fire, having been quiet until now. "We take nothing from this land. We are only passing through. We shall be gone before the sun clears the horizon."

Kolo was staring at the old man, seemed to silently scold him for daring to speak without permission. There was an anger in his eyes that Shaddock couldn't quite understand. Then the young breed wrinkled his nose with disdain and ignored him. Garton went on talking.

"Let's get this straight, you old coots. You're here right now, this minute. And that's trespassing. Now, you got a choice in front of you. You can either pay whatever fine we set . . . or we'll drag your sorry asses all across the state of Nebraska. And whichever way, we still get paid." He gauged the look in Shaddock's eye, then shifted his gaze to the Sharps rifle and the big horse pistols, still in their holsters on the ground. "I hope that wasn't a foolish thought in your eyes just then," he said, smiling. "I really do. 'Cause my boys'll cut you in two 'fore you get halfway to them guns."

"I wouldn't dream of it," Shaddock replied. His hand had slid down his side to the tail of his shirt, bare inches from the hidden pistol.

"Make your call," Kolo prompted, fixing the cowboy with that icy blue gaze. "Now."

The muscles in Tolman's hand were tensed up, and he was past the decision stage, all the way to the act itself. But just as his fingers slipped under the shirt and prepared to dart for that birds-head grip, George Atwood suddenly barked again.

"G-g-g-god-d-dam-m-mit!" He grabbed off his hat and threw it to the ground, his face beet red and seething with anger. The disguised girl was still looking at him, wide-eyed, and this time she was unable to avert her gaze. Their eyes were locked on each other, and she looked as if she might faint at any minute. "W-w-w-what's the m-m-matter with you! Y-y-y-you d-d-don't l-like the w-way I t-t-talk? Think it's f-f-funny? Well, d-do you!"

"The g—I mean, the boy didn't mean anything, mister," Shaddock said.

Even Kolo tried to calm him down. "It's just a kid, George. Let it go already—"

"No!" Atwood was livid. He nudged his horse sideways onto the old cabin's floor, brushed back the tail of his coat so Willie could see his holster clearly. "You g-g-got a r-real f-f-fancy rig. You th-h-hink you're p-pretty f-fast, huh? Well, y-you try m-m-me, okay?" He took the rawhide loop off the hammer of his Colt. "C-c-c'mon, b-boy. D-d-draw, d-damn y-you!"

The attention was on the two of them now, so no one saw Shaddock grab for the Merwin and Hulberd .44, draw it out of his pants, and hide it behind his leg. His plans had changed; he'd have to kill Atwood first, and just pray that Rexer and Lansdale were taken by surprise. If not . . .

He watched George closely, studied the twitch of his arm, the tension in his gun hand. He knew the second that it would dart for the Colt's grip. . . .

Tol lifted his pistol and aimed, but he wasn't fast enough. Someone else fired first, and he barely caught sight of the muzzle flash from the corner of his eye. But he still wasn't sure he believed it. George Atwood's hand was barely to his gun when Willie Ducane finally snapped out of her trance and reacted by instinct. She drew her pistol and rocked back the hammer all in one fluid motion, fired as soon as the barrel cleared leather. And before the plume of fire had even erupted from the barrel, she was already raking her left hand across the top of the pistol, fanning back the hammer, and letting it fall again for a second shot less than a heartbeat after the first.

One bullet hit George Atwood flush, right between his left collarbone and the muscle of his shoulder. The heavy slug jerked him sideways in the saddle, toppled him backward even as his horse spooked and bolted forward. That sudden movement took him out of the path of the second round, which zinged harmlessly past his shoulder and instead hit the crooked-nosed Lansdale square in the forehead. It made a dull popping sound on impact, snapping his head back and knocking his hat off but not taking him out of the saddle. He actually straightened up for a moment there, raising his head to look at the men around him. But his eyes were already glassy and rolling up into his head, just fields of white beneath the puckered and leaking wound in his brow. A spasm racked his body, a last gasp, and then his muscles went limp and he slid off his mount, hit the ground like a bundle of wet rags.

The echoes of the gunshots faded into the distance, and all was silent in their wake, except for the moaning Atwood. All eyes were on Willie Ducane, who stood with smoking gun in hand. She was just as surprised as everyone else present, if not by her speed, then the deadly results that she had wrought. Even Tol was stunned. At least till he saw Rexer slowly unfold his arms and then suddenly grab for his own pistol. Tol raised the Merwin and Hulberd and fired, flinching from the heavy recoil and the gout of flame that jumped from the barrel. But he hit the gunslinger dead center, just above the sternum, and Rexer gasped just once as he went down.

Garton and Hinchberg were slow to react, just now drawing their own weapons. But before Tol could turn his pistol on them, No Moon dropped a pinch of powder into the fire before him and set off a startling flash, followed by a thick plume of smoke. It startled the two, gave him enough time to grab his Winchester from under the blanket and open fire. He caught Garton in the side of the head, sending the man with the Henry rifle flying, and then he levered a new cartridge into the action and turned it on Hinchberg. The hulking man took the round full in the chest at close range and staggered back, dropped his pistol and his glasses. But he did not go down. No Moon had to fire two more times before the outlaw would collapse.

Tol could barely see; the powder flash had surprised him as well, and his vision now swam with spots of bright orange. He turned away, rubbing at his teary eyes, and he barely saw Hephaestus Sipes coming at him, drawing his own gun, a Colt Dragoon every bit as large and ancient as the cowboy's own LeMat. Shaddock brought up the stubby Merwin and Hulberd, but he did not fire; he knew Sipes was reacting hesitantly, else he'd already have had that big horse pistol out by now. So instead he just charged the stockier man, howling like a banshee. Sipes was caught off guard by the attack, and Shaddock just swatted him across the face with the short barrel of his pistol. Hephaestus dropped his dragoon and lurched to his knees. "Sorry about that, friend," Tol muttered over the groaning man.

"Shaddock!" It was No Moon yelling, and his tone was strident. Warning him. In that instant he realized he'd made a major mistake, and perhaps a fatal one.

He'd forgotten about Kolo.

Pounding hooves suddenly bore down on him from behind. He whirled around with his gun out, but the charging palomino was only a few feet away, almost ready to trample him. At the last minute it veered away, and that's when he saw Kolo leaning out of the saddle toward the cowboy, wielding that wicked Bowie with at least a foot of gleaming blade. He slashed at the cowboy's throat, his arm all but a blur, and Shaddock could only throw up his arm in a feeble attempt to fend off the attack. Steel sparked on steel as the knife struck the upraised pistol. But just as quickly Kolo reversed his slash with a backhand motion. This time the razor edge sliced into Tolman's face, splitting the length of his right eyebrow and grating on the bone beneath.

Shaddock winced and grabbed for his lacerated brow as the half-breed passed him by, heading for where his brother lay writhing in the grass. No Moon stepped into his path, bringing the Winchester up for a quick shot. But Kolo just gave his horse the heel and rode right into the old Sioux, knocked him sprawling. Then there was nothing else in his way. He rode straight for his moaning kin. "Give me your hand!" he yelled, until George finally climbed to his knees and reached for help.

But Kolo hadn't counted on Willie Ducane still standing there.

"Shoot him!" Shaddock yelled as he fought to clear the blood from his eyes. That alarmed Kolo; he finally noticed Willie, saw the pistol still smoking in her hand. And for an instant their eyes met, locked onto each other so fiercely that neither seemed able to move.

"Dammit, shoot!" Shaddock had gotten to his feet and was weaving toward them, trying to aim with his other eye. But his shouts seemed unable to break the trance that Willie was caught in. She wouldn't move. Not even when Kolo grinned and went back to helping his brother. He dragged George up and draped him across the saddle before him, then spurred his horse to a gallop. Not once did he look back to see if Willie would shoot.

She did not even raise her pistol.

The palomino headed for the open prairie, following the spooked and riderless horses of his confederates. He was joined by one other rider, Hephaestus Sipes, who had recovered from the cowboy's blow enough to catch his own mount and was fleeing hell-bent for leather. Tol Shaddock wiped enough blood from his eyes to fire a few random shots in their wake. But the Hulberd gun was not very accurate at a distance, and the rounds went wild.

He quickly pulled the kerchief from around his neck and wound it taut, tied it around his head to cover the gaping cut above his eye, pressed it tight to stem the flow. And then he turned on Willie in disbelief. "You had a clear shot," he questioned. "Why didn't you fire? Why?"

"I don't know . . ." she stammered at first, shaking her head in bewilderment. "He . . . he . . . didn't have a gun, and . . ."

Tol's jaw hung slack. "He what? What the hell are you . . . ah, never mind. They haven't got away yet." He stalked back across the campsite, shouted, "See to the Indian," over his shoulder as he retrieved his Sharps rifle. Then he strode quickly beyond the cabin walls to where he'd been shooting earlier.

There he had no trouble sighting the two horses that sped out across the open ground, back to the east, where they had come from. Right along the line of old fenceposts, he thought with relish. That would make estimating distance all the easier. Ride harder than that, you little bastard, he thought as he knelt on one knee and mopped a rivulet of blood from the side of his face. Try to outrun this . . . He raised the heavy rifle to his shoulder and peered through the Vernier sight, estimated their distance and speed and how far he'd have to lead them. Five hundred yards . . . no, coming up on five fifty. He eased back the hammer and pulled the set trigger. Six now. Took a deep breath and held it. Seven. Coming up on eight . . . Then he squeezed the main trigger.

Something hit the barrel just then, jolted it skyward at the exact moment that the hammer fell and sent the round uselessly into the morning sky. Shaddock lowered the rifle and blinked at the figure standing over him. He'd been so intent on his target that he'd failed to notice Willie Ducane's approach. But it was hard to ignore her now, after she'd grabbed the rifle barrel and spoiled his shot. "I coulda had 'em," he said, glancing over his shoulder to see the riders growing even smaller in the distance. He'd never be able to reload in time. "I had 'em measured out just right. . . ." He looked up at her. "Why? What the hell were you thinking about?"

"You were gonna shoot 'em in the back," she said in disbelief.

"So?"

"But you ain't dirty that way. Are you?" Her voice was shaky and desperately in need of conviction. "Tolman Shaddock ain't no damned backshooter. He can't be. . . ."

Shaddock stood wearily, the muscles of his face taut with

barely controlled anger. "Come with me," he said, grabbing the girl, pulling her after him so hard that it jerked the hat off her head. He all but dragged her back into the camp, led her past the recovering No Moon, who was sitting up now and trying to straighten his jangled senses. He took her straight to the limp bodies sprawled in the grass and grabbed her by the hair, forced her down to stare into Lansdale's white eyes and gaping forehead.

"You see that, girl?" He gritted his teeth, making her stare at the corpse despite her struggling. "This here's real. It ain't no book with a lot of made-up horseshit in it. It ain't a bunch of rules about what's fair and what ain't. The only thing that matters is who's still standing when it's all said and done. Look at that poor bastard you killed—it don't matter to him whether you shot him in the front or the back or wherever. The only thing you gotta know is that he woulda done the same thing to you if given the chance."

She finally wrenched herself from his grasp and stood looking away, trembling. She took one last horrified peek at the man with the broken nose and gaping forehead, and then her stomach started to turn and she dropped to her knees, retching.

Tol stood over her, now feeling more helpless than angry. What's done is done, he told himself. You didn't have to be so hard on her. She's just a child. . . .

Yeah. A child with the fastest draw he'd ever seen. And if she didn't learn some hard lessons now, she might not live through the next go-round.

No Moon drew up beside him, holding his ribs painfully. He seemed to echo Tol's very thoughts when he said, "Those men will be back, won't they?"

"Oh, yeah. You can bet on that. If they don't have any more men, they'll get 'em some. And they'll be back. We'd just better not be around when they do." He knelt down beside Willie, who'd given up all her stomach had to offer and was now hunched over, sobbing. "You gonna be all right, missy?"

"I . . . I suppose," she stammered in a weak whisper. She looked up at him meekly from the corner of her eye. "I've never killed anyone before."

He nodded, putting a reassuring hand on her shoulder. "Don't worry. You'll get used to it."

They packed their gear quickly and ran the horses down, which had been spooked by the gunfire but fortunately hadn't wandered far. They were in the saddle and riding west by the time the sun cleared the horizon completely, just as No Moon had predicted. It rose steadily behind them, framing the flock of buzzards that had begun to circle in their wake.

At least they looked like buzzards.

Chapter 11

Shaddock kept them at a full gallop most of the day, and by late afternoon he was confident that they'd put a wide enough berth between themselves and their pursuers, whether they be Sheriff Tuttle's posse or the Atwoods. Still, whenever he chanced a look back across the prairie, despite the visual reminder of just how wide open it actually was, he just couldn't shake the feeling that they were being watched. There were no more bird shapes in the sky, at least that he could see. Still, he felt vulnerable being out in the middle of nowhere with hardly any cover to speak of, with most trees and hills seeming like distant geographic anomalies on the far horizon. So he kept up their jarring pace and would not relent.

Neither Willie nor No Moon complained. In fact, neither had said a word since the battle with the outlaws some eight hours before. Not even when they stopped at a spring-fed pond around noon to water the horses and let them cool down. Tol was a little worried about the Indian; he had taken quite a shot from Kolo's horse, and he favored his ribs on the right side. Might even have something broken there. But he was a medicine man, wasn't he? If anything's wrong, he should be able to treat himself.

With Willie, on the other hand, he could find nothing physically wrong. She had come through the fracas unscathed, at least on the outside. But she still looked downcast and troubled, and he knew it was the shooting that had rattled her. You pushed her too hard, he told himself. You shouldn't have railed at her so for spoiling your shot. She didn't know any better; after all, despite the lightning gunhand and the hardy looks, she's just a town girl, pure and simple. She's too civilized to the hard ways of the frontier. You should be explaining it to her instead of dressing her down.

But she's a strong girl, he countered. She can take it. Still, when he glanced back at her and saw the stormy expression on her face, and the conflicting emotions that roiled beneath, he wondered if he'd judged her incorrectly. She's got the tools, he knew. Quick wits and a way with a horse, a draw that would put most trick shooters to shame. But it takes more than that to make it out here, even these days.

Especially where they were going.

It took grit and instinct, and a steely resolve for self-preservation. He began to wonder if she possessed such qualities. *If killing trash like Lansdale and his ilk would bother her this much, how would she react the next time? Would she draw and fire, or . . .*

Worry about that when you come to it, a voice counseled. You've got yourself to think about now. Or hadn't you remembered that you're an old man these days, fragile and feeble and unaccustomed to spending so much time in the saddle. Your back is creaking and your butt doesn't feel like it belongs to you anymore. Add to that the lack of sleep in three days time, the two different battles against man and spirit, and a weaning from the liquor bottle after more than a decade of immersion. The question should be, how are *you* doing?

But Tol's only answer to that was a weary grin. He had aches and pains, sure, too numerous to count, and he'd rode the last few miles with his senses dulled and his eyelids at half mast, remaining just alert enough to keep the bay mare in a westerly direction. But despite it all, he felt more alive now than he had in a long, long time. His shaking had faded and he still felt vigorous despite his lack of sleep. And the hot, familiar smell of cordite still hung in his nostrils. It was as if the gunfight had awakened him, pumped his veins full of life and cleared from his mind the cobwebs that time and the bottle had spun so efficiently. Most of all, he was going somewhere, and not just down the road to the next small town, the next lackluster audience to clap at his tired old exploits. This time he had a purpose.

That purpose just might get you killed this time, the voice warned.

The cowboy shrugged it off. Everybody dies sometime or other, he thought. At least this way I might go out shooting. At least it might count for something.

That was how he always expected to go anyway—riding into the fray, his guns blazing. Perhaps that's why the fictional Creekmore massacre had always appealed to him so. Facing death head-on was ever better than wasting away over the years or dying in bed, surrendering to sickness the same way his old friend J. B. Omahundro, the notorious Texas Jack, had given in to pneumonia. He'd been fine—Tol had seen him just a few weeks before. And then . . .

Nope, not me, Shaddock had declared upon hearing the news. I'm making that decision for myself. Heaven or hell, I'll be going in a blaze of glory.

Don't be too anxious, said the voice with a cold, humorless chuckle. You might get your wish.

That chuckle bothered him more than he cared to admit. To get his mind away from such thoughts, he slowed the bay for the first time in many miles and surveyed the landscape before them. The other two stopped alongside him, looked around as if he'd spotted trouble. "We've pushed 'em pretty hard," Tol said, stroking the mare's thick neck, wet with foamy lather. "And I think we could use a rest ourselves. What do you say we find us a place to bed down for the night?"

Willie glanced nervously behind them. "Are you sure nobody's behind us?"

"No," he said matter-of-factly. "But we've gotta stop sooner or later, and so it might as well be now. If we can find us a good enough campsite . . ."

He turned his attention back to the land before them. More of the gently rolling grassland marked their path to the west, the swaying blades all but glowing in the waning light of the day.

Tol resented more open ground; he still couldn't shake that feeling of being watched, and he kept looking skyward, expecting more of the witch's leather-winged spies to be circling up there. He'd have preferred the cover of forest or hill country, anything that might hide them or give him a wall that he could put his back to in case they were attacked.

But on the other hand, the open country presented them with no obstacles, and the horses could really cut loose and travel as they had most of this day. *We've gone at least twenty miles*, he thought. *Added to the ground already covered during the escape from Barlow, that should put us somewhere very close to the Wyoming boundary, with the long-flowing Platte a few miles to the south and the town of Torrington westward. We've made good time*, he figured. *Depending on just how far that particular stretch of the Rockies is, we just might make it in the next two days.*

If nothing else gets in your way . . .

Shut up. He jerked his mind back to the geography. There was a ravine running about a hundred yards to the south, a natural trough running east to west where the land had shifted ages ago and then pinched back together. It was now a snaking home for thick weedstalks and thorny tendrils of wild shrubbery. At least it interrupted the monotony of the land, he thought. To the north was a line of hills that looked like mountains at first glance, until one realized that they weren't so far from there, only a mile or so out of their way. The lower slopes were coated in sparse pine, but higher up there were patches of gray rock peeking through, especially at the top of the first hill, where jagged shards pointed skyward and formed a natural crown.

"How about up there?" he suggested. "The rocks will hide any campfire, and we should be able to see for miles around. That'll tell us for sure whether we're being followed or not."

"Sounds like a good idea," No Moon said. He was still holding his side, but no longer wincing quite so noticeably. "We should take the time to heal our wounds." He motioned toward Tol's head. "I can stitch up your cut, if you want."

Shaddock reached up to gently prod the laceration in his eyebrow, found it not as tender as it had been but still willing to nag him angrily. At least the bleeding had stopped; the kerchief was stiff and crusty, grafted to the edges of the cut. Even the slightest movement of his brow caused a slight but harsh tearing sound, and the numbness flared into full-fledged pain again. He would take the Indian up on his offer, even though he dreaded a sewing needle more than a bullet. *If only I had a bottle,* he started, but then he reconsidered. *Nope, you've gotten past all that. No more bottles, ever. You'll just have to set your jaw and take it.*

"Well, let's get at it, then." He reined the bay in a northerly direction, and the others rode alongside him.

Willie's face was still pinched and worrisome, as if some dark thought were niggling at her insides. "You all right, missy?" Shaddock asked.

She did not look up immediately. But she must have felt his gaze lingering on her, and finally she shrugged. "I ain't hurt," she said, "if that's what you mean."

"Well, you don't look so well." He was silent a moment, trying to choose his words carefully. "Lookee here, girl. I been meaning to tell you something. I'm sorry for how I acted back there, manhandling you and all. That wasn't proper, and I apologize for it."

She almost smiled. "I'm not brooding, if that's what you think. You were right and I was wrong—I should be the one apologizing. If I hadn't stopped you from shooting them . . ." Then she looked away. "None of it's like I expected, that's all."

Tol understood then. "You mean killing a man."

She nodded. "I read about it so much. And when I practiced out in the fields, it was such a game. I'd pretend that some can or target was a famous pistol fighter like John Wesley Hardin, and I was facing them down in the middle of the street. But this was different. It was cold and hard and it won't leave me alone. Every time I close my eyes I see that man's face as I shot him. . . ."

Tol could tell from the quaver in her voice that she was close to tears, and that's why she wouldn't look at him. "Willie Ducane, don't you be running yourself down over this," he told her in a scolding voice. "It ain't like you killed an innocent man. They was all dogs and cutthroats, and I doubt that their own mamas would even mourn their passing. Hell, you did a service to the community. If Roscoe Tuttle finds that trash back there, he's liable to pin a medal on you."

She couldn't even manage a smile this time. "I know they were outlaws. But it doesn't make me feel any better."

Shaddock felt bad that he couldn't cheer the girl, and he thought about changing the subject. But No Moon, who had been listening quietly, was already ahead of him. "I have seen many soldiers in my life," he said from where he rode along on the other side of her, "and many men who lived and died by the gun. But I have never seen a man draw a pistol as fast as you, Willie. How did you gain such speed?"

The cowboy agreed. "Damned fast, girl. One of the fastest I've seen, if not *the* fastest."

She looked back and forth between them, and for the first time her brow unknitted itself. She actually blushed a little. "It's nothing, really. I just practiced a lot, out in the fields away from town. There wasn't nothing else to do in Barlow, you know. Just reading and shooting. And I got pretty good at it." Her eyes went to Shaddock. "Am I really the fastest? Even more than Bill Hickok himself?"

At the mention of the name he spat from the corner of his mouth. "You don't make high comparisons, do you? Bill Hickok may be fair with a pistol, but he's also the lyin'est bastard I've ever had the displeasure of knowing. And them Eastern reporters swallowed every drop of his horseshit like it was sweet preserves or something. I'll tell you the truth. Ever heard of his gunfight with the McCanles at Rock Creek Station? Well, that was during my wandering years, after I left the sheriffing trade and before I ended up as civilian scout for the Army. I was there at Rock Creek when it happened, and I seen the whole thing. So I know the truth.

Them boys was unarmed and Hickok still shot 'em, with him hiding behind a curtain to boot. It don't take no fancy pistol shooter to bushwhack somebody."

"What's the matter with a little bushwhacking?" Willie asked, and there was meaning in her eyes. "You said there weren't any rules out here on the frontier. You remember, live or die, and that's all?"

He grinned. She was trying to twist his words back on him. "I ain't saying them boys didn't deserve it," he told her plainly, "and if'n he thought they were that big a danger, then I say hell yes, shoot 'em from behind a curtain. Better yet, get yourself a Sharps like this here and pick 'em off from as far away as possible. But don't lie about it. Hickok's bragging was just plain deceitful."

Willie shook her head in exasperation. "Shaddock, for a man with no rules, you sure are fussy about the ways people act."

He shrugged. "When you're a couple hundred years old like me and Pappy over there, you've earned the right to be fussy." Then he leaned over toward Willie and whispered in a conspiratorial tone, "Was there really nothing else to do in Barlow? No boys at all?"

"There were boys," she agreed with the same sigh that she had used each time her father broached the subject. "But none that I had a mind for."

"Shame," said Shaddock. "But that's just a matter of time. Some young buck'll come along and catch your eye right quick, and then it'll be time to hang up the gun and tie on the apron. Maybe that's already happening . . ."

"What's that supposed to mean?"

He kept his eyes on the hill straight ahead. "Well, I caught a glimpse of the way you and Kolo looked at each other back there. Maybe that's why you couldn't shoot. You were too busy being sweet on him—"

"That's a damn lie!" she snapped, her face beet red and angry. "He didn't have a gun, that's why I didn't shoot him. You don't know what you're talking about; maybe your eyes are going bad or something or . . ." Then she saw the smirk on the tall cowboy's face, realized he'd just been teasing her. She also realized that her response had been way too pronounced and even she wondered why. She fell silent, embarrassed and brooding while Shaddock guffawed loudly.

The hill that drew them was, on closer inspection, a tall precipice some sixty feet high, capped by a layer of natural sandstone that had kept this particular chunk of earth from being eroded like the rest of the plain. Only stone showed on the facing side of the monolith but as they skirted its edge they saw a grassy slope most of the way up its back, with even a few sparse trees growing there. It wasn't so steep that the horses couldn't climb it, Tol thought, at least halfway up. So he put his heel to the bay and sped her forward, around to the slope and then up its incline a little more than halfway. There they found a shoulder of dry grass which was level enough to set up camp on.

"This oughta do," he said, swinging out of the saddle. "Afraid we're still open to sight, so we'll have to run a cold camp tonight." He carried the Sharps in the crook of his arm as he handed the bay's reins to Willie. "You take care of the horses, girl. I'm climbing up top to take a look around." He glanced at No Moon. "Up to a little climb, old man?"

"If you are, old man," came the Indian's answer.

There was a path for them to climb, a series of jagged outcroppings barely a few inches wide that formed a crude ladder of sorts, all the way to the top. No Moon led the way, moving up the rocky escarpment with such speed and sure-footedness that it seemed he already knew just where to put his hands and feet.

"Yes, I have been here," he told Shaddock when the cowboy mentioned his obvious familiarity. "When I was much younger. These were some of our favorite hunting lands. Many animals came in this area to be near the river." He pointed south, in the direction of the meandering Platte. "I took my first antelope from just below us here, with my bow. I came upon it at the same time as a Pawnee youth, a sworn enemy. But I brought it down first, and caused my rival great shame that day. My father was very proud." The Indian's ascent had slowed somewhat with the reminiscence. But now the smoky tendrils of memory were behind him again and he continued climbing to the rocky crown.

Once there, he offered a hand to the cowboy and pulled him up as well.

The sight from the top of the butte was inspiring, even to someone as jaded by time as Tol considered himself to be. The landscape swept away as far as the eye could see, a carpet that undulated with the breeze, its length and breadth interrupted only by a distant clump of windbreak trees or, even farther, another ridge like the jutting rock that they stood upon. The ravine that they'd noticed to the south was nothing more than a small vein from up there, a meandering line of overgrowth in the body of the grasslands. "It is still beautiful," No Moon whispered from right beside him. When Tol glanced over at him, he thought he saw a tear forming in the corner of the Indian's eye. "This is native land. Or was. Seeing it should make my heart sing again. But instead there is only pain for what is lost."

"I know what you mean," Shaddock said. And he really meant it. For he missed those older times just as keenly as the Indian did. He had not suffered as the red men had—his people were not dwindling from the face of the earth—but he was just as much a stranger to these changing lands. It wasn't the same, none of it. No matter how expansive the plains before them now appeared, he could still feel the closeness of man, encroaching around him, choking off his air. Now there were too many towns, too many miles of barbed-wire fencing, too many signs that read PRIVATE PROPERTY—NO TRESPASSING. If only this Ghost Dance were on the level, he thought, he'd surely have tried a few steps himself. To have things back the way they had been . . . the plains crawling with big shaggies, the land as clean and unblemished as when he had first laid eyes upon its majesty. He would even have welcomed the return of the decimated Indian tribes. Though he'd fought the savages throughout the frontier at various times during his life, he'd always held a grudging respect and admiration for their kind. They were good custodians of the land, and there was honor among them. At least you knew where you stood with an Indian, he thought. He only wished he could say that for the whites he'd known in the years since.

If only the dance was for real. He felt very old then, and he almost reached out and put a hand on the Indian's shoulder. But he didn't.

There was a distant growl to the west, the dying echoes of thunder. They looked in that direction, but all they could see was a line of dark clouds edging the horizon, waiting for the sun to sink behind them. "Sounds like a storm," Tol said, disturbed. "If it don't come this way, we'll probably be riding into it tomorrow." He didn't like the idea of that; he had seen plenty of prairie storms in his days as a drover along the Chisholm Trail, and he'd never really shaken the fear they instilled. But he could do nothing about it, he told himself adamantly. You got a job to do, remember? You got a purpose here. "Well?" he said, turning back to the east. "Can you see anyone following us?"

No Moon wiped the mist of memory from his eyes and swept them slowly back and forth across the land already traveled, pausing to study two trees in the distance that were the only possible hiding places in that wide-open sprawl. "Nothing," he reported. "I see nothing."

"Well, so far our luck's holding," Tol said. "Who knows, maybe Tuttle and his posse will run into the Atwoods and keep 'em busy, least till we can get where we're going." He looked at the Indian. "Think we'll make it?"

"I came to Barlow in three days. With one day in jail and the same number back . . . it will be close. But if we move as quickly, and find no obstacles in our way . . ." He looked to the west, searching the darkening horizon just below the falling sun. "It does look like a storm building there," he reported, and his voice held the promise—or the warning—of something more.

"What? You don't think this Dee-Bo-Ha is behind it . . . do you?"

The Indian shrugged. "I do not know, Shaddock. She is a crafty one, and she knows we are coming. I expect she will try to stop us one way or . . ." His voice trailed away to nothing. Tol saw from the corner of his eye that his lips were still moving, but no words would form. His back had gone rigid and the color seemed to bleed from his face.

Shaddock's gut twisted at the intimation. "What is it?

What do you see?" When No Moon didn't answer, he stepped behind the smaller man, tried to follow his gaze. "What the hell are you seeing . . ." he asked the silent Indian beside him. "I just don't—" And then he saw it too. The dark figure of a man, like a Negro in black clothes, wading through the knee-deep grass, moving as if at a dead run. Tol's breath caught and his heart squirmed up into his throat. The thing he watched was not a man, was not even human. It had two arms and two legs and it walked upright, but that was where any similarities ended. It was black as pitch, like a shadow pulled loose from the ground, and its flesh appeared oily and gleamed in the sunlight. Long quills sprouted from its back and arms like some nightmarish porcupine. The shoulders and chest and arms were massive, fully twice as large as the biggest man he'd ever seen. And that made its head look all the smaller in comparison. A knotty lump of ebon tissue jutted outward from just above the chest, looking more like a tumorous growth than a head. He saw no eyes or ears or mouth on that lump. But that did not seem to bother the creature or hinder its progress. It plowed across the fields with a purpose, powered by legs that did not know fatigue.

Tol stared at the monster, feeling a cold familiarity seep through him, a numbing fear from his past. And suddenly he was deep within Paha-Sapa again, staring at the murderer of Jubal Turner and the soldiers, hearing insane laughter bubble from the darkness of a devil's heart. . . .

"Siyoko," No Moon finally whispered, his voice full of fear. "It is true. A Black Heart Devil. I had not expected this. I had not . . ."

It was a few moments before Shaddock could find his own voice, and even then he had to steel himself against screaming outright. "Wha-what do we do?" he wanted to know, even as he watched the thing trudging through the grasses about six hundred yards out, moving relentlessly eastward.

Eastward. "It is not coming toward these rocks," No Moon observed in a dread whisper, afraid it might somehow overhear them even at that extreme distance. "It is traveling in the direction we came. Perhaps if we are very still, it will pass us by." He knelt down on the rock and then lowered himself onto his stomach, his eyes still locked on their quarry. Tol did likewise, keeping his Sharps rifle at the ready. It would do little good against such a creature—he knew that firsthand. But holding it gave him a slight comfort just the same. He thought of crawling back to the edge and calling down to Willie, signaling her to stay put and keep the horses quiet. But he could do nothing lest he attract the beast's attention. He didn't dare move, didn't take a deep breath—his fear was that great, that palpable. It sat on his back and strangled him, gouged him with bony heels. For down there on the plain was his worst nightmare come back to haunt him. This was the thing that had forced him into a bottle for so long, that made him deny his past and live by some Eastern reporter's fictional rules. And he knew deep down that it had come for him again.

The Black Heart Devil waded blindly through the grasslands of the Sand Hills, its path never faltering, never deviating in any other direction. It passed the tall rock without turning toward it or even acknowledging its presence, kept right on striding toward the east. When it was finally past and moving away from them, Tol allowed himself to exhale. That was close, he thought, his hands still sweating on the stock of the Sharps. That was very—

The Devil stopped.

No. It couldn't have heard me breathe. Could it?

He couldn't pull his wide eyes from the creature as it stood stark still in the middle of the meadow. What's it doing, he wanted to ask, but he dared not make a sound, and he doubted the Sioux would know anyway. They were side by side on the rocks, and Shaddock was sure he could feel panic, perhaps outright terror, emanating from the other man as well. All they could do was watch. And pray.

The beast still faced eastward. But with an agonizing slowness it began to move. First to the right, then to the left. Till it faced the hill. Tol still could see no face on its smallish head, no eyes to see them or ears to pick up their labored breathing. *But somehow it knew they were there. How? How . . .*

He glanced over his shoulder, into the sky above them.

And he saw the black specks circling high up. They had been watched all along.

No Moon tensed alongside him. Tol knew immediately what had happened.

The Devil had taken a step toward them. When Tol turned to look, it took another. Then another. It was coming.

No Moon rose onto his knees. "We must go at once. Hurry!"

"You go first," Shaddock said as he eased back the hammer on the Sharps. "I want to give this bastard something, from me to him."

"But that won't do any good . . ."

"It'll make me feel better," he muttered as he raised the Vernier sight behind the breech and estimated the distance to his approaching target. Maybe there's a part of it that's vulnerable, he thought, trying to convince himself as he adjusted the sight. Maybe I was shooting wild back then, maybe the pistols just didn't have the gumption to do major damage. He braced the big-bore, centered it on that massive chest in the distance. Maybe I'll hit something important this time.

Ease back the set trigger to lessen the main pull. Exhale. Then squeeze . . .

The gun roared and the recoil pounded his shoulder, shook him so bad that the impromptu bandage tore away from his brow and a trickle of blood rolled down his cheek in response. But Shaddock ignored it. His attention was solely on the dark figure, his concentration so focused that he was sure he heard the sharp slap of the .50-caliber bullet striking home.

The demonskin rocked back on its heels from the impact. But it recovered quickly and did not move another step. At least at first. A heartbeat later it grabbed for the wound in its chest as if a fire had flared to life inside it, and a muffled scream rolled across the plain, a deep and painful sound without benefit of a mouth to free it. The beast staggered a few steps to the side, looked as if it might topple to the ground at any moment. But then it whirled around and began to run full out, even faster than before, heading to the south this time. In scant moments it covered the open ground to the ravine, and without warning it jumped into the weeds and overgrowth and disappeared from view.

Both old men were speechless. "What the hell did I hit?" Tol wanted to know. "I must've done something right," he mused, patting the big rifle. "Maybe it's the bigger bullet or—"

"Sunlight," the medicine man surmised. He was looking away toward the setting sun, barely a hand's width from the dark clouds lining the horizon. "That must be it." He caught Shaddock's puzzled expression. "Don't you see? The Devil is only a skin, a thing. What lurks inside, its heart, is a living shadow. This one is most definitely Dee-Bo-Ha's. Your bullet cannot harm a shadow, but it still leaves a hole behind. A hole that lets the sunlight through. And what is a shadow's only enemy?"

"Light." Tol was finally grasping the other's logic. "So it ran for cover before I could put any more holes in it."

"Or until that hole can heal."

The cowboy nodded. It made more and more sense. He thought back to the battleground in the Black Hills, and the black goblin that he fought there. That's why it didn't come out when the soldiers first attacked, he realized. It wasn't dark enough yet. It couldn't take the chance of getting shot and letting light into its heart. And when he shot it across the fire? It grabbed the wound, covered it until it could heal over. And it never opened its eyes or mouth until it was past the fire, with its back to the light. . . .

"What are we waiting for?" he said, itching for a fight. "Let's go down there and ferret the son of a bitch out. It'll look like a sieve when I'm through with it."

"There's no time," No Moon advised. He motioned to the setting sun. "Once it is dark, it will be too strong to stop. We must move while we have the chance." He headed for the edge and the rocky ladder they had climbed.

"But where can we go?" he called after him, looking skyward at the circling specks. "Those damned things up there will lead it straight to us. Where the hell can we hide from it?"

No Moon looked back at him, and Tol could see that the

fear was lessening in his face. There was still a glint of it in his eye, still very alive, but the rest had been subjugated beneath an iron will. This man was a survivor, he knew. A warrior. "Not a place to hide," he said flatly. "A place to set a trap."

No Moon was climbing down the rocks, as nimble as a mountain goat, and Tol had to scramble after him.

Willie was alarmed by their urgent manner when they reached the lower slope where they'd left her. She had already started setting up camp when they abruptly grabbed up the saddles she had laid nearby and started readying the horses once again. "What's wrong?" she wanted to know even as she grabbed up her own things and began readying the tired Buck once again. "What did you see up there, a ghost?"

"You could say that," Tol said, and an icy shiver ran along his spine.

In just a few minutes they were ready to ride. No Moon swung into the saddle, his face pinched with concentration. "A Black Heart Devil," he muttered, still unable to dismiss his surprise at such a sight. "I underestimated this witch. She is powerful. I have known of only one other *wicasa wakan* who could summon such a demonskin. And that was my father."

"Don't forget that stumpy little shit I killed in the Black Hills," Shaddock said as he put a boot in the bay's stirrup and hauled himself up. "He did a pretty good job of it, let me tell you."

No Moon did not change expression or even turn to look at him. "Yes, I know," he muttered over his shoulder. "Sky Falling Man *was* my father." Then he gave his Appaloosa the heel and started down the slope at a hurried clip. Willie followed after him, leaving a stunned Tol Shaddock in their wake.

Chapter 12

The earthen house had been a family's home once, when a wagon from Indiana strayed away from the Oregon Trail in search of a homestead. They had carved a large single room from the side of a gentle slope, firmed up the perimeter with heavy bricks of sod and soil, and planted a string of Christmastime firs on either side and all around the rear for a windbreak. They supported the ceiling with heavy beams, some of which they brought in from the town of North Platte while the rest were scrounged or stolen from other abandoned cabins in the area. And when the wood ran low, they constructed wide doors for the entrance from the bed of the wagon itself. Their work was slipshod and hurried in the face of a bad winter, but it was proven sound by the years to come. For it still stood today, some twenty years later, long after those original owners were but a memory. Whether they died in the silence of the prairie or were taken prisoner by the bands of Northern Cheyenne and Pawnee who wandered these lands at that time, no one would ever know. But the house remained in mute testament of their passage.

The grasses grew thick across the old soddy these days, and the pine trees had grown tall and strong and held the wind at bay. The big double doors were still there, though hanging crooked now in a buckled framework and rotting from the ice and rain. It saw occupants infrequently now, only when ranch hands used it as a line shack while herding, or when passing fugitives took advantage of its shelter and isolation.

Or when travelers happened by. The three who stayed

there this night did not care about the people who had come before, or about the musty stink within or the way the doors wouldn't latch and banged softly on cracking leather hinges. All they cared about was that the sun had just slipped from the sky, and that darkness now spread across the land like a giant's shadow.

The night was upon them. There was not much time.

No Moon stood on the sloping grassy roof, lit by the glow of Hanhepiwi, the Night Sun. Hurry, he urged himself. It's well past dusk now. The Devil will be here. Hurry! But he knew he could not leave, not until the task was done. He had to be thorough, or they did not stand a chance. He reached into the pouch on his side and took out another small handful of sweetgrass and sage and powdered bone, the same mixture that had served him so well back in Barlow. Then he held it out and sprinkled it lightly over the grass. Not too much in one place, he cautioned. There isn't so much that you can waste it. Just a light dusting, all over the roof . . .

Something howled out on the prairie, in the extreme distance. It was only a dying echo that reached him, a faint, shrill cry. But it still brought him rigid with alarm, and the spirit knife was already clutched in his left hand. Stupid old man, he sighed. You are as skittish as a colt. It was a coyote, nothing more. But next time it might not be, *so hurry up!*

He sprinkled the crown of the hill, right up to the rusted metal smokestack that blossomed a few inches above the grassline. Then he began to back down the rear toward the trees, off the roof of the soddy and onto the hill proper. That's when he heard the soft tearing sounds from just below him. It drew his attention to the base of the hill, where he saw the grass moving, bowing outward as if some new tree were straining to break through. Then a square thatch tore loose from the surrounding sod and lifted up, swung straight back on itself till he could see the underlying board beneath it. It was a trapdoor attached to a wooden frame, just as black and rotting as the larger doors out front.

Tol Shaddock poked his head out into the cold night air, his forehead still wrapped in that bloody rag so that it obscured one eye. "I told you," he said, grinning at No Moon. "These old soddies usually had an escape hatch in case of . . ." He stammered then, trying to find a better way to put it. "Well, you know. Indian attack." He looked at the powder the Indian was still sprinkling about, then glanced around them at a nighttime cast silver by the waxing moon. "You almost done?" he asked anxiously.

"Yes. The whole roof is covered."

"And you think that'll stop it?"

"Yes." He tried to sound hopeful. "The powder will strengthen the roof enough." But his confidence flagged, and his statement came out as more of a question, at least to himself. Will it be enough? Will it really?

Don't think that way. You have to believe, or the spirits will have no respect at all. And if they will not give their aid, what chance do any of you have?

It will be enough. It will be . . .

Shaddock pulled the trapdoor back into place as No Moon walked back across the roof and down the incline on one side, then rounded the front to where the doors hung askance. Deep down he wished for a bolt on those doors, a heavy crossbar of iron to throw when the Devil arrived. But he knew even that would not stop such a creature, and he felt ashamed for letting his fear get the better of him. There is strength in the magic, he assured himself. But you must have faith. Besides, he thought as he edged past the door and slipped inside, the idea isn't to keep Dee-Bo-Ha's demon out. It's to keep it in.

There were no furnishings in the hovel, no benches or cots or anything at all. There was not even a stove for the smoke pipe in the roof to be connected to. Which was just as well, since anything at all in the cavelike structure would have been an obstacle. There was barely enough room the way it was, what with two men and a girl and three horses sharing the same quarters. It was cramped and uncomfortable to be sure, and getting the skittish horses to go inside had been no small chore. But No Moon knew better than to leave them outside during the night; even Tol remembered the fate of his Mose back at Barlow. The Black Heart Devil would kill the horses if it could, because that would most definitely stall them, keep them from reaching the foothills of the Rockies. That way the Dance of the Ghosts could go on uncontested. . . .

Willie and Tol came out of the back just then, squeezing around Buck and the mare and getting an irritated snort from the latter. Both man and girl were covered in soil and pulling cobwebs from their hair, and from the smell, they had probably crawled through not a small amount of animal spoor as well. "Messy business," Shaddock said, grimacing as he brushed at his clothes. "But at least there is a way out back there." He glanced over at Willie. "You sure you're up to this, girl? If you ain't, you just say the word and I'll take your place."

"I have already told you, Shaddock," No Moon said, growing impatient with the cowboy's stubbornness. "You and I are too old for such a task. She is young and fast. Willie must be the one."

The girl nodded her agreement. "Don't worry about me, Tol," she said, patting him on the shoulder. "I'll be fine." But there was a momentary flash of fear in her eyes as she turned away from him. She drew her Peacemaker and opened the loading gate, checked the cylinder for the ninth time. "Well, I guess I'm as ready as I'll ever be. Give me a signal when it's time." She gave them a forced smile and then squeezed past the horses once again, heading for the pitch darkness in the rear of the room.

"I don't like this," Tol repeated as he followed No Moon to the door.

But the Indian ignored him. There were more important things to do. He bent down in the doorway of the hovel and drew his hunting knife, used the steel blade to gouge a small furrow in the soil just deep enough so that a misstep by them or the horses wouldn't break the line. Then from the leather pouch he produced a small drawstring bag, poured more of the powder into his hand and then sprinkled it in the furrow all along the threshold, forming a solid line of white in the dark and tamped-down soil. He thought perhaps he should bring out his pipe and smoke some *kinnickkinnick* as offering to the spirits, to better attract their attention and their aid. But there was no time for that. He only hoped the spirits would understand.

He took out the *wagmuha,* shook it four times slowly. Then he began to chant in the mystery tongue of the *wicasa wakan,* low and whispery. I ask the Great Mystery, Wakan Tanka, to aid me in this time of need. For I am a warrior and a medicine man of the Oglala, and while I would stand alone against any man, I cannot act so against the *wakan* forces before me. Inyan, the rock, please strengthen me for the battle that is to come, and Maka, Grandmother Earth, look upon me with favor and show me courage beyond my own. From Skan the force-giver and Wi the Sun I ask for speed and protection against the evil that I face.

He addressed the others as well, Tate the Wind, Wakinyan the Thunderbird, and so on, until he had invoked all eight of the personages who made up the whole of the Great Mystery. They answered him in eight voices that were but one. They granted him all he asked, for he was an old *wicasa wakan* and had come before the spirits many times, had celebrated them and given them befitting respect. As he chanted, he could feel the powder between his fingers moving, each grain of crushed bone and dried sweetgrass and other herbs becoming hot against his skin with power, just as the handfuls he had sprinkled on the roof would be strengthened as well. The barrier he formed would hold against the Black Heart Devil . . . for a while at least.

He sat back from the line, sighed with fatigue. Such concentration had taken much from him, and the exhaustion had caused his bruised ribs to hurt again. But he ignored it. Tol Shaddock was standing beside the door, looking down at the line he'd carved and planted in the dirt, remembering the similar circle back in Barlow. "I did not learn all of my father's ways," No Moon said. "But protecting lines like these were his specialty. And he did show me that. This was good for us."

Tol frowned. "I don't think this'll work," he said, "the plan, I mean. You oughta seal that trapdoor too, so it can't get in at all."

No Moon sighed wearily. He'd explained this before, but

the cowboy was thick-headed and refused to understand. "That would do us little good." He went through it yet again. "The Devil does not need to kill us, at least not right away. Dee-Bo-Ha needs only to delay us, keep us from interfering with the ceremony. If we seal this room up, the Devil will just wait us out until it is too late. No, we must trap it here, or we will never reach the mountains in time." He looked toward the back of the room, where he knew Willie to be hiding in the pitch blackness. "The Devil will come for me—I am sure the lizard birds have told her we're here. But I have not seen them since before we arrived; they would not know about the trapdoor. So Willie should be able to slip out and get its attention, lure it around the back and inside. And while it is distracted, you flush the horses out while I go around the back and seal that door as well."

"Trapping Willie in here with it, you mean."

No Moon pointed at the grainy white barrier. "Willie can cross this line. The Devil cannot."

Tol's frown deepened. "I don't know . . ." was all he would allow.

The Indian read his expression, and he understood then. He reached out and touched his shoulder. "You think highly of the girl, don't you? Well, do not worry. She is young and fast as the wind, and she has rare courage. Wakan Tanka should look favorably on her for this."

The assurances were met by silence at first. Tol just shrugged his ignorance of such matters and walked through the gloom of the soddy to stroke the bay mare's nose and keep her calm. But after a few moments he asked, "How do you know this Wakan Tanka character isn't helping the witch instead of us?"

No Moon flinched. For at times, this Shaddock seemed very astute in the ways and beliefs of the Human Beings. And he had raised a question that the medicine man would rather have not dealt with. "I . . . doubt that," he finally volunteered. "I have called on the spirits and been in their presence many times throughout my life. And the things I felt in that mountain lodge were very different, very . . . unsettling. I do not know what forces she commands." He shrugged, hoping he sounded indifferent and not as worried as he actually was. "But I could be wrong. The *wakanpi*, the spirits and all higher beings, are fickle. They are not good or evil. They are simply *wakan*. Mysterious. They exist. And they do not care whose side they are on, good or bad, red or white. All that matters to them is who calls them, who shows the most respect and gives the most offerings and recognizes their worth. Perhaps this Dee-Bo-Ha has curried much favor with Wakan Tanka. Who am I to say? But the spirits still hear my calls. They give strength to my spells and my magic lines, do they not?"

"Wait a minute," the cowboy said skeptically. "There aren't any good or evil spirits? Then what's that thing following us if it's not evil? Or the one I saw in the Black Hills?"

"A skin. That is all. It is the shadow within that makes it live. In Paha-Sapa you saw the horse soldiers slaughtered by such a beast, so you knew it had to be evil. But how did my father see it? How did he see the unprovoked attack on the men and women, the children who were with him? How did all the Lakota tribes see the greedy white miners who defied the treaty and stole from our sacred land? To them, the Black Heart Devil would have been a protector, a guardian. So the shadow within it was evil only in your eyes. Such things depend on which side of the stream you stand. But this Dee-Bo-Ha . . . that is a different story. She is an evil one. She has twisted the minds of many powerful shamans, and she has sent spirits to destroy me, a Human Being and her own distant kin. This is evil, Shaddock. And if we do not stop her, I fear it will spread all across the land."

Shaddock spat in the gloom, punctuating his own feelings. "All this talk of Indian gods and spirits sticks in my craw, you know. Take this Ghost Dance . . . I mean, am I really supposed to believe that the red man's gods are so powerful they could sweep the white man off the face of the earth? Come on! If that's the case, how come they didn't help you'uns out during the Indian Wars? How come there ain't too many of you around these days, and you're all wasting away on the reservations?"

The Indian turned his questions back on him. "How

come your Jehovah did not stop the slaughter in the great war between your gray and blue coats? Many thousands died, and for what? Who knows such things? Such is the way of gods, I suppose. You have your Great Mystery, just as we have ours. I can only guess at why they did not help us. In the past, most of the tribes throughout the land were very proud at heart and thought they could fight the invaders off. But then they saw the numbers of the white man like locusts on the wind, and they were afraid in their hearts. By then the spirits had become angry because the warriors had not been singing their songs and asking for protection in battle, and their ears became deaf to such things. Besides, many of the Human Beings never had faith to begin with. Many have adopted the white man's beliefs. Only the medicine men held true. And there are not many of us remaining."

The bay snorted just then and tried pulling away from the cowboy. But Tol scratched behind its ears and whispered to it, and the animal calmed down. Then he asked, without looking at the Indian, "Why didn't you tell me you're Sky Falling Man's son?"

No Moon smiled. "I was afraid you would not trust me. That you might think I'd come seeking revenge."

"Did you?"

"Once. It was I who found my father and the others, and I swore to kill the white man who did this. But the spirits were not with me, for I could not find you these many years. Then, when I found the paper on the fencepost days ago, just when I needed such help, I knew then the spirits had saved you for just this time."

"So they had this in mind all along, did they?" Tol mused. "Well, I wonder if they already know what the outcome's gonna—"

The bay suddenly neighed in alarm, bumped up against the other horses, and they screamed as well, deafening the men in the limited area. Tol was busy trying to calm them before one could kick out in panic and hurt another, but No Moon was facing the entrance. He was standing defiantly just across the threshold with his grandfather's spirit knife in hand when the doors jerked outward, torn from their leather hinges and cast aside like sheaves of paper. The doorway was filled with darkness, for the hulking figure there completely blocked out the moonlight.

The horses reared in terror despite Tol's efforts, banging their heads on the low ceiling. But No Moon stood his ground. He watched as a dark hand reached out, tested the barrier he had constructed. The air above the powdered line seemed to ripple like the surface of a disturbed pool. But it held firm. The hand came no closer. Still, the phantom did not back away because of that. It stayed right there, filling the doorway with its presence. A voice whispered then from its unseen mouth. It was light and feminine in tone but with a steely edge. *"I have come for you, Oglala,"* the witch said from a mountain far away. Her laughter rippled through the hovel like a cold wind.

Chapter 13

Crouching in the dank and the dark, Willie Ducane heard the horses become agitated and she felt their fear like a physical wave. She knew then that the Black Heart Devil was nearby. She felt low along the wall for the wooden slats that marked the frame of the escape tunnel, moved over into its mouth on her hands and knees. But she didn't go out. Not yet, she thought. Not until No Moon gives the signal . . .

A whisper floated through the soddy then, found her in the darkness and raked her nerves with abandon. *"I have come for you, Oglala,"* came that soft voice, sounding female on the surface but something else beneath. Something not even human. It planted the seeds of fear in the pit of her stomach, made her feel weak and dizzy, disoriented by the blackness that held her so totally. Don't go out there, said the voice of reason and common sense. For whatever spoke those words is out there now, waiting.

Calm down, she countered, taking a deep breath that barely whistled past the heart clogging her throat. You have to do this. They're counting on you. Now, go, before you lose your nerve altogether.

She no longer needed to wait for a signal. It was time. She took another breath. Mouthed a silent prayer. Then crawled into the tunnel.

Willie immediately hated that cramped place. It was like crawling through a long, dark coffin, where the bones and dried matter of the dead crackled under her palms and knees. The scent of damp soil assailed her nostrils, even more so than within the soddy earlier, and mingled with it was the spoor of some unknown animal. It's a den, she had to remind herself from before. Some prairie animal had been using this tunnel, living here, and its bones or those of its prey were the brittle things that snapped beneath her weight. But the thought sickened her just the same and served to counteract the fear. It urged her onward more quickly till her outstretched hand finally found the wire loop on the trapdoor.

She paused there, pressed her ear to the edge of the wood, and listened. But there was nothing to hear.

"I have come for you, Oglala. . . ."

Willie mustered what courage she could and eased the door outward. *Just a bit at first, enough for a quick look . . .* She feared that a loud creaking sound might mark her exit, but the hinges were leather thongs instead of the hardware she'd sold at the general store. They cracked with age and one was broken clean through, but they made no sound at all. She looked out through the blades of grass that framed the edge of the hole. There was nothing in sight except the pine trees along the rear of the hill, cast silver in the moonlight and swaying to the tune of the evening breeze. So far, so good. She breathed deeply and eased the door out farther, all the way back until it was wide open. She looked all around, along the treeline and up the slope of the hill above her. Nothing. Only then did she dare to climb out, leaving the door open for her return. She scurried quickly to the trees and into their protective folds, where there was at least a modicum of concealment.

So far, so good, she kept repeating to herself, trying to dredge more courage from the depths of her soul. But with each trip to the well she came back more dry than the time before. Slow and easy. The natural urge was to draw her gun, to have it in her hand for reassurance. But she fought it. Tol said bullets don't hurt it anyhow, and besides, the ratchety sound of that hammer coming back will be deafening in this quiet. And that might just bring that thing running.

That threat was enough. She did not touch the Peacemaker on her thigh. But her hand would not move far from it.

Step by step. Just find the damn thing first . . .

She moved back into the trees farther, found them planted in two staggered rows to form a corridor of prickly limbs. That should keep you hidden, she tried to reassure herself. And having a barrier on either side gave her some sense of security. At least she wouldn't be out in the open. Her movements were painfully slow as she tested the ground with the toe of her boot, afraid of the abrupt sounds that stepping on twigs or dried needles would make. But gradually she made her way around the hill to the side of the soddy, almost within sight of the front.

And what will you find there, she asked herself deep down. What does it look like? Tol had been very evasive, describing it only as a black goblin covered with long stickers. But she had seen the fear in his eyes, and that spoke much more than any of his words. What will it look like, she persisted. Or more important, how will you react? Like you did in Barlow, when those spirits appeared before you, when they murdered Pa? Will you freeze again, squalling like a child?

She hoped not. But there was no way to know. Not until she actually saw the creature. And to her surprise, that realization sparked a morbid curiosity within her. Enough to overcome her fear if only for a moment; just long enough to move a little farther along, to reach out and brush aside the branches for a first look . . .

A yell shattered the crystal quiet of the night. At first it seemed to come from off to her right, from behind the hill, where she'd left the trapdoor open. It sounded like Tol, shouting her name. And just a moment later it came again, only this time it was from the front of the soddy, from the open door, and it was No Moon's voice. Much clearer. She could even hear the fear in it. "Willie!" he called. "It heard you! It's coming! *Run!*"

The words stabbed through Willie's ears and struck a chord of terror so pure that it almost blinded her from within. She wanted to scream, but her voice was suddenly a razor blade, threatening to leave her throat in shreds with the merest sound. It's coming, her mind repeated, as if she had failed to understand the urgency before. But the natural instinct for flight was muted by the fear that gripped her, locked her muscles in place. Only her eyes moved, from one corner to the other, searching the shadows around her for any sign of Shaddock's black goblin. When do I move, where do I go—

From behind her. A giggle of anticipation. Almost girlish.

There was no thought then. Only reaction. Willie dropped to the ground like a stone and rolled to one side, beneath the lowest limbs of a pine, even as something massive lunged over her and into the next tree in line. There was a crashing sound as limbs and needles rained down all around her, but she was too busy moving, snaking through the debris and out of the first tree row, into the open and facing the side of the sod house. Now, run, dammit, it's right behind—

A new crash deafened her as the fir tree she'd just crawled beneath splintered in two, the upper half tearing away from the trunk and tipping over in her wake. And she didn't have to look back; she could feel that thing as revealed through the new rent in the treeline, forcing its way through the limbs, coming after her.

Willie was suddenly running, gathering so much momentum from her fright that she leaned too far and almost fell onto her face. Her hands flew out to stop her, and suddenly she was scrambling spiderlike around the base of the hill, searching in the moonlight for the blessed sanctuary of the trapdoor. A sudden fear lanced through her—it was behind you, what if it found the door already and closed it—but she forced it down by sheer willpower alone. It'll be there, Tol wouldn't let it be closed, it'll be there!

There were no sounds behind her, no thundering footfalls as befitted the massiveness of the thing that had lunged through the trees. But it was there, she knew, right behind her. And it was gaining.

She rounded the hill farther and there, lit in bright silver, was the underside of the trapdoor with its wire loop laid wide open, the square of darkness yawning beneath. This time she did not think of the small, hated space, that long, dark coffin that had repulsed her so before. Instead, it was blessed sanctuary as she dived into the hole, squirmed through it as fast as she could, yelling to Tol and No Moon, "It's coming! It's coming!" But she could barely hear herself over the frenzied neighing of the horses inside. A little farther, she thought, groping along the dirt walls as she moved, until her hand caught the wooden frame on the inside wall of the soddy. Just one more good pull and—

Something caught her foot.

Her leg was jerked violently out from under her, pulling her grip loose from the wooden frame and slamming her to the ground. The air rushed from her lungs and her head swam. But she was not too dazed to realize that the grip on her foot was still there. Or that she was being dragged backward through the tunnel.

Panic flashed through her as she screamed and clawed at the walls, felt her fingers dig furrows in the dirt and dead roots as she scrabbled for some sort of purchase. Her hand caught hold of one of the planks overhead and for a second or two it gave her some support. But then it jerked loose from the wooden supports with a dull popping sound and a cascade of dirt came down on her head. She couldn't hear herself screaming as the inexorable pull started again. . . .

"I've got you!" came a voice from the mouth of the tunnel as a strong hand clamped around her outstretched arm, slid back to her wrist, and then held tight. She recognized Tol's voice in the darkness, could imagine him bent up against the back wall of the soddy with his long legs braced for a tug-of-war. But in this game Willie was the rope. She gasped as the struggle began, locking her free arm around her shoulder so the limb wouldn't pop from its socket. But she couldn't take any such precautions for her leg. In that massive grip it seemed to be stretching ever longer, and her hip joint cried out from the pressure. Another minute and she knew it would give with an audible crack.

Point your toes, someone seemed to whisper in the darkness. She looked around, in front and behind her, before realizing that it was her own voice she heard, coming from deep within. Point your toes, it said again, so calm and collected, the voice of reason. But Willie still didn't understand the cryptic message. Her body had to react without conscious approval, pointing both of her feet just as straight as they could manage.

The boot on her imprisoned right foot slid just a bit, an inch, maybe more. But with the next strong tug, one that would most certainly have torn her leg loose from its moorings, the boot slipped completely off into the giant hand that held it. Suddenly she was free on the one end, and on the other Shaddock's straining now found little resistance. He jerked her halfway out of the tunnel, and she climbed the rest of the way on her own. She was in the soddy, trying to stand on her numbed leg. The horses were gone, having fled out the front of the house during the struggle. So the only sounds were her and Shaddock's panting, and the creak of the planks and tunnel-framing boards behind her as something big squeezed through. . . .

It's coming!

"Run!" she screamed at Tol, starting forward on her own but wincing from the soreness in her leg. She faltered at first, but then Tol's strong arm was around her waist and all but picking her off the ground. They both headed for the square of moonlight outside the sod doorway.

Willie chanced a look backward, not knowing what she expected to see in that near-absolute gloom. But to her horror, she could make out something. Two slitted eyes and a mouth coming out of the tunnel, rising, pressed against the low ceiling of the room. Each orifice was blacker than the darkness surrounding them. As black as the dirt of the grave, she thought. And her skin crawled as those eyes locked onto hers and they came charging across the hovel after the two of them.

"Faster, Tol!" she screamed, looking to the soddy's doorway but finding it so far away, a small dot of light at the end of a long corridor of darkness. Her hand dropped to her thigh and brought out the pistol, and she put it back over the cowboy's shoulder and fired once, twice, three times at the oncoming phantom. But all she heard was that gleeful laughter again, and the eyes bearing down on them, overtaking them—

"Get ready!" Shaddock warned her, and then with a sudden jump they were sailing through the air, out of the blackness and into the cold wash of moonlight. They came down hard, but the cowboy rolled before impact and took the brunt of it himself. Then they tumbled head over heels and ended in a sprawl on the grass outside.

Willie recovered as fast as she could, whirled on the doorway behind them with her pistol at the ready. But there was nothing there that she could see. Only the darkness within. It seemed to ripple a moment, but then she blinked her eyes and it had stopped. Was that thing still in there? Or was it going out the back even now, circling around to find them? She looked around for the Indian, but there was no sign of him. "Where's No Moon?" she panted. "Did he make it or—"

There was a female wail of rage from within the soddy, mingled with something primeval and far more frightening. And she knew then that No Moon had completed his task. The trap had been sprung and the Black Heart Devil was still inside. A massive fist struck one of the walls of the house, sounding like a dull crack of thunder, and then there was another in its wake and another. More blows of frustration and anger fell, a rain of them. Willie began to worry. For in the face of such fury, she knew the earthen house would not stand for long. . . .

"It will hold," No Moon said as he came around the side of the hill house. He was carrying his pouch on his shoulder, and a boot in his hand. He handed the latter to the girl. "I strengthened the roof and walls with the same magic that seals the doors. It will not escape. Not right away at least."

Shaddock was just climbing to his feet, still groggy after that hard landing. He looked out into the prairie. "Well, I'd better go round up the horses," he sighed, starting on foot. But Willie limped over to stop him.

"Let me worry about that, Tol," she said. Then she let out a shrill whistle. Immediately there was a neigh from out beyond the treeline to the left and in a few moments Buck came running to his master's call. She caught the horse's bridle and rubbed his nose in reward. "I'll round up the others," she said, hissing as she pulled her boot back on. Then with Shaddock's help she climbed up into the saddle and set out to look for the missing mounts, leaving Tol and No Moon alone before the open hovel.

They stared into the absolute darkness there, neither man saying a word at first. The hammering on the walls and ceiling had ceased. There was no sound in there. No movement. "You sure that trapdoor's sealed real good?"

The Indian nodded. "It is still in there, Shaddock. Against the rear wall. Watching us."

From the depths of that stygian dark came a voice, soft at first but growing in pitch and losing any semblance of humanity to become a banshee wail.

"This will not hold me for long, Oglala. Your magic will weaken with distance and then my servant will be free and I will move like the wind to find you. You will not stop me, old man. You will never stop meeeeeeeeeee!"

Tol held his ears against such a sound, to no avail. He could not shut out that hideous shrieking. But No Moon did not move a muscle, nor did his expression change. If he was still afraid of this Devil, he did not show it. There was instead a steely resolve in his gaze as he said in a calm but determined voice, "We shall see about that. We shall see."

Chapter 14

It began to rain shortly after midnight, not too hard but enough to soak the riders despite the slickers they wore, courtesy of the Barlow General Store. The cold was intensified by the dampness, and before long they were frozen clear through, right to the marrow. But they did not let that stop them. They rode hard and fast most of the night, for they were eager to put as many miles as possible between them and the soddy. For despite the fact that their pursuer was still imprisoned behind them and falling farther and farther away, its memory still hung in their minds and haunted their thoughts, making the chill in the air that much colder.

When the sun rose behind a low ceiling of gunmetal-gray clouds, it found the three at a temporary camp beneath a tall overhang of sandstone that kept the rain away if they sat right up against the rock. The eroded cliff in turn stared out over the wide and wandering Platte River itself. The ribbon of lazy water was eternally slothful, never hurried, and it would take a torrent ten times that falling now before it would awaken and rise above its banks.

"A foot deep and a mile wide," Tol had told them when they decided to camp there. "We should have no trouble fording it. But for now, we need a fire. And at least here we'll have wood to burn." He was looking out into the Platte, to a small island ringed in stiff reeds. There were birch trees growing on that hummock of soil, and some of their fallen branches had already washed to the shore of the river like driftwood. Tol gathered a small pile of these and set about making a fire. But the sticks were just too wet; after an entire box of matches, they still refused to hold a flame. So the cowboy finally gave up in disgust. He grumbled, pulled the collar of his coat and slicker up, lowered the big flop hat over his eyes. "We'll rest here for a couple of hours," he had announced, "and then we'll be on our way again . . ." The words were barely out of his mouth before he was asleep.

Willie could barely stay awake herself. The exhaustion was ever-present now, as familiar to her as the soaked-through clothing that she wore, and it was becoming increasingly harder to remember what it was like to be well rested. There was the hunger, too, gnawing at her insides now more than ever. It was that and the chill of the wet morning that finally forced her to give in to the weariness. Her eyelids lowered all the way, and for a while there was blessed numbness, so deep that even her father could not taunt her.

She dozed for several hours, adrift in a cocoon of warmth. But when she finally roused, she was startled to realize that the warmth had not faded with slumber. There was a campfire crackling before them, chasing away the dampness. The same pile of sticks from before . . .

She looked to Tol and found him still snoring beneath his hat. It was No Moon who sat awake on the other side of her. He was sharpening a stick with his knife.

"How?" she said, pointing to the flame. "They were too wet. Weren't they?"

No Moon gave her an exhausted grin, seemed barely able to lift the corners of his mouth. He picked up a discarded twig and twisted it between his thumb and fingers, muttering in Lakota all the while. And as she watched, a spark danced between his fingers and the stick. It grew steadily, birthing a blue flame. And then he tossed the stick into the campfire, and the flames grew stronger still.

Willie moved over near the fire to warm herself and gave the medicine man an appreciative nod of the head. She did not bother asking him how he did such things. She had come to expect such miracles from him.

No Moon finished whittling the stick across his lap, seemed satisfied with the point he had formed. Then he reached behind him, produced the two pheasant that he had already dressed, and skewered them with the makeshift spit. Willie gaped, entranced and excited as he hung them over

173

the fire on two forked sticks. "But how?" she stammered. "Where . . ."

The Indian pointed off to the island in the middle of the Platte. "They were over there," he said, "hiding in the weeds."

"But I didn't hear any gunshots."

"No, you did not." His weary grin returned. "They offered themselves to me, for we will need our strength on the remainder of our journey." Then he sat back against the rocks, began whittling on another stick to pass the time.

"You never fail to surprise me, old man," she said appreciatively as the hollow in her stomach grew worse in anticipation. She took off her gloves and rubbed some feeling back into her hands as she waited for the birds to cook. Despite the slicker, she was wet clear through and her clothes weighed an extra fifty pounds at least. Her feet ached and her bottom was becoming quite raw from the endless hours in the saddle. But even taken together, such were the least of her worries compared to that bone weariness deep inside her. The few hours sleep had done little to allay it. She wondered if all adventurers and drovers and range riders felt as bad as she did and if they ever got used to it.

Yes, of course, said a cynical voice inside her head, one that sounded very much like her own. Cowboys face ghost-white demons and shadowy devils every day of the week, sometimes twice on Sundays. So get used to it, girl, if that's the life you want.

No thank you, she decided. The general store and its mundane rituals of stocking and restocking and not a hint of adventure at all was beginning to look more inviting than she'd ever known it could.

"This is what gave your state its name," said No Moon, still carving the end of a long birch branch. "The word Nebrathka is Siouan, you know. It means 'flat water.'" He nodded his head, agreeing with himself, and continued his whittling. But his words seemed distant, detached.

"Are you all right?" Willie asked, reaching over to touch his arm.

He looked up for a moment, just long enough to give her a

glance. Then he went back to his work. "I am fine. Just thinking."

"Shouldn't you try to get some sleep? You look tired."

"I have rested. But I will sleep when this is over. For if my concentration should lapse, the Black Heart Devil might become free too soon. Dee-Bo-Ha can move quickly in such a skin. I must hold it prisoner for as long as possible."

"What if it gets out and comes after us? What do we do next time? Trap it again?"

He barely shook his head. "She will be watching for such a thing. No, next time we will have to destroy it."

That surprised her. "Can it be done?"

No Moon shrugged. "I don't know yet. But I have an idea." He looked all around, as if about to share a secret. Then he held up the stick he'd been working on, as if it were a king's scepter. It was still a birch branch, had not changed much since he'd brought it back from the island. The smaller branches and knots had been smoothed off, and he had cut two notches in it, one just short of each end.

"What is it?"

He didn't answer right away. He simply reached into his shoulder pouch, where he stored his magic. He produced a roll of what looked like aged brown twine. "There is magic in this," he said, unwinding the thin but stout buffalo sinew to show there was a loop on each end. "This is the string that was on my first bow, when I took the antelope from the Pawnee brave. Did I tell you this story, or just Shaddock? Ah, it does not matter. What matters is that it held my aim true, and sent the arrow in its flight. There is a spirit in this string. Its name is Elya-eh. It told me this, though I do not know what it means." He stood and hooked one loop in the notch at one end of the stick. Then he stepped around the birch branch with his left leg and hooked it with his toe, leaned on it until it bent far enough to hook the other loop. It stayed in a horseshoe shape, and the string was very tight. When he plucked it with his finger, it made a solid thrum that seemed to please his ear. "Not bad," he said, obviously pleased with his impromptu bow. Then he put it aside and started work on the reeds.

Willie was silent a moment, watching him split the end of the reeds and insert eagle and crow feathers from his bag to help the arrows fly true. And she waited for some bit of wisdom that she hadn't caught yet. But finally she could wait no longer. "A bow and some arrows?" she said with confusion. "That's your plan? I don't understand . . . what can a bow do that our guns can't?"

The Indian shrugged. "Maybe nothing. But maybe everything." He looked up and grinned before going back to work, and Willie didn't bother asking more. She didn't have to know exactly what No Moon meant to do or how he would do it. Just the fact that he had a plan was enough. She felt more than reassured in his presence. She felt safe, like a little girl sitting on a parent's lap, listening to the soothing lullaby of a powerful voice.

No, she thought. Not my father's lap. Someone else . . .

She watched the man as he worked and she studied his face. The strong, weathered features were like a mask cut from grainy leather, except for those timeless eyes that had seen the death of his own world and the birth of another, and maybe even beyond the both of them. And she felt a familiarity somehow. "You remind me of someone," she said, without even knowing who it was.

He did not look up from his work. "Is that right? And who would that be?"

The way he spoke, the timbre in his voice, chased the mist from her memories and gave her the answer she'd been seeking. "My grandfather," she said, "on my father's side. His name was Gunther Ducane. He came from the old country across the ocean and settled in Pennsylvania. That's where we lived until I was four, when my parents came west. We were headed for Oregon, you know." She thought back to those times, barely visible through the eyes of a child. "I don't remember much about Grandpa. He was strong but in a quiet kinda way, like you. And when he grinned, it meant something." She saw the same expression on No Moon's face and it almost made her laugh. "You remind me so much of him."

"To my people, grandfather is *tunkashila*. It means much

respect. This is how we address the spirits sometimes. By comparing me to your *tunkashila,* you do me a great honor."

The girl nodded, blushed a bit. "What about you? Do you have any grandchildren of your own? Maybe a granddaughter my age?"

His grin faltered somewhat with that question, but he propped it back up for her sake. "I had a son once," he said slowly. "But he died while fighting with Red Cloud at the Powder River. He went with many coup that day, a warrior with honor. But in the end he was just as dead. I only hope he finds good game in the hunting grounds beyond the Far Pines." He paused then. The weight of the past was heavy on his heart, and he did not like the burden it gave him. For he could feel the distant Devil straining against his bonds, searching for any weakness. He let the painful memories slip away and turned the conversation back to Willie Ducane. "You came west with your father and mother? Where is she? Did we leave her in Barlow?"

Now it was the girl's turn to turn solemn and introspective. "Mama died in Illinois while trying to give birth to little Gunther, but he never got borned neither. So then it was just Pa and me. But the both of them dying like that kinda took the wind out of his sails. He didn't talk about Oregon much after that. He started slowing down. We made it as far as Barlow, which was just a little speck of nowhere when we came across it. But that's where he decided to put down roots."

"Did he ever recover from your mother's death?"

"Not really. But more from little Gunther's than Mama's. See, he'd always wanted a son. Somebody to carry the Ducane name. When he didn't get one with me, he was after Mama right away to have another, a boy this time, had to be. She tried back in Pennsylvania a couple years after I came, but that was a stillbirth and a girl, anyway. Then little Gunther finally came, but it was such a hard birth. . . ."

No Moon nodded with understanding. "So you became the son your father never had."

Willie shrugged. "I suppose you could say that. It was a good substitute at first. But for the last couple years Pa was after me to be more ladylike, to wear dresses and frilly things, to brush my hair up in fancy ways to get the boys' attention. But I didn't see the sense in that. I mean, what's a fancy dress gonna get you in Nebraska? It gets dirty and it tears when you step on the hem, and you can't run for fear of tripping on the blasted thing. I just never had any use for it, you know? Now, don't get me wrong—I ain't ashamed of being a girl. Actually I like being who I am, and I wouldn't have it no other way. But I never saw why a woman couldn't do the same kinda things that a man could do, if she had the talent, that is. I could be a drover or a ranch hand if I had a mind to. Does that sound wrong to you?"

No Moon thought hard about that. "The women of our tribe are not warriors," he finally said. "They keep the lodge for their mate, and prepare his meals, and they bear him many children." He glanced over at Willie. "But you would make a better brave than most I have known. Perhaps if you take a mate, he can stay with the children?" Then he grinned again, actually laughed out loud, which she had not heard him do before. And the sound of it was so merry and full of life that she couldn't help throwing her arms around his neck and giving him a hug.

"What's this about?" Tol said as he roused just then, wiping the sleep from his eyes. "See here, girl, get away from him. Don't you know he's old enough to be your grandpa?"

"It ain't that way, you old coot." Willie laughed as well, and after the last few days it was a strange sound to her ears. Strange but welcome. "We were just talking. Isn't that right, grandfather?"

No Moon just smiled while Tol shook his head without understanding. "Well, better get started . . ." he said, tilting the hat back from over his eyes. And that's when he finally felt the heat and saw the fire burning before him, and the birds roasting over it. "How the hell—" he started. But then he looked at the knowing smirks the other two wore and sighed. "Forget I asked. Just cut me off a piece and hurry!"

While they were eating, No Moon finally got to tending Tol's knife wound. Tol hemmed and hawed at first, hesitant to face the much-feared sewing needle. But once the Indian applied some of the herbs from his pouch, the pain eased considerably. In fact, they deadened the wound so much that he barely flinched as the needle cinched up his eyebrow. Once that and the pheasant were finished, they begrudgingly put out the fire and gave themselves back to the cold drizzle.

Shaddock took measure of their position as they crossed the Platte. They were in Wyoming by now, he estimated, just southeast of Torrington. There was still quite a bit of prairie to cover before they would reach the foothills of the Rockies. So as tired as they still were, even after the brief rest, they set their mounts to a brisk gallop and steered them to the southwest. And as they rode the clouds overhead thickened and grew darker still.

They came to the fence first.

It was a series of sturdy posts sunk deep and strung with three strands of heavy-gauge barbed wire, running east to west and as far in each direction as the eye could see. The boundary of someone's ranchland, they surmised, intended to keep the cattle from wandering. But it had failed to do its job. At one fifty-foot section the fence had been torn down, the posts uprooted or splintered, the wire bent into harsh tangles or snapped completely in two. The stampeding longhorns must have hit the fence like a whirlwind to destroy it so completely. But the wave of bovine muscle had not gone without casualties. There were three steers caught in the tendrils of the barbed wire, their legs tangled while the rest of the horde trampled them to death. And one other cow lay some twenty yards away, as far as she could crawl with a broken fencepost protruding from her chest. The rest of the cattle had gone on, scattering into the Wyoming plains.

"What do you think stampeded them this bad?" Willie wondered aloud.

Tol nodded. "I'll give you three guesses. This is the quickest path to those mountains. And so it'd be the quickest path for the Devil to come for us. It probably passed through here two nights ago, before we saw it yesterday. And it must have scared the shit out of them poor beefs." He shook his head at the waste—juicy steaks just rotting away to nothing, said his still-half-empty stomach— as he reined his horse back along their path.

It wasn't even a mile till they found more carcasses. Only these cattle hadn't been killed in a frenzied run for freedom. Tol walked his horse slowly from animal to animal, noting their wounds. And his stomach turned even further. One's head was turned around backward. The next had been gutted with one of its own horns, the broken weapon still sticking from the animal's side. The one after that appeared fine, kneeling down in the grass as if pausing to rest. Except its head now sported a gaping hole between its eyes in the shape of a massive fist. The eyeballs themselves must have blown out from the impact, for the sockets now stared vacantly up at him. They reminded him of other sockets, other dead faces that littered the ground beneath one of the peaks of Paha-Sapa.

"Why," he muttered. "Why would it kill so many, so senselessly?"

"Practice," said No Moon flatly. And that made it seem all the more chilling.

Willie was visibly worried. "That Devil . . . It isn't here, is it?" she asked No Moon in an urgent voice. "I mean, what if it got out . . ."

"It is still there," he assured her in a weary voice. "I can feel it testing the barrier now and then. We can go farther still."

Tol was thinking of the scene that must have played out here; the mad squalling of the cattle as this dark destroyer wandered into their pastureland and began slaughtering right and left. And he fully understood the destruction of the fenceline. If it had been in his way, he would have plowed through it as well. "Christ amighty," he sighed. "It's like it was killing anything that got . . ." Then the meaning of his own words sank in. Killing anything that got in its way.

What if that included people?

Willie read his wide-eyed expression. "Where there's cattle, there's usually a ranch nearby. You don't think it might've—"

"There's one way to find out," he said, pointing to the
southwest. "It would have to be along this path. And if there
is a ranch . . ." He didn't finish his thought, for he was
already giving his horse the heel. The bay was running
almost before the order was given, bolting out across the
bloodstained pastures, with the others galloping frantically
after her.

They rode into a deep depression that was plugged with
slaughtered longhorns and kept going up the rise on the
other side. It was just beyond that, at the foot of a long and
gentle grade, that they saw the houses and corrals of a cattle
ranch. Wagon ruts ran away from the main house and off to
the northwest, presumably to a more substantial road that
might lead to Torrington or some other small town. There
were no signs or brands in sight, nothing to tell them the
name of this spread. And there was no life either. No
movement. The only sound was the raindrops slapping on
their slickers and hats. It was like a ghost town down there,
Tol thought, as fingers of dread gripped his heart.

"Should we go down?" Willie asked.

"We had a hand in this, in a way," Tol said. "I suppose we
owe it to whoever's down there to check on 'em." He looked
to No Moon. "Are you sure it isn't free?" The other nodded.
"Then let's take a look and be quick about it. We got a lot of
riding ahead, and we can't waste too much time here." He
started down the grade, but this time Tol didn't try to ride
ahead as was his way; he went down with the others, side by
side. Whatever happened here was already over; no amount
of hurrying could change that. And after seeing those
mutilated cattle, he was not particularly eager to survey
these results.

They rode up the wagon path around a decent-sized
corral, where a horse lay gutted in plain view, and then they
passed the bunkhouse and main barn beyond that, with a
tackroom out back. The ranch house itself was a two-story
structure with a wide, covered porch that went all around
from the looks of it. It was not the fanciest cattle ranch Tol
had ever come across, but it was surviving well enough. Or
at least it had been. It didn't seem natural seeing it this way,

so still and quiet. It raised the hackles on his neck. "Hello in the house!" he called. "Or anyplace else. Give a yell if you hear us." He listened intently, but he expected no reply, and that is just what he received.

He turned to his companions. "Like I said, we can't waste too much time. You two go look through the bunkhouse while I check in here. Give a yell if you find anybody. We'll doctor them if we can, or help 'em on their way if called for. But we ain't got time for burying nobody." The girl and Indian nodded and reined back toward the bunkhouse as he dismounted and stalked up onto the porch.

The front door was shut but not latched well—it swung open as he knocked. Even standing on the threshold, he could tell the interior of the house did not feel right. A thick silence hung in the air like a pall, and he knew that to enter would be like wading in deep water. We kinda owe 'em, he repeated. So he swallowed his fear and drew one of the LeMats from habit, thumbed that big hammer back before stepping inside.

There was a shallow entryway where a few heavy coats were hung on long wooden pegs, and a mirror on the wall where he saw his own reflection and regretted it. There was no denying the look on his face, a mixture of disgust and fear, and he stepped quickly past to avoid seeing it again. He found himself in a long open room with a fancy stone fireplace and wood mantel at the far end. The furnishings were well beyond Tol's station: a well-upholstered settee and plush high-back chairs, as well as a masterly leather throne with a stocked liquor cabinet near at hand. But none of it held the cowboy's attention, not even the bottles that once would have forced him to his knees in gratitude. He passed them by as he stalked silently through the house, into an empty library, then back through the big chamber and into the dining room, moving toward the kitchen.

The buzzing of flies reached his ears, very loud to be heard over the patter of rain on the roof. It was coming from the archway ahead of him. Don't look, his mind warned. You know what happened here and you know what you'll find, so just leave now, leave before you lose your nerve. But

Tolman Shaddock had never been one to heed the tenets of common sense. And so he went carefully into the kitchen.

Where he found a slaughterhouse. The back door no longer existed, and walls and cabinets were painted in violent splashes of crimson. The floor itself was awash, with blood standing at least an inch deep in places and congealing like old syrup. Through the swirling clouds of greenflies Tol could see that there were people afloat in that charnel stew. Or pieces at least—an arm here, a torso there, a head in the corner. Tol couldn't tell how many people in total, but he could guess from the battered and twisted faces that there were at least four. And one of them had been a child. The cowboy turned away and retched in a corner of the dining room.

There's no one to help here, he knew. Siyoko and its mistress had been too thorough for that.

He waited until the heaving had eased, and then he went back through the house and out onto the porch. The fresh cold air cleaned the smell of blood and maggots from his nose, brought him back to his senses. It was stupid to come here, he cursed himself. You've wasted too much time already. Get the others and get on your way. "Willie!" he called. Their horses were tied to a hitching post outside the bunkhouse. "There's nothing here. Come on, you two, let's get moving!"

No answer. Only the *pop-pop-pop* of the rain on the porch roof.

A cold notion settled in the back of Tol's mind. Are you sure the barrier's still holding, old man? "Willie! No Moon! Come out!"

Still no answer, no sign at all. His mind raced. Could the witch have tricked him? Could he have thought the Devil was safely locked away in that soddy when it was free all along, following after us, waiting for just the right time to—

That's crazy. No Moon's the *wicasa* whatever, not you. You gotta trust him. You do trust him, don't you?

Don't you?

"Willie!" His eyes were everywhere as he walked away from the house, stopping beside the bay just long enough to holster his pistol and retrieve the Sharps rifle instead. "No Moon!" He went straight for the bunkhouse, no longer slow and wary but with a long, determined stride fueled by panic and anger. He came to the door and saw it was open, went through with the rifle leveled at the hip. A cloud of flies swarmed around his head, and the smell of blood and death was in his nose once again. He didn't have to look to know what was around him in this room—it was worse than the kitchen, and his boots were already sticking to the floor. But he forced himself to look nonetheless, to search the horrified faces and parts of faces he found, praying silently that none of them would be fresh or female or Indian red.

When he was finished he'd counted twelve men altogether. And none of them had been Willie or No Moon.

Then where were they?

He went outside and looked all over the spread again. There was only one place he hadn't looked yet. The barn. The door was standing ajar. And it hadn't been when they rode in.

Is the barrier still holding, old man?

He could still hear Sky Falling Man's laughter coming from two mouths at once, and a girlish giggle from the darkness of the soddy. And for the first time in his life he wanted to run from a fight, wanted to get on his horse and ride like the wind and never look back, not once. But he thought of Willie and No Moon, and he knew that leaving wasn't an alternative.

Well, if you're gonna go, get it over with. Just make sure it's on your feet and fighting.

He thumbed back the big Sharps hammer and crept closer to the barn. Closer still, till he could peek around the door that stood open.

Nothing. No sign of the Indian or the girl. No sign of . . .

His eyes shifted to the stalls lining each side of the barn, and he was startled to see movement. Horses. There were horses there, alive—he could see the flicking ears and manes above the walls that divided each stall. There were at least seven, maybe eight. But why would the Devil have killed all those people, he wondered, and every steer it could lay its hands on, yet leave these animals alive?

He crept into the barn and looked over the door of the first stall.

The horse he found was an exhausted roan. It was still saddled, still bore the lather of a hard ride. So that's it, he realized. The Devil didn't kill them because they weren't there. Whoever's been riding this horse arrived not long before—

A door creaked at the far end of the barn, where the tackroom was located. But to Tol it was as loud as a gunshot. He whirled around with his rifle poised at the hip, and found himself pointing it at No Moon. The Indian was standing in the doorway, his hands at his sides, a blank look on his face. Willie was just behind him, her face hovering just over his shoulder. Tol sighed in relief, started to lower the Sharps.

"Goddamn you two," he cursed them with a grin, "you gave me a fright, disappearing like that. What the hell were you . . ." But then he noticed Willie's knitted brow beneath the brim of her hat, and the fact that they stayed right in the doorway of the tackroom. He knew something was wrong. The big-bore came back up in alarm.

Willie and No Moon were shoved out into the barn, followed by one man. Then another. Then two more and three more after that. They were all hard-looking characters with guns in hand, a motley crew that reminded him of those notorious thumpers they faced back in Nebraska. In fact, two of them were downright familiar. The wild-eyed man holding a pistol to Willie's head looked suspiciously like Stutterin' George Atwood. He even had his other arm, where Willie had shot him, tied up in a sling. Standing beside No Moon was a young man who shared his dark skin cast. And he kept fingering the hilt of the Bowie on his belt.

"Hello ag-g-gain," Atwood managed to say, smiling humorlessly. "Are you g-going to k-k-kill us all with that one b-bullet, old m-m-man?"

Shaddock smiled. "Not all. Just you." He raised the Sharps to his shoulder, pointed that yawning bore right at the outlaw's face. "Let them go," he warned. "Now."

"You're c-crazy, old m-m-man," George said. "But I th-think you'd really d-do it." His eyes left Shaddock for a moment, slipped just past the old cowboy's shoulder, and he gave an almost imperceptible nod. But Tol caught it. And he knew exactly what it meant. He cursed himself for an amateur, just started to whirl about, when a rifle butt landed at the base of his skull.

Pain flashed through his head for just a split second, and then there was blackness. He didn't even feel the ground rush up to meet him.

Chapter 15

"Sorry about that," said a voice that through the miasma of Shaddock's recovering senses sounded almost familiar. He opened his blurred eyes and tried to force them into focus, and that's when he saw the big features of Hephaestus Sipes looming over him, grinning. "I say I'm sorry I had to tap you like that, Tol," said the old outlaw. "But I guess I owed you at least one." He motioned to the cut on his swollen cheekbone where the cowboy had struck him with a pistol barrel. It was just beginning to scab over. "You feel like sitting up, old hoss?"

Shaddock realized he was lying on his side with his arms bound tightly behind his back. He nodded and let the big man pull him up to a sitting position, leaning him against a low wall of stone no higher than the middle of his back. He immediately felt heat directly behind him, heard the crackle of flames in a fireplace. Where the hell am I? he wondered. And in his quest for an answer he fought off the lingering fog of unconsciousness and looked around to get his bearings. He was sitting against the hearth of the main room in the ranch house. His arms were indeed bound behind him, but then, so were Willie's and No Moon's; the Indian was on the floor a foot or so along the hearth, nursing a split lip, while the girl sat in the closest of the high-back chairs. She appeared to be all right, but she no longer had a hat to hide her hair—it spilled down around her shoulders and commanded the attention of the men at the far end of the room. Tol's coat and guns and those of his friends had been gathered up and piled on a table across the room.

He recognized George Atwood, sitting in the master's leather chair, nursing a bottle of rye from the liquor cabinet. His right arm wasn't in its shirt-sleeve; it was hanging in a sling against his chest. His shirt was buttoned only halfway, so Tol could easily see the bandages around his neck and shoulder. Despite that, a small spot of blood had seeped through to mark where the girl had shot him. He took a long swig from the bottle and glared at Willie ominously, while she tried not to meet his gaze.

His half brother stood across the room with some of the other men, speaking to one with pock-marked cheeks in particular. The conversation appeared to be growing rather heated, for Kolo's brow was furrowed with growing anger and his steely blue eyes flashed. The scarred man saw it, too, and backed down rather quickly.

Tol counted heads. Besides the two Atwoods and Sipes, there were three others. That made six in all. But he remembered counting eight horses in the barn. That meant two others were around somewhere, probably standing watch outside or bedding the horses.

"You'll be okay, Tol," Hephaestus Sipes was saying. "I tried not to hit you too hard. An' you got a pretty thick skull anyway." He knelt down, whispered confidentially, "I don't bear you no ill, friend. I know you coulda shot me dead back there an' I appreciate the thought. I guess us old boys gotta stick together, huh? So I tried to talk George outta coming after you like this, but he's not one to forget. You'uns really pissed him off. Especially that boy." He glanced over at Willie. "I mean gal. Lord, who'd a' expected that? It's gotta be stickin' in his craw worse'n ever."

"Get me a gun, 'Phaestus," Tol whispered back. "Slip it to me when you can."

The old man's crooked eyes let him watch Tol and his cohorts at the same time. "Oh, Tol, I can't be doing that. . . ."

"You know what's gonna happen here, Sipes. They're gonna kill us sure as there's a tomorrow, and if that loon gets his hands on the girl . . . At least give us a fighting chance. That's all I'm asking."

The bearish old man stroked his wide gray beard. "Dammit, old hoss, I ride with this bunch—"

"W-w-what's with all the w-whispering, S-Sipes?" George Atwood blurted out.

"Why, nothing, George," Sipes said with a big grin. "Just comparing stories about the old days. You want to hear 'em? Some a' these are a real hoot—"

"Just sh-shut up, you ol' s-son of a b-b-bitch." He took another swig of rye and went back to scalding Willie with his glare.

Sipes sighed as he turned back to Tol. "Ain't no love lost there," he said softly. He glared back at Atwood a moment, considering. "I ain't promising nothing, Tol," he whispered. Then he got up and went back across the room to his comrades.

"Are you well?" No Moon asked as soon as the lumbering outlaw had departed.

"I'll live. How long have we been here?"

The Indian nodded toward the window behind Shaddock. It was dark outside. "You've been out for a while."

Dark already. How many hours? "The Devil," he asked anxiously. "Is it still . . . ?"

The look in No Moon's eyes was answer enough. "One of them hit me," he said, "and my concentration faltered for just a moment. But it was enough."

Shaddock's insides went cold despite the fire so near at hand. "But it won't catch up with us, not for a while. We rode all night and the morning too."

"But we stopped to sleep," No Moon reminded. "And we watered the horses a few times. The demonskin needs no sleep. It never tires. It keeps on until its task is finished." There was panic in his eyes. "We have to get to our weapons before it gets here—"

"I said I don't like it!" someone suddenly barked. It was the man with the scarred cheeks that had argued with Kolo before. He had stood in the corner and steamed until his courage was ample enough to stand up to the younger half-breed. "I don't like staying here. It's like a goddamn butcher shop in there"—he motioned through the dining room to the kitchen archway—"and there's bodies every-place. What are we staying around for? What if neighbors come by or lawmen or something? I say we ride hard and put this place behind us. I don't wanna hang for something I didn't do."

"It is kinda creepy," another said softly, unable to keep his eyes off the kitchen doorway. "And it's getting kinda rank in here."

Kolo didn't say anything. He just looked at the other man standing nearby, a bandy-legged brushpopper with fancy studded chaps and a hand-rolled cigarette between his teeth. "Me?" the man asked, looking around. Then he grinned. "Shucks, pard. Dead don't bother me none. I'm just glad to be under a roof for once."

"I s-said we s-s-stay!" George barked without taking his eyes off the girl. "And th-that's f-f-final! T-tell 'em, C-Clancy."

The half-breed nodded, then turned an angry glare back on the two who'd complained. "George done told you, Citro. And Farris, that goes for you too. We're staying. Now, go help Kisner with the horses. And keep your mouths shut. Understand?" He fixed them both with that icy glare, but evidently there was something in the scarred man's eyes that he didn't like. His hand went to the massive knife on his belt. "You got trouble, Citro?"

The scarred man glared back, and for an instant his hand twitched and Tol would have sworn that he'd go for the six-shooter on his belt. But the dark young man before him was imposing despite only average height, and his icy look seemed to inspire second thoughts. Just the fact that he carried only a knife spoke to his abilities with it—at that close-up range Tol knew the other outlaw would not stand a chance. And Citro must have realized that too. For he finally held up his hands in surrender, nodding for Farris to do the same. They went through the entry hall where the mirror and coats still hung and out onto the porch.

The breed watched after them, and his hand stayed on the hilt of his knife for a long time. Shaddock had faced many skulkers and backstabbers like this Citro over the years, and he knew the man would never actually stand up to the younger Atwood again. Instead, he would keep silent until the day he could shoot the boy from a distance. Of course, Tol also knew that Kolo would cut the man's throat long before that day ever came.

"The boys've got a point, Kolo," Hephaestus Sipes said, nodding. "It is a little unnerving, camping here with them corpses everywhere. What you think killed 'em like that?"

The breed shrugged. "Who can say? Border gangs maybe—meaner ones than us. Or maybe some renegades off the reservation." He looked over at No Moon sitting by the hearth. "Hey, old man. You think any of your boys coulda done this?" He laughed out loud before turning his attention to his half brother. "What about you, George? What do you think?" But the other Atwood was too busy glaring at Willie to answer.

"You were here first," Tol reminded them. "How do we know you didn't kill these people?"

Kolo shrugged. "You don't." He came closer, stood beside George's chair, and stole a quick drink of rye. "We rode hard and fast to catch up with you, Mr. Shaddock. Thought we'd lost you there a few times." He looked at Willie and shook his head. "I swear, I never expected this. A girl. And with a draw like that. George here's jealous, girlie. He wishes he had your gunarm."

"An' mayb-be I w-w-will yet," Atwood stammered in a growl, releasing the bottle long enough to draw a knife from his boottop. But Kolo put a hand on his arm, and the older of the two begrudgingly put it back. "A g-girl shot me," he moaned in anger, "a g-g-g, a g-god-d-damned girl . . ."

The breed ignored his mutterings. "I want to know something. Just where are you three going in such a hurry?"

Tol laughed. "You'd never believe us."

"Try me."

He looked the young man straight in the eye. "There's a demon from hell on our tail, the same one what murdered these ranch folk. And it'll keep on killing anything in its way until we get to the Rockies and put a bullet in the witch that called it up. You follow me, son?"

A sly grin spread across the half-breed's face and then he broke into raucous laughter. "That's a good one, old man. Now, let's have the real reason." When Tol shrugged, he looked to No Moon and then to Willie. And in the girl's eyes he saw it was the truth. "You don't actually believe that crap he just said, do you?" He backed away, still not sure how to take them. "Either you're shitting me royal . . . or you've all lost your goddamn minds."

"B-b-bitch," George Atwood was still muttering. He felt his shoulder, flinched at the pain that even a gentle prodding brought. And then his anger grew even hotter. "Y-y-you think you're p-p-pretty fast with a g-gun, huh? With th-that f-f-fancy rig 'n all. Well, here's y-your chance to p-prove it." He stood out of the chair and wobbled slightly, dropped the rye, and let it roll leaking across the floor. His good hand hovered above the handle of his gun. "G-g-go on, C-Clancy. G-give her a g-g-gun."

"Let it go, George," the breed said.

"What? Y-y-you giving the ord-ders n-now, b-b-boy?"

"You can't fight her, George." Those blue eyes bore into the other man, even through the haze of liquor. "She's faster than you, even when you're sober. She'll kill you, like she almost did last time. So let it go, you hear? Please?"

The older man glowered for a moment and spat on the floor. But he didn't question his kin. He stalked over to the chair where the girl sat, stood in front of her as if daring her to look at him. But the entire time Willie's eyes were rooted on the floor. "L-l-look at my sh-shoulder," he growled. "Look what you d-done to m-me. I s-said l-look, d-d-damn you!" He cuffed her hard along the ear, snapping her head back, and then he grabbed her by the throat. Both Shaddock and No Moon struggled to get up, but it was Kolo who moved like lightning. He grabbed his brother and pulled him back, put himself between them.

"I said no, George." He was adamant. "She's just a girl!"

Atwood stared at him, uncomprehending. "S-so? Sh-she's the one that sh-sh . . . that sh-shot me! W-what's wrong with you, b-boy?" George stepped around Kolo, approached Willie again even as he continued talking to the breed. "Y-y-you ain't wanting this one f-for y-yourself, are you? This s-scared l-little g-girl, Clancy?" He reached out and held her chin a moment, with Willie squirming to get out of his grasp. Then his hand slid down across her chest, cupped one of her breasts. And a crooked smile curled one corner of his mouth. "Hell, m-maybe you ain't s-so l-little at that." He jerked at her shirt, popping two buttons into the air, and when she tried to pull away he brought a hand across her mouth. She cried out. Stutterin' George laughed. "Yeah, I'm g-g-gonna like this," he said, that smile spreading all across his face.

Kolo reached out to restrain him. "George, I said let it go—"

"Don't f-f—d-don't f-f-fuck with m-me, C-C-Clancy!" the man whined, turning on Kolo in a rage. And though the half-breed could have drawn that knife in a split second and carved his brother seven ways to Sunday, he didn't. In fact, he cowered beneath the older Atwood's anger. "I'll g—I'll g-g-get you an-nother g-girl, Clancy. This one's m-mine."

"But—"

"You s-sassin' me, C-Clancy? You want m-me to l-leave you behind? 'C-cause I'll do it. Y-you want that?"

The breed said nothing. He just hung his head. "No, George. Don't leave me alone. No, George . . ."

"Then sh-shut up!" He glared at the younger man until Kolo retreated a step or two. George smiled in victory. "That's b-better." He turned back to his prisoner, smiled like a rattlesnake. "C-c'mon, girlie. L-let's find us a s-s—a s-soft p-place. . . ."

Willie didn't wait for him to reach for her again. Instead, she rolled back in her chair and lifted her knee up clear to her chin. And then she pistoned her leg out as hard as she could and drove a boot heel into George Atwood's bandaged shoulder.

On impact his eyes went wide and he let out a strangled squeak as he crumpled to the floor, moaning. She forced herself up out of the chair and aimed another kick at him, this time meaning to split his lip all the way to the eyebrows.

But Kolo had gotten over his surprise and was starting toward her. He had just reached out for her when Shaddock stuck out his feet and tangled them with the half-breed's, tripping him up.

"Run, girl!" the cowboy shouted, and Willie didn't need to hear it twice. She bolted toward the entry hall with her hands still bound behind her.

Hephaestus Sipes just laughed and made no move to stop her, but the bandy-legged man did. He spat out his cigarette and came forward with a wide grin in expectation of a good wrestling match with the buxom young thing.

Willie gave him no such chance; she lowered her head and plowed into him like an ornery bull, splitting both lips with her forehead and bowling him over. He rebounded off the wall and sank down, dazed and spitting blood, while Sipes laughed even louder.

The girl rounded the corner and found the front door standing wide open to the drizzly night air. But to her dismay she also found the other outlaws on the porch, rolling cigarettes and swigging their looted liquor. Citro and Farris were just turning to see what the commotion and laughter was all about when she burst past them, running as hard and fast as she could. The bunkhouse, she thought at first, but then she remembered the corpses there and changed her mind. Think, dammit, think! She could already hear the surprised men hooting behind her, the slap of their boots in the mud as they gave chase. The barn! Head for the barn!

But there may be someone there. Kolo said a man named Kisner was tending the horses—

What other choice do you have? Move!

A voice rang out behind her, a shout strangled by pain and rage. "L-l-l-leave her b-b-b-be!" George Atwood yelled. "The b-b-b—the b-bitch is m-m-mine!" She dared a glance back and saw where the others had stopped, looking back themselves toward the house. Atwood was in the doorway, holding his shoulder as he walked slowly, deliberately after her.

If I can just get loose of these damn ropes, she thought, and she tried to reach her hands around to the watch pocket on her jeans but couldn't manage it while running. Please, just give me enough time. . . .

The barn door was standing open, just like they'd left it, and a light was on inside. The horses were snorting and fidgeting already, and she figured that either the shouting had spooked them or maybe the other outlaw had. Well, you can't worry about him now, she told herself. If he gives you trouble, just kick him in his privates and make it hard, so he can't get up. She rounded the door and burst into the barn, startling the horses even more and half expecting a pistol barrel to be staring her down. But she couldn't see the man, nor much of anything else. Most of the barn was in shadow; the only light was that of a kerosene lantern hung on a peg just inside the door. She looked from stall to stall, expecting to see a cowboy hat bobbling up and down amid the horses as Kolo's man spread more straw. But she didn't see any. Maybe he's back at the house, or asleep up in the loft.

"I'm c-c-coming, y-y-you bitch! An' I'm g-g-gonna s-s-skin you alive!" He was halfway there.

Willie hurried to the far end of the barn, where the tackroom door still stood ajar. But she feared the missing outlaw might be in there and so she ducked into an empty stall instead and pulled the door halfway shut with her foot. There in the darkness she could finally put her plan into action. When Kolo and his men first captured her, she'd held her breath as they stripped off her gunbelt and taken the hunting knife, fondling her as they did so. But they never touched the watch pocket, where she kept her pencil stubs and the small folding knife that she used to sharpen them. She twisted and contorted to reach that pocket, feeling the stout hemp bite into her wrists and her shoulder creak from the strain. A little farther, a little . . . Her finger slipped into the pocket, touched the knife. Now another finger . . . that's it. Now just pinch and lift, slowly . . . She held her breath as the little knife slid out, a little farther, a little . . . Then her finger slipped. The knife teetered on the edge of her pocket for a second, and in a panic she made a grab for it. Got it! She sighed in relief as she pressed it against her palm.

At the other end of the barn the door swung even wider. "Come and g-get it!" her tormenter called.

Willie's mind raced. Open it, hurry, start cutting! There's not much time! She pinched the blade and unfolded the thing, then turned it in her hand and laid it against the ropes and began sawing, back and forth, back and forth, as quick as her wrist could work it.

Footsteps were muffled by the sawdust and straw covering the barn floor. But she could hear them nonetheless, each pounding in her ears like the peals of a bell. He's coming! Faster, dammit! Faster! She could hear his breathing, raspy, almost panting, checking each stall as he came.

A strand of the rope gave under the knife. She felt it. The tightness lessened a little, but not enough to pull free or break. Keep at it, keep working . . .

"You c-c-can't hide f-f-f-for long," he said in a light singsong voice that could not mask the maniacal menace beneath. He was so close, maybe the next stall. Maybe—

The door jerked open, and Willie flinched. In the bare light she saw only the right side of George Atwood's face, livid, drawn tight like a mask of madness. One eye even twitched uncontrollably. He was protecting the right side of his body, which sported a large spreading stain that looked black in the lamplight. Her kick had torn his wound wide open.

At that moment her ropes gave way. Her arms came out from behind her, and he saw the tiny knife in her fist. One side of his mouth pulled back in a cruel smile. "Mine's bigger," he said, holding up his "Arkansas Toothpick," its blade limned in silver from the distant lamplight.

He lunged at her, slashing, and she barely ducked beneath his attack. She stabbed back at him with her own knife, feeling foolish at the size of her weapon but thankful to have one at all.

Atwood wasn't his brother's equal with a knife, but he was more familiar with it than his opponent. He started to lunge again, but this time slashed downward, raking the point across the girl's shoulder. It was not deep, but the pain blinded her and made Willie drop her knife. That's when he came back across her face with the butt of his weapon.

The brass pommel struck her across the cheek and split the skin, sent her staggering backward only to fall in a puddle of wet dung. The outlaw just laughed. He turned and plunged the "Toothpick" into the door of the stall. Then he started to unbutton his trousers.

"I'll t-take you r-r-right here," he growled as he came into the shadows after her. "An' I'll b-be in y-you when I c-c-cut your throat. . . ." But once his eyes adjusted to the gloom, he stopped. His brow furrowed. "Wh-wh-what the hell . . ."

Willie looked at herself, found her shirt and skin stained black. But it wasn't dung as she'd thought; she could tell that by the smell. This was a warm, nauseating aroma, so familiar . . . Just like the bunkhouse. Oh, God, she thought as she tried to get up, but her hand came down in the muck on something cold and wet, something she knew without looking was a face. The eyes were open beneath her palm, and her fingers had slipped inside a still-screaming mouth. . . .

George Atwood took a step closer, stared at the remains strewn all around her. "K-K-Kisner?" he gasped. He began to back away slowly.

He had reached the doorway of the stall, when there was a sudden cracking sound and his chest exploded outward. A spray of blood and bone fragments hit the wooden wall as he jerked and twitched, and a crimson dribble ran from the corner of his mouth. His movements ceased, and he just hung suspended in the air, his boots not even scraping the ground. Something had impaled him from behind and still protruded from just below his sternum, and for a split second it seemed to Willie that he'd grown a new arm from the middle of his torso.

But then she realized that this limb was coal black and the flesh not completely solid but runny and viscous like tar. And long porcupine quills extended from the forearm. The massive fist was closed, but as she stood there, too stunned to move, it opened for her examination. In the center of that black palm was George Atwood's heart. The glistening muscle gave one last twitch of life and was still.

The girl's wide eyes traveled up from the hand, past the dead man's shoulder and still farther, into the darkness above him. To her horror, the shadows there blinked at her. Ebony eyes unsquinted, and a mouth every bit as dark gave her a toothless smile. And then laughter bubbled out of it, sweet and lyrical and chilling to the soul.

The seeds of fear in Willie's stomach were in full bloom now, unfurling tendrils that sought to enfold her muscles and hold them in place. But she fought them off. By instinct she lunged for the front of the stall, hit the ground, and rolled just beneath George Atwood's dangling feet, out into the open barn beyond. Then she was back up and running full tilt for the door so far away. But even as she ran, she remembered the race around the soddy only the night before and she knew that it was so much farther this time, and that she didn't have a chance in hell of making it. Any moment that bloodstained talon would land on her shoulder, jerking her back into the arms of night. . . .

She kept running, tears streaming from her eyes as she waited for the touch of doom. But she was almost to the door now, barely twenty feet to go, and still there was nothing. Past the last stall, past the lantern and its glow, and out into the night. Only then did she realize she was not being followed. Turn and look, said the voice of caution. Make sure it's back there and not circling around to meet you.

She had to fight the impulse to run, and somehow she managed to slide to a stop beyond the open door. Then, choking down her fear, she looked back into the depths of the barn.

The spiny goblin was still there, all nine feet of it, exactly where it had previously stood. It still held George Atwood on its arm like an oversized bracelet, letting him swing back and forth. And it was still watching her as well. When it was sure it had her attention, it held the outlaw's heart out for examination once again. Only this time it squeezed the thing, pulped it into a squishy mess that dribbled from its fist. Then the demon cackled anew in that high-pitched woman's voice.

Willie bolted for the ranch house, not daring to look back again. But the laughter followed along, and it whispered in her ear. *"Tell the Oglala,"* it said. *"Tell him I'm coming."*

Chapter 16

"Kolo!" Citro called through the open doorway of the ranch house. "You better get out here!"

The half-breed came out onto the porch, along with Hephaestus Sipes and Jeter, the man nursing two split lips. There they found Citro and Farris and another outlaw, Maclay, holding Willie Ducane by the arms. She was panting and wild-eyed, covered from head to toe in blood and foul matter and holding a shallow knife wound in her shoulder. But she didn't seem concerned with the cutthroats that held her. She was frantically twisting in their grasp, staring back over her shoulder at the barn across the ranch grounds.

Just seeing her startled Kolo, and after that the true meaning of her presence caught him in the heart. He looked to the barn as well, but George wasn't in sight. There was only the open door, and the lantern light that spilled outside onto the dirt. "Where's my brother?" he said frantically as he came toward Willie. He drew the Bowie from its sheath. "You better tell me and fast—"

"Dead," Willie stammered, lucky to be forming a coherent word at all. "It . . . it killed him. Killed them both . . ."

"Both?"

"Kisner's bedding the horses," Sipes reminded them.

Another look at the barn, then at the girl's bloody clothes. There was too much to have come from her wound alone.

And he still remembered the efficient way she'd dealt with George once before, and put a round in Lansdale's forehead. "You little slut," he growled, laying the knife blade against the girl's trembling throat. "If you've done anything to him, I'll—"

His words were interrupted by the laughter. It was soft, like a whisper, a woman's silky voice that barely issued above the clamor of the snorting and fretful horses. But they all heard it nonetheless. It took their attention away from the girl, turned their eyes to the barn again.

As they watched, a shadow spilled through the barn doors and into the lamp's oval of light. It was long and indistinct, except to Willie's eyes. A moment later the lamp glow winked out, leaving darkness behind. But the woman's chuckling still lingered, playing on the night air like a lilting tune just the slightest bit off key.

No one said a word at first; it was enough just to hear that eerie sound. But finally the laughter died away, and the night was too silent after that.

Hephaestus Sipes cleared his throat, whispered, "What the hell was that?"

"Somebody's out there," Kolo said in confusion. Then he remembered that George was still missing and he turned on Willie angrily. "Who the hell's out there?"

The girl just shook her head. "It killed them" was all she would mutter. "It killed them both. . . ."

"Goddammit!" He pulled the girl out of the men's hands and shoved her toward the bandy-legged Jeter, who caught her with an arm around her neck. "Take her inside," he ordered, thumbing the razor edge of his knife. "Keep an eye on all of 'em. The rest of you, come with me." Then he pushed through their ranks and led them off into the night, toward the now-darkened structure that lay just beyond the bunkhouse.

The outlaw named Jeter tightened his hold, cutting off Willie's air. "You're gonna regret hitting me, bitch," he snarled, spitting blood from his torn lips. He all but dragged her back across the porch and into the house.

She came into the main room backward, pulling at his arm and gasping for breath. So she didn't see Tol and No

Moon right away. By the time he turned her around, her vision was beginning to swim and the edges had grown fuzzy and dark. But she managed to glimpse her two companions by the fireplace, standing but still bound tightly. Shaddock had an angry look on his face, and in that one brief instant Willie knew that he was about to charge and attack the man, to free her from that merciless grip. But with his hands tied like that, he was destined to fail. You're the only one with your hands untied, she railed at herself. Do something, quick!

The numbing fear she'd felt outside was all but forgotten as she threw all of her weight forward and jerked on the wiry man's arm, catching him by surprise with her speed and strength. Before he knew it, Jeter was off balance, dropping his grip on the girl's throat and sailing over her shoulder. Willie didn't hesitate; the moment he hit the ground she attacked, pummeling and choking him, trying to reach the outlaw's holster. But Jeter wasn't as careless as before. This time he already had his hand on his gun.

She had to settle for his beltknife instead.

The outlaw jerked away from her and whirled about with his pistol raised. But Willie was that much faster. She ducked beneath his gun arm and lunged, stabbing with all the strength she could muster.

Jeter squealed. He dropped his gun and clutched at the knife blade that was now wedged hilt-deep in his floating ribs. But he couldn't pull it free. He cried out again, staggered a few steps and then collapsed, his body stiff, his limbs twitching. He gurgled once and was still.

Willie crouched there, gasping for breath. Her sudden anger was gone, replaced by the cold realization of what she'd done to survive. She looked down at the motionless figure beneath her, and at the blood that spattered her hands. "Lordy," she muttered. "I didn't mean . . ." Then she remembered where she was and why she'd come, and the fear sprung on her anew. "It's here!" she hissed to Tol and No Moon, afraid to let her voice rise above a whisper. She glanced fearfully at the windows. "It's in the barn. It said it's coming. . . ."

"Willie!" No Moon snapped. His tone was sharp and got her attention. "There isn't much time. Get the knife. You have to cut us—" He halted. His eyes moved past her, up over her shoulder, and she felt her insides go cold all over again. She turned slowly, expecting that black goblin to be standing in the doorway behind her. But instead it was Hephaestus Sipes. He had a large skinning knife in his hand.

"Stand back, old son," Shaddock said in a threatening tone. He turned sideways, and Willie saw that though his wrists were still bound, he had retrieved one of the LeMat pistols from the table across the room. "I couldn't shoot while the girl was a-rasslin'," he explained, "but I got a pretty clean shot at you."

Sipes forced a grin. "Relax, Tol," he said, holding his arms out. "You got me all wrong." He came across the room, unmindful of the barrel pointed at his belly, and stopped beside Willie. He looked down at the motionless Jeter. "Good work," he said. "I never liked old Dick much." Then he walked on to Shaddock and No Moon. "I'm on your side," he said solemnly, "'cause something ain't right here. All these bodies. And old George disappearing. I figure you know what's going on." He grabbed No Moon by the shoulder and turned him around, cut through his bonds with one slice of the blade. He turned back to Tol and that big ten-shot gun. "Well? You gonna shoot me or let me get you loose?" When the other man didn't move, he held up his hand as if taking an oath. "You got my God's-honest on this one, friend. 'Cause to tell you the truth, I'm just about scared shitless right now."

A gunshot rang out in the night, startling the lot of them. Almost immediately there were others, five or six, right after the first. Shouts. A strangled cry. All from the direction of the barn.

"We must hurry," No Moon said to Tol.

Shaddock looked at Sipes again, then turned and stuck out his arms. For a split second Tol wondered whether he was making the right choice or not. But the blade cut through in one quick movement and he was free, massaging his numbed arms. "What do we do now?" he asked.

The Indian was already moving across the room toward the table where their coats and weapons were piled. "Willie, go lock the door."

"A door won't stop that thing—"

"Of course it won't. But we don't want to make her suspicious, do we? Now, hurry!" The girl nodded and quickly ran into the entry hall as he picked up the big-bore Sharps and threw it to Shaddock. But No Moon did not bother with his own Winchester. Instead, he picked up the bow and reed arrows that he'd constructed along the banks of the Platte River.

"What's that gonna do?"

No Moon paid little heed to Shaddock's question. He pointed to the kerchief around Sipes's neck. "Take that off," he said, "and cut it into strips."

The old man did just that, as quickly as his knife could work. Especially after more gunfire crackled outside. Another scream rang out, one of pain and torment. Sipes handed over the rags and put away his knife in favor of a pistol.

The medicine man took a strip of kerchief and tied it around the point of one arrow, leaving a little tail of rag to hang loose. By this time Willie had returned.

"What did you see out there?"

"Some muzzle flashes out back of the bunkhouse," she said, breathing hard from sheer terror. "I didn't wait for any more." She went to the table, retrieved her Colt, and strapped it on. "The door's bolted. You want me to check out back or—"

"There's no time," No Moon said. He had nocked the arrow in his makeshift bow and stood facing the fireplace, the rag at the point held just above the flames. "All of you, stand before me, facing the door. You must block the light so it will not be afraid to come in."

The three lined up as he suggested, side by side, Shaddock's back against No Moon's. "Now what do we do?"

"Prayers never hurt," the Indian said.

"Yeah," Tol muttered, "but to whose God?"

The medicine man didn't answer this time. No one spoke at all, and a silence settled that was defied only by the popping and cracking of the fire behind them. The room was mostly dark, sheathed in their own shadows as they blocked the flickering light from the hearth. Only the ceiling danced with light. Tol didn't like the silence, and he didn't like the dark. He could tell Willie and Sipes felt the same way. They stood right against his side, shoulder to shoulder, and he could feel the tenseness in their muscles, could feel the tremors of growing fear.

You're waiting to die, said a cynical voice in the back of his mind. You're standing here all quiet and still, like a sheep with its throat bared to the wolf. Because there's nothing you can do. No weapon you can use. Not the buffalo gun in your hands, or the Indian's ridiculous bow. That damn thing probably won't even shoot straight. He glanced over his shoulder at the old red man, saw him standing with the bow and nocked arrow before him, the rag-wrapped tip still hanging just above the flames. A fire arrow, the voice sighed. What does he think that will do? You know yourself the Black Heart Devil doesn't burn. How long did you leave it in that fire in the Black Hills, hoping it would catch and curl up and disappear to ashes?

Stop it, he thought. No Moon knows what he's doing. Trust him. He's earned that much.

Hidden behind the looming Shaddock and unmindful of the doubts that ran through the cowboy's head, No Moon stood in the glow of the fire, eyes closed. The fingers of his right hand caressed the taut sinew that he'd carried since childhood. He spoke deep down, in a voice that only he and the spirits could hear, in a tongue that was neither white nor Lakota but something taught him ages before in the *hanblechia,* his first vision. The same time that Elya-eh came to him and agreed to live in his bowstring.

I have not called upon you for some time, patient friend, he said deep down. But I have carried you faithfully, and given gifts of *wacanga* and sage in your honor. Now I am calling on you to aid me as you have in the past, as you did that first day in the meadow by the great rock, when you helped me take the antelope and made the Pawnee swallow his pride. There is an enemy coming. Aid me, O Elya-eh. Aid me . . .

There was a commotion outside. A pounding on the great

door, over and over in a frenzy. And as soon as it stopped there, it started again elsewhere. This time at the window. A fist struck the glass, cracking one of the panes. "Help me!" came the muffled voice of Kolo. They could barely see his face pressed against the glass, leaving a smear of blood behind. "It's coming! Help me!" He whirled around, looked behind him. "Oh, my God!" they heard him gasp. Then he was gone from the window and back at the door, pummeling it with maniacal intensity, his voice no longer forming words for their ears but instead sounding like one long yewl of terror.

Willie couldn't stand it. She heard that voice and the panic in it, and she felt as if it were her own, as if she were still standing by the barn door as the goblin laughed and dangled George Atwood from its massive arm. We can't ignore it, she thought as she looked to Shaddock. But he didn't seem to be listening. The only movement that he made was to thumb back the hammer on his buffalo rifle.

Kolo's voice was a wail in her ears. *"Help me, it's coming! Oh God, it's coming! Help . . ."*

Willie was moving before she even realized it. She broke away from the others and ran full tilt across the darkened room and into the even darker entry hall, ignoring the shouts from Shaddock and the other man. Her hands were on the heavy drop bar that she herself had swung into place only minutes before, and she threw it up and jerked the door open. A figure lurched through the doorway, startling her, but then Kolo sprawled on the floor and scrambled across it like a crab, babbling all the while. "It's coming, it's right behind me, right behind—"

Willie looked through the crack in the door even as she started to push it shut. She saw that the cloud cover had broken up if just for a few moments, allowing a smattering of moonbeams through to the earth below. One of them struck the ground out by the empty hitching posts no more than twenty feet from the porch, casting the damp ground in a blotchy shade of silver. And into that light stepped a shadow of ill proportion, a massive torso on spindly, doglike legs. The hulking figure was bringing something behind it.

Willie didn't have to see them completely to know what the Black Heart Devil was holding. Two of Kolo's men were being dragged by the ankles through the dirt, their shattered bodies leaving a dark track through the moonlight.

The shadow looked at her, the black-speck eyeholes winking open on the knobby head that jutted almost from its chest. And when it saw her, the mouth opened as well, wider and wider, yawning like the flexible jaws of a serpent but even more malleable without bones or joints to impede it. Through that maw Willie could see all the way to the creature's core, to the complete and utter darkness that had once been a woman's shadow, and she felt a cold emanating from there like a gust of arctic wind.

The shadow silently dropped its broken burden and took a tentative step past the hitching posts, then another that brought it to the end of the laid-stone walkway.

It's coming, it's gonna be here in less than a minute, so shut the damned door, shut it and bolt it and run like—

The shadow lunged up the walk, bent into the charge and almost on all fours as it came at the porch like a spiny locomotive. The movements were so swift and silent that it was just a dark blur to Willie's eyes, and she wasn't sure what she was seeing or if the moonlight was just playing tricks.

"Willie!" It was Tol's voice from behind her as he lunged against the door and slammed it shut, jerking the crossbar into placed with a thunderous crash. Then they were both moving, scrambling back across the entry hall in a blind panic, pausing only to grab up the gibbering breed, one on either side, and all but carry him the length of the big room.

They were little more than halfway to the fireplace where Hephaestus and No Moon waited, the latter still facing the fire, when they heard something hit the door behind them.

With a crash, shards of oak and splinters rained through the entry hall, bouncing off the walls with hollow reverberations, accompanied by the tinkle of a shattering mirror. The cacophony did not give Shaddock and the girl pause; instead, it spurred them on even faster. As they reached the hearth, Willie took Kolo's full weight and held the babbling half-breed up beside her as Shaddock shielded the light from the hearth as before and took his buffalo rifle back from Sipes.

Tol focused his attention on the darkness that marked the entrance. He found himself looking into the depths of his own shadow and that of the others, splashed all about the walls and even on the arch they'd just come through. It was littered now with the remnants of the door, and a stray spark of firelight glittered on a broken shard of mirror, at least until Sipes moved even closer and butted up against Shaddock's side. Then there was only darkness.

At least until something even darker stepped into view.

It came around the corner slowly, filling the archway, its shoulder scraping the ceiling beams overhead, the tense spines gouging at the wood and leaving furrows as it passed. The thing's eyeless, featureless head jutted forward and down, looking to Tol like a new fist was growing from the middle of the thing's chest. But then it opened one eye, just a slit, enough to make sure there was no light in the room. It was apparently satisfied, for both eyes opened wide along with the mouth, revealing a stygian gloom that was nigh absolute.

"Where is the Oglala?" the shadow of Dee-Bo-Ha demanded from within its demonskin.

Tol's finger tensed on the trigger of the Sharps, and he was just about to fire from the hip. But No Moon's voice was almost against his ear, just loud enough for him to hear. "Not yet," he said, and Shaddock steeled himself to obey.

"I said where is the Oglala!"

The voice was pitched and frantic as the goblin advanced into the middle of the room. A swipe of one massive arm knocked furniture spinning in all directions, smashed one chair to kindling, and disemboweled a couch so that downy feathers rained all around like midnight snow.

"You will all die this night," it decreed. *"And the old man will be last so he can watch it all—"*

The witch was still talking when No Moon turned and thrust his arms between Willie and Tol, holding out his bow with the string drawn to his cheek. The arrow was poised, its head wrapped in a strip of rag that in turn was wrapped in a plume of angry flame. The sudden flare of light took the Devil by surprise; the eyes and mouth vanished, closed over by the roiling flesh of its face. It tensed to spring. . . .

At that moment Tolman Shaddock knew what it was that No Moon had in mind. For he remembered shooting this demon the day before, and what happened when light seeped into the wound. Before No Moon could even tell him to fire, he brought the rifle to his shoulder and squeezed off his single round. A thunderous roar filled the room as the rifle bucked in his arms and almost threw him back into the fireplace. A licking tongue of blue fire shot from the big-bore, almost reaching to the Black Heart Devil itself, and it left a ragged hole in the creature's oily chest. Light poured into the wound from the glow of No Moon's arrow, and the creature flinched, reached to cover the wound until the undulating skin could reseal it properly.

But by then the medicine man had already fired his arrow.

With the echoes of the Sharps still ringing in each person's ears, no one heard the soft *thhpptt* sound of the bowstring's release, or how it played in the air like the tiniest ring of fairy laughter. But they saw the arrow fly, streaking across the short distance like a shooting star. As they watched with wide eyes, that glowing missile plunged straight through the already-shrinking hole that Shaddock's blast had wrought, past the wriggling flesh and into the dark abyss beyond, into the Black Heart of the Devil. The moving edges of the wound ran together and sealed over completely, leaving no scar or sign of the arrow at all.

The goblin flinched. Jerked. Staggered back a step or two. Tremors began to heave within that massive chest and travel outward into its arms and legs, growing in violent force as they went until the beast sank to its knees beneath their weight. Its knoblike head thrashed across its chest, as if in torment, and when it could fight it no longer, the eyes and mouth opened wide and a soul-wrenching scream rang out, high and hollow, slicing through all present like an angry razor.

They could see that there was no longer an ebon void behind those eyes. The inside of the creature was lit up, glowing like a star in the darkness. Dee-Bo-Ha's voice continued to scream in agony as the inner fire kept growing, till a tongue of flame licked out of the creature's mouth and seared the vision of those watching.

Abruptly the scream broke, as if there were no more voice left to feed it. The chilling sound began to fade, leaving only the echoes to play in their ears. With it went the fire that raged within the Black Heart Devil. The light inside grew dim and barely flickered, until it seemed to go out all at once, like the snuffing of a candle. But it was different in there now. The blacker than blackness that had dwelled within and taunted them was no longer there. Instead, it was just . . . empty. And to emphasize that impression, the hulking form began to collapse on itself, sinking to the ground and folding over without substance until it was little more than a puddle of obscene tissue and spines.

An empty skin.

No Moon was the first to move. He stalked cautiously away from the fire, across the room to the remains of the goblin. He reached out and prodded those noisome folds with his bow. The skin seemed to squirm a bit but nothing more. He sighed and relaxed, let the tension ease from his shoulders. "It's over," he said.

The other two old men exchanged wide-eyed looks. Hephaestus Sipes looked petrified with surprise. Willie tugged on Shaddock's sleeve and motioned for help with Kolo, who was hanging on her shoulder and still mumbling like a man in a stupor.

The Oglala looked down at the demonskin again and whispered under his breath, "We are coming, witch. We are coming!"

We are coming . . .

The words echoed as if from a great distance, but they might as well have been spoken right into her ear. Dee-Bo-Ha still would not have heard them. Not over her own screams.

There was a fire inside her, smoldering in her chest and spreading from there to engulf her completely. Eating her alive. And despite her vast powers, her magic, she was powerless to stop it. She twitched and writhed and cried out in agony. Help me, master, she screamed silently. This is not what I was promised! Not what I was promised at all.

But there was no answer. Only the pop and crackle of the flames that sheathed her.

They burned themselves out after what seemed like an eternity, and in their wake she lay spent and moaning. Her breathing was shallow, unsteady, her senses scorched beyond feeling. Her vision swam with dancing spots of red and orange, even behind closed lids. And she kept them closed too. She did not dare to look at herself, for she already knew what awaited her gaze; black and cracking flesh where beauty had been, the stubbled remains of her raven hair. To lose what she had hoped and prayed and faithfully served for. It's not what you promised, she sobbed. Not the life you promised.

Open your eyes.

It was not a voice that spoke to her but a sensation, like the touch of a cold hand. She had felt it so many times before that she did not think about it or consider its message. She simply obeyed.

Her eyes fluttered open, blinked themselves into focus. She was lying on her back, staring up at the hide covering of the small conjuring lodge. Tendrils of smoke curled overhead, and at first she thought they rose from her baked flesh. But then she caught the sweet, pungent smell and she knew they must be coming from the small firepit beside her. Hesitantly she held up her arm to look at it, and to her surprise there was no black crust to assail her. Instead, her flesh was still soft and smooth, red with life. She stared at it incredulously, even as the scalding pain lingered deep within her. She reached up to touch that unblemished skin, saw that her other arm was still supple and beautiful as well. Her hands ran all over, stroking her naked, trembling form, finding naught but buttery softness that tingled at each touch. Her hair was still intact, though plastered against her head and shoulders with perspiration. I'm not burned? Then, what . . . ?

Images flashed before her mind, scenes that were disjointed but oddly familiar and becoming even more so as her scrambled senses slowly pieced them back together.

Figures standing against a hidden light, their features lost in shadow. A flare of light stabbed into her like a knife, and she had to close her eyes to fend off the brightness. In that brief instance she saw that an arrow held the hated light, and a crude bow supported the missile in turn. And behind that she saw the face of the Oglala. . . .

It all came back to her. She sat up on the small mat and turned to the wall of the lodge behind her. The dim glow of the stones in the firepit glowed there, flickering ever so slightly. Enough to cast her shadow. If she'd had one.

She felt the burning deep within her again, a spark fanned and glowing along the angry fissure where her shade had been torn away. She knew that this pain would never leave her. You will pay for this, Oglala, she promised. I will try again. I will summon something even more deadly, a demon that you've never heard of. Perhaps I'll choose from another world entirely and then—

No.

That cold hand again, touching her soul.

It is time.

Time, she thought, incredulous. So soon? How long was I away? She climbed to her feet and draped the feathered robe around her bare shoulders, stepped through the lodge flap and into the cold of the night. Her eyes rose skyward. Heat lightning was flashing up in the sky, traveling from one horizon to the other, playing across the underbellies of clouds turned bloated and angry. They were moving, those clouds, like a storm gathering strength. But only in a long, languid spiral. Its center was just over the flat summit of the spire. As she watched, there was an ear-splitting groan, as if the earth itself had cracked open. But it came only from the tower above her. Rifts had begun to show in the walls of the granite obelisk, forming a ragged spiral from top to base. And in those fissures, the rock continued to move, to grate and slide on itself with cataclysmic intensity. When it finally stopped, the lower lip of each crack now jutted out from the rest of the rock, a natural ledge that ran all the way to the flat summit.

"The Stairs to Heaven . . ." Dee-Bo-Ha whispered. "It is time." She smiled, her flesh tingling not from the cold but

210

from the anticipation of what was to come. Her anger with the Oglala and his helpers was forgotten, for they were no longer of consequence. Why worry about them, she thought. They are too late. The Dance is about to begin.

The robed ones came to her side and fawned over her as she walked to the larger lodge. They held the flaps apart so she could enter. But she went in alone.

There were even more of the harbingers now, such a mass of entwined coils and limbs that the medicine men were barely visible in their midst. But their chants still rang in the smoky air, and she could feel their power amplified all around her. She began to pick them out one by one, still squatted before the firepit and staring into space, oblivious of the inhuman figures that squirmed around them, giving obscene caresses and drinking from their veins.

"Enough!" she called in a voice that rang above all else. All movement stopped, all sound. Even the low chanting of the men. They turned to look at her, both glazed human eyes and those that had never suffered the daylight. And they waited for her words.

She graced them with a smile. "It is time."

The salamanders blinked and the few features they possessed tried to echo that smile. They began to untangle themselves from the motionless men, and one after another they slithered back into the firepit, diving in headfirst. There was a plume of hissing smoke and a foul stench that rose to mark each creature's passing. But finally they were all gone and there remained only the medicine men and Dee-Bo-Ha.

She looked them over, and they her. In their eyes was a living hatred that might have cowed any other who had fallen beneath their glare. But she knew it was not intended for her. Their attention was still turned inward, focused on whatever images the visions had left in their minds and hearts. They sat naked on their small hide mats, their leathery flesh pricked and torn by needlelike teeth, their loins matted with whatever gummy excretions their attendants had produced. But they also sported paintings across their bodies, strange symbols and drawings that were inked in blood and etched by inhuman hands. They looked haggard from their ordeal, just a group of wizened old men who swayed with exhaustion and might drop at any moment. But the twisted expressions of anger on their faces said they would not fall. These were not ordinary men; they had much power beyond the simple confines of flesh and bone. And they would not fail her. She knew that.

"The ghosts are calling," she said softly. "The Dance begins."

The naked men stood slowly, oblivious of the scream of muscles that had not moved in six full days. They fell silently in line and shuffled to the mouth of the lodge, through the flaps that the robed ones still held. Without another word of instruction from the witch, as if the command were already known deep within them, they turned as one and started the trek toward the Stairs to Heaven.

Chapter 17

Hephaestus Sipes put another splinter of wood into the fireplace, feeding the flames to a brighter blaze. But no matter how warm the air became, it simply wouldn't chase away this strange chill from his old bones.

He couldn't help but sneak another sideways glance at the puddle of spines and ebony flesh that still lay on the floor just where it had fallen. He'd never seen anything like it, that was for sure. Not in sixty-five years on this green earth, and didn't hear of anything like it either. If it hadn't been lying there as living proof to what went before, he'd have thought he was dreaming, maybe sleeping off a bad drunk somewhere. He walked over to the demonskin for the third time in the past fifteen minutes, close enough to nudge it with the toe of his boot. A tremor went through it, the reflexive wriggle of a snake that doesn't know it's dead yet.

But this thing was different, like a snake that might have been dead, but with a skin that just went on living without it. The idea raised the hackles on his neck and fascinated him at the same time. He poked at it again, watched it flinch.

"Saw a buffalo that moved like that once," he said to no one in particular. "It was dead, no two ways about that. What was moving was the layers of maggots under the pelt." He grimaced as if the memory had brought a smell along with it, and he backed away. "I'll tell you, if I hadn't seen all this . . ."

The others weren't paying him much attention. They were situated all around the big room, silent to a man and girl, immersed in their own dark thoughts. Shaddock was standing at one of the windows, staring out into the damp nighttime outside, while Willie had finished changing into clean clothes and was now letting No Moon tend the wound in her shoulder. Atwood's knife hadn't gone too deep. Only a few stitches were necessary. Kolo had ceased his desperate mutterings and sat silently in one of the chairs that hadn't been smashed, flicking his thumb against the razor edge of his knife. No Moon had offered to tend the gash in his scalp but had not received an answer.

Sipes pointed to the demonskin again. "So this is what you came here for? To kill this thing?"

Tol sighed. They had already explained it to him twice. But Hephaestus just didn't seem to grasp the scope of it all. In a way Shaddock couldn't blame him; it had taken him a while to accept it himself. So he tried not to get too impatient with the man's questions. "The Black Heart Devil was sent to keep us from reaching the mountains, Sipes. Remember?" But the crooked-eyed old man just scratched his beard and looked at him in confusion. "All right, I'll go through this one more time. . . ."

Kolo suddenly looked up, turning his icy gaze on Willie Ducane. He did not wear a hateful expression, or one of menace. In fact, there was no emotion on his face at all. It was blank, as if any feelings he'd once had had been bled away by whatever horrors he'd faced out in the dark. But that did not make his eyes any less unsettling. He just looked at her for a moment, quietly. Then, in a near whisper he asked, "Where is my brother?"

He's lost his mind, she thought. Doesn't he realize what went on here? "Listen to me," she said slowly. "He's dead, remember? I told you, that thing, it grabbed him and—"

"I want his body."

"Oh." She blushed a little. "Last time I saw him . . . that thing killed him out in the barn."

The half-breed didn't nod or say another word. He simply rose from the chair and started for the door. Shaddock called after him. "Wait up. I was just gonna go check the horses."

But the young man was already through the archway and into the littered entry hall, heading out the hole where a heavy door used to stand.

"Think I'll go anyway," the cowboy said. He pointed to the empty skin. "You want me to take care of that?" he asked No Moon. "I could drop it down the well, or bury it, or something."

The Indian kept tending to Willie's shoulder. "I will deal with it," he said without looking up. Tol just shrugged and went on.

"Hold up there, Shaddock," Sipes called. "I'll go with you. I could use some air." He didn't say that his real desire was to get out of that room for a few minutes, away from that moving pelt. It was beginning to give him the willies.

They went out onto the porch, and their eyes immediately fell on the bodies out by the hitching posts, the ones Siyoko had dragged toward the house just before breaking in the door. Sipes studied the two shattered forms, fighting gloom and bad eyesight and the condition of their faces to make an identification. "That one's Maclay," he said, forcing back a gag. "At least I think so. About his size. As for this other, I doubt even his sweet mama could pick him out. What a god-awful mess!" He looked toward the barn, just an indistinct shape in the midnight gloom. "Where's Kolo?"

Tolman could see a little better in the dark than the other. He barely made out Kolo walking away from them. He was halfway across the ranch grounds, almost to the barn. In just another moment he went through the open door and disappeared inside. Tol was in no hurry to follow him. "He'll be communing with the dead," he advised. "Let's give him a minute or two." So they took their time walking in that direction, first stepping over the two corpses that blocked the end of the walkway.

It was still cold and damp out, misting lightly, just enough to soak through their coats and sting the skin, to make them wish they'd gone back for their slickers. But the ceiling of clouds overhead appeared to be breaking up. There were patches of starlight in places, winking down at them, telling them that the foul weather was clearing and at least they wouldn't be riding in rain tomorrow. Tol felt the tension easing from his neck and shoulders, replaced by a numbing fatigue that made him want to lay down and sleep for a week. But he willed that exhaustion back, barricaded himself against it. Don't give in yet, he warned. There's more to come, maybe even worse than this. You can sleep in a little bit, 'fore the ride starts again. But not too much. You can't give in.

The bodies by the porch must have been Citro and Farris, for they found Maclay near the door of the barn. Or at least his upper half. They never found his legs. Both the men passed him by rather quickly, as they'd seen their fill of slaughter that night. They went on into the barn.

Kolo was sitting on the floor in a quagmire of straw and blood, holding George Atwood's limp form across his lap. He tenderly picked the flecks of grime from the dead man's face and pushed back what hair he had, and the other two would have sworn they heard him humming softly. They just watched, not saying a word.

After a while Kolo stopped humming. Without a word to the other two, without even acknowledging their presence, he laid the elder Atwood aside, gently, as if afraid to wake him. Then he stood and went along the stalls, searching until he found the appropriate horse. It was the same sturdy Morgan that Tol had seen George riding when Willie shot him. They must have run it down after it spooked. Kolo led it out into the middle of the barn and made it stand very still, even when he dropped the reins. He went back to his brother's body and lifted it up, wrestled with it until he could sling it over his shoulder. It was even more of a struggle getting it over the horse's back. Again, neither Tol or Hephaestus offered any help, nor did the breed ask for any. Panting heavily, he finally used a leather thong to tie the hands and feet of the corpse and keep it from falling off the horse's back.

He went into another of the stalls after that and came out leading his own fiery palomino. It wasn't saddled—Kisner had been bedding the horses when he was killed—but Kolo found his rig perched on a wooden rail nearby and remedied that quickly enough. The horse was soon ready to go.

But Kolo wasn't, not yet anyway. He stalked about the barn silently, searching in earnest, until he found what he was looking for—a shovel that was used to muck out the stalls. He took it and swung himself up into the saddle, leading his brother out of the barn and into the night. He turned away from the ranch house and went out toward the pasturelands, the palomino moving at a slow walk. He was not eager for what must be done.

The other two watched after him. "Where will he go after this?" Tol wondered. "To get more help?"

"Not likely," answered Sipes. "This was it. There ain't no gang anymore. Only him and me."

Shaddock looked over at him. "And what about you, old son? What are you gonna do from here on?"

"Well, that's a good question," the bearish man said, scratching his taut whiskers. "Thought I might tag along with you'uns, if you don't mind me."

The idea took Tol by surprise. "You ain't thinking right, friend," he told him flat out. "Maybe you really didn't understand what I told you back at the house—"

"I caught more than you figure, Tolman. It's been sinking in on me ever since we left the house. You're going to the mountains to stop this Indian witch from starting a Ghost Dance, she being the one who sent that boogerman after us." He grinned, showing his bad teeth. "See, this skull ain't quite so thick as it looks."

"Knowing that, you still want to go?"

"Why not? Ain't nothing keeping me here. Nothing keeping me nowhere. What I'm saying, Tol, is I'm an old man and I ain't got nowhere else to go. So might as well be with you."

Shaddock just shook his head. "Maybe you don't know what we'll be getting into. No telling what kind of demons and spirits are waiting on us there. And I'll tell you straight, 'Phaestus. There's every chance that we won't be coming back from this one."

If the idea frightened the other man, he didn't show it. In fact, he dismissed it with a shrug. "You ever think about growing old, Tol?"

"I hate to tell you, Sipes, but we're already old."

"No, I mean really old. Weak, shaky. When your bones break too easy and you can't get around by yourself, let alone get on a horse. Well, I've thought about it. A lot. And I don't cotton to the idea. I don't have no family to speak of, nobody to take care of me when I get infirm. I can't get work, not on a ranch or even a farm, not at my age. And I surely don't want to end up in one of them homes for the aged—I heard about them places. No thank you."

"So where does that leave us?"

Hephaestus smiled. "Live hard for as long as you can, and go down fast. Why you think I've been running with these pups lately? Sure wasn't the money. Hell, in all their jobs, they never came close to that one haul I made in Texas when you shot off my ear. Naw, I figured that it'd come down to a fight with the law sooner or later, and that's where I'd meet a dignified end, as the good Lord intended all along. I kinda hoped you'd be the one to shoot me back where we knocked heads, but I guess it just wasn't my time. Now here you are, heading off to fight the heathens one last time—by God, if that ain't destiny, I don't know what is."

"Wait a minute," Tol said in confusion. "Let me get this straight. You want to go because you figure it's a good chance to die?"

"More or less."

"Well . . . that sounds reasonable. I think. But you won't be too disappointed if I don't join you."

"Up to you. We all got different callings, you know."

They busied themselves with checking the horses. The animals were all in good stead, a little skittish but calming more and more now that the Black Heart Devil was a fading memory. Two of the outlaws' horses were particularly antsy and kept the others somewhat riled. Sipes discovered that those were the closest to the stall where Kisner's remains were, and the scent of blood was frightening them. So Hephaestus moved those two out into the middle of the barn while Tol covered up the grisly remains as best he could.

"We're lucky," he said as he mopped the cold sweat from his forehead and leaned on the pitchfork. "That thing was in here, right here. It couldn've killed the horses at any time, just like the spirits did back at Barlow. Could've kept us from reaching the mountains in time. But that witch was too intent on killing us. That's the biggest mistake she's ever made, I'll promise you that." He thought about that and found himself grinning.

"What is it?"

"She made a mistake. Don't you get it? All this time I've felt like . . . I don't know. Like we're fighting the Devil himself or something like him, like he's watching us all the time and knows what we're thinking. But now I know we're just fighting a woman. And that she makes mistakes. For the first time it seems like we might live through this." He turned back to spreading straw over Kisner's body, and didn't see the dejected look on Sipes's face.

They finished feeding the horses, even the ones that no longer had masters, and as they left the barn they secured the doors so prairie scavengers drawn by the scent of blood wouldn't bother them. Then they went back to the main house.

They found No Moon sitting up by the fire. He looked drawn and tired, his craggy face sporting even more lines than normal. In the reddened light of the flames, Tol thought he looked very much like his twisted-up father. His lids were heavy but he refused to let them fall. Willie, on the other hand, had no such willpower. She had curled up beside No Moon with her back against the hearth and was already fast asleep, snoring softly.

"I said I would take the first watch." No Moon nodded toward the dozing girl. "You should do the same."

"In a minute," Shaddock said. He noticed that Jerry's body had been disposed of. The demonskin was gone as well. The floor was empty now. "What did you do with it?"

No Moon ignored the question. "Get some rest. It will be dawn soon."

It was just after midnight. Willie had been awake for only an hour or so, for it was her and Hephaestus Sipes's turn to stand watch. No Moon was leaning against the hearth with his head pitched over onto his shoulder, snoozing lightly, looking just like Grandpa Gunther napping after Sunday dinner a lifetime before. Shaddock had made a bed on what remained of the couch, even though the back was shattered and the legs broken so that it leaned drunkenly. He was sprawled out with his feet dangling over the far end, and occasionally he grunted and struck out at enemies that faced him in the battlefield of dreams.

Sipes's head dipped again, and he fought to lift it back up. He was in the chair just across from her, a shotgun in his lap. But despite all his protestations, he couldn't fight off the onslaught of slumber. His eyelids sagged and his head began to dip once again, a protracted process that ended with his chin on his chest. And this time it didn't rise again. Willie didn't bother to wake him. She could stand watch for the both of them. The short rest she'd had was enough for now, and her shoulder was nagging her anyway. She just wondered if the pain would somehow hamper her gunhand—

Something small buzzed through the air, passed a foot or so above her head before hitting the wooden mantel with a soft thud. A bug, she thought as she stood to inspect where it had landed. But then she saw a familiar hilt protruding from the wood there, its small blade buried more than halfway. It was the folding knife she kept in her watch pocket, the one she'd lost in the barn while fighting with . . .

Oh, God, she thought, whirling around and drawing her pistol in a heartbeat. For somehow she expected to find George Atwood come back from the dead, leering at her despite the massive hole in his torso. But she saw that wasn't the case. Kolo was standing in his brother's stead. The breed was wet from head to toe, dripping on the polished hardwood floor, and his clothes were stained with fresh mud. Even his face was streaked with soil, and in the flickering glow of the fire, it almost looked like warpaint. He wasn't threatening her; indeed, if he'd wanted, he could have put the folding knife in her eye as easily as in the mantel. And she knew it. He did not even look angry anymore. But she kept her gun out just the same.

"I am coming with you," he said in a hard-edged voice. "But only if I get the witch."

"Nope," Willie said flatly. "She's mine."

Kolo seemed surprised by that. "But . . . she killed my brother."

There was anger boiling in her suddenly. She looked at his mud-stained face and saw him from earlier in the night, when her arms were bound and that stuttering bastard was pawing her and this man stood and watched.

"She killed my pa," she told him in a low whisper that wouldn't wake the others, "and that's what she'll pay for. Your brother was a no-account clod of horseshit, and he don't deserve avenging. He was a rapist and a murderin' outlaw, as crooked as a barrel of guts. Just like you. And I'll tell you flat out, mister. If that thing hadn't killed him, I woulda. And I'da enjoyed it."

She saw a spark of rage flash in Kolo's cold blue eyes, and the muscles of his hand flexed as if reaching for that great knife on his belt. But her sudden smile caught him off guard.

"Go on," she urged, even as she uncocked the Colt and slid it back into the holster on her thigh. "I'll even give you a head start. Just 'fore I blow your head off."

They stood for a moment staring at each other like statues, the anger between them a palpable thing. Then the half-breed turned and stalked back out through the archway. She heard his boots on the porch this time, followed by the hoofbeats of his horse as he rode away in a fury.

Willie stood there, still seething inside. But at least it took her mind off the pain in her shoulder.

Chapter 18

A rooster crowed from a chicken coop out behind the house, heralding the sunrise and startling all of them in the process. Tol took satisfaction in hearing that sound. So the Devil didn't kill everything on this ranch, he thought. She intended to but she didn't. Another mistake. Their prospects were looking better all the time.

"Rise and shine," Willie said as the cowboy roused from his makeshift bed and rubbed the feeling back into his sore muscles. She had found some coffee in the kitchen—how she'd had the nerve to look was beyond all of them—so a fresh pot hung in the fireplace. She was sipping from a cup over by the window, where the first sparks of morning redness could be seen in the sky. "Clouds have moved on," she said. "Pretty cool, still, but looks like we'll have a clear day for riding."

Tol looked around. No Moon was already up and securing his bedroll. There was no sign of Hephaestus anywhere. "Where'd Sipes go?"

"Wrangling breakfast, I figure. He lit out of here the minute he heard that rooster crow." She moved closer to the sofa and bent for a conspiratorial whisper. "The Indian's acting kinda fidgety," she said softly. Then she went for more coffee, as if afraid the Oglala might hear anything more.

Tol looked at No Moon, and he understood the girl's concern. The Indian's brow was pinched as if in worry, and the lines of fatigue in his face had not been relieved by a few hours sleep. If anything, he looked more haggard than before. Even as he retrieved his bowstring and tossed the makeshift bow into the fire, Shaddock could see that he was favoring his side again, the same injury he'd received from being run down by Kolo. He had been so busy protecting them that he hadn't taken the time to treat himself.

No Moon's concentration broke, and he looked up to find Shaddock watching him. "Did you say something?"

"Nope. Just wondering if you're okay."

He tried to smile, but it came out as a wince. "I will have to be. This is the last of the seven days. We have to ride like the wind if we are to reach the mountains in time." He stood up and shouldered his pouch and his bedding. But when he reached for a third pack, Tol could hear him grunt from the strain. The cowboy moved to put a restraining hand on the Indian's shoulder.

"I'll get it, No Moon. You're carrying enough." He bent down for the bundle, and for the first time he realized that this was not something they'd carried with them before. It was a bedsheet that had probably been retrieved from one of the rooms upstairs. It was rolled up to a length of about two feet, and tied off at either end with leather thongs. "What the hell's in here anyway . . ." he said as he reached down and poked the bundle with a finger. And beneath the flannel sheet he felt something squirm. "Damn!" he said, jumping back. "It's that damned demonskin! I thought you said you'd taken care of that thing!"

"I have," he said calmly. "I readied it for the journey. The skin is a *wakan* thing, Shaddock. There is much magic there."

"Are you crazy? That thing damn near killed us!"

No Moon sighed impatiently as if arguing with a child. "That was Dee-Bo-Ha. The skin did only what her shadow commanded. She is the evil. This is just part of the Great Mystery. And perhaps it can be of help to us."

"Well, to hell with that. I don't want to be near the thing. I ain't carrying that thing, no thank you. I'd just as soon step in shit as—"

"I did not ask you!" the Oglala barked, his face drawn tight in an angry mask. It was the first time he'd raised his voice to either of them, and it took both man and girl aback. But just as quickly as the fury came, it subsided. His face was again stony and implacable, though hints of pain showed through the cracks as he held his injured side. "Willie will carry the skin." He looked at her. "Won't you?"

"Uh . . . yeah. Sure." She walked over to the bundle and picked it up gingerly by the rawhide straps. There was a longer thong tied to one of the end pieces and hanging loose at the other, and she used this to sling the bundle across her back like a quiver of arrows. It wriggled against her, but she forced a smile and said nothing.

Hephaestus Sipes came through the archway carrying two chickens whose necks he'd already wrung. He also had his pistol out. "I hate to tell you'uns this," he said, "but I think something's in the barn with the horses."

Tol felt his insides shrink. What now, he wondered with dread as they all scrambled through the entry hall and out onto the porch. I should have stayed up there with them, he chastised himself. I should have kept an eye on them. But I just thought that after the Devil was gone, we wouldn't have to worry, at least not for one night.

All eyes were on the barn. But in the morning gloom, through the ground fog that had yet to be burned away by the sun, they saw that the structure was no different from the way they left it last night. The doors were still closed. The horses made no sound. "I'm telling you, I heard something," Sipes said defensively. "I was right out back there and I heard one of the horses start to carry on. Startled me, I'll tell you. Almost peed down my leg."

"Well, I don't see nothing," Willie said. "Should we take a look?"

Tol had just finished buckling the gunbelt that he'd grabbed on the run, and he drew one of his big horse pistols. "Might as well. We gotta get 'em saddled and ready to go anyway." He stepped off the porch, still watching the barn. "Willie, you and 'Phaestus go 'round the back. I'll take the front door and—" But he never finished his commands. In midsentence both barn doors came swinging open, their hinges squeaking angrily.

Shaddock and the others stopped in their tracks. Now what, he wondered, looking to No Moon for some clue. The worried look on the Indian's face gave him no solace. Did he know something was coming? Is that what made him lash out just now? "Everybody back into the house," he said, ushering them all onto the porch. "Whatever it is, we'll have a better chance holding it off from in there."

A horse snorted from out in the barn, and another after that. But there were no neighs of terror or panicked thrashings against the stall doors as there had been the night before. Finally, one of the horses came out into the open at a light canter. It was a familiar palomino, and Kolo was perched in the saddle. He was holding the reins of Shaddock's bay mare, already saddled, and in line behind it was little Buck, No Moon's Appaloosa, and Sipes's weathered old buckskin. He brought them straight across the grounds and right up to the hitching posts outside the ranch house, the ones farthest from the bodies on the walk.

Kolo fixed them all with that icy gaze, a white man's eyes in a ruddy native face. But he didn't say a word. He had tied a bandage around the gash in his forehead and washed away the mud of the grave. He had even changed his shirt. He still wore the Bowie on his belt, but now he also wore his brother's six-shooter and carried a Henry rifle that he had taken from one of the dead men. He looked each of them over carefully, but still he remained silent.

No Moon looked at the half-breed. "Have you eaten?" he asked. "We will be traveling very fast and with few stops. We will all need our strength. Come inside, please." He went back into the house, and the others followed behind. But not Kolo. He stayed on his horse, stoic. Unmoving.

They roasted the birds in the fireplace and ate quickly, without words. This was the final day, and that fact was weighing heavily on all of them. Each person was alone with his own thoughts. Even Willie, though hers kept drawing her back to that hitching post outside. She tried to tell herself she was just worried about little Buck, that's all.

When they finished eating, they gathered their gear together and went to mount up. No Moon climbed into his saddle with gritted teeth, refusing to give his pain any voice. Willie went straight to her own pony, but in passing the motionless breed she tossed a bound-up napkin into his lap. "I hope you choke on it," she growled under her breath.

Kolo opened the bundle and found two drumsticks within. He nodded, wolfed them down in the same silence as before.

"Ride hard," No Moon told all of them when he was ready to go. "We have far to travel this day."

When the sun cleared the horizon, it found the ranch empty again. It had returned to the dead, but with five new hands signed on and a sixth in a shallow grave somewhere in the pastures close by. The men and girl who had been there were already a mile or more to the southwest and moving farther away with each passing minute.

They rode all morning, giving their mounts little or no respite. Especially No Moon. He almost stood in the stirrups, his body crouched down near the horse's neck for speed, and Shaddock's bay was hard pressed to keep up. Something was driving the Indian, that much was obvious. He does know something's going to happen, Tol decided. But what?

There was no way to find out now. His voice was drowned out by the thunder of their horses' hooves, and No Moon's attention was focused directly ahead, on something beyond time or distance. Shaddock could only swallow his apprehension and follow along.

The sun edged farther in the sky, reached its zenith, and passed it by. And still they were on the move, their speed diminished only by the obvious fatigue of their mounts. No Moon remained in the lead, pushing his froth-stained Appaloosa as hard as he could, and Tol had already made up his mind that he'd have to jerk the reins from the Indian's hands before his horse collapsed under him. At that moment, No Moon finally eased back in the saddle and slowed his mad flight. They came to a stop in a creek bed whose spring had dried up long ago.

"We will rest the horses here," No Moon said to them in a clipped manner, wheezing slightly from the strain of the ride. Tol would have sworn he saw flecks of blood on the Indian's lips. No Moon dismounted and turned away, busy with pouring canteen water into his upturned derby for the Appaloosa to drink from.

Willie did likewise, letting Buck drink appreciatively

from her cupped hand as she put the canteen to her own lips. But she was conscious all the while of Kolo's stares. He'd watched her all morning, ever since they left the ranch. His glances were furtive at first but became more open, till he was outright defiant about it. As if goading her to face him. Well, if that's the way he wants it, Willie thought, so be it. She turned on him with a fiery glare.

"What the hell are you looking at?" she snapped.

If she expected to be met with like brusqueness, she did not find it. His face remained impassive, his eyes not boring into her but watching with a childlike curiosity. Almost shy in a way, he flinched when she turned on him. But his flinty outlaw nature reasserted itself and he continued his stare. "You didn't know him," he said softly.

"Know who?"

"My brother."

"I knew as much as I needed to know, thank you." She touched her bandaged shoulder and felt the pain as a reminder.

"No, I mean from before. He wasn't always like that. Just in the last couple years. When I was little, George looked out for me. He raised me when my ma died and our pa ran out on us. He was a good man. But folks—white folks—they wouldn't leave us alone. Nobody wanted a half-breed around. And George couldn't hold a job for all the grief they gave him, on account of his funny talk. We didn't start out to be no outlaws. We're just what people made us to be."

Willie was surprised by all the words that seemed to rush from the young man all at once. She could feel a sincerity in his voice, and saw glimmers of pain and humiliation in his eyes, still burning after all these years. For a moment she felt sympathy for this poor soul . . . but then she squeezed her shoulder again and felt the pain flare, gritted her teeth against it. Remember who you're talking to, she snapped. This ain't some poor orphan boy begging for a crust of bread and a warm place to sleep. "I don't care," she said in a merciless whisper. "You might have been the sweetest little babies to ever be weaned from the tit. It don't make no nevermind to me. All I know is you went wrong somewhere along the way. You turned into murderers and cutthroats, and you hurt people. And there ain't no excuse for that."

Kolo drew back as if slapped. There was confusion in his eyes. He obviously hadn't expected such a sharp response. "I . . . I done things I ain't proud of," he said. "I won't deny that. But—"

"But what?" she prodded him. "Speak up. Why is it so important that I know all about you, huh? What do you want from me? Forgiveness, or . . ." Her eyes widened. She looked straight at him, deep into those pale blue eyes. "That's it, isn't it? You want me to forgive you. The both of you."

Kolo's mouth thinned to a line, and his eyes turned cold as ice again. He jerked the reins and led his palomino a short distance away.

"Looks like you hit a raw nerve," said a voice from behind her. Hephaestus Sipes came walking over, leading his buckskin with a hatful of water. "Yeah, I'd say you got that boy plumb figured out."

Willie shook her head. "No, I don't think so. One minute he's hard as nails and one of the devil's own, and the next he wants to be like a lost little boy."

"Well, you gotta know where a fella's been 'fore you can know where he's going. Clancy there may be a little slow and simpleminded at times, and George was certainly the smarter of the two. But the boy was the real leader of that gang. He held us together, treated everybody fair. George, hell, he was a crazy man. Nobody'da followed him at all if it weren't for Kolo. That boy coulda had the whole gang to his ownself, shut George out completely. But that weren't his way. Besides, that loony Atwood was all the family Kolo'd ever known, the only one he ever trusted. And now that part of him's gone. Darlin', I suspect you're right—that boy is pretty much lost. And you can't go on too long in life without trusting somebody—that'll drive you crazy for a fact. So for some reason he's picked you to lead him back, to take his brother's place. But first you gotta forgive him."

Willie scoffed. "Well, if that's what he wants, he can go whistle down the wind. I ain't taking no killer to my bosom.

Why, except for that crazy brother, I doubt he's ever loved anything in his life."

Kolo glanced over at her just then, as if he'd somehow heard her words even over the distance between them. But then he just looked away.

Shaddock led the big bay up the bank of the draw to where No Moon watered down the Appaloosa. The Indian's attention was still focused away on the southwestern horizon. "What is it that's eating you?" the cowboy asked. "You've been as nervous as a whore in church all morning."

The other man glanced at him, pursed his lips as if torn over whether to air his thoughts or not. "Since I awoke," he said in a low tone, "I've felt that something was wrong. I sensed movement in the night. And I heard voices. I was not sure what it meant then. But now I think I know." He pointed off to the horizon. "Do you see that?"

Tol looked there, but he could see nothing. Just a small bank of dark clouds edging the sky some miles away. "You mean those clouds? So what? Another storm coming through?"

No Moon licked his finger and stuck it in the air. "The breeze is blowing to the east. But those clouds aren't moving."

"But what does that mean?"

A chill seemed to go through the Indian as he gave voice to his fears. "I think the Dance has already begun. We will rest here a little while longer. But then we must ride again. We are running out of time."

The mountains were in sight now, a series of jagged spires against the horizon. But the closer they came to that range, the more clearly they could see the storm clouds that roiled directly above. They were deep and angry and moved contrary to the breeze, circling the mountains in a slow spiral, like a whirlpool growing in the heavens themselves. It was like nothing any of the riders had seen before, and it filled them all with a cold sense of dread. But it did not slow their advance. They pushed their loyal steeds with the same anxiousness as before. Maybe even more, since the sun was beginning its evening descent. It would disappear behind those clouds in just a few hours. And that idea held more terror for them than anything else.

No Moon began to ease up on his horse, pulled back on the reins until the wheezing animal was almost at a standstill and those behind him had to do the same or run him down. "What is it?" Shaddock asked in a worried voice.

"Oh, my Lord!" Hephaestus Sipes exclaimed, pinching his nose. For at that moment the breeze picked up and buffeted their hair and clothing, and it brought something else as well. A warm, putrid stench that almost colored the air around them. "Whew!" the bearish man snorted, and even the horses seemed irritated by it. "I ain't smelled nothing that bad in years. We used to get them foul winds in the old days, remember, Tol? When everyone and his dear old granny was a-running to cash in on the buffalo hunts? They'd shoot them big shaggies from horseback and from the tops of trains, thousands of 'em at a time. And then they'd strip off the hides and leave the rest to rot in the heat. Terrible smell. Just terrible." He took his hand from his nose, tested the air again, and almost retched. "But I do believe that this is worse. What the hell could be causing that?"

No Moon reined his horse forward at a cautious walk. Shaddock followed next, and the others fell into line after him. They went another hundred feet or so and found themselves on the top of a rise. The ground sloped sharply downward from there and formed a plain that spread out before them, reaching all the way to the foothills of the mountains.

Except this grassland was colored not green or yellow but a lumpy shade of brown. And it was moving. Undulating like the waves of an inland sea.

Tol couldn't make out much. His eyes were watering too badly from the stink. It was even stronger here, almost overpowering. "What is that down there? Cattle?"

No Moon had a terrible notion. And the flock of buzzards circling above the herd only served to reinforce it. "The Ghost Dance promises the return of the buffalo," he said in a weak voice. He smelled the air, almost gagged. "But the witch never promised they would be alive."

"Buffalo?" Willie was incredulous. She had taken her kerchief from around her neck and tied it over her mouth and nose to fight the stench. The others did likewise. "Are you saying that those things down there are—"

"Still dead," he finished for her.

Tol couldn't believe what lay before him. An entire herd that swept all the way to the mountains, to the left and the right as far as the eye could see. The biggest herd of shaggies he had ever seen. And every one of them rotting on the hoof? "How . . ." he started, but his voice cracked like a fearful old woman's. "How do we get through those things?"

No Moon wasn't paying any attention. "They are not the children of Tatanka the Buffalo. He would not allow such a mockery. These are Dee-Bo-Ha's bastard offspring." Then, to himself, he muttered, "I wish I had more time. Well, the spirits will understand. . . ." He reached into his shoulder pouch and took out the gourd rattle and a small pipe carved from buffalo bone. He carefully filled the pipe bowl with *wacanga* from one of the many hide pockets inside the pouch, then produced a flame to light it, even though Tol knew he had no match in hand or even a stick to rub this time. He closed his eyes and puffed on the pipe and blew a ring of smoke on four occasions, then shook the rattle four times sharply. And then his voice rang in the fetid air, not a cry or shout but a steady droning song in a language that none of them understood. He sang for just a few minutes. Then he opened his eyes and put away the rattle, shook out the pipe and stowed it as well.

"So?"

"Tatanka has answered," No Moon told them. "He understood the urgency of my call, but I am to make twice the offering when next we speak. That is only fair."

"What did he say?" It was Kolo this time, taking the others by surprise.

"That we can go now." The medicine man nudged his horse and the animal reluctantly started toward the lip of the slope.

"Now, wait just a minute!" Tol called, reining his own horse around to block the other's advance. "Just how are we supposed to get to the mountains? Go around? Who knows how far this herd stretches."

No Moon nodded. "You are right. That is why we must go straight through." He looked back at the others. "Do not worry. Tatanka will conceal us from their eyes. He promised me this." He guided his horse forward once again, around the bewildered cowboy and down the hill toward the grazing land of the dead.

The rest hesitated at first. But one by one they slowly followed after him.

Chapter 19

No Moon was anxious. He knew that time was fleeting; one glance at the waning sun told him that. It descended steadily toward the west, and before long it would disappear completely behind the storm clouds that churned above the mountains some two miles distant. He watched those clouds shadowing the crusty peaks below them, saw tendrils of lightning crackle along their dark and swollen bellies. Were they moving faster now? Was the evil building? How far had the Dance progressed, or, more important, how much time did they have left? We've got to reach them, he thought urgently, we have to put a stop to this obscenity before it's too late. But it was no use. There was still that ocean of moving forms that blocked their path, a brown river of decay. The smell was growing worse with each step they took, reinforcing his unease.

Have faith, he counseled himself. You are not without power. You have courageous allies, men and girl alike, who are still at your side despite the horrors that await them. And you have heard the powerful words of Tatanka, the true

spirit of the prairie. The Buffalo God has promised to
conceal you from these false children, these mockeries of his
own kind. His strength will not fail you.

Yes, No Moon agreed, trying to sound convinced. With
the good will of the spirits and the Great Mystery, we will
ford this obstacle. And we will reach them in time. We will.

But despite his assurances, he couldn't shake the cold
touch of fear at the back of his neck.

They rode on in silence, and grew steadily closer to the
herd itself. The buzzards were just overhead now, real
buzzards this time, swimming through the rancid air like
dark spirits. The birds' ranks had swollen in size in the time
it took the riders to come this far. But those numbers were
nothing when compared to the vastness of the herd itself. As
they drew still closer, they found that to their eye the plain
no longer existed; there was only the bison, as multitudinous
as the grass of the prairie and stretching beyond the bounds
of sight. Even the mountains were a distant image now, just
dark and indistinct shapes along the horizon, shimmering in
the fetid vapors that rose up from the body of the herd.
Animal noises came out to greet them: the bawling of cows
and calves, the bellows of irate bulls. But the sounds were
not right—all of them could tell that, even Willie, though
she had never seen or heard a bison in her life. These calls
wavered and warbled and yet they carried not a hint of life.
They were just hollow sounds, echoing across the flatlands
like ghosts to the ear, melding with the drone of a million
flies.

The riders choked down their fear, resisted the charnel
stench, and continued their advance. They didn't stop until
they were no more than a hundred feet from the edge of the
herd. Not till they could clearly see the individual animals.
And those animals could see them.

Two in particular stood on the periphery of that great
gathering, and there was no question that their attention
was focused on the riders. One was a bull that stood some
six feet at its shoulder hump, with a massive head and short
curving horns. A powerful animal, or at least it had been
before its death. The thick pelt of shaggy hair was moldering

with age, and parts of it had already been sloughed off. That revealed the flesh beneath to be shriveled and sagging like a collapsed bladder, and it seemed to writhe before their eyes with parasitic movement. The animal was slow, its actions stiff and stuttering, hindered by muscles long atrophied. But that did not stop it. The bison still pawed the ground and snorted with lordly arrogance, though presence alone was its most terrifying aspect. The cow standing alongside it was not quite as decayed. But its legs were splayed wide and its sides were swelled to grotesque proportions, inflated by the gasses of putrefaction. Both animals watched them with red eyes sunk deep in hollow sockets.

Willie held the reins taut to control little Buck's skittishness. But she knew just how he felt; she could feel the panic rising like bile into the back of her throat, and she pressed the kerchief against her mouth to smother the urge to both retch and scream. And the others reacted the same way, fighting their mounts and their own revulsion. Hephaestus Sipes moaned under his breath and muttered "sweet God amighty" over and over. Kolo looked around anxiously for support, but his brother was nowhere to be found.

Shaddock fidgeted in his saddle and brought up the Sharps in anticipation, even thumbed back the hammer. But No Moon's horse was right beside him, and the Indian put a hand on the cowboy's arm. He didn't say a word, but somehow Shaddock knew to wait.

The red eyes stayed on them, unblinking. But neither of the animals advanced, nor did they mewl a warning to the rest of the walking carrion there. And after a while they just turned away without interest and melded back into the herd.

"What the hell . . ." Tol whispered.

"Tatanka has concealed us," No Moon explained in a low voice. "They look upon us, but we are not what they see. Perhaps they see themselves, or others of their kind. I do not know. But we must take advantage while there is still light. Come." He urged the Appaloosa onward. It did not want to go at first, but the Indian gave it the heel once more and it obeyed. Tol went next, and Kolo after him. Neither Sipes nor Willie were eager to follow along, but the girl held back longer and the bearish old man was forced to go next. By the time her pony fell into line behind the old buckskin, No Moon was already nosing his way into the herd itself.

The buffalo didn't move at first, didn't even seem to notice his presence. But slowly they parted and allowed him just enough room to slip through. The others followed behind, staying as close as they could. Willie brought up the rear, and when it was finally her time, she swallowed her revulsion and urged little Buck forward. But as soon as they were past, the animals along the edge unconsciously closed ranks and she soon found herself hemmed in on three sides by death on the hoof. Why didn't you let the old man go last, she cursed herself, trying to keep her eyes centered solely on Sipes's back. Maybe if I don't look at them, she thought, but just as quickly realized the futility of such a plan. It was like a sailor trying to ignore the churning waves around him. All she could do was close her eyes, but that would cut her off from her friends, and she couldn't risk it. Not for a second. Face it, girl, she told herself. You're in this up to your neck. And it may get worse 'fore it gets any better.

The buzzards were flying lower now, several of them actually swooping down over the backs of the bison and raking their talons through the decomposing hides, as if they were about to snatch the monsters from the ground and carry them away for supper. Tol motioned silently over to the right, where one of the birds had actually landed on the shoulder hump of a large female. Its bald head and beak were thrusting deep into the flesh of the creature it sat on, disappearing completely for a moment, only to jerk back into view with a new morsel hanging from its curved beak. And still the buffalo didn't move. It was not a pleasant sight, and the men started to turn away in disgust. But their eyes were drawn by a new horror. The animal behind the female did not make a sound; it simply lurched up off the ground and onto the other big shaggy as if trying to mount her. But instead, its fur-fringed mouth yawned wide open and clamped down hard on the dining buzzard. It squawked and screamed, its talons raking the muzzle that held it, tearing clear to the bone. But the animal did not flinch or let go. Instead, it sank back into the rest of the herd, dragging the bird along until they were both out of sight. The screeching abruptly stopped. But the other sounds did not. The tearing of flesh. The crackle of small bones breaking. Others were attracted by the scent of blood, and the bison there began fighting among themselves, butting and snapping at one another in a sharklike frenzy. But it was a small meal. The struggle did not last long.

Even after the ranks of the buffalo had calmed and the ocean of brown was once again without ripple or disturbance, Willie and the others were still numbed with dread. No one moved or said a word; they simply stared at the blighted legion around them, more terrified than ever. Buffalo are supposed to graze, aren't they, Willie thought. They eat grass, not meat. The image of those great flat teeth clamping onto the buzzard and dragging it down replayed itself in her mind over and over. Only now the picture had changed, warped itself until she saw the animal rise up and clamp onto her own arm.

Fear coursed through her like specks of ice in the bloodstream. What if the spell wears off, she fretted. If we get right out in the middle and then Tatanka's concealment fades? Or even worse, what if there were never a spell at all? Wouldn't it be just like the witch to try to fool No Moon, to tell him what he wanted to hear and lure them out into the middle of this horde, only to abandon them there and laugh as they were consumed? She shivered at the thought and hugged herself. The ice was spreading.

A shadow fell across her from above, and the beat of wings filled her ears a split second before something struck her head in passing, knocking her hat completely off. She recovered quickly and searched the sky for her attacker, but there were so many of the buzzards circling about that she couldn't be sure which was the culprit. The only thing she could be sure of was the stinging pain in her scalp, and a sticky warmth spreading there. She reached up to touch the tender lacerations, and the fingers of her glove came away crimson. "Bastards," she said, letting irritation force her fear aside for the moment. She put a hand on her gun butt. "Just try that again, I dare you. . . ."

No Moon had started forward again, threading his way

through the bovine ranks, and each rider moved tentatively after him. But they hadn't gone a hundred yards before one of the buzzards swooped down over the herd again. It came in low, just above the sea of molting fur, and veered to sweep right across their line. The half-breed saw a dark blur from the corner of his eye and managed to duck down and avoid talons that slashed at him. And then it was past them and rising back into the crowded sky above. But this time it had not gone unseen. There was no mistaking those long, leathery wings, or the gray-green cast of its reptilian skin. One of Dee-Bo-Ha's gargoyles, just like the spy that Tol had brought down a few days ago.

Willie's eye followed the creature closely as it weaved through the flock of buzzards, and she saw how even those menacing birds of prey shunned it and altered their flight when it came near. But there were some shapes aloft that didn't avoid the lizard thing's company. Three others of its own kind joined it and hung there in the air, beating their wings and glaring down at the riders so far below.

How do they see us? Willie wanted to know. Aren't we protected by Tatanka? Or is that only against the other buffalo?

Her hand was still on her pistol, and she would have drawn and fired already had not the lingering fear of the bison given her pause. How will they react to the gunfire, she wondered. Would it frighten them, stampede the cadaverous beasts in every direction? Or would it attract them, like the squawks of the dying bird seemed to do?

Before she could decide, the silence was shattered by the sharp crack of a rifle shot.

No Moon had watched the lizard things as well. But he had held no such reservations over bringing his Winchester to bear. The blast was jolting in the quiet, and its echo rolled across the plain like low-level thunder. The buffalo were startled, especially since they could not see from whence the sound came. Those nearest drew quickly away from the horses and pawed the ground with uncertainty. But they did not stampede as Willie had hoped. They stayed no farther than thirty feet away, and there they waited.

No Moon fired again, bare moments after the first blast, and this time his aim was on the mark. One of the flying reptiles jerked with the impact of a .44 slug, and its wings folded limply as it fell from the sky like a rock. It came down somewhere out in the thick of the bison horde, and they fell on the tidbit with ravenous abandon. The other three gargoyles did not wait around for the Indian to adjust his aim; they shot off across the sky in three different directions, arcing back and forth until they could lose themselves in the buzzard flock.

"What the hell's going on?" Hephaestus called out, a quake in his voice. He was looking all around in a blind panic. Willie moved her horse up alongside him and drew her pistol, determined to guard the old man against those darting monsters. In fact, all of them moved into a rough circle, covering each other's backs as they scoured the heavens for some sign of their tormentors.

"Look out!" Tolman's warning was almost too late. But No Moon had already sensed the danger bearing down on him, and he dropped low and halfway out of the saddle to avoid it. The hurtling form skimmed just above him, needlelike teeth flashing. But Kolo was next in line, and his big Bowie flashed just the slightest bit faster. The blade sliced through scale and muscle and hollow bone, and the creature spun off in one direction while its wing went another. It came down in the open away from the horses, twitching and flopping in pain. At least until one of the braver bison darted out to grab the lizard and just as quickly drew back into the pack.

The half-breed had no more than cut the beast before another was attacking Shaddock, landing on his shoulder with pin-point accuracy. Talons dug through his coat and deep into his trapezius muscle while teeth sliced his ear open, all in an eye blink, before he could react. He grabbed both of its flapping wings and struggled to hold it away from him, but the creature was strong for its size. It jerked and snapped at his face, its jaws foamy with his own blood.

Willie snapped off a quick shot over Tol's shoulder, completely by instinct. Her round struck home; the lizard bird's head popped like a firecracker, and Shaddock found himself holding aloft a twitching corpse. "Thanks," he nodded, throwing the thing away with disgust.

"One more," No Moon said, levering another round into the Winchester's chamber as he searched the skies above. The buzzards had moved farther away now, frightened by the roar of the guns. But they did not flee. Not when the stink in the air held so much promise. Like the buffalo, they just circled a little farther out, waiting to see what came next.

Whack! The fourth lizard came from nowhere, and it struck Hephaestus Sipes full in the face and dug in deep. Its leathery wings enfolded his head like a shroud, and they couldn't hear the man scream. The force of the attack knocked him sideways out of the saddle, right into Willie, who still rode alongside him. The pony and buckskin both neighed in surprise and jolted forward, out from under their ill-balanced riders, and the two went tumbling to the ground.

Willie was back on her feet quickly, turning to the old man and the thing wrapped tightly around his face. His muffled screams goaded her on as she tore at the thing and wrenched at its wings, prying them back from around his head. Just as quickly, that sinuous neck turned on her and silver eyes bored into her with rage. It bit at her fingers, leaving one of her gloves in tatters until she could release a wing and grab it firmly by the throat. By then Hephaestus himself had a firm hold on it and was pulling it loose, disengaging the hooked talons from his bloodied cheek and brow. When he pulled it far enough away, he produced a knife from his boot and plunged its point into the lizard bird's torso just below the throat and ripped downward. The thing squealed and fought all the harder, but its life was steadily belching out onto the trampled grass, a gout of blood as black as pitch. Its limbs lost their strength and the gutted animal quickly went slack in their hands.

Willie threw it away from them and turned her attention back to Sipes. "Are you all right?"

His face was torn all over, one cheek flayed to the bone, a brow bitten in two. He wiped the blood from his eyes and looked at her, gave a weak and painful grin. At least he hadn't been blinded. But then his crooked eye wandered to the side and saw something, and when it drew enough of his attention, the grin seemed to slide off his face. He was looking past her shoulder.

The ice was back in her blood, freezing her from within. She turned slowly, afraid of what she would see.

Their spooked horses were nowhere to be seen. And neither were their friends, for that matter, at least at first. There were only buffalo surrounding them. Hemming them in. The animals had moved in while they fought the lizard bird, were less than fifteen feet away. Their red eyes watched the two hungrily. Willie searched the herd for some sign of Tol and No Moon and found them off to the left, their mounts caught in the rush of shaggies that had surged forward. They were fighting to get back to her, but the horde was too thick to wade through. She could see the dread etched on the Indian's face, and she knew they could not reach her. Not in time.

Red eyes were still on her, fiery orbs in maggoty sockets. She knew that they saw her now, saw her clearly. The spell was gone, at least for her and Sipes, as long as they were off their mounts.

Or could it be the lizard they're after? It was a desperate thought. But they had gone after the others. Maybe they were smelling the blood. . . . She picked up the carcass and heaved it at the line of rotting bulls as hard as she could. It landed near them with a wet sound. The beasts ignored it. One of them finally did reach out to bite down on a limp wing and pull the small feast back into the pack. But the others did not fight over it. Their gaze would not leave the larger meal to come.

"Here," Hephaestus said as he got to his feet. "You might need this." He had picked up her Colt and was offering it to her. His own horse pistol was out in one hand and his knife in the other. "Not that I figure it'll help much. Sorry bastards, the whole lot of 'em." He looked behind them, found the animals edging closer until he hollered like a madman and forced them back a step or two. He put his back to Willie's so they could watch all sides. "Tol Shaddock!" he yelled. "Goddammit, I don't want to go this way! Get us out of here!"

"We're coming!" the cowboy called in frustration as he kicked at the animals in his path and prodded them with the butt of his Sharps rifle. But the big shaggies didn't acknowledge his presence. Their only thought was getting to the front of the line. Where the food was.

Two of the buffs charged suddenly, but it was only a feinting attack and stopped just short of the two. Willie fired just the same, putting five more rounds into the nearest forehead. From the sound, it was like shooting a rotten melon. The beast shook its head drunkenly and edged back into its place in line, waiting for another chance.

Another charged in from the other side, almost reaching Hephaestus Sipes this time. But the bearlike man hollered and lashed out with all his considerable strength, and the animal retreated with a knife protruding from its eye socket.

"We won't last long this way," Willie said as she flipped open the loading gate of her Colt and took more rounds from the loops on her pistol belt. But she had barely gotten two into the cylinder when the biggest buff on the line, a bull swelled even larger with unvented gases, roared and came straight for her. And this was no feint. It was not going to stop—

Something jolted her from behind, knocked her sideways to the ground, and she feared that another had attacked from her blind side. But she looked up to see that it was only Hephaestus Sipes. He had shoved her out of the bull's path to take its charge head-on himself.

The animal hit him like a freight train, knocking the wind from his lungs and driving him savagely to the ground, trampling him with great splayed hooves. The old man cried out in pain, pointed his gun at the monster that loomed over him. But before he could fire, its long-whiskered jaws clamped down on his entire arm up to the elbow. There was a gnashing sound, the pop and snap of bones grating together. Hephaestus's cries choked off, and all the blood ran from his ashen features. The animal began to shake him like a toy.

Willie leapt to her feet in a panic and jammed her gun into the beast's eye socket, as far and as hard as she could manage, and then fired the only two shots she had. The thunder was muffled, and she saw the rounds come tearing out the far side, carrying shards of bone and ropy tendrils of gray matter as well. But the buff did not let go of Sipes. Instead, it thrashed even harder, butting her aside and wrenching the gun from her hand, leaving it permanently wedged in its own ruined socket.

But Willie wouldn't quit. She threw herself at the animal again and pummeled it with her fists, tearing through the hide and brittle muscle, feeling the mealy life beneath squirm in her hands and the time-softened bone sink in with each blow. But all to no avail. The animal would not release its prey.

Even then, from the corner of her eye she could see the other bison moving, coming closer, one in particular bunching for a charge. And her ears caught the thunder of hooves behind her, bearing down on her. But she wouldn't stop fighting. Not until the end—

An arm snaked out around her middle and caught hold, jerking her off the ground with no warning. Then she was moving, being carried toward the buffalo that she'd seen ready to pounce. She lifted her legs and sailed over the top of him, and the bull looked around stupidly for a meal that had vanished before its eyes.

Kolo gave one last tug and pulled her all the way into the saddle with him. Then he wheeled the palomino into a tight turn, given the scant room the gathering buffs allowed, and headed back for Hephaestus Sipes. But Tolman Shaddock was already there.

The cowboy leaned out of the saddle, held out a hand to the man still struggling on the ground. He could see that Sipes's arm had been all but bitten in two—only strands of muscle and ligament kept him imprisoned now. "Grab hold!" Tol yelled, straining to reach the man.

Hephaestus looked up through a haze of blood and pain. He started to reach out just as another of the dead shaggies nosed its way in and bit down on the man's left leg, just

241

above the ankle, squeezing out another anguished cry. Shaddock wheeled around and fired with the Sharps, blasting a massive hole in the skull of the second animal. But it did not avert the thing's attention.

"Not like this!" Sipes was crying over and over. His eyes found Tol's for a moment and held there, pleading. "Not like this . . ." he said again, a faint whisper this time.

The cowboy understood. He drew one of his big LeMat pistols, aimed carefully, and fired just once. Hephaestus Sipes went limp and cried out no more.

That didn't stop the buffalo. More and more of them crowded around, forcing Tol's horse aside. But he didn't fight them anymore. He turned the bay and rode back to No Moon and the others.

"I couldn't help him," Willie was saying plaintively. "I tried . . . tried . . . . But I couldn't help him . . ." Tears rolled down her cheeks and she buried her face in the half-breed's shoulder. Kolo looked around at the others, unsure of what to do. Finally he just held her and said nothing.

No Moon took up the lead once again, and they slowly threaded their way through the herd toward the mountains, leaving the feeding ground behind. The tumult in the ranks died and the agitation eased, so that the animals were not so bunched up and the horses could move a little faster. Still, it took them almost two hours to navigate the ocean of animals. During that time the sun disappeared behind the storm clouds and took its light with it, leaving a dusky gloom over the land. That rendered the herd a single all-encompassing shadow, so that only their eyes could be seen, glowing in the darkness. But somehow it was better that way; it saved the riders the constant sight of decay. Only the smell remained, and they had almost gotten used to that.

Willie heard a familiar snort behind them, strained her eyes through the gathering gloom to see that loyal Buck was following in their wake. The buckskin was there as well, both still hidden by Tatanka's spell. But she did not consider trying to switch back to her own mount. The fear of losing her balance and falling back into that horde again was too great. She was still shaking from before, and it was a comfort to be riding with Kolo. To not be alone.

For his part, the half-breed did not complain about having to ride double. He also didn't take his arms from around her, not until they reached the far edge of the herd.

The horses stepped anxiously out of those tight and fetid confines, into open ground, where the air was not quite as leaden with the reek of decay. But their riders' relief was tainted by the loss of Sipes. Tolman kept looking back across the herd as if expecting to see some sign of the old man. Willie quietly transferred back to little Buck's saddle, then dug in her pack for the extra Colt that she'd taken from the general store's display. Kolo watched her intently.

No Moon was looking elsewhere. His face was a mask of concentration as he considered the task before them. They stood at the foothills of the mountains, beneath the rocky crags and peaks with slopes coated in bristling pine. But above it all was the gathering storm. It seemed so much larger this close up, its spirals decidedly faster than before. The lightning seared his vision, left a sulfurous odor in the air that was somehow more unsettling than the stink from before. *Has it gone too far? Is there still time, or—*

No, there has to be time! We can still make it if we hurry!

Without warning, the Indian put his heel to the Appaloosa's flanks and bolted toward the hills, taking the others by surprise. They quickly gathered their wits and set off after him, worried by his urgency and at the same time sped on by their desire to leave the filthy herd far behind.

They followed him up a rise that was little more than harsh brush growing from sediment pockets in the austere rock, and the horses found slow going in the loose shale and shifting dirt. No Moon was already over the top and out of their sight. They kept doggedly at it, reaching a flat, shelflike area where scrub grew dense and thorny. Mountains loomed before them, rugged escarpments that eschewed any thought of gradual rise. Instead, they seemed to burst straight upward out of the earth, defying anyone who traveled this way. There were no rises or slopes that the horses could muster, or even handholds within view should they want to climb. The only avenue open to them was a narrow pass between two of the sheer walls.

It was dark in there, infested with shadow. Even when the lightning flashed again, it was too well shaded for any illumination to reach. Tol tried to penetrate the gloom, but it was no use. "Do you suppose he went in there?"

"There's nowhere else he could have gone," Willie answered. "Except down."

There was movement in there, and a form came hurtling out of the shadows toward them. Tol fumbled for his pistol and Willie already had hers in hand when they recognized the Appaloosa. It hurried past them and down the brushy grade, and they noticed that it was barebacked. No saddle. No Indian.

Their eyes returned to the pass, just as a sharp command issued from within. "Hurry!" came No Moon's disembodied voice. "We must go on!"

The three swallowed their apprehension and moved forward, into the gloom.

The Indian was waiting for them within, standing next to his saddle and bedroll. He had discarded all but his shoulder bag, which was ever present on his side. As they drew nearer he pointed to the rear of the pass. The walls came together back there but did not close off entirely. Instead, they formed a steep grade that could be traversed on foot, and at the top was a natural arch of stone through which they could see scrub and weeds growing. The trail he had told them about.

"Leave the horses," he ordered hastily as he started up the rocks with a nimbleness born of urgency. "Tatanka will still protect them. Quickly!" He was already close to the top before they could climb out of the saddle.

Willie started to leave her packs and saddle on little Buck for the trip back. But the doubts were quick to assail her—what if you don't need them again, what if you never come back—and she remembered that No Moon had freed the Appaloosa. It was a harrowing thought. But she agreed that it would be best for little Buck. So she dumped the saddle and gear and took off his bridle as well. "There you go, fella," she said, stroking the tired horse. "Wait for me, okay?"

It snorted softly and nuzzled her cheek.

"Come on, Willie," Tol said. He and Kolo were standing at the edge of the rocks, about to begin their ascent. He was carrying the big Sharps, and the breed had his Henry. Their faces were drawn and serious, and they looked ready for war.

She wondered if she looked anything but scared.

They led the way and she tried to keep up as well as she could. But she hated leaving her faithful pony behind. She kept looking back over her shoulder, only to find that it hadn't turned to run like the Indian's horse or even the bay and palomino. Buck still stood watching after her.

The last time she looked back, the gloom had resettled in her wake and she could barely make out any details down there. But slowly the scene came through to her, and she stood in stunned silence. There was no longer a floor to the pass down there, or a loyal horse waiting for his master. She saw instead a dark and primordial ocean, chopped with waves and foaming against the rock, rising steadily. And to her eye the waters seemed to churn with life, teaming with forms both ancient and arcane, things that had been once and might be again. They rose up from the water to stare at her, serpent creatures with spinal fins and vestigial limbs and wide, soul-hungry eyes. They looked at her and called to her, whispered her name in wet and gurgling voices. . . .

Then there was a flash of lightning from above, searing her vision with just a glimpse. And when she blinked her eyes back into focus and gazed down again, it was a rocky pass and no more. Little Buck still watched after her and snorted with concern.

Settle down, she told herself, trying to chase the clammy chill from her arms and legs. You're seeing things, that's all. Just your imagination. Now, get moving before you lose the others.

She turned to climb again. And that's when she saw Kolo standing just above her. His eyes were wide as saucers. For he had been looking back. He'd seen it too.

Without another word they both hurried after the cowboy in a blind panic.

The sun finally slipped beyond the edge of the world, and night claimed the land once more. But in one area of the Rocky Mountains, it mattered little. For there night had come early. How long it stayed was yet to be decided.

Chapter 20

The storm was building, growing angrier. There was no rain yet, but the wind was certainly picking up. It whistled up the trail behind them and buffeted the four against the rock, making their hurried climb that much more tiring and dangerous to boot. Thunder rolled around them, vibrating the air, sounding to Tolman's ear like rich and mocking laughter. The darkness was deepening as well. The men and girl had stopped once again to wait for the lightning to come, for only then could they see where they were and what lay ahead. Feeling along the trail for where to step had worked so far, but the higher they got, the more treacherous such blind progress became.

Willie's hair was whipping around in the stiff wind, getting into her eyes and mouth. But all she could do was push it away. She had nothing to tie it back with, and no hat to contain it. Her scalp was aching as well where the talons had raked her. But she had to ignore that too. All that was important was getting to the top of the rock they were on.

"How much farther?" she asked, having to put her mouth right to Kolo's ear to be heard over the squall.

"Not much, I think" was all the half-breed could say. "Wait for the lightning again. Then we'll know."

She looked around at Tol, could barely make out his

features next to her in the dark. "Where's No Moon?" she called even louder.

The cowboy pointed ahead of them, knowing that she could barely see his finger and nothing beyond that. "He went on ahead," he wheezed, then punctuated that with a racking cough. "I don't know how that old fart's doing it. After all that riding and now this climb . . . I'm dead on my feet. I don't know if I'll make it much farther. . . ." He propped himself on the barrel of the Sharps and tried to catch his breath, but the wind stole it away again.

Willie took him by the shoulders and shook him. "You can't give up on us!" she said firmly. "We ain't come all this way to give up! You got that? You hear me?"

Before he could answer, there was a flash of lightning, splitting the air around them, and a split second later came the crack of thunder. The bolts grew across the bellies of the clouds like yellow ivy, and their momentary light allowed the three to take stock of their situation.

Since leaving the archway of rock, the trail had led them beyond the foothills and into the heart of the mountain range. It snaked through the cleft between two towering crags and up the shoulder of a pine-covered ridge, to the rocky outcropping they were trying to conquer. The darkness had slowed their progress, but to Tol's mind, it did have its advantages—it concealed the altitude to which they had climbed, kept them from knowing exactly how far they had to fall if one step was in the wrong place. And when this newest bolt lit the scene, he was careful to keep his eyes focused straight ahead. There he saw that their hand-over-hand traveling had not been in vain; the crest of the rock was within sight, no more than twenty yards above them. There was no sign of the Indian, but Tol put that from his mind. He couldn't worry about that now. First things first. Once the lightning was gone and the blackness had returned, he concentrated on the image of their objective, kept that scene lit up in his head and before his mind's eye, searching out the handholds and the good footing.

"Come on," he told the other two as he started once again up the jagged slope. He felt Willie's hand on the back of his gunbelt, and he figured that the breed was probably holding her in turn. He led them forward, but at a brisker pace than before, afraid that the image would fade from his mind and leave them stranded again, waiting for another bolt of illumination. There wasn't time for that. They'd waited long enough. They had to find No Moon.

They were almost to the top when Kolo dug in his heels and pulled them to a halt. "Wait a minute," he called. "What's that sound?"

Tol couldn't hear a thing, not over the whistling of the wind and the rattle of his own breathing. He tried to tune out the former and held his breath, strained his ears . . . but it was no use. All he could make out then was the beat of his own heart.

No, wait. A throbbing sound to be sure, but not the laboring of his pulse. This was steadier, more rhythmic. A drumbeat. Coming from the other side of the rock they were climbing.

Cautiously Tol and the others felt their way to the crest and peeked over at the scene beyond.

The darkness was not so dense or clinging there, so they could make out the geography readily enough. Below was a canyon, looking like a massive wedge had been chopped from the mountains by a titan's ax, leaving a wide meadow in its wake. A gradual slope led down from where they stood, the only obvious path into the canyon. The other walls were very steep, simply tiers of solid stone, and they in turn were whiskery with thick brush and pine saplings where the soil was deep and fertile enough. The far end of the canyon was blocked by yet another natural obelisk that jutted into the stormy sky, this one even higher than they presently were. But all of this was so much detail, mere elements captured in a quick glimpse before the eye was drawn elsewhere, into the cleft below. For that was where the bonfire burned, the huge pyre in the center that chased away the darkness. It was also where the drumbeats and the dancing took place.

Where the tipis were.

The empty valley where Dee-Bo-Ha's two lodges had sat alone was now full with other structures, tipis and wigwams and wikiups, from stone wall to stone wall. Dark figures danced between them and gathered before the fire, smudged with shadow to their distant eyes but clearly bearing full headdresses of feathers and beads. They waved lances and cudgels and bows with fervor and screamed into the night. There were at least a hundred of them, maybe more. No one could see where the drums were playing, but their sound throbbed in the air, growing ever louder.

"Over there," Willie whispered into Tol's ear, and pointed just down the slope from them at a stand of scrub brush. Tol's eye picked out the figure crouched hiding behind it, and he recognized No Moon. They tried to signal him, but the Indian was staring out over the festivities below and not looking back.

They went down the slope after him one at a time, first Willie, then Kolo, with Tol bringing up the rear. Each made it to the cover of the brush. Shaddock crouched next to No Moon and watched the shadowy figures down below, half expecting one to point in their direction and sound the alarm. But they had gone unseen.

"Thought we'd lost you for a minute there," he whispered to the Oglala without having to strain, for they'd left the howling wind on the other side of the rock. He motioned to the scene below. "Is this the Ghost Dance we're supposed to stop? I thought you said there was only nine of these medicine men?"

"Those aren't the medicine men," No Moon said, his voice flat. "This is more of the witch's prophecy. Look at the tipis and their paintings. Do you see? That is not one tribe down there, but many. Lakota, Cheyenne, Arapaho, Pawnee, Blackfoot. Separate tribes, united only in death. This canyon was empty before. They have come here since. Just like the buffalo."

Just like the buffalo. Tol remembered the herd they had passed through, that ocean of molder and decay. He sniffed the air to be sure. It wasn't as strong as before; the winds around these mountains did not let the stench hang in the air like a pall. But it was there nonetheless. His eyes followed the warriors prancing around below, silhouetted against the roar of the flames. He could see the way they moved, the stuttering, jerky quality to each shadowy figure's step. And their screams were hollow. Devoid of life.

His skin began to crawl. He wondered if these dead men dancing below would be as decomposed as the herd had been. If their hair would be sliding off in clumps or their sallow flesh twitching with other forms of life.

"Then where are the medicine men?" Kolo asked.

No Moon pointed to the tower at the other end of the canyon. "Up there."

Shaddock pulled his attention away from the grisly scene that lay below and, in doing so, he finally noticed the rock that the Oglala was referring to. Really noticed it this time. It was a tall plateau that erosion, and perhaps less natural forces, had carved into a wholly unique obelisk. It was round-sided and essentially smooth, except where cracks had occurred all around it and shifted, forming a narrow ledge running clear to the top like the stripes on a barber pole. And at the top . . .

Tol's breath caught. The flat summit of that tower, where the Stairs to Heaven led, was centered exactly beneath the eye of the storm. The cyclonic clouds turned everywhere but there, and when they weren't flashing mightily with lightning, he could see a flickering light playing on them from below. "There's a fire up there," he said slowly. "That's where the Ghost Dance is?"

No Moon nodded. "That is where we must go." He looked at the trail into the valley, where he'd walked to the lodge of Dee-Bo-Ha. It was a natural progression to the Stairs from there. "But if we can't go through the valley . . ." His brow was knitted with frustration.

Shaddock pointed to the walls of the canyon. "What about those ledges? Some of them look like they reach all the way to the other side."

"But they're mostly overgrown," observed Willie. "You can't tell by looking if the stone's weak or barely wide enough for your boot. For all you know, the weeds might be growing out of the rock in places there, with no ledge at all."

"You got a better idea?"

The girl just shrugged and said nothing.

No Moon looked to the tower again, just as a flash of lightning lit his face and illuminated his fear. "We must go now," he said. "Before it is too late!"

"Then that settles it," Tol was adamant. "We'll try the ledges. But we better split up."

"What?" Willie exclaimed.

"Just hear me out, girl. If we all go one way, and that one doesn't pan out, then we've just wasted too much time. And if those things down there are anything like that herd . . . well, maybe it's best if we split up. Then the chances are twice as good that at least some of us will get over there and stop this thing." He looked to No Moon. "What do you think?"

"There is wisdom in your words, Shaddock," the Indian nodded. "I will go with Willie along the south wall." He put a hand on the cowboy's shoulder. "May Wakan Tanka smile upon us this day." He nodded to Willie, and the two of them started across the slope at an angle, headed for the wall.

Are you crazy? Tol asked himself. Splitting up like this? What if you and Kolo make it to the far side and No Moon doesn't? This witch has already raised an entire herd of buffs from the dead, and a small army of Indians from the looks of it. What could you do to stop her without him?

The cowboy set his jaw. Whatever I can, he told himself adamantly. I've got my guns and my wits, and they've got the job done for sixty years. That'll just have to do.

"We'd better get moving," Kolo prodded him. He agreed and followed after the half-breed as they set out across the slope in the opposite direction.

They reached the northern wall of the canyon unseen and settled on the third ledge as their best avenue, about thirty feet above the canyon floor. Tol would have preferred to go higher, as far from the tipis and the dancing phantoms as possible. But the third ledge looked to be the longest, reaching most of the way to the plateau, and its ample overgrowth would give them suitable cover. And that was the most important thing.

"We'd best crawl most of the way," he whispered to the stoic young man with him. "It'll keep us out of sight. And whatever you do, keep your eyes facing forward and don't look down. Remember them damned shaggies. Hell, I got a feeling what's down there'll be even worse. And neither one of us needs to be looking at 'em. Got that?"

The breed nodded sullenly. Then he climbed out onto the ledge with his Henry rifle, dropped down onto his hands and knees, and crawled into the thick of the brush. Tol waited until he had moved some small distance ahead before following.

The overgrowth was dense, and it fought their every movement; thorns snagged at their clothing and stung their hands and faces. But neither of them cried out or gave any voice at all to their discomfort. Each was so choked with fear that it was doubtful they could have made a sound if they'd wanted.

Kolo stopped a moment and tried peering through the brush, but Shaddock prodded him in the rear with his rifle barrel. "I was just looking for Willie," the outlaw whispered defensively.

"Her and the old man can take care of themselves. Now, get moving!"

The cowboy glanced through the weeds and briars himself, just a quick look to gauge how far they had traveled. He could see the bonfire much closer now, almost parallel with them. About halfway, he thought with grim satisfaction. So far, so good. He moved a little farther along, paused with gritted teeth to pluck a tendril of thorns from his cheek. Not much farther . . .

Kolo had stopped up ahead and was waiting for him. "Cover's thin up there," he said, pointing to a ten-foot stretch where the weed growth was scant and the ledge more open to view. The light was brighter there as well, that close to the bonfire. All the better to see them. He looked to Shaddock for a solution.

The old man shrugged. "Ain't much choice. We gotta keep going. Just stay low to the ground and crawl as fast as you can. And don't look down."

The younger man nodded his understanding. He slid the Henry up ahead of him, across the perilous stretch of open rock. Then he got down on his stomach, took a deep breath, and scrambled as quickly as he could, slithering from side to side like a great lizard. He didn't exhale until he was safely on the other side.

The chanting and screams did not change from below. There were no sounds of alarm. Tol sighed. *Now, old man, if only you can move that fast.* He edged out into the open, scrunching down as low as he could manage, and he started across the ledge with his rifle held out before him. *Ten feet, just ten feet, how long can it take? Just keep moving as fast as you can . . .*

And don't look down.

Even as the cautionary words echoed in his mind, he could feel himself disobeying them. His eyes were drawn to the corners by some macabre curiosity that he neither understood nor could control. Before he realized it, he was looking out over the dancing throng below.

In the flickering light of the bonfire, he saw that the red men had become white, stricken with the pallor of death. They stamped and swayed in a staccato manner, fighting the handicaps of atrophy and rigor mortis, and their blighted bodies still bore the marks of their individual fates. Some were pocked with bullet holes that bruised darkly around the edges but no longer bled, while others had been slashed and stabbed by the cavalry saber. But the vast majority of those present bore the mark of a more insidious weapon— the reservation—upon their gaunt and ravaged forms. His eye centered on one of these, a young girl dancing just before the fire and well lit for his observation. It was apparent that she had starved to death; she was barely more than a skeleton wrapped in brittle tissue that cracked at the joints as she jumped and capered about. The child that she clutched to her sagging bosom was just as emaciated, except for his stomach, which was bloated and appeared ready to burst. The sight brought horror to Tolman's mind, not just that they were dancing long after their death but that they should have died in that manner at all.

The girl and child turned just then in their aimless dancing, unconsciously facing him so that the firelight played upon their features. But the cowboy managed to avert his eyes just in time to avoid seeing them. He knew if he saw their sallow and haunted faces, with eyes that glowed red like the herd's, he would not be able to hold back a scream. Get moving, damn you, he cursed himself. Hurry, before they see—

The drumbeats stopped. The singing and crying out stopped. There was a sudden and threatening silence in the canyon.

Oh, my God . . . did they see me? He couldn't bring himself to turn back, to look and find out. He pressed his face into the rock and scrunched back across the ledge until his side was as tight against the wall as he could manage, and he waited and prayed that those damned drums would start again.

But the silence lingered.

Look at them. You have to look . . .

He forced his eye open, turned his face back to the canyon.

The resurrected Indians had all stopped, were standing stark still in the silence. He dreaded their white faces, the red stares, for he knew he would see the same obscene hunger there that had dwelled in the herd. But there were no faces. He could see only the backs of their heads. Their attention was instead focused on the opposite wall of the canyon. He followed their gazes, scanned that tiered escarpment for some movement.

He found it on the fourth ledge. It was the most over-grown, clogged with weeds and small pine saplings, enough for a man to crouch behind. Was that where No Moon and Willie had gone? He wished now that he'd kept an eye on them, so he'd know for sure. He was just about to look elsewhere when his eye noticed the cascade of dirt and pebbles leaking down to the bare ledge below, skittering across the rocks. Then a few more pebbles fell farther along the ledge. Stopped. Still more, even farther.

Something was moving on the ledge. Someone.

What if the Indian doesn't make it? What would you do then?

Tol knew the answer deep down. Against the witch he wouldn't stand a chance. But No Moon would. So it was he who had to reach the tower and its ledge. Shaddock's responsibility was to see that he made it there.

The cowboy got to his feet without a second thought, stood up in plain sight.

Kolo couldn't believe it. "Get down, you old coot!" he growled.

But Shaddock stood his ground. He scanned the figures below and decided on a beefy male this side of the bonfire, wearing the elaborate war bonnet of a high chief, though of what tribe he couldn't be sure. He kept his eye locked on that motionless figure as he thumbed back the hammer on the Sharps and raised it to his shoulder. Then he yelled, "No Moon! Willie! Get moving!" just before he squeezed the trigger.

The roar that followed was nothing compared to the thunder that kept booming around them, and the muzzle fire a poor substitute for the lightning. But it still echoed all around the canyon, and drowned out the thwack of a lead ball striking home. But the damage it caused could not be ignored. The impact jerked the chief clear off his feet and threw him forward. Straight into the bonfire.

There was no scream as Tol half expected. The man he'd shot simply crawled back off the pyre with most of his face now a gaping exit wound and his bonnet aflame, with fire licking along his arms and shoulders as well. He staggered blindly until the flames consumed him and he fell. But even then he crawled about, pitifully silent.

None of the others rushed to his aid. They did not spare a glance in his direction. To a man and woman and child, all had turned completely around to seek out the source of the gunshot, and they found him standing open against the rock three ledges up. Tol stiffened at the sight of them, at the eerie sensation once those unblinking red eyes were riveted to him. He saw in them exactly what he'd expected—the same as the buffalo before them. Hunger, both unnatural and without limit. Only seeing it in human faces was infinitely worse. The thought made his spine go cold and his blood as thick as paste. He just stood and stared back at them, and it wasn't until a hand landed on his shoulder that he could break free of his trance.

Kolo was standing beside him. "You're crazy," he said. "But I think I know what you're getting at." A half grin curled his lip as he levered a round into the Henry's chamber. "So let's buy 'em some time already." He didn't bother to aim. He just started firing into the throng below, picking his targets at random, and kept firing even when he saw that his shots had little effect. The rounds ripped through torsos and shattered limbs and knocked the Indians to the ground. But they would not stay down. When he finally came up empty, there were just as many watching them as when he began.

He immediately began to fumble for extra cartridges. Sweat was beading on his brow, sliding down his face. "What now?" he asked.

Shaddock was searching the far wall, looking for some sign of Willie and No Moon. Had they made it farther along yet? How much more time did they need? But he could find nothing. Damn! He let his gaze drift back across the hellish ranks below, and that's when he saw one of them move. A shirtless brave, his chest shredded by artillery fire and his skull glaring where his scalp had once been, took a tentative step toward the wall where the cowboy and outlaw stood. Then another step. A girl followed him, and an old man after her. Two shriveled children came forward, almost dragging themselves. Grinning.

"Good God, here they come," Kolo whispered. "We've really stepped in it now."

"Start moving," Tol said, reloading the big-bore even as he nudged Kolo along the ledge. His eyes were focused ahead, to the end of the canyon where the base of the plateau lay. "If we can get to that ledge where they can't surround us, we may be able to hold 'em off."

They had just started to wade through the stickers and weeds, knocking them aside with their rifles, when a communal whoop came from below. It must have been the signal to attack, and Tol half expected a hail of arrows to pin them against the rocks. But the dead natives must have been too caught up in the sight of food, for they came scrambling toward the wall, clambering up it hand over hand. Some ran ahead before starting to climb, hoping to head the two off. Tol fired on the run and hit one of them dead center, knocking him off the wall. But the warrior was just as quickly back up and searching for more handholds. The ledges below were swarming with white, grinning faces and fiery eyes, coming steadily closer, and Shaddock came to realize that they weren't going to get out of there alive. This is it, he told himself. Looks like your ass really does belong to ol' Joe Hayes after all. No Moon, you sorry old heathen, I hope to God you make it, 'cause I'd hate to die for nothing.

A pasty hand snaked out from under the bushes and clamped around Shaddock's ankle. He cursed and struck blindly through the foliage, felt the butt of the rifle strike something with a sickening crunch. But it could not stop his momentum or regain his stolen balance. He lurched to his left through the leaves and thorns and fell over the lip of the rocky shelf and into open space. He was not airborne long; he must have struck the next ledge down, but he couldn't be sure because the impact stole his breath and filled his mind with the blinding colors of pain. He bounced along the wall for a split second more, bruising and scraping his limbs, and then he hit the ground. That final blow was punctuated by the distinctive crack of a back breaking. He felt the numbness in his body and limbs and knew what fate had befallen him.

Not like this.

He could still hear Hephaestus Sipes's last words as he was being eaten alive. And now here he was, crippled and helpless, awaiting the same fate. If only Kolo can still see me, he thought, if only he can help me the way I helped Sipes . . .

Someone uttered something guttural in his ear, grunting in a language that he did not understand. It took him by surprise, triggered reflexes that should have been paralyzed. Before he knew it, he was scrambling off to the side, his limbs still numb but functioning just the same. He looked back to where he'd landed, blinking his eyes into focus. And that's when he saw the Indian he'd landed on. The brave was sprawled on his stomach, flailing at the ground, digging at it with his fingernails. For he had not only absorbed the brunt of the cowboy's fall, but it had been his back that had broken so audibly. The fracture must have been clear through, for despite the fact that his upper and lower halves still moved, they could not do so in unison. It merely flailed about uselessly. It couldn't even drag itself after him.

Shaddock regained his wits quickly in the face of such fortune and renewed danger. He looked up to the ledge from whence he'd fallen. He was amazed to see how far up it was and how he'd survived such a fall, as well as escaping the horde of dead bodies that still clung to the escarpment there. They looked up and down now, from Tol to Kolo, as if unsure which direction to go. The half-breed made the decisions for them; he resumed his barrage of gunfire, drew their attention back to him. But a few started down again, intent on the lanky cowboy below.

Kolo's bought you time, urged the voice of reason. Don't waste it. Move now, while you've got a chance.

He looked around, saw that he was lying at the edge of the flat area, faced with a line of cocoonlike tipis. But just beyond them he could see the Stairs to Heaven.

More gunfire reached his ears just then, several shots in rapid succession. But they didn't come from the canyon wall behind him. These issued from far above him, on the tower itself. He turned his eyes skyward, had his vision seared by yet another flash of lightning. In that flash he saw a body leave the ledge up near the top. It hung for a split second before crashing to earth somewhere beyond the canyon. Too fast for Shaddock to make out any details. *No Moon? Willie? No, it couldn't be either of them, it—*

Almost immediately a second figure toppled from that granite spire, just like the one before. But this one needed no lightning to mark its descent. For this body was sheathed in flames. The arms were windmilling madly even as the fiery form disappeared into the darkness outside the canyon.

It wasn't them, Tol concluded quickly. It couldn't be. They ain't dead yet and neither are you, so get up and get moving, dammit, while you got the chance!

He scooped up the empty Sharps and was already moving, weaving through the native tents, not daring to look anywhere but at the base of the tower. He was limping badly from a gash in his knee, and his hip was on fire, maybe even cracked. But you can't stop now, he urged. Keep going, keep going, not much farther . . .

Something moved in the tent directly ahead. The flap was opening even as he drew nearer, and he saw the dark forms that stepped out into the night. They were barely lit by the bonfire behind him, but he could see that they were stout and strong and not as decomposed as most of the others he'd seen so far. These were warriors, and they were armed—one wielded a knotty cudgel, while the other had a long-bladed knife. They saw Shaddock and came forward to meet him.

Kolo's rifle rang out once again. But this time Tol heard the bullet whir over his head like an angry bee, saw it tear the face off one of his assailants. But the blow didn't give the cadaver pause. Instead, the two came straight ahead, moaning hungrily.

Tol's natural panic was drowned beneath a wave of growing anger. I've come too far, he thought. I've seen too much to be stopped now. Not now.

With an animal growl from deep in his throat, he lifted the empty rifle overhead and charged into battle.

Chapter 21

"No Moon! Willie! Run for it!" The crack of the big-bore echoed all around the canyon.

No Moon moved from his crouch. He immediately grabbed Willie by the arm and started through the covering weeds, threading his way around the pine saplings that blocked their way. She fought him at first, for she'd heard the cowboy's bellowed command and wanted some sight of him, and of the outlaw as well. But the Indian drew her relentlessly on and would not let go. He knew what Shaddock had just done for them—it was a noble act, more selfless than he'd known from any man. And in that moment he wanted to be with him, standing shoulder to shoulder with the white warrior, facing whatever fate the Great Mystery had decreed. But he knew they had to go on. If they didn't, Tol's sacrifice would be for nothing. No, he couldn't let this opportunity slip away. The price was too great for that.

He didn't look to the right or the left; he just kept his head down, tried not to make too much noise and bring attention back to them. They moved quickly along the ledge, behind cover as much as possible, until it grew sparse and they found themselves almost to the tower of dark stone. The ledges all but ran together; it was no more than ten feet down a steep slope to the floor of the canyon. When they slipped down, as quietly as possible, neither of them could ignore the scene spread before them.

The resurrected natives were oblivious to the presence of the Oglala and the girl. Their attention was centered elsewhere, on the far wall just as No Moon had expected. For up there in plain view stood Tolman Shaddock and the half-breed, defying the dead things below with their mere presence. Offering themselves up as sacrificial sheep to buy a few moments of time.

Get moving, old man. They're doing this for you.

No Moon took Willie's hand and led her to the base of the Stairs to Heaven. It was just a narrow ledge, no more than a foot at its widest and considerably narrower in some places where the stone had crumbled away. It wound upward around the shaft of the tower at a much steeper angle than he'd previously thought. It would be hard just making their way up it, let alone moving quickly.

Willie clutched at him. "One of them's looking at us!" she said in a terrified whisper, motioning to the closest tipi some fifteen yards away. An old woman stood leaning on a long stick, her face withered yet inset with eyes of fire. She was watching them.

The medicine man put a calming hand on the girl's shoulder, drew her after him as he started up the inclining ledge. "They will not follow here," he assured her. "The magic is too great. They cannot pass. Come, we must hurry!" He let go of her and concentrated on his own ascent, clutching his tender ribs.

Willie was staring across the canyon again. She watched as Kolo began firing the Henry rifle into the crowd. "We can't leave them!" she cried after the old Indian. "They might need our help!"

He turned on her with an angry glare. "That's their concern, girl," he said. "Look up"—he pointed skyward— "up there. That is ours."

She did that, craned her neck back and spied up along the stone wall behind her. The storm clouds were spinning actively, their revolutions growing ever faster, so that she felt immediately dizzy for having cast her eyes to the heavens. Just above the mountain, at the very epicenter of the storm, she saw that the clouds were taking shape, forming a tornadolike funnel. The sight filled her with so much dread that it jolted her when No Moon caught her hand again.

"Now do you see?" he said hurriedly, his breath a wheeze of exhaustion. "This is our task. Yours and mine. Come." He started climbing the ledge once again, and this time Willie followed after him.

She cast one last glance back at the two men on the ledge, saw that the Indians had yet to move toward them. They'll be all right, she thought, trying to sound confident. They're tough, they can handle themselves. She thought of the funnel cloud forming above her and hurried her ascent.

The ledge wound around the rear of the tower, away from the canyon and the limited light that the bonfire provided. In the resulting darkness the two had to slow down and feel their way along, to make sure the stone was secure and solid before committing a foot to it. Just when their advance slowed to a veritable crawl, the lightning would flash and show them the way, when they needed it most. As if . . .

Willie went cold at the thought. As if it's supposed to light the way. What if it's true, she dared to ask. What if the witch is letting us come? What if this is all a trap, and whatever she has waiting for us up there is ten times worse than what Tol is facing even now?

In front of her, No Moon had stopped his advance and crouched against the wall of the tower. She would have bumped into him in the dark had she not heard his breathing, a painful rattle from deep in his lungs. "Are you okay?" she asked, trying to help him up. But the old man just waved her off and stood again under his own power.

"I . . . will make it," he assured her. "Do not worry." He started up the ledge again, motioning for her to follow. Willie wanted to help, to let him lean on her for support. But the trail of stone was too narrow for them to move side by side, and she doubted the proud old man would have allowed her anyway. All she could do was stay close behind him.

The next revolution of the Stairs brought them back to the glow of the bonfire, though it was far below them now, and its dim light cast their shadows on the tower as looming monstrosities. Willie noticed just how far they had come; the canyon walls were well below them, and they were nearly as high as the rocky ridge they had crested when they first set eyes on this towering plateau. They were no longer protected from the wind—up here it lashed at them mercilessly, threatened to flick them into space like bothersome insects. Willie wiped the hair from her eyes and pressed herself flat against the smooth walls of the obelisk, or as flat as she could manage with the demonskin still strapped to her back. It wriggled madly against her like a puppy eager to be put down, and if she'd given it any thought, she might have loosened the straps and let the horrid bundle fall. But her mind was elsewhere.

Listening to the gunfire from below.

Her eyes started to stray beyond the lip of stone where she stood, but she managed to catch herself. *Don't look down, whatever you do. It's a long drop from here and you never have been too good with heights. And besides, you don't want to see what's going on down there. You may not like what you find. Just remember, Tolman Shaddock was fighting and surviving before you were ever born. And as for that lawless half-breed, why would you worry about him anyway? It's not like he means anything to you, right? You got a task to do, just like No Moon said. So keep your mind on that and don't look down.*

But despite her own advice, her eyes kept creeping, inch by inch, to the ledge and beyond. She had to wrench them away by sheer force of will. She looked instead out into the darkness, out past the ceiling of clouds just above. To her surprise, she could see beyond the initial peaks that they had passed in coming here, all the way to the plains so recently traveled. The sky there was crystal-clear, and that left the earth below bathed in star- and moonlight. She could make out the sea of buffalo, even larger than before. And past that . . . there were lights. Hundreds of flickering campfires lit the open countryside for miles, growing in number even as she watched. And those lights let her see the tipis. So many of them . . . just like the canyon below. But on a far grander scale.

Lightning flashed just then, a stuttering bolt that seared her vision twice. But in the scant time between those arcs of bright yellow, it seemed as if the world changed before her eyes. One minute the plain was there, repopulated. The next it was gone, lost beneath the same primordial ocean she had seen rising in the foothills earlier. There was the second flash, and the world was back to normal, or at least the nightmarish semblance she'd come to expect. The buffalo were back, and the tipis. And their number was still growing.

She forced her eyes shut, squeezed them until tears broke and slid down her cheeks. This is our task, she told herself over and over as she felt her way along the ledge. It isn't over yet. We can still—

She bumped into something. No Moon, standing frozen against the rock. "You see it too?" she asked, sure that he was looking out beyond the storm as well, paralyzed by the scene sprawled beneath the dark mantle of night. But his eyes were elsewhere. Locked on the ledge farther along. She followed his gaze and saw the dark pair blocking their advance.

Surely more of the same, she thought. Death shambling on two feet, cadavers like those below who did not have the good sense to rot in peace. But a scar of lightning across the bloated heavens showed these things to be different, at least in their dress. Both were swathed from head to foot in long woolen robes. Their faces were hidden deep in shadowy hoods, their hands likewise lost in the folds of voluminous sleeves. Only steel issued from the latter, reflecting the light of the bonfire from below. Each held a dagger at the ready, and their feral hissing sounds seemed ill-fit for human vocal cords. They stalked down the ledge in single file, preparing to strike.

Willie pushed No Moon back against the rock and drew her pistol in a single smooth motion, fired as soon as the Colt's barrel cleared the leather. It struck the first of the two robed ones in the upper chest and jolted him, halted his advance by a step. But he came straight on again.

She fired again, putting two more into the heart area. When the thing still didn't stop, she aimed higher and emptied the rest straight into the darkened hood at almost point-blank range. But their assailant did not stop. Frantically she drew back the gun, prepared to bash in whatever skull lurked beneath those folds of dark cloth. But No Moon just brushed her back against the tower, letting the robed figure stagger blindly past them. It went off the ledge and into space. And it did not utter a sound all the way down.

The second attacker was coming now, mere steps behind the first, and Willie knew there wasn't enough time to reload. She fumbled for the knife in her boot even as the robed one lunged with his own, aiming for No Moon, since he was the closest. But the blade did not reach its target. The exhausted old man moved much faster than she expected; he caught the wrist of the knife hand and held it, struggled to keep the blade mere inches from his chest. The sleeve slid back from the bare arm that he kept imprisoned, and they both saw its gray-green hue, how the flesh overlapped itself in small reptilian scales. No Moon sneered; another of the witch's inhuman servants. The notion sparked a revulsion that gave him new strength. He not only held the knife at bay now, but began to mutter under his breath in the Lakota tongue.

Willie was just moving to swat the robed attacker with her Colt when the Indian's curious behavior stopped her in her tracks. More magic, she thought, and hesitated to get closer for fear of spoiling whatever he had in mind. The way he was talking seemed vaguely familiar to her somehow.

She noticed that he was not just holding the thing's

mottled wrist but rubbing it as well, kneading his thumb and fingers against that glistening lizard skin. She remembered seeing him do that along the Platte River, when he twisted a twig between his fingers.

And started a fire.

The blue flame came to life with a whoosh, enveloping the talon and knife alike, melting them together into a lump of tissue and steel. It took a moment for the shock and pain to travel; then the creature threw back its head and hissed in agony. The thrashing dislodged its dark hood and they saw its face, the familiar snout with its needled teeth, the slitted lizard eyes. It was an obvious relative to the flying gargoyles, or perhaps one of their very own somehow warped by the witch's foul sorcery. But whatever its genesis, the flame was proving it mortal enough.

No Moon let go of it, allowing the blue fire to race down its arm to the sleeve of its robe. Once the fabric was ignited, there was no stopping the flame. The creature was soon sheathed in a cocoon of crackling heat. Its cries dried up with the shriveling of its lungs, so when it finally staggered beyond the ledge and plummeted into the darkness, it fell as silently as its cohort.

"We must hurry!" whispered No Moon, looking anxiously at the roiling sky above. The battle, which had lasted scant seconds, seemed to have stoked a fire of urgency in him, for he drew her up the narrow path after him, not even allowing her time to reload. Not until they had made another revolution of the obelisk and found themselves on the dark side once again, just below the flat summit itself, did she manage to rearm her gun. Another ten feet was all it would take. Ten feet . . .

The wind whistled around them, harsh and unrelenting. But somehow they managed to hear something else above its squall. A low, tremorous drone. Voices, intermingled and chanting to an unknown rhythm. No Moon did not recognize the tongue in which they sang, but something about it sent shivers racing along his spine. His eyes drifted up to the storm once again, and this time he noticed that the lightning and thunder came in direct relation to that very song; they mimicked its pitch and resonance, accentuated the power in its mysterious words. They are doing this, he knew. The medicine men. *You must stop them, open their eyes to the trickery that has been done them. Before it is too late . . .*

Willie had just loaded the last cartridge and snapped shut the Colt's loading gate when No Moon motioned her near. He took a knife from his belt, not the spirit stone but a simple steel blade, and he used it to slice the straps that held the bundle on her back. He slit open the sheet as well, revealing the oozing black of Siyoko's skin, which he allowed the wind to help unfurl before him. Then he held it out to her. "Put it around you," he said into her ear.

The girl wrinkled her nose at the prospect. "That thing? It's bad enough to carry it. But to wear it? I don't think so."

"Do it. There is great magic in this hide. It may yet protect you from what we will face up there."

She pushed his own hands back toward him. "Then you wear it. It'll give you a better chance against her."

"You need it more."

He would not take no for an answer; Willie could see that in his eyes. So she sighed, allowed him to drape the horrid thing around her shoulders, tying the sleevelike arms around her neck. The thing was large enough to envelop her completely with its legs dragging the ground behind her. And it seemed to wriggle with glee at her closeness. Willie winced. It was like wearing a coat of maggots. But she kept her chin high and gave No Moon an appreciative nod. "What about you?" she asked. "Won't you need some protection?"

He touched the bag on his shoulder. "I have my ways. I have Elya-eh, who has helped me before and may yet again. And my *sicun* is still full of power. And I have the spirit knife given me by my father, the greatest of the Oglala shamans, he who was killed by the great white warrior Shaddock. And now that same warrior has given himself for us. These are *wakan* things, Willie. Magic. So we will not be fighting alone. There is more power around us this night than the evil you see here." He managed a smile, touched her on the shoulder. "Do not worry, granddaughter."

Willie tried to look confident. But all she could manage was worry.

The Indian straightened and took a deep breath, ignored the rasping pain in his side. They stalked quietly up the ledge until they were on the flat table of rock itself, and the lightning flashed to herald their arrival.

Chapter 22

There was no wind on the plateau.

Willie and No Moon realized it as soon as they set foot on that flat expanse of ancient rock. It was like passing over the threshold between worlds; the buffeting ceased immediately and the howls changed as well, muffled as if by an invisible wall. An eerie stillness took its place, so sharp and crystalline that it seemed to magnify the sounds that remained. The crackle of flames. The chanting.

The summit of the tower was perfectly flat, more than one hundred feet from side to side. There was a circle painted in the center of the rock, with a second circle within that, and between their two lines were strange signs and symbols that No Moon did not recognize. At the heart of the inner sphere was a bonfire whose flames leapt high into the air, defying the winds that swirled everywhere but there. Surrounding that pyre, moving within the confines of the painted circles, were shamans from nine of the great western tribes. Their naked bodies were tattooed with the same runic characters that lay beneath their feet. Each of the old men looked weak, exhausted; their trudging movements could barely be called a dance. But their voices were still strong, calling out into the night with their mysterious song, and their faces were still twisted in fury. Indeed, their anger remained a palpable thing. No Moon could feel it heavy in the air of the plateau. It and something more . . .

"Up there," Willie whispered from beside him. He looked

up to see the funnel of clouds that they had witnessed from the ledge below. It was becoming pronounced, lowering slowly but surely. Its focus was the fire directly below it, at the center of the circles and the dancing men.

No Moon rushed forward, tried to look directly into the faces of the men as they danced along. "Stop this!" he called to the Cheyenne medicine men, first Cold Eyes and then Buffalo Hump. "You do not know what you are doing! The woman has tricked you!"

But he could not gain their attention. He started to step into the circle to face them but thought better of it. He was wary of those forboding symbols. So instead he grasped the chin of the next man in line, the Crow called Smoke, and turned it to face him. To his dismay, the man's eyes were glazed over, blind to him. Whatever Smoke was seeing, whatever twisted his face so, came not from without but within.

"They cannot hear you, Oglala" came a soft, sultry voice. He looked up, through the ring of dancers, and finally saw someone else standing on the far side of the plateau. She came out from behind them and let his eyes, and Willie's, fall on her unfettered.

Willie wasn't sure just what she was seeing. The woman before them was dressed in a long robe of eagle feathers that swept the ground at her feet, so only her face was visible. But that image seemed to shift as she watched. One moment it was Indian in hue and structure, the high cheekbones and straight nose, turned up just at the end. But then the raven hair shifted a bit, lightened to an auburn like her own and the skin color paled as well, became a rosy pink with freckles across the nose and cheeks. And when the woman smiled it was warm, almost loving, just like how Ma used to—

No! The girl gritted her teeth, felt the anger rising within her. *That isn't my mother. My mother's dead and you can't fool me, you bitch. So just stop it right now.*

Dee-Bo-Ha's countenance shifted again, back to the ruddy complexion and noble features. She was still beautiful, almost too much so. But Willie knew that this was just another of her many faces. And in knowing, she could look beyond it to what lay beneath.

The witch must have sensed this, for she fixed the girl with a lethal glare.

"Let them go," said No Moon in a threatening tone.

"I do not hold them." Dee-Bo-Ha gave a wan smile. "They do what they wish."

"But only after you've tricked them. Are the pictures still in their minds? Enough injustice and slaughter to fuel their anger, to make them useful to you? I can allow this no longer."

She fixed him with her arrogant gaze. "You have no say in the matter. Besides, the ceremony is almost complete. It is good that you have come, Oglala. You are just in time to see the return of the Old. And the coming of the New." She looked up reverently to the roiling heavens above.

Willie's lips pulled back from her teeth in a silent snarl. Her anger had reached its zenith, the spark fanned to a white-hot flame. The evil behind her father's murder now had a face that she could see, and that allowed the grief and loss and frustration to come together in one concentrated emotion—rage. She picked out a target on the woman's feathered robe, a spot right between her too-damned-perfect breasts. And then she raised her pistol to fire.

But inexplicably there was no hammer to cock; instead, something pricked the pad of her thumb, and the pain brought her attention to her extended hand, and to what had once been a Colt Peacemaker. Now there was something else clutched in her fist—coils of sinuous muscle and dark green scale, at least three times around the width of her hand. Along its back was the flexible barbed fin that had stung her. Where the barrel should have been was now a long, serpentine neck, one that turned on itself so the wedge-shaped head could look back at her with wide and hungry eyes.

My God, she gasped. For she had seen the thing before. It was one of the snakelike creatures she had seen in the foothills, rising from that black abyss of an ocean.

The thing seemed to acknowledge her recognition. It smiled at her, showing multiple rows of razor-edged teeth. And then like the snap of a whip it struck, burying those same teeth in the fat of her palm.

"Oh, God!" she squealed, her eyes filling with tears as the

pain rose up her arm like liquid fire. She could feel the teeth ripping through the thick muscle of her hand, notching the bone beneath. And still it chewed even harder, sinking yet another row of teeth into her flesh, until she had to grab at its flat head to keep it from thrashing about and tearing her hand to pieces. "God, it hurts!" she cried. "Get it off me!" The sight of her own blood spurting all around, staining her jeans and coat, panicked her all the more. Her vision began to swim, and her legs buckled. That's when No Moon caught her.

The Indian immediately grabbed for her wrist, caught the snakelike thing right behind its head. He tried to strangle it, but the flesh was malleable, like wet clay. It just oozed between his fingers and continued to chew on her. In desperation he dug his thumbs into those wide, colorless eyes, pushed even harder until he felt them squish and finally pop. The thing opened its mouth and made a horrid gurgling sound, and he immediately jerked it away from her, letting Willie fall to the ground in numbed shock. The thing was still writhing and fighting him, trying to wrap its coils around his arm or turn its head far enough for the teeth to find purchase. He didn't have time to summon the fire spirit as he had with the robed thing on the ledge. He just wanted to be rid of this foul animal. So he turned and flung it as hard as he could across the plateau, directly at the witch.

Dee-Bo-Ha showed no alarm. She simply reached up and caught the serpent, then casually rolled it into a ball. When she opened her hands again, it was not to reveal green scales but blued steel. The inanimate form she held was that of a Colt Peacemaker, nothing more.

Willie watched her in disbelief, then looked again at her blood-stained hand. The bite wound in the palm was vicious and gaping, still bubbling blood. It was no illusion. She pinched it beneath her other arm and gritted her teeth, not only against the pain, but the beautiful witch's mocking laughter.

"Guns are very dangerous, my dear," she said. "You could have been hurt." Then Dee-Bo-Ha laughed all the harder and tossed the revolver over the side of the cliff. When she turned to No Moon, she no longer showed even the pretense of humor. "You are powerful, Oglala. But you are nothing compared to me."

He was not cowed by her boasts. "We shall see" was all he said.

The woman sneered in contempt. She took a deep breath and blew it out, directly at them. It came across the open space between them not as a breath but as a plume of crackling flame. Willie barely had time to duck her head and throw her arms up in defense, unwittingly covering herself with the still-squirming skin she'd almost forgotten about. The air hissed all around her and she could feel the heat building, stealing her breath. It was gone as quickly as it came. She lowered the living cloak.

Wisps of exposed hair on her scalp had been singed to the root, and a few of them still burned, so that she had to swat at them to put them out. But otherwise she was unharmed. The skin had indeed saved her, just as No Moon knew it would.

No Moon! Oh, no, she thought as she turned to him, remembering how she'd urged him to take the skin instead of her. He'd been standing right next to her . . . there was no way he could have avoided it in time. Indeed, he had not. Her eyes found him singed black and smoking. At least his clothes were. Even the derby on his head. But his skin and hair were unmarked.

I have my ways, Willie remembered him saying. And now she believed it.

"You will have to do better than that, woman," he called to Dee-Bo-Ha. Willie saw that even the witch wore a shocked expression.

Dee-Bo-Ha wasted no more time with boasts; her jaw seemed set in desperation as she muttered an incantation beneath her breath and extended a hand into the air before her, then slowly clenched the fingers together in a squeezing motion. Willie gasped, grabbing for her throat. It felt as if she were being strangled, even though there was nothing around her neck. Nothing touching her at all. But her air was being closed off just the same. She saw Dee-Bo-Ha's fist tightened and tried to rise, to run for the woman who was killing her. But she could barely make it to her knees.

No Moon felt the stricture of magic as well, gulped in what breath he could. But he would not go down. Instead, he started across the plateau in strong, measured strides, and drew his hunting knife as he went. Dee-Bo-Ha's face drained of color, and this time it was not an illusory effect; the cords in her neck were straining from the pressure she exerted in squeezing the open air, an effect mimicked by her magic. Yet it still did not stop the Oglala. She knew then that she had underestimated her opponent once again, and this time she may not have a second chance.

No Moon's quickness closed the distance between them, and he was almost on her. He even reached out, took hold of her velvet-soft throat. But then . . . pain. The same he had felt all during this journey, ever since the half-breed's horse had driven him to the ground. It flared in his ribs once again, but this time it was stronger, more intense than ever. And it grew. It moved up across his chest and infected his heart as well, felt as if a spike had been driven through his sternum. His left arm throbbed without mercy and then went numb, dropped to his side. Then his other arm. The knife clattered to the ground, useless. There was no air, none to breathe, and his temples throbbed to the irregular drumbeat of his own heart. He sank to his knees and then onto his side, wincing from the pain.

Air came finally as the spell on No Moon and Willie was released; he hungrily gulped it in. But that did not ease the fire in his rib cage. He looked up, saw a face looming over him, backlit by flashes of lightning. . . .

Dee-Bo-Ha wore a gloating look of victory, even if it wasn't her hand that had brought him down. "What's wrong, old man?" she chuckled. "You look ill. But do not worry. I will not let you die. Not yet. Not until I have had my fun. Now, what should we do first? Should I take away your skin, peel you one layer at a time? Or I could turn you inside out, leave you lying in a puddle for the birds to pick at. Or perhaps you should go with the others. For I promised the master ten souls in the first place and—"

She was interrupted by another clap of thunder. But this one was not muffled by whatever unseen wall surrounded the plateau. It was loud and sharp, leaving a ringing in the ears that masked the *thwack* of a heavy bullet striking Dee-Bo-Ha's chest. The witch was jerked out of No Moon's line of sight.

The chanting abruptly stopped, and the dancing as well. The medicine men stood frozen in the glare of the bonfire. But Willie noticed that the men were shivering where they had not before. One of them moved his hands down to cover his nakedness while others began to look hesitantly around them, wide-eyed, as if awakened from a deep sleep. The Crow that No Moon had spoken to before now noticed the blood paintings on his scarred flesh and wiped at them in disgust. The spell over them was broken.

But by whom?

Willie turned to where she'd seen a momentary flash from the corner of her eye. But there was no one else on the plateau. Nothing there at all . . . except the barrel of a rifle. A yawning big-bore, leveled on the very edge of the rock, still smoking.

As she watched, a familiar face peeked up over that rim. Tolman Shaddock limped the rest of the way up the Stairs to Heaven and onto the rocky table itself, leaning on the Sharps for support. He was battered and bruised, his gray hair pulled loose in tufts and his mustache crusted with blood. His coat hung about his lean frame in tatters. But he was very much alive.

He stopped, took the time to lever open the breech of the rifle, expelled an empty casing, and loaded a fresh round. He looked at Willie and nodded a greeting, let a smile curl the corner of his mouth to see that she was still alive. But his business was not finished. He hobbled across the open rock and approached the prostrate form of Dee-Bo-Ha.

The witch was sprawled on her back, the feathered robe thrown wide to reveal her exquisite nakedness beneath. It also showed the sizable hole in her left breast. Clearly a mortal wound. Except this woman was still moving. She writhed drunkenly, her eyes wide with disbelief, glazed by that hated sensation of pain.

She fought to rise. Shaddock stepped back from her, the Sharps leveled at his hip as she made it to her knees, so the blood ran down her bare stomach in a glistening stream.

"No . . ." she stammered, her voice wheezing from a deflated lung. As she spoke again, her eyes were not on Tol. They rose to the churning heavens above. "Please!" she beseeched the tempest. "You promised me life! You . . . promised me . . . flesh! I have served you . . . well, I have done . . . all that was asked. Do not let them take this away! I . . . want to live! Have mercy! Have—"

She never finished her plea. Shaddock raised the rifle and fired, putting a .50 round into her forehead. At that range it didn't leave much behind.

The body jerked and went limp, crumpled backward. But something else was left in its wake.

The thing was shimmering and translucent, a bit of temporal mist that somehow held shape and substance. Tol remembered the spirits in Barlow, the ones that consumed Russell Ducane's soul and reshaped his body. He knew that this was another of their kind, and always had been. So that was what she had meant by being promised flesh—the witch's humanity had been a ruse all along. This was her true identity; a spectral creature wholly different from the fleshly disguise it had taken on. There was not a hint of humanity in the visage before them; instead, it was a wispy amalgam of animal shapes every bit as horrifying as They-Who-Follow-Behind. The face was long and lupine, with flicking ears and a tooth-lined muzzle. The arms were equally thin and curiously manlike, save for the talons at the end of each finger. All of this was covered in dense, bristling fur, at least halfway down the torso. There the coarse dog hair gave way to dark scales that glistened in the firelight, and they in turn sheathed the long, sinuous coils of a serpent.

The *nagi* that had been Dee-Bo-Ha writhed in its impotence and defeat. It turned its eyes skyward and wailed pitifully, finishing a plea that had started in its previous form. But when that was over, those wide and soulless eyes turned on Shaddock, and there was no mistaking the vengeful anger it their gaze. The image of Russell Ducane's screaming soul being consumed was fresh in his mind as Shaddock started to back away, knowing even as he did that there was nowhere he could run from such a being.

The *nagi* hissed, coiled itself as if to strike. But the blade of a stone knife slashed through its torso from behind, dissecting it somewhere between the jackal and snake segments. The phantom separated, screaming, and then it faded from view. That left only No Moon, wavering on unsteady legs. He wheezed painfully with a hand still clenched to his chest. But he stood nonetheless.

"Tol!" Willie called. She ran to Shaddock's side and threw her arms around him, wincing at the pain it caused her hand. "I didn't think I'd ever see you again."

"Well, I had a helluva time catching up to you'uns," he sighed. "I'm just glad I got here in time."

She pulled away from him, asked hopefully, "What about Kolo? Is he—"

The cowboy frowned. "The shooting stopped before I was halfway up here," he whispered. "I could hear 'em whooping and screaming down there, but . . ."

He didn't bother finishing. He knew she understood; he could see the tears welling in her eyes. He didn't know she'd had such feelings for the breed. From the way she wiped her face and stared at the wetness on her hand, he doubted that she'd realized it either.

No Moon stood over the witch's dead body, facing the naked and shivering medicine men. He was steadier now; the pain in his chest had subsided, at least to a point where he could tolerate it. But his left arm was still without feeling, hanging useless at his side. He slipped the spirit knife back into the sheath on the rear of his belt, then pointed to the corpse. "Look closely," he told the silent old men. "See what your anger and your thirst for vengeance brought about. Look how you almost damned us all."

"No Moon!" Shaddock was pointing up at the clouds above them. "The witch is dead, isn't she? Why isn't that going away?"

It was true. The clouds above were still churning and spinning, just as before. Perhaps even faster now. And the twisterlike cone was still descending toward the center of the mystic circles. No Moon watched, and he remembered snatches of Dee-Bo-Ha's words. They hadn't meant anything to him at the time. But now their meaning was becoming more and more apparent. *Promised my master ten souls . . . the return of the Old, and the coming of the New . . .*

Something's coming, No Moon realized with dread. The witch's "master" is coming!

"It's supposed to be over," Willie stammered as her fear continued to grow. "Isn't it over?"

The old Indian shook his head. "The ceremony has gone too far," he said, swallowing hard. He looked at her, the color draining from his face. "I fear it is just beginning."

Chapter 23

The men and girl on the plateau stood dumbfounded. They watched in numbed silence as the dark clouds twisted together at their center and lowered a tapering tendril down toward them. The lightning flashed like the blink of a giant eye, and when the thunder came again, Tol would have sworn the laughter in it had returned, rich and mocking.

"This is it, then," Willie whispered. "We've failed. All this was for nothing."

No Moon gave her a quizzical look as if unable to comprehend the surrender in her words. Then he forced a smile. "The spirits have been with us this far," he said. "Perhaps they will stay with us yet." He turned on the trembling men behind him. "We are the most powerful of ten tribes. We may yet hold this evil in check."

"But how?" asked the one called Atawai of the Navaho far to the south. "We are as bare as birth, without our tokens and fetishes. What magic could we bring to bear against such as this?"

The Oglala limped over to him, fixed him with a cold glare. "You summoned the damned thing with nothing, did you not? You can fight it the same way. All of you, stand before me here. And put out your hands."

The naked old men did as they were told. In the flickering light of the bonfire they stood in a line, and each extended his right hand, palm up. No Moon picked up his hunting knife where he'd dropped it earlier and limped to the head of the line.

"Each of you knows of the circles of protection against spirits who would do us harm. We have different patrons whom we call on for strengthening such bonds, but the magic is still the same." He looked up to the descending funnel. "We are of different tribes. But to whatever is coming, we are only one. We are men. And our blood will be as one."

With that, he upended the knife and drew the blade along the line of open hands, slicing the palm of each one in turn. The old men flinched but did not cry out; they accepted the Oglala's word and held true.

When the other nine were finished, No Moon cut his own hand. As the blood seeped out and ran down his wrist, he held it aloft for all of them to see. "Draw a new circle, around the witch's own. Hurry, while there is time!"

The ten of them fanned out around the mystic spheres where the dance had taken place, and each used his lacerated hand to smear an arc of redness on the rock. Some were shakier than others from the cold and their own terror, but the finished lines, when connected, formed a circle to match the two within. Then, as if each sensed what the Oglala would instruct next, they sat down cross-legged outside the lines they had just drawn. No Moon did the same, even though it seemed to make his pain flare. He gritted his teeth and tried to force it aside.

"Call to your patrons," he told them. There was urgency in his voice, for the swirls of descending cloud were already touching the ground around the fire. "Summon any spirits who might give aid. We will need them now as never before." Then he closed his eyes and began to chant.

They all did. They were low murmurs at first, mutterings in ten different tongues that could be discerned only by the ears of each speaker. But their pitch and rhythm melded with time and the words all seemed to slur together, at least to the other two watching. They became a soft trilling sound, a hum of power.

"Look!" Willie whispered to the cowboy standing beside her. She pointed to the circle of blood, and even Tol gasped when he saw that it was glowing. First a dull red color and then brightening to blue and then finally white-hot. Willie could feel the energy emanating from the Indians' circle of protection. But would it be enough? She pulled herself close to Tol. "What happens now?" she asked.

"I don't know, missy," the lanky old man replied. "But I don't think it'd hurt to pray a little."

The revolving column of smokelike darkness lowered into the center circle, surrounding the bonfire, and having that light at its core now changed the shade of the cloud from ominous black to ethereal white, almost glowing. The inner sphere filled quite quickly and spilled over into the second, obscuring the painted symbols and icons there. Then on past the second circle, beyond the perimeter of the Ghost Dance itself. But the cloud halted once it reached the bloodline. Whispery tendrils of fog extended out like delicate fingers and prodded along the line, touched at it. But they did not pass over.

The cloud looked like a cylinder of milky whiteness spinning before them now, reaching high into the gathering dark above. Lightning flashed in there, within the circle itself, and the center rumbled with thunder. But it was no longer laughing. This was a growl of irritation. Of rage. When the next clap sounded, it was stretched out of shape and bent into syllables, into booming words that rang in their ears but were understandable just the same.

"Release me!"

Willie and Tol flinched at the sound of the voice, if it could be called that, and the medicine men did likewise. But they did not let it break their concentration. Each kept his eyes closed and his mind focused, and the burning line of blood remained bright.

"There's something in there!" Willie whispered. For there was definite movement behind that smoky curtain; shadowy forms moved against the bright heart of the fire. Long spindly limbs, some with multiple joints like an insect while others were fluid, as supple as a serpent's coils. But of one thing they could be sure: whatever owned those limbs had to be huge.

"Release me!" It called again, and the rock beneath their feet seemed to tremble with the impotent anger it conveyed. But No Moon and the others remained stoic, offered no reply other than their continued chanting.

Willie summoned her courage, stepped a little closer to the apparition. Tol tried to pull her back, but she had her mind set. "Ju . . . just who are you?" she stammered in as strong a voice as she could muster.

Something issued through the swirls of fog, far enough to be made out. At first it looked like a single lidless eye as large as her fist, extended on a long stalk like some monstrous insect. But then in a heartbeat the thing changed shape, became a human head on a long, wattled neck, and the face emblazoned on it continued to shift. It changed from young to old, to different races and genders, all in less time than it took her to blink. The final image was Willie herself, a mocking version of her own face with a smile drawn back into a hideous rictus and the eyes glowing with evil intent. The horror receded into the fog like a retreating worm, and Willie could finally breathe once more when it was out of sight.

"I am the all and the one" came that terrible voice. *"What was and what will be again. In the times before, when the mouth of man had yet to form, I was known as Azathoth, and also as Shub-Niggurath, the goat of the woods with a thousand young. But since then your kind has known me by many names, a thousand times a thousand more. Ra. Odin. Zeus. Kali. Cernunnos. Quetzalcoatl. Yahweh, the God of Abraham, and my own nemesis as well, the Fallen Angel."* The eye stalk reappeared, barely visible through the fog. It was looking past Willie to the tall cowboy behind her. *"Some would call me Lucifer,"* it said directly to him as it changed shape again, this time to a burned-red face with pointed goatee and ample set of horns. *"Satan. Scratch. Mephistoph-*

eles. But you may call me ol' Joe Hayes." And then the face mocked them with laughter as the swirling cloud reclaimed it.

It was moving about in that column of smoke, whatever it was. Its sheer size blocked out the glow of the hidden bonfire as it passed before it, approached the barrier where No Moon sat. It stopped just short of showing itself again. But its shape was still evident, looming over him. The Indian's eyes remained tightly closed; if he sensed its nearness, he gave no sign.

"I shall solve your great mystery, Oglala," it told him. *"For I am Wakan Tanka. I am also Iktomie the Spider-Man and Tatanka the Buffalo. I am even such a little thing as the spirit in your bowstring."* It became a sly whisper then. *"Is this not the voice of Elya-eh? Listen, Oglala. Is this not the voice you heard in your Hanblechia, and every one after that? I have tricked you ever since that first Vision Quest. All these years and you never knew."*

Shaddock saw that No Moon was breathing harder than before. His downturned face was twisted with pain, and one hand clutched at his chest. But he did not cry out. He did not break the cadence of his chant, and the light of the circle did not waver at all. Frustrated, the unseen creature moved on to the other old men seated around it. *"I am Coyote, the Trickster, and Tirawa Atius, and the Great Flame, Giver of Life, and a legion of others. And each time you have called upon me, whatever the guise, I have laughed at your ignorance and led you further into the dark. I am all you know and have ever known. But I am not alone. There are others. They follow behind me, the Leviathans of old, who held dominion in this world before your kind crawled from the cold womb of the ocean. And they shall possess it again. It is useless to oppose them. Release me now!"*

One of the medicine men stopped chanting, and the blood barrier flickered because of it.

Longer Tongue of the Minneconjou looked up out of reflex, his eyes wide with terror. In the next instant, before the others could take up the slack and restrengthen the circle of protection, the thing calling itself Joe Hayes struck.

Something long and thin shot from the smoky cylinder, so fast that they barely had time to see that it was a limb with three joints and a chitinous covering, like the shell of a beetle. Three pincerlike fingers clamped onto Longer Tongue's head and jerked him into the whirling cloud before he had time to scream or even utter a sound. The bloodline flared back to life a split second later. But it was too late.

The Minneconjou screamed long and loud from the depths of the white void, and the tone chilled the blood of all present, white and red alike. But as they listened, the cry changed, stretched and warped and dropped in timbre until it became the thunder, and within it the satisfied laughter of the unseen devil itself. *"So goes the one,"* it taunted, cold and cruel, *"and so will go the rest. The gate will open. You cannot stop it."*

Willie was still staring at the empty spot where Longer Tongue had sat mere moments before.

The gate will open . . .

She looked away instinctively, out into the night. And there she saw that primordial ocean once again. It was much higher now, covering all but the plateau and the tallest peaks around them. And it was becoming more and more real with each passing moment. The snake things were singing out there, joining their wet voices in chorus to herald the opening of the floodgate, as monstrous forms began to break the surface, the leviathans from before, rising anew from the stygian depths in their corrupt majesty.

Willie forced her eyes back to No Moon, searching for some sign of hope or reassurance. But instead she found the old man struggling to keep his composure. To simply survive. The veins in his neck and temples were bulging from the strain; it was all he could do to enunciate each syllable of the chant. The cold realization came to her: he won't last much longer. But how can I help him, she thought frantically. How?

It probably wouldn't hurt to pray a little. . . .

Willie didn't question the idea. She simply moved closer to the circle, almost to No Moon's side, and fell to her knees, clapped her hands together as she did every Sunday in the

Barlow church. Only this time she called on a different God. This time she really meant it. "Oh, Wakan Tanka," she pleaded earnestly. "I ain't one of your people, but I'm calling on you just the same. This man has served you well. He has remembered you and given offerings in your name. You must help him now, strengthen him against this evil."

"I have already told you, child," the cloud thing boomed. *"I am Wakan—"*

"No!" Willie got to her feet, stood angry and defiant against it. "You are not the Great Mystery! You are no one's God. A devil, maybe, but no God! 'Cause if you were, you could come out of the circle right now." There was no answer from the swirling white, no movement in there. And Willie felt her confidence grow. "Did you hear me, Mr. Hayes? If you are Wakan Tanka, and all the other Indian Gods, then how are they holding you there? Where are they getting their power, who are they calling on? You ain't answering, Mr. Hayes. C'mon, dammit. Come out of there now!"

"Silence!" it roared, with a flash of lightning to emphasize its anger. Only this was not just heat lightning, a simple flash to sear the eyes. It was a crackling bolt of energy, and it snaked out of the cloud column with a mind of its own. Willie barely turned to run before it struck her square in the back.

Tolman saw her drop like a rock; it felt like the arc of lightning had struck him as well. No, no, don't let this happen, he was saying to whatever God might listen as he ran to the girl's side and pulled her into his arms. The smell of singed hair hung heavy around her, and he could see bright red burn marks along her jaw and neck. But she was still breathing. Strong, too, despite what he had seen. Her eyes were open but spinning crazily, trying to focus again. "Wha-what was . . ." she stammered, unable to get her bearings.

"I don't know how you did it," he told her, almost crying in relief. "That shoulda burned you to a crisp. I mean . . ." He felt her squirming in his grasp and started to put her down. But he realized it was her black cloak that moved so, wriggling against his hand. *The demonskin!* He pulled it off her and held it up, tried to find the place where the bolt had struck. There was no mark. *It wouldn't burn, just like the one in the Black Hills so many years ago.*

There's magic in that skin. Maybe we can make it work for us.

Shaddock looked to the old Indian, still fighting his mumbled war, still losing. They were powerful men, these great shamans. But they were just too old, and too exhausted to carry on such a fight. The glow of the circle was beginning to dim even now, and it was only a matter of time.

But what if they had a chance, he thought. One shot at sending that damned thing back where it came from, without it fighting them? Could they do it? Would they even know how? There was no way he could answer that; this Indian magic was all incomprehensible to him. He had only one thing to rely on.

Trust No Moon. He hasn't steered you wrong.

Shaddock smiled. For the first time since killing that witch, he felt he had a use in all of this. He had his own plan.

"I'll trade you for this," he told Willie, draping the skin of Siyoko over his shoulder as he laid the Sharps down beside her, unbuckled his gunbelt, and did the same. "Take care of 'em, missy," he said, patting the big LeMats, "and they'll take good care of you."

"Tol? What are you—"

"No time, little lady." He unfurled the skin and put it around him, even up over his head. The feel of that living wrap made his flesh crawl, but he tried to ignore it. "I'll be seeing you." He gave her a wink and turned away.

Willie wanted to cry out, to call him back to her side. But she feared it might draw the demon's attention, and the lightning, to him. All she could do was watch.

He moved silently and close to the ground, sneaking up on the Oglala just as he did so long ago in his Indian-fighting days. Once he was close enough, he reached up and drew the stone knife from the back of No Moon's belt. The flat obsidian felt good in his hands.

He took a deep breath, let it out, then jumped up with his

living armor pulled close around him and let out a war cry—*"YEEEE-HAWWWW!"* And ran headlong for the circle.

The lightning struck before he got two steps. It hit him in the shoulder, a jolting blow. But the demonskin blunted much of it and kept him from burning, and his momentum was already too great to stop. The energy was still crackling around him when he leapt across the bloodline and disappeared into the swirling fog.

The thunder voice of ol' Joe Hayes shattered the high air of the plateau in reaction, enraged at such an unexpected attack. Other horrid sounds issued from that obscured battleground, animal squeals and screams and moans that defied description. Willie felt her throat constrict. What they must be doing to him in there, she thought. For even her worst nightmares could not produce sounds like those. She could see something thrashing about, something huge with limbs that flailed the air around it. And then one cry rose above all others, even above the roaring of the demon itself.

"YEEEE-HAWWWWW!"

She saw it then, just a quick glimpse but enough to haunt her the rest of her days. The creature was like a monstrous spider twice the size of the biggest draft horse she'd ever seen, with a swollen abdomen and long, segmented legs like the one which had taken Longer Tongue away. But that wasn't all. A massive humanlike torso grew from the thorax as well, complete with a human head and arms. But it had no face. There was only a mouth, wide and howling, and a forest of eyes waved around it on long tentaclelike stalks. The torso was raised high and the head was thrashing wildly, spraying the air with yellow ichor. The source of its rage and pain was in sight as well. Tolman Shaddock was clinging to the back of the thing's neck like a bronc buster. The demonskin trailed behind him as he stabbed away with the spirit knife, driving it home again and again, ripping huge gashes in that festering hide.

The cloud swirled again and the combatants were lost in the void once more.

"Now!" the cowboy yelled from within. "Do it now!"

No Moon apparently understood. He stood up, straight and tall, his pain shunted aside by sheer force of will. This was their chance; struggling with Shaddock had weakened the demon's defenses. They had to act now or never. The Oglala's chant rang in the air like an anthem, shouted to the four winds as he extended his hands into the air, at least the one that still obeyed. And the other eight did the same. They rose almost as one and mimicked his movements, still calling out in different tongues yet hearing their words somehow fit together as if part of the same song.

No Moon took a step toward the glowing bloodline, and the others did the same. And in reaction, the circle drew away from them. It shrank in on itself, all the way to the outer sphere that Dee-Bo-Ha had drawn. Another step, and the line moved again, even farther inward, past where the runic symbols and signs had been painted. And in its wake the rock was now seared clean.

The medicine men advanced farther. As they came, the cylinder of smoke shrank as well.

It grew thinner and thinner, and the battling shapes and shadows still inside changed with it. When the old men finally came shoulder to shoulder, the blood circle was little more than a hand's width across, and the column of smoke barely as thick as a sapling, all the way to the heavens. No Moon bent down and put his hands around its base, slowly brought them together. The column dwindled away to a bare thread of smoke, nothing more, and even that rose skyward, out of his grasp.

The howl of the wind died. The lightning no longer flashed, nor did the thunder come again. There was only silence. The spiraling clouds overhead slowed their revolutions, began to break up and dissipate before their eyes. And the twinkling of stars began to peak through, a million lights embedded in the ceiling of the sky. Hanhepiwi was there as well, hanging nearly full just shy of its nightly zenith.

Willie blinked her eyes, unsure whether this was really happening or just a last wishful thought before dying. She peered out into the night. The surrounding peaks and the distant plains beyond were well lit by the moonglow; she could see they were unmarred by what had transpired. The ancient ocean was gone without trace; likewise the rotting herd and the spreading rash of tipis that had stretched to the horizon. The world had returned to the way it was.

She knelt down, lifted the heavy gunbelt left beside her. "Tol?" she called, turning back to where the medicine men still stood. "Where's Tol?"

No Moon looked at the rock beneath his feet. He was standing where the bonfire had burned earlier. But there was no sign of it now, not even a blackened scar on the surface. Just like there was no sign of the cowboy who had saved them. "He is gone, Willie," he said helplessly. "I'm sorry."

The girl sank to her knees, unable to hold back her tears. The old man went to comfort her. But the pain came back before he could take a step, just as sharp and debilitating as before. Maybe even a little worse. "Willie . . ." he whispered just before he collapsed.

Chapter 24

Willie sat on the cold stone with the stuporous Oglala across her lap, holding him close. "No Moon?" she whispered into his ear. "Please . . . answer me!" She shook him gently, but he would not rouse. "Don't leave me like this!"

Shadows loomed over her; she looked up into the staring faces of the other Indians, gathered all around the two of them. "Help him," she begged. "I think it's his heart, the way he grabbed his chest, and . . ." But none of them moved. They just looked at her. "You're medicine men, aren't you? Then don't just stand there, for God's sake! Help him!"

Nothing. Just glassy stares and shivering silence. Willie saw her own reflection in their wide and frightened eyes, and it finally dawned on her just how shattered this nightmare had left them. These once-proud men stood naked before her, painted and humiliated, their very grasp on reality tenuous at best. Every year of life was a scar on their tortured faces. They were lost souls, all of them. And they were actually looking to her for some sort of direction.

They would be of no help to No Moon. They couldn't even help themselves.

"Go on," she told them. "Leave. Get your clothes, if you had any to begin with. Hurry, before you freeze your asses off."

Running Thunder blinked, nodded sullenly, and turned away. The others followed listlessly, unable to function singly for now, only as a communal whole. They went to the edge of the plateau and started down the Stairs to Heaven in single file, leaving Willie and the Oglala alone beneath the starry mantle of the night.

She sat and rocked the old man gently, stroked his silvery hair. "You'll be fine," she whispered. "Yeah, just fine. You're strong. You can get past this. But you've gotta hang on. Do you hear me? Hang on, old man. Please."

What if he dies? she asked herself. What if you're left alone again? First Pa, then Kolo and Tol, and now No Moon. And when he goes too, what will you do then?

I won't do anything, she snapped defensively. Because he's not going to die. He'll get through this, you wait and see. He won't die like Pa did. I'll take care of him. He's gonna be around for a long time.

No Moon's skin was turning cool beneath her hands. "Getting kinda nippy up here," she told him, pulling up the collar of his coat and then her own as well. "We're gonna need us a fire. Yeah, gotta get you good and toasty. I think I got a match in here somewhere." She patted her coat pockets, finally found the tin box where she kept them. "There we go. Now, the question is, what do we got up here that'll burn?" She looked around the barren shelf of rock in frustration. But there was nothing. Just them and Dee-Bo-Ha, and she doubted the witch's body would burn well. She considered going down to the canyon for some wood, but it would be a struggle wrestling an armload back up the ledge. Besides, it would take her from No Moon's side for too long.

She finally remembered the oilcloth in her inside pocket, the one that held her journal papers and other personals. She unwrapped it but left most of the things in place, the pictures of her parents, the handbill for Colonel Brady's show. The only item she took out was the small diary. She leafed through it slowly, reading the entries and the small-town monotony that lay beneath the words. It occurred to her how quaint her writings all sounded now, how foreign to her, like scenes from a stranger's life. She realized how little those pages held for her now.

Her father's words came back to her. *You'd do well to get your nose out of the past and start looking to the future.* And that made her feel better about what she had to do.

She tore the pages from the book, one after another. It pained her wounded hand to do so, but she managed. The paper was piled beside them while Willie struck a match, shielding it against a wind that no longer blew. She put the flame to the pile and watched as they grew in the shreds of her past. It was a small fire and provided less heat than she'd expected. But it was reassuring to her; it made Willie feel a little less helpless.

No Moon roused then but only for a moment. He moaned softly before sinking back into the depths of unconsciousness. Still, it was a sign. He was fighting.

"Can you hear me?" she called to him over and over. "It's Willie. I'm right here."

One of his eyes fluttered, opened partway. A corner of his mouth twitched. But the other side of his face remained dead, sagging, and motionless. He cleared his throat and looked up, let that single eye linger on her face, and she began to wonder if he recognized her at all.

"I . . . cannot be dead yet," he winced. "It hurts . . . too much."

"Don't you even talk about dying." Willie tried to sound optimistic. "You got a long ways to go yet. A long ways."

The old man shook his head. "Maybe it would be best," he whispered. "There are worse things than death, you know."

"Oh, yeah? Name one."

There was pain in No Moon's eye then, but not the physical kind. This went deeper than his fractured heart, straight to the core of his being. "Not knowing . . ." he began, "what lies beyond the Far Pines, once we have left this world. I used to know of the great hunting grounds, a new life after this, one that was open and free. I even saw it once, or thought I did, while I hunted in Paha-Sapa. But maybe I was just dreaming." He looked at her, held her gaze. "What if the demon spoke the truth? That voice . . . I have heard it before . . ."

"Yeah, whispering in the night, like all devils. Trying to fool you and trick you. You saw it, old man. It couldn't come out of the circle, could it?"

"No. Because we held it there. But what if it was us all along? What if the magic was in each of us instead of in the spirits, if our ancestors had it in the beginning and created the Great Mystery to explain it so we would not become too prideful and full of ourselves? Willie, I have heard that voice." He sighed, gritted his teeth in pain and frustration. He took her good hand in his own. It was very cold. "I am so tired," he whispered. "I will sleep a while. Will you stay with me?"

A tear slid from the corner of her eye. But she still shook her head. "Yes, *tunkashila*. As long as you want me to."

He gave her a half smile, as much as his paralyzed lips could form. He laid his head in her lap and relaxed. Sleep came upon him quickly, quietly.

Willie stayed with him, just as she promised. She fed the fire as long as she could, until the paper was all gone. Then she watched it slowly go out.

Sometime later the absolute quiet of the plateau amplified the shuffle of footsteps growing louder, climbing up the spiraling ledge. One of the medicine men, she figured, had come to his senses and was returning to offer his herbs and his aid. But the face that rose above the edge of the rock and into her view was much younger, and much more scarred to boot. Kolo's face was scratched and bitten and his dark hair matted with blood. But at that moment Willie couldn't have seen a more beautiful sight. He approached her, limping even worse than Tol had, with his clothes hanging in tatters around him. The holster on his hip was empty, but he still carried that damned Bowie in his fist.

The girl was shocked speechless by his appearance. Is he real, she wondered, or some ghost come back to haunt me? She wished she could touch him to be sure, to throw her arms around his neck and cling to him for dear life. But she didn't move. She just stared at him, until he looked at himself self-consciously. "What?" he wondered. "Do I look that bad?"

"No," she answered. "You look fine. I just never expected to see you again, that's all."

He laughed at that. It was a rich sound, celebrating luck and life, and it sounded foreign in the silence of the plateau. "I didn't expect to be seen, I'll tell you that." The outlaw began to chatter then, uttering more in the next few moments than he had since she first set eyes on him. The exhilaration of escaping seemed to have loosened his tongue. "When Shaddock started up here, I saw there was just too damn many of them things to fight. And when my guns went empty, I started to think I was a goner for sure. All I could do was slip back into one of those crannies 'tween the rocks down there and cut at anything that reached in." He massaged his aching arm, peeled his fingers away from the knife's handle one at a time. "Got pretty tired, I'll say. This damn Bowie started to feel like it weighed a hundred pounds or so. But then, just when I was giving up hope, the goddamn things just up and disappeared. Figured it was you'uns' doing up here, but I stayed low just the same. Didn't poke my head out until I saw them old men coming down the way. They went down through the canyon—there ain't nothing there now but those two lodges in the middle —and they went into the bigger one, got some clothes, and went on up the other side. And then I came up here." The half-breed looked around the empty plateau, let his eyes linger on the remains of Dee-Bo-Ha for a moment before continuing his search. "Where's that old coot Shaddock anyway?"

"Gone," Willie said. "But he saved us. Him and No Moon." She stroked the old man's hair with reverence.

Kolo watched the Oglala, hoping for some movement. But there was none. "Is he . . ."

Willie just nodded. "About a half hour ago. Just slipped out of him. He's looking for a better place, I suppose."

Kolo nodded in understanding. He came over and lifted the old Indian's head, let her slip from under him. They both laid him gently on the rock.

"Maybe we should take him down from here," she wondered, "give him a proper burial."

Kolo shook his head. "It ain't their way. I hear the Sioux put their warriors up on platforms. I don't know just why. But one thing's for sure—you can't get much higher than this." He turned to the other body on the plateau. "That the witch?"

"Yes."

He pursed his lips. "She sure don't deserve to be up here. Not with him." Going over to the corpse, Kolo dragged it to the edge and pushed it over. Then he came back to Willie's side, stooping along the way to pick up a burned and battered derby. They returned it to their fallen comrade's head.

Willie took the leather pouch from No Moon's shoulder, sifted through its contents. She took the *sicun* bundle from within and put it in one of No Moon's hands. And in the other she placed the coiled bowstring from his youth. "Watch over him, Elya-eh," she whispered to it. "Show him to the hunting ground, and bring him many antelope." Then she turned away from him and did not look back.

Kolo retrieved Tol's gunbelt and the Sharps rifle, and they descended the Stairs to Heaven for the last time.

The night was utterly quiet in the empty canyon. But to their ears, the beat of drums and the echoing howls of the dead still lingered, just beyond earshot. It gave speed to their stride. They went straight across the flatland, past where a bonfire had burned, past the empty lodges and whatever dark secrets they still held. Then up the slope at the far end of the canyon and over the top, back along the mountain path.

When they came through the rock archway and descended the slanting stone into shadow, Willie hoped to hear a snort of greeting from below. But there was only silence. When they reached the bottom of the pass, she saw her saddle and the others as well. But there was no sign of little Buck.

"The medicine men," Kolo guessed. "They were coming this way. They probably grabbed all our horses."

"Not Buck," Willie said. She hadn't given up on the fiery pony. Not just yet anyway. She slipped two fingers into her mouth and gave a piercing whistle, one that ricocheted off the rock around them. Then she listened.

Nothing.

"I told you. Them horses are miles away by now."

Just then a neighing answered her from out in the night, and the girl shot Kolo a smile.

The pony came galloping into the gloom of the pass, snorting and prancing like an excited pup. He ran right to his master and nuzzled her face with his nose, forced a laugh from her. And the sound of it surprised her as much as Kolo's had on the plateau. She'd begun to think she would never hear it again. The nightmare's over, she reminded herself. Time to get on with living.

She was busy saddling Buck when she caught a glimpse of Kolo from the corner of her eye. He was going through Tol Shaddock's packs. A hard thought went through her mind— once a thief, always a thief—but then she tried to temper it. Tol's gone, she told herself. Don't seem too proper, but it ain't rightly stealing. "Looking for something?" she asked.

When he turned around, Kolo had a powder flask and Tol's pouch of lead shot in his hands, with the rest of his loading gear. "I figured if you're gonna be keeping these old antiques of his, you better have the things to load 'em. A gun ain't much use empty, you know." He walked over to Buck, draped the gunbelt with the LeMats over the saddle horn and stowed the rest of the gear in the side packs. Then he looked at Willie, saw that she was blushing. But he hadn't known her previous thoughts, so he paid it no mind. He just held up the Sharps rifle. "Couldn't find no more shells for this. Must've taken 'em with him."

"Bring it along anyway," she said as she finished cinching Buck's straps. She stepped into the stirrup and climbed aboard, then held out her good hand to the outlaw.

The half-breed smiled, didn't bother with the hand up. He just jumped up onto the pony behind her, had to keep a good hold around her middle to keep from sliding off. She didn't complain. "So," he said before she had even given Buck a nudge, "where are you headed?"

"I don't rightly know," she replied. "Up till now I ain't give it much thought. There's nothing back in Barlow for me, not anymore." She smiled at a notion. "Maybe I'll go to Oregon. My pa always wanted to go there. I could see it for him. What about you, Kolo? Where are you going?"

The breed just shrugged. "I can't tell your horse where to go. So I guess I'm headed wherever you are." He didn't sound too disappointed with his predicament.

They rode out beyond the pass and onto the scrub shoulder of the foothills, under the light of the stars once again. The plains spread out below them, a rolling carpet of grassland limited only by the reach of their eyes. Willie turned Buck around and looked back at the mountain range behind them, looming high overhead, an eternal monument to the *wicasa wakan* she had left in their care.

But what about Tol, a voice asked her. Who'll remember what he did here?

She looked back over her shoulder at the empty rifle that Kolo carried, and she knew what she must do.

"What are you up to?" he asked as she slid out of the saddle and took the rifle from his hand, drew the Bowie from his sheath as well. She went to the edge of the brush-strewn shelf that they stood on, right along the slope to the prairie below. And she began to dig with the knife. She gouged a narrow hole in the soil, hissing from the pain it caused her hand. But she didn't let that stop her. She dug until she was a foot down, upended the rifle, and shoved the barrel into the ground, pushing the loose dirt in around it and packing it down hard.

Kolo watched with curiosity as she took a paper from the inner pocket of her coat. It was Bill Brady's flyer that she'd taken from the window of the general store. She also took a pencil stub from the watch pocket of her jeans, used the little folding knife to sharpen it for writing. Then she went to work on the flyer.

"I still don't get what the hell you're up to," the half-breed sighed.

"Making a headstone," she told him. Once she was finished, she held the poster up against the wooden stock of the battered Sharps and stuck it there with the whittling knife, pounded it deep with the butt of the Bowie. It held firm. The paper would not blow away easily.

She went back to the horse, let Kolo pull her up into the saddle. Then she turned and appraised her work. The words on the page had not been changed; they still heralded the Western legend of Tolman Shaddock, hunter and lawman and Indian fighter. His exploits with the Orlen brothers and the Creekmore massacre were still intact. But a last adventure had been added to the list.

RASSLED THE DEVIL, the sign now read, AND RODE HIM BACK TO HELL.

Kolo looked at the words, squinted his eyes at them. But it was all chicken scratching to someone who couldn't read. "What does it say?" he asked sheepishly.

"The truth," she told him. "The God's honest truth."

She took the reins and urged little Buck down the slope. The pony snorted and seemed only too eager to obey.